THE SILVER STAR RANCH ROMANCES

THE COMPLETE SERIES

SHANAE JOHNSON

THOSE JOHNSON GIRLS

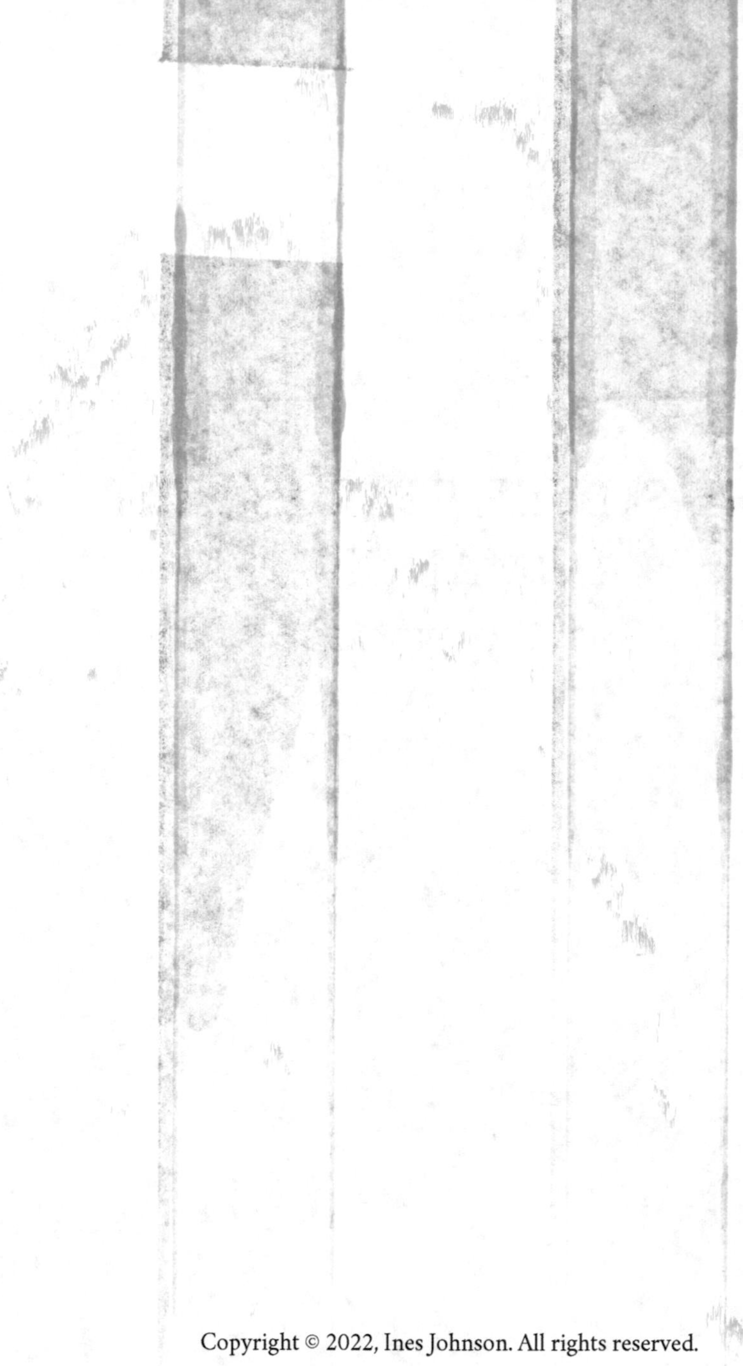

SHANAE JOHNSON

HIS Pledge TO Honor

A SILVER STAR RANCH ROMANCE

CHAPTER ONE

 *S*cout Silver walked the length of the solicitor's office. The office wasn't on the main street of the small Montana town she'd lived all her life in. The town was only considered small due to its population. The square footage of Honor Valley could fit the island of Manhattan inside a couple of times. But the people could all fit into the high school football stadium with enough elbow room to be comfortable. Though they'd all likely be hugging each other while mixing and mingling.

So, no, she didn't have to drive the thirty minutes it would take her to get into the heart of the town to handle her business. She'd only had to saddle up a horse and ride next door to her neighbor's at the Flying Cross Ranch.

Scout hadn't even bothered to knock at the front door of the Matthews's homestead. The massive door was always open. She'd walked right in and let herself into the converted formal living room, which served as Haran Matthews's office, to wait.

Instead of waiting in one of the six chairs pulled into the room, she paced.

The familiar surroundings should've eased her spirit. There was the ancient oak desk under which she'd never been found in games of hide and seek. The well-tread afghan of fading reds and blues whose patterns she'd focus on when she was being scolded for some childish indiscretion that had never been her idea, yet she'd taken the blame to protect the younger, guilty party.

It was the pictures on the wall that had always fascinated her most. She looked up at those now. Most of the pictures featured tall, uniformed Black men in black and white reproductions and sepia-toned prints. The black and white print was a snapshot of the 9th Cavalry Regiment known as the Buffalo Soldiers; the all-Black soldiers who fought in the American Civil War. The sepia-toned photograph was a picture of the Tuskegee Airman; another all-Black force of airman from the century just past. The third picture was in full color. It featured a skinny Black man with his arm around a barrel-chested white man. Both men sported the modern camouflage style of military fatigues, handle-bar mustaches, and broad, toothsome grins that told the viewer that they were solemnly up to no good.

Scout reached her hand up to the picture. With a tremble in her index finger, she traced the line of the white man's smile. She tried with all her might not to blink because whenever she did, the picture of her father faded in her mind.

The door of the office opened. Scout jerked her hand away from the photograph on the wall. Her features went carefully blank. Her eyes trained on the afghan as though expecting punishment for the indiscretion.

A white man with a handlebar mustache did not enter the room. Nor did a whiskered Black man. The door opened to reveal a head of dark brown hair much like her own. But Saylor's hair was pulled back in a tight ponytail rather than loose and down her shoulders like Scout's.

"We're the first two to arrive?" asked Saylor.

"Just like always." Scout opened her arms to her younger sister. The two eldest of the Silver sisters embraced in the empty room, holding onto each other like they were all they had because now that was true.

"I still don't understand why we're here?" said Saylor. "The General's funeral was three months ago."

Scout shrugged helplessly. "I didn't even know he'd left a will. The only thing he owned was the ranch, which he signed over to mom after the first time they got divorced."

"No, that was actually the second time they got divorced," Saylor corrected.

Saylor scratched at her nose. When she did so, Scout noticed the bags under her sister's eyes. Either Saylor wasn't sleeping well, or she had been crying last night. Scout wouldn't be surprised if both were true. Though she doubted the tears had anything to do with their father's death three months ago.

General Abraham Silver's daughters had been prepared for this day since their birth. Their father, who'd enlisted right out of high school, had been one of the original Navy SEALS. By the time Scout was born, he'd been leading elite covert operations for a decade. His life was in danger more times than it was not.

"Father Matthews didn't tell you anything?" asked Saylor.

Scout shook her head, her gaze returning to the picture on the wall. She eyed the sly smile of the man with his arm around her father. Just like the biblical brothers in the Bible, Haran Matthews and Abraham Silver had been like true brothers. So much so that Abe's daughters had always called their father's best friend and neighbor Father. It was a happy coincidence that the veteran and lawyer was also a man of the cloth.

"If there is a will," said Saylor, "do you think Cruella will contest it?"

Scout cringed at the mention of their father's second wife. That divorce had been a battlefield with many casualties, namely the children. Their stepmother Catherine had tried to take the ranch in the settlement, which had been the main reason why their father had signed the Silver Star Ranch over to their mother the second time they'd remarried.

"I don't know," said Scout. "But I have a bad feeling about this."

"Cruella didn't even show up to the funeral. But I know Mareen's here."

As though she heard her name being called, the product of that second marriage walked into the door. Mareen's elegance preceded her as she framed the doorway.

As always, her head was high. The makeup coating her porcelain skin was perfectly done to accentuate the crystal blue eyes they all shared. Instead of cowboy boots like Scout wore, or penny loafers like Saylor wore, Mareen wore six-inch stilettos, which were entirely impractical on a ranch. She had for a short time, but then she'd chosen sides. And that side had been away from the ranch with her high society mother.

"Ladies," Mareen said.

Ladies. Not sisters. Not family.

Though Saylor and Mareen could've been twins with how much they favored. Instead of a ponytail, Mareen's hair was coiffed in a perfect bun. Scout knew the woman's eyesight was as poor as her sisters, but Mareen wore contacts.

Irish twins was a term Scout had heard whispered behind the hands of the town gossips. Ghetto twins was what she'd heard thrown at Saylor's back in the halls of school. Both Saylor and Mareen were technically the second eldest of the Silver sisters. Both women were twenty-five. Born the same year. But to different mothers.

Scout and Saylor shared a look. Scout motioned her head for Saylor to say something. Saylor raised her brows and shook her head. Scout rolled her eyes.

Mareen turned to glance at them. Just in time for Scout and Saylor to straighten and smile blandly. Suspicion cut the corners of Mareen's blue eyes, but like always, she said nothing, offering her older sisters the silent treatment.

The three eldest Silver sisters were saved by a clamor coming through the door. It was the youngest three Silver sisters. The identical faces of Tilly and Gunny came through the door first. Their blonde hair a hallmark from their mother -their father's third wife.

Well, technically Roxanne had been their father's fourth marriage. After the General left Mareen's mom, he'd come back home. For a short time. But her parent's second marriage lasted the blink of an eye.

The timeline was all too confusing when Scout was busy learning Algebra, so she'd stopped trying to work out the equation and all its variables. She was simply thrilled to have two new products of the complex math; Gunnery and Artillery.

Yes, the names were tragic. All their names were tragic. It just proved how head over heels each of her father's three wives must have been for him to allow that ink to dry on the birth certificates.

Scout had vowed at a young age that she would never be that head over heels for a boy. She'd had a couple of boyfriends over the years. But each relationship had confirmed her commitment to never get married and save herself the drama that the institution caused.

Surprisingly, her sisters didn't share the same view. Saylor was head over heels with a man who Scout knew was a one-way ticket to a divorce attorney. Luckily, Scout doubted the philanderer would ever take her sister down the aisle. Then there was Mareen, who sported a blinding rock on her left hand.

"I'll bet dad left us all a secret stash of money," said Brig, the youngest and last of the six Silver sisters. "You know he didn't trust banks. He probably left piles with Father Matthews, and that's why he's called us here today."

Brigadear Silver looked exactly like Scout and Saylor with her dark hair and light eyes. Because, like Scout and Saylor, Brig shared the same mother and father. After his third wife, which was his fourth marriage, Abraham Silver came back to his first wife once more. Apparently, the third time was a charm because they stayed married until her mom died ten years ago.

But once Sarah Silver was laid to rest, the girls rarely saw their father again. He dove into his work with the military, rarely surfacing for more than the occasional phone call with his girls.

"Hey Mareen, you came back," said Brig, her bright eyes glowed as she flung herself at Mareen.

"Of course, I did." Mareen offered her youngest sibling an awkward pat on the back and a tight smile. There was some give to Mareen's smile.

Brig was a force of nature. She was also too young to have felt the carnage of all the adults' emotional warfare. But honestly, Scout simply doubted the young woman cared.

Brig took the seat next to Mareen and began chatting away about her studies at the state school she was attending. Mareen tried to hold her aloof composure. But it was slipping under Brig's easygoing, tornado-like friendliness.

The door opened for the fourth time. Part of Scout worried that they might be introduced to a seventh sibling. But no, it wasn't another pale-skinned woman with brown hair and blue eyes that entered. It was a dark-skinned man with a handlebar mustache. The grin that had always hinted at mischief was thin right now.

Scout had always viewed Haran Matthews as the strongest man she knew, stronger even than her father because he had come back home to raise and care for his family. Father Matthews was from a line of warriors. His great grandfather was one of the Buffalo Soldiers depicted on the wall. His own father had been one of the Tuskegee Airmen.

But Father Matthews looked small and tired today. Scout had to remind herself that he had lost his best friend. The weight of the loss, and whatever their father had tasked him to do in his absence, was clearly heavy on his shoulders.

He looked around the room, not quite meeting any of the girls' eyes. That's when the bad feeling in Scout's stomach increased. There was one seat left open, but she wanted to pace the floor. She wanted to crawl under the massive oak desk and hide. Instead, she trained her gaze to the floor and counted the patterns on the rug. Whatever Father Matthews was about to tell them, she knew she would be in trouble.

Father Matthews rounded the desk. He looked pointedly at Scout. Finally, she took the seat. Once she was seated, he sat too.

"Girls, I have your father's last will and testament here." Father Matthews took a deep breath before continuing. "He's left you all equal shares of the ranch."

"But I thought Mom left the ranch to Scout?" said Tilly.

Tilly and Gunny's mother had died shortly after their birth. When their father had shown up on his ex-wife's doorstep with two infants in tow, Sarah Silver hadn't blinked an eyelash. She'd taken the bundles in and raised them as her own.

"When your parents remarried the last time, the property became both of theirs," Father Matthews was saying. "When your mother died, it reverted back to your father."

Scout sat forward. She hadn't known that. All this time, she'd been carrying on running the day to day operation of the Silver Star Ranch as though she were the sole owner. She'd converted the homestead into a horse rehabilitation ranch and taken on injured, abandoned, and discarded horses and gave them a place where they could heal and recover. The business didn't make her rich, but it paid the bills, including the education of her sisters.

"Well, I'm giving my part to you, Scout," said Gunny. "You've taken care of all of us since mom died."

"I agree," said Tilly.

In her peripheral vision, Scout saw Brig and Saylor both nod their agreement. Mareen's chin didn't dip. It remained high, and she stared straight ahead.

"I'm afraid it's not that simple," said Father Matthews. "You see, your father left stipulations. One of which being that the will couldn't be read until three months after his passing. The other stipulation..."

Father Matthews set down the stack of papers. He closed his eyes and pinched the hairs at the edge of his mustache.

Scout had seen her father make that same motion. He often did it when he was arguing with her mother. Or when he was disciplining one of his daughters. Again, Scout's gaze tracked down to the afghan, seeking the pattern while she awaited a punishment for an act that wasn't her doing.

"As I said, your father wrote that the land reverts to each of his daughters equally. However, before any of you can sell or transfer your portions..." Father Matthews took another gulp, still avoiding each of their gazes. "Before any of you can transfer your ownership, you'll have to get married."

There was silence in this room that had always been filled with so much laughter, a little scolding, and the deep baritone of Father Matthews telling stories of old to his children and the children of his best friend.

"Married?"

"Married!"

"Married."

Only Scout, Saylor, and Mareen remained mute at the proclamation.

Father Matthews held up his hand as though he weren't done. But what more could there be?

"If you're not all married within the year of your father's passing, the land goes..." And now Father Matthews did look up. He looked up to Scout. "...to his second wife, Catherine."

CHAPTER TWO

Lincoln Rawlings rolled his head around his neck. The popping sounds of the tendons there set his nerves on high alert. Gunfire had been a constant siren call in his living quarters for years, never allowing him to fully relax where he lay his head.

For a second, his brain fogged, casting his mind back into the dark cloud of battle. Head on a swivel was a common phrase in the military that meant stay alert, danger was ever-present. But looking out at the Montana sky, he knew no danger was present. The Purple Heart Ranch was one of the safest places in the world, especially when it came to Wounded Warriors like him.

He didn't have to stay alert. He didn't have to stay on guard. The only conflict existed within him.

Linc tilted his head back. He let the tendons snap, crackle, and pop while he bathed in the rays of sunlight. The brightness of the light only barely penetrated the ever creeping darkness in his mind. Linc knew that pretty soon, the fog born of war, the shadows that had seeped into the corners of his brain and begun eating away at his attention, at his retention, that blackness would one day swallow him whole, leaving nothing behind.

The bark of a dog caught his attention. The tiny Irish Terrier looked up at him with large eyes on his small head. Its front paws pressed into the ground as though it stood at attention. It had no hind legs. Instead, there was a wheelchair attached to its limp back legs. The wheels came to a halt as the dog sat its rump on the ground.

Linc had to force himself to let out the breath he held as the dog sat. Many dogs in the military were trained to sit when they detected the chemicals that made up a bomb. But the dog in the wheelchair apparatus wouldn't have passed muster to be a field dog. Just as Linc no longer passed muster to operate in the field.

His operating days were over after the doctors had operated on him. His body was whole, intact. It was his mind that was no longer cleared for duty.

Rolling his head again, Linc heard the tendons in his neck pop once more. The dog gave a pitying whine. Linc bent down and gave the pooch a scratch behind the ears. After the petting, the Terrier raised his rump and set his wheels in motion. Mission accomplished, he trotted off, having gotten what he came for.

Mission accomplished. Those words sounded like an echo in the hollow caverns of Linc's brain. He was supposed to be on a mission… but the details were hazy.

Linc rubbed at his brow, trying to remember what he'd come outside for? His duffel bag was at his feet, as though he were ready to be spun up and fly out to some distant land. There were car keys in one hand. He was cleared to operate an automobile, but he couldn't remember where he was meant to go?

Pressed into the flat of his palm behind the set of keys was a yellow square of paper. The adhesive at the top of the note stuck to the top of his palm. There were words scrawled across the center in a bold, blocky script.

Mission Objective: Silver Star Ranch.

Task: Keep Your Pledge to the General.

Linc's fogged mind cleared. Those words were enough to remind him of what he was meant to do, what his mission was, his final mission. He hefted up his duffel bag, clenched the car keys in his hands, and marched across the yard to the ranch's clinic.

Passing the nurses and doctors, Linc smiled blandly. It was hard for him to keep names and faces straight. These were the men and women who had helped him heal after his mission. He didn't want to appear rude to them. He wanted to appear healed. Though he would never truly be that again.

Reaching his destination, Linc didn't bother knocking on the door. It was ajar, and it was filled with five other men. One man sat on the bed. lacing up his boots. It was a slow-going job as he only used one hand for the job. Jefferson's left hand lay limp on the mattress as he struggled.

None of the other men made a move to help. None of them made it appear that they noticed the struggle. Jeff was the only one in their unit who'd walked away with a visible wound. The other men were able to hide their scars, but only if they didn't look each other in the eyes.

Once Jeff was finished, Linc asked, "Ready to go?"

Carter and Truman, the closest to the door nodding. Grabbing their duffels, they fell in with Lincoln. Wilson, who stood at the window, pushed off the wall. He reached for his duffel, and then for Jeff's before clenching his hand into a fist and drawing away. Jeff pretended not to notice and hefted the bag on his back with his right hand.

"We missed the funeral," said Jeff.

That couldn't be helped. They had all been laid up in a German hospital at the time of General Silver's funeral three months ago. Last month, they'd been sent to the Purple Heart Ranch to work on their internal wounds. Each man had balked at the idea of coming to the rehabilitation ranch. But it had been an order, the last edict of their commander in chief.

General Silver had been fond of calling his unit the President's Men because each of the soldiers had the name of a president. Linc had wondered if the general had handpicked the boys for that very reason. Whatever the general's selection process, it had been spot on. The six men had worked together seamlessly over the years, executing the toughest missions the military had thrown at them.

Until the last mission. The one that had nearly taken their lives. The one that had cost them their most valuable player; the general himself.

"The Silver Star ranch is 312 clicks from here," Linc began. "We'll take two vehicles and drive out. We should arrive at 1100."

"This isn't a mission, Linc," said Wilson. "We're out of the military."

That was true. Each of the president's men had received a medical discharge after their time in the German hospital. Along with that honorable discharge, each man had received the Silver Medal of Honor for the heroic attempts they'd all undertaken in their last battle.

"All I want to do is rest," said Jackson. There was a touch of gray sneaking into the hairline at his temples.

"All I want to do is find a good woman and make some babies," said Carter as he ran a hand through his overly-styled hair.

Truman remained quiet. Like Linc, both of them wanted back in the military. But the only way that would happen is if they took a desk job. That was a slow death.

"We made a pledge to do this," said Linc.

That shut them up. Even three months later, they all still felt the loss of their leader acutely. Linc was sure each man could still hear the explosion that had taken their leader from them. All they had left of him was the pledge they'd made, the pledge to check in on his six daughters and see if there was anything that the President's Men could do for the girls.

"Let's gear up and roll out."

CHAPTER THREE

"Gunny, pick up," Scout hissed the order into the cell phone.

Normally, she was lucky to get three whole bars on the device. The service on the Silver Star Ranch was notoriously hit or miss. But it was a cloudless day. A flock of five birds flew in formation, mirroring the strong signal on the face of her phone. The only problem was the electronic chirping of the ring tone from the other end of the phone.

"Gunnery Ulysses Silver, you better pick up this phone or so help me—"

A long beep cut off Scout's threat to her sister. Scout yanked the phone from her ear and glared at the device. With a huff, she hit redial.

"I know you're there," Scout huffed into the receiver. In response, the phone rang and rang again. "They get cell service out in the middle of...where is she again?"

"The Namib Desert," said Brig as she led a tall Thoroughbred to the slow feeder.

The once-proud racehorse walked slowly on the lead, his head hanging low. Scout winced as she watched the horse's large, soulful brown gaze narrow as though each step were painful.

They probably were. Heathcliff had come to them after losing his tenth consecutive race two years ago. His owner had been fed up and ready to put the horse down now that he was no longer profitable. Scout had convinced the wretched man to give the horse to her. She and Saylor had slowly nursed the weary horse back to some semblance of health, though he would never race again. Which was for the best.

No one here would try to coax any horse to be all it could be. Only to be what they were. The Silver Star Ranch was a place of rehabilitation, of reform, maybe even a bit of revitalization. But not restoration.

The horses that came here had been broken, either in body or spirit, by the humans who had owned them. Scout had no interest in patching them up and sending them back. Here the animals would live out the rest of their days at peace as they healed from the inside out.

Originally, this had been a working cattle ranch. But on her twenty-first birthday, just three years after her mother's passing, and her father's continual absence as he took on mission after mission with the military, Scout had sold off the cattle and transformed the land into a rehabilitation ranch for retired and abused horses.

Her father had balked at the idea, insisting she would fail. He'd also insisted it was high time she got married and let a man run the ranch for her. She'd told him that if he wanted a man in charge, then he could come home and run the place himself.

He hadn't come home. Their calls became fewer and further between. Until there were none, and he was gone.

Scout sniffed and rubbed at her nose. She blinked a couple of times, trying to clear whatever dust was in the air. The bleep of the voice message indicator rang in her ear, announcing that her sister would not be taking her call anytime soon.

Scout had the urge to slam the phone down. But she didn't dare. She didn't want to startle the magnificent creature on her own lead.

And so she disconnected the call and turned to a problem she could solve.

Bingley had chunks missing out of his blond hide. A result of getting caught in a wire fence for hours. The Sorrel horse was still a beautiful animal with its flaxen coat and mane. Because of its coloring, the Silver sisters had named it after the equally flaxen hero of their mother's favorite novel.

"Don't worry, boy," Scout soothed. "I'll figure it out. I won't let anyone take any of us from our home."

Bingley pawed the ground. He shook his head back and forth, a low whine escaping his mouth. Scout wondered if he doubted her? It was more likely the horse's deep-seated distrust of humans. He'd been badly treated. The gashes in his skin had come from the neglect of his former owners. The wires had dug deep and held fast for hours before anyone had noticed.

Even today, the animal startled easily when it felt confined and cornered. Both Brig and Scout made sure to keep in the horse's eyesight as they tended his wounds, wounds they'd have to tend for the rest of the horse's natural life. The owners had discarded the animal when he had lost his looks. But to Scout's eyes, the male was still beautiful with his healed scars.

All of the two dozen horses on this ranch had stolen into Scout's heart over the years. She and her sisters had been the ones to nurse each and every one of them out of the dark and back into the light. They had given love and attention, kindness, and care when the ones who had originally taken on the job had turned their backs.

And now her father thought he could force his daughters' hands? Do away with all the good they'd done all because he never got the son he craved. Not if she had anything to do about it.

But what could she do about it? Father Matthews had shown her how the paperwork was all there. There were no loopholes. Either she and her sisters got married, or they'd lose it all.

"Gunny said she would be out of pocket for at least a month," said Brig.

They didn't have that much time. Already two weeks had passed since the reading of their dad's will. They only had a few months left before the end of the year. And none of his daughters had any prospect of marriage. Except for Mareen.

Mareen was scheduled to have a winter wedding just before Christmas. Scout only knew because she'd seen the announcement in the society papers. None of her sisters had received an invitation.

What Scout was more surprised by was that the wedding was still on. She wouldn't put it past Cruella to push the wedding back a few weeks so that the ranch would come to her. But she supposed her stepmother knew her ex-husband's daughters too well. She knew that there was no way the five opinionated, loud-mouthed, unfinished girls could land a man in three years, let alone three months.

Rehabilitating these animals had become Scout's life work; Saylor's too. They weren't going to give it up because of a man. All she had to do was find a husband. How hard could that be? People married every day. And divorced the next day—if her family was any example.

However, Scout was having problems finding a man to leg shackle. She wasn't exactly sure where to go about finding one for herself? None of the boys in town would do. She'd grown up with them. Beat them at one too many sports. Raised her hand to answer every question they got wrong. Surprisingly, boys didn't like that.

Maybe she should go out of town? But where would she go when she got there? A bar? She wasn't much of a drinker. A night club? She was even less of a dancer. And she had nothing to wear.

What was her father thinking? It's not like men fell out of the sky.

The sound of boots on the ground had Scout turning around. Walking up to the fence where six of the tallest, broadest men she'd ever seen in her life. The one in the lead was a beautiful specimen.

He wasn't the tallest. The brown-skinned man at his left had a few inches on him. But the guy at the center had a larger than life air about him. His dark gaze was clear, focused. The pectorals of his broad chest were clearly defined by the tan shirt he wore. Resting against the center of his chest was the unmistakable rectangle of dog tags.

Soldiers.

What were soldiers doing on her ranch? What were six soldiers doing on her ranch? Right after the reading of her father's will and the crazy edict he'd laid out for his six daughters?

Bingley must have had the same tingling of suspicion race across his back because he pawed at the ground some more. His head shook more forcefully in the lead. He couldn't see the threat that was coming at his flank.

Before Scout could grab her wits, the horse reared up on its hind legs. Bingley broke free and took off. Scout's feet were slow as she made to scramble after Bingley. But apparently, there was no need as the six soldiers entered the enclosure and spread out around the horse.

CHAPTER FOUR

*L*inc hadn't grown up with horses. None of the President's Men had. But when they'd become a unit under the General, it was one of the first things Silver had insisted his men learn; how to ride but also how to manage a horse.

"In a herd, there's always a passive leader, and there is always an alpha leader," General Silver was fond of saying. "The alpha horse is warm-blooded and bossy. They'll push and shove their way to the front. The other horses will get out of their way, but rarely do you see them follow the alpha."

When that mighty blond horse reared up on its hind legs, Linc didn't need to call out an order. He silently, slowly moved into the enclosure. His men fanned out behind him, following in his footsteps.

"The passive leader concerns himself with the herd," General Silver had taught them. "They are watchful of events and will stand by if another horse is separated or in distress. It is for this mindset of unity and egalitarianism that other horses willingly follow them."

When the blond horse had startled, it had nearly knocked over the woman who held it's lead. In that instant, Linc's full attention switched from the troubled horse to the woman.

It was her eyes. Even from yards away, the brilliance of their blue struck him. Linc's shoulders snapped straight when that startling gaze settled on him. He had the drive to rear up onto his toes and paw at the ground at the sight of her. He wanted to growl gleefully in the air to all around him. He wanted to follow her around the enclosure until he had her full attention.

But something was blocking his way to her. It was the tetchy, blond horse that was now loose. Linc had wanted to spring into action and head straight for the blue-eyed angel. He almost had. It was Jefferson's hand on his shoulder that held him back.

Linc had nearly forgotten the General's training. You never charged a nervous horse. Only an alpha would make such a foolish move. You approached the horse calmly, quietly, passively, letting it see that you meant it no harm.

Without a word spoken, the six soldiers spread out around the enclosure. Slowly, quietly, calmly. From the corner of his eyes, Linc could see that even their breaths were in sync. The President's Men moved as a unit toward the beast, cutting off any route of escape.

The horse slowed its nervous motions, but it didn't stop. Its head swayed right and left, a sign that it was still anxious. Jefferson's voice rose up. His tones calm and soothing.

"Lower you heard, boy," Jeff said. He lifted his right hand, his left arm hanging limp at his side. "It's all right. We're friends."

As if in a trance, the horse began to heed Jeff's command. Linc took the opportunity to sidestep that action and move around the horse to the woman the horse had broke from.

For the first time, Linc noticed there were actually two women. Neither had moved from their spots at the far side of the enclosure. They both stared, blue eyes agape at the six men surrounding their horse. It was clear these were two of the general's daughters. If not for the brown hair and proud chins, it would be the blue eyes that told him. Linc had never seen another shade like it.

He did a quick visual check of the woman on the other side of the fence. She was younger, a bit of youthful roundness still clung to her cheeks. Her shock was quickly wearing off to be replaced by amusement and something akin to devilry, a look the general used to get in his eyes before calling an audible change in the mission plan.

Linc's gaze skated past the younger Silver to the woman inside the enclosure. Once again, his gaze found hers and held. And held.

The constant fog that had settled around Linc's head since that last op dissipated and cleared as he looked down into her clear blue gaze. With the fog of war gone, everything made sense to him again. All of his thoughts fell into alignment. All of the tracks of his understanding and reasoning synched up and arrowed at her.

Linc's hand itched for his pen and sticky notes. He wanted to be sure he didn't forget anything about her. Not the fact of the tilt at the corner of her right eyelash. Not the notion that her nostrils flared as she exhaled. Not the matter of how the center-left of her lush lips pursed as she took his measure.

He stood at attention for her. His shoulders were back. His chin was high. But he didn't avert his gaze as he'd been taught at the military academy. No, he looked directly into that blue gaze, hoping he passed muster, while he waited for any order she might give. Because he knew, without question, that he'd take on any mission this breathtaking creature assigned him.

"Who are you?" she demanded. Her voice was haughty. Her words clipped. Her tone demanded an answer.

Linc couldn't hide the smile that split his face. She was definitely the General's daughter. Likely the eldest. What was her name? He knew the General had told him. He'd told them all his daughters' names. But the details weren't ones that Linc kept at the top of his list of sticky notes.

"Your father sent me," he said.

At that, her gaze narrowed even further on him. That right eyelash lifting higher. "Let me guess; he sent you to marry me."

That had not been the reason for the mission here. Had it? Linc wanted to consult his notes.

He sent you to marry me.

Linc didn't feel the need to reach into his pocket. His mind was clear. His synapses were firing. In fact, they were rewriting his purpose for being here, on this ranch, in real-time. Across the front of his brain, Linc saw a new web of objectives and tasks arranging themselves. His new mission objective was clear as the light of day, clear as the blue of her gaze.

He sent you to marry me.

Lincoln Rawlings was a soldier first and foremost. He was a man who lived for the next mission. His commander had sent him here as his final mission. But General Silver had not been clear on his objective as he lay dying from his injuries.

He sent you to marry me.

Linc wouldn't need a reminder that this is what he was meant to do with his life. General Silver's daughter's features were burned into every part of his brain, including the parts that weren't working optimally. More importantly, her suggestion was a command he wanted to follow. A mission he was eager to take on. A task he was already tactically preparing for.

He sent you to marry me.

That hadn't exactly been the General's last edict to his men, but every part of Linc was happy to follow this order.

CHAPTER FIVE

"Lincoln Rawlings, ma'am."

It was just three words, but Scout heard the lazy Southern drawl in them. The sound sent a shiver across her shoulder blades. The tall, broad soldier dipped his head, more like a Victorian gentleman would've done in a ballroom upon meeting a young debutant.

Scout was no such flowery miss. So she wasn't sure why her hand raised, knuckles up, as though she were expecting a kiss, instead of palm out, as though she was expecting a quick handshake.

"Scout Silver," she announced, leaving her hand the way it was and waiting in breathless anticipation to see what he would do with her offering.

Lincoln Rawlings didn't disappoint. He took her fingers in his. He didn't lift her hand and bring her knuckles to his lips for a light kiss. Nor did he turn her palm over and crush her fingers in a rough handshake to prove his manliness.

His pinky was the first to make impact. The smallest of his digits spanned the length of her entire hand. That first finger curled at the base of her fingers, just under the webbing where the top of her palm met the calluses just below four of her digits.

Next came his ring finger, which Scout had the presence of mind to notice that it was, in fact, ringless. His middle finger was long enough to wrap around the outside of her thumb. His index finger curled up in a come hither motion as it connected with her own index finger. But he was not done.

His thumb brushed over the back of her hand. It gently caressed the harsh hills of her knuckles until it came to settle in the fleshy valley between her index finger and thumb, making a loop with his own index finger.

This was worse than a gripping handshake. This was better than a courtly brush of lips. Scout felt pulled to this man, lassoed with the ropes coming taut around her. She felt herself coming to heel. She felt herself wanting to follow his lead.

With that last thought, she snatched her hand away from him. Lincoln Rawlings let her go with no resistance. Scout hid her hand behind her back, as though it was a separate entity from her. All the while, the heat he'd ignited with his touch spread like wildfire up her arm and throughout her entire body.

"Scout?" Lincoln said with a grin. "Right, I remember now. You're just as your father described you."

Part of Scout wanted to reject that notion; the idea of her father speaking about any of his daughters for any reason. When he was away, which was most of the time, he treated them as though they didn't exist.

But then there was the other part of her, the part that wanted to know everything her father had said about her to this man. Had he spoken of her in a proud manner? Did he tell Lincoln about her accomplishments? Had he known about her accomplishments? He couldn't have. She'd stopped bothering to tell him years ago. It wasn't like he showed up for any of them.

"Tall, long mane of hair," Lincoln was saying, "and long legs like a colt."

Scout bristled at that. Her father had called her his little colt when she was a child. But that was many years ago. She wasn't sure if she liked Lincoln Rawlings thinking of her as a gangly-legged pony.

"We were his unit." Lincoln spread his arms to encompass the other five men.

Four of the men were resting hips and shoulders against the fence. They all stood, partly watching Lincoln and Scout as they talked, partly watching as the fifth man led Bingley around the enclosure. The horse was calm on the lead, not pulling or even swaying his head.

Scout noted that the man who held the reins was only using one arm to do so. The other hung unnaturally limp at his side. She didn't stare. She had better manners and had seen worse injuries.

"That's Jefferson with the horse," Lincoln said. "And this is Wilson, Jackson, Carter, and Truman."

"Nice to meet you." That came from Brig. "I'm Brigadear."

Brig had tied up Heathcliff and was leaning against the other side of the fence nearest the men. The girl always had been boy crazy. Brig's gaze lingered on the dark-skinned man who stood at the edge of the bunch. There was a touch of gray just above his ear, though he didn't look much older than Scout.

Scout would be the first to admit that the Silver sisters had daddy issues. But Brig seemed to tend toward men who were a bit too old for her. Each of her crushes had always been on her male teachers and not on the boys sitting next to her, jockeying for her attention.

Scout made it a point to glare at the older man; Jackson had been the name Lincoln had called him. For his part, Jackson gave a shake of his head and stepped back from Brig.

"Hey, wait," said Brig, "aren't all those names of the U.S. Presidents?"

"Yup," said the man Lincoln had pointed out as Carter. "Your dad was fond of calling us the President's Men."

"That's cute," Brig said, but her gaze skated past the young Carter with his sculpted hair and landed back on Jackson.

"Funny how you six show up so soon after the reading of my father's will," said Scout.

"We're sorry we couldn't get here sooner," said Lincoln in that sultry voice of his. His gaze was cast down, as though in shame. "Your father made his men pledge that, should he die in combat, to check on his daughters at the Silver Star Ranch, and see if they needed anything."

"How convenient," Scout scoffed as she made her way over to Jefferson and Bingley. She took the reins from the man and turned to lead the horse to the fence. As she did, she looked the six men up and down again.

These were exactly the kinds of men his father wanted for sons. Loyal soldiers, following his orders without question. That hadn't worked so well when her father had produced wily daughter after daughter. So this was his plan to finally get his daughters to heel, marrying these six men and put the ranch in their control.

She could see the general's signature all over this. A contingency plan in case he died. Six husbands for his daughters.

Fat chance that would work. Even if Lincoln was the walking epitome of everything that Scout found attractive in a man. She would never marry him for the sole reason of him being her father's choice.

But at the same time, he was her only choice if she wanted to save the ranch. Could she go through with a marriage to a man set up by the father who had abandoned her?

"We're here at your convenience," Lincoln was saying. "We've all recently separated from the service after..."

Lincoln looked away from her. His mouth shut, and his hazel gaze darkened. It was as though a storm cloud moved in in real-time. Scout had the urge to turn his face back to hers and wipe the look away.

"We have some downtime," said Jefferson, coming to stand beside Lincoln. "We figured we'd come here and help out around the ranch in any way you need."

"In honor of my father's last request?" said Scout.

Lincoln turned back to her. The fog in his gaze lifted. "Yes, ma'am. Anything you girls need. We owe it to the general. We gave our word. A soldier's word is his bond."

Not for all soldiers. But fine. Scout had some jobs that they could do around the ranch while she decided whether or not they passed muster for the job she needed them for most.

CHAPTER SIX

*S*crape. Whoosh. Thud.

The sound of the metal tines hitting the dirt over and over again was surprisingly soothing to Linc. The scent of manure in the air wasn't that much of a bother. The clunking sound the heaps made when sent the heaps into the trash can was oddly satisfying.

"I'm sure this isn't what the General had in mind when he told us to check on his daughters," Carter grumbled.

Scrape. Whoosh. Splat.

Carter dropped his shovel to the ground with a yelp. He lifted the toe of his designer cowboy boots for inspection. "Man, I got horse droppings on my boot."

Linc turned from the male and continued his work. For a man who had crawled through a field of bloodied bodies slogged through the harsh jungle, and even waded bobbing refuse, Carter was extremely fastidious when he was out of fatigues.

The six of them were fresh-faced, well-rested, and up at the crack of dawn. Linc had woken confused in the small log cabin behind the main house of the ranch. But after he'd looked over on the nightstand at the note he'd left himself, his mind instantly cleared.

He'd been looking at that note for months. This morning he was able to check off the first tick on his mission objectives. Reaching for the pen next to the stack of stickies, he put a bold checkmark next to the words Pass Patton.

General Silver had been fond of naming each step of a mission objective or task after other generals and military figures of history. The Patton Objective was the first phase of this mission. They'd arrived at the Silver Star Ranch and met the general's daughters. But somehow Linc knew, their work here wasn't done.

Next objective; Stonewall. He needed to find out what Scout Silver was hiding. Because he knew she was hiding something behind those bright blue eyes. But he had no idea what it could be or how to break past her defenses.

"Does anyone else feel like we walked into a trap?" Truman yanked a length of rope from the tack wall and set about rewrapping it. He made concise circles, but he winced each time he brought the rope up to his shoulder.

Linc's brain focused on the man's wince. The synapses in his brain misfired a few times before the connection was made. Truman pinned down under a heavy pillar, a fallen wall. The man's left hand empty of the sniper rifle always at his side. That was the last time Linc remembered seeing Truman lift a weapon.

"Marriage?" said Truman. "You heard her say that, right?"

Linc's mind traveled back to yesterday. The sight of Scout Silver standing in the sunlight was as clear as a new day in his usually foggy brain.

He sent you to marry me.

Linc had not forgotten those words. They'd played the rest of the day and into the night on a loop inside his head. That was part of his Stonewall Objective; to find out what Scout Silver meant when she'd said those words.

"Didn't we escape all that nonsense by leaving the Purple Heart Ranch," Truman was saying. Marriage was the last thing the man wanted. What Truman wanted was for his shoulder to heal properly and to get back into active duty.

For himself, Linc knew that active duty was no longer in question. Not with the lag time in his thinking and the constant tangle of his thoughts. He was grounded for the rest of his life. What he would do with it, he had no idea.

"Do you really think the general would've wanted any of us for his daughters?"

Linc wasn't sure who'd spoken. Often if he wasn't giving his full attention, he missed these kinds of details. What he was more interested in focusing on was the question itself.

"General Silver was a smart man." Those placating tones were all Wilson. "He was a brilliant tactician who was always two and three steps ahead of the enemy."

"These aren't the enemy," Carter piped in. "They're his daughters."

"Right, his daughters." The cynicism in Truman's voice was hard to mistake. "Who he told us all about."

A large part of their job as soldiers was to hurry up and wait. In those long, waiting hours, the General would share stories about his daughters. Linc knew a lot about Scout. He knew she rescued horses. He knew Saylor was a vet who specialized in large animals; a livestock veterinarian he thought it was called. He'd heard tales of Mareen Silver winning medals in dressage, though Linc still wasn't clear on what that was. Something or other about horse dancing. He knew the twins had done horse vaulting, which he'd figured was akin to gymnastics on a horse. And the youngest, Brig was studying equine therapy at college.

"Then he made us promise to come here in the case of his death," Truman went on. "And the first thing out of his eldest daughter's mouth was marriage."

He sent you to marry me.

Linc shook the thought from his head. "None of us are fit for a wife."

It was true. The blast that had taken the General from them had left wounds too deep to heal any time soon. Definitely too deep to bring a woman into any of their spheres. But even as he thought of all the negatives, the possibility of it thrilled Linc.

He sent you to marry me.

Linc had no trouble remembering each of those words. The flare of her nostrils as she said them. The pull at the corner of her eyes as she'd sized him up.

Had that been hope in her blue eyes? Had it been anger? He couldn't be sure.

"But I'm happy to do any work we can for these girls," said Linc. "It's the least we can do for them."

A silent agreement settled in the barn. They each knew why it was the least of things. Because they had failed to do one thing. They'd failed to save the girls' father. If that mission hadn't gone wrong, the general might be here now mucking out these stalls himself.

Linc lifted his gaze as a truck ambled down the road. Two women hopped out to unlatch the gate. When the gate swung inward, he saw the silver star emblem of the ranch. It still galled Linc when he thought about the honor ceremony where they'd each received the Silver Star Medal. The medal was for their bravery in that last mission. Brave they'd been, but the mission had not been accomplished. They'd lost their commander. They'd each lost a part of themselves.

Linc turned his attention back to the horses. At least this was one mess that he could clean up. He'd only make a mess if he even thought about anything more than his duty to Scout Silver.

Linc caught a heap of manure up into his shovel and tossed it. The movements were practiced ones from his time at the Purple Heart Ranch. He'd loved working with the horses there. They were uncomplicated animals. They didn't require words to understand them. He need only look into their eyes and see what they needed.

The horse in the back stall stuck his head out. It had a dark mane of hair that was the color of midnight. But its large eyes were brown and fathomless.

No. Not fathomless. Linc saw confusion in those depths. He watched the horse gaze around at the walls confining him and then lower his head. The magnificent beast pawed at the ground and shook his head from side to side as though in a panic at the confinement.

Linc didn't think. He reacted. He dropped his shovel and went to the stall.

The gold plate on the stall read Wickham. Linc put his hand out to the horse. Wickham backed up. His ears went flat to his neck, a sure sign of aggression.

Linc held still, breathing calmly in and out, and waited. It took a few tense moments, but slowly the horse's ears relaxed. It took first one, then another tentative step toward him. Wickham dipped his head, as though sniffing Linc's palm like a dog would a new friend.

Apparently, Linc passed muster for the horse. Wickham nudged Linc's hand up and onto his long nose. Linc obliged, patting the horse's muzzle. Even being so bold as to scratch behind the horse's ears, which didn't flatten again.

Wickham raised his soulful gaze to Linc. The communication between man and horse was clear. The horse needed to get out of this confinement. He needed some space to roam. Linc understood the sentiment perfectly.

CHAPTER SEVEN

"Who called the hot guy brigade?" asked Tilly as she tossed her bag down on the kitchen counter. Her blonde hair hung down in lush waves over her shoulders as her blue eyes widened to take in the sight out the back window.

Saylor, who was on Tilly's heels, had her head craned over one shoulder like an owl trying to determine if it had found a new sparkly treasure or if there was danger afoot. "Are they here for lessons? Or… something?"

Saylor's brown tresses were pulled back into an orderly queue that rested between her shoulder blades. Those blades were tense at the same time as they sagged forward. It hadn't escaped Scout that her sister hadn't come home last night.

"They're not here for lessons," said Scout. "But they are here for something."

She stood at the large picture window in the kitchen that sat over the huge farmhouse sink. Saylor came up to her right shoulder, Tilly came to stand at her left. Brig stood on tippy toes to look over Scout's shoulder.

"Well?" said Tilly. "What are they here for?"

The men in question had been set to mucking out the horse stalls when they woke at the crack of dawn this morning. Scout had startled to see them coming out of the cabins that arced around the big house.

There were six cabins. The General had had one built for each of his daughters on their thirteenth birthdays. It had never occurred to him to wait until the more monumental sixteenth birthday. Nor did the idea of jewelry or a car ever enter his strategic mind.

No, General Silver felt that the pinnacle year of any child's life was when they turned thirteen. And homeownership was his idea of a meaningful gift. In his defense, each of his daughters had a pony before they could walk.

"The General sent them," said Scout.

"Sent them for what?" asked Saylor.

"He sent them to marry us," Brig squealed behind Scout's ear.

Scout ducked her head just in time for the barrage of sonic sounds to assault her. There was Brig still squealing her eagerness. There was Tilly's shriek of indignance at their father's heavy-handedness. There was Saylor's blaring silence as her gaze swung from the window to Scout and back again.

The six men were out of the barn. They lined their shovels up against the wall, just like toy soldiers. Scout didn't doubt that the interior of the structure would be entirely spotless. They were the General's men, and she knew first hand that General Silver did not suffer uncleanliness.

What she wasn't expecting was for a couple of the men to remove their shirts from their bodies to wipe the sweat from their brows and neck. Lincoln Rawlings was one of the strippers.

Her ears were ringing. But not from her sisters' chatterboxes. Each Silver sister was quiet as they took in the scene of bare, man flesh before them.

Muscles. Lots of muscles. Biceps glistening in the late morning sun. Chests rising and sinking with deep breaths and gulps of the lemonade Brig had set out earlier. A few pats on the back, as though for a job well done, but more than likely for a well-delivered jab between friends. And then, the kicker.

Lincoln Rawlings smiled. Grinned was more like it. That's when the morning shifted to afternoon, and the sun shone brightly in the sky. So bright that the rays passed through the glass of the kitchen window and warmed Scout all the way through.

"Dad sent us a squad of men?" said Tilly, all hints of indignation had slipped from her voice.

"Hmmm," hummed Brig.

"They said they're here to marry us?" said Saylor, her shoulders now straight.

"Hmmm," repeated Brig.

"No, they didn't say that," said Scout. "But the timing of it…"

"You think dad planned this?" said Tilly.

"Wouldn't be the first time the General tried to move his family around on a chessboard."

"I'll marry one," said Brig, raising her hand.

"You are not getting married," said Scout. "You're too young."

"I'm a college senior," Brig countered. "And besides, if we don't do this, then we lose the ranch."

Scout pinched her earlobe. She caught sight of Lincoln dipping back into the barn. As he went, he pulled his shirt back over his head. Scout sighed… in relief, of course. Barns were messy places, and she didn't want to be responsible for dry cleaning.

"I'd never marry a soldier," Tilly was saying.

"But you'd marry a Russian mobster," said Scout.

"Sergei is not a mobster."

"Where's his picture."

Tilly pinched her lips together in the way she'd done since she was three when she was trying to explain her child logic to an adult.

"Ordering up a male order, Russian groom is not how we're going to deal with this either." Scout put force into her voice. But she was dealing with one of General Silver's daughters.

Though she pitied any scam artist who thought they could worm their way into this family, she kinda hoped one would try. The

Silver sisters had terrorized the valley for years. Teachers groaned when they learned they'd have one in their classrooms. Coaches' hair turned gray when they learned one of the girls might be on their team for the season. Heaven help them if they had to deal with two at a time.

"I promised I'd get married. It's not like I have to stay married. Our parents certainly didn't."

But that's not how Scout wanted to treat a marriage. She wanted to get into a relationship and stay there. Just like this had been her home all her life, she didn't want to bounce around in a relationship.

"Well, I certainly don't need to marry one of them," said Saylor.

The three sisters turned away from the window and looked at her. Really looked at her. The tension in Saylor's shoulders was gone, but she wasn't relaxed. She was never relaxed. Looking into her eyes, Scout could always see the truth.

The bags under her eyes weren't going down, letting Scout know that she'd faced another sleepless night last evening. Her blue eyes were red and puffy, not shining and bright. What had that creep done now?

"Nick is thinking about proposing," said Saylor. Her voice didn't go shrill with delight. It wobbled with uncertainty.

"He said that?" asked Tilly.

"Well, I brought it up, and he didn't shoot it down. So..." Saylor let that linger, her gaze on the ground.

"So, he's thinking about it," said Brig. Her tone was a clear attempt to be helpful to her older sister, but the hard glint in her blue eyes gave credence to what Tilly and Scout were both thinking.

Nick was Saylor's first boyfriend. Though it had taken him years of clandestine dating before he allowed her to call him that. Years while he was dating other girls right under Saylor's nose. But just like now, Saylor's gaze was down on the floor. Scout hated that her sister thought she only deserved the scraps on the floor.

Maybe marrying one of the guys outside wasn't such a bad idea. Especially if Scout could thrust Saylor onto one of them. But not

Lincoln. Maybe the soft-spoken Jefferson who had been so good with her horse the other day.

Lincoln was walking back out of the barn. But he wasn't alone. He had a horse on a lead. A dark horse who was already starting to tug.

"Scout, what's wrong? Your face just went pale?"

"It's Wickham."

CHAPTER EIGHT

hen Linc had stepped out of the sun and back into the barn, the dimness of the space had confused him. The sticky note at the top of his post-its gave the objective to clean the stalls. But looking around, they were already mucked. So what was he doing back in here?

At the back of the barn, he heard a pitiful whinny. The fog cleared from Linc's brain and his steps became purposeful. He marched to the back and up to the horse.

William? No, Wickham was the name emblazoned in the door to the horse's quarters. Linc felt like he should know that name, but he didn't want to press his brain too hard. He'd completed the task given to him this morning by Scout, but he wanted to do more.

After giving Wickham a reassuring pat on the muzzle, Linc turned to the tack wall. He'd had Truman organize the equipment there into a more logical array. They'd hung saddles and bridles up on the wall instead of posting them on the portable saddle racks. Now there was more space on the floor. They'd added more hooks to hang halters, crops, reins, and girths. He'd made a note to build some wall-hanging cabinets for additional storage.

With his way cleared, Linc reached for a halter. Turning back to

Wickham, he held up the device. The horse's large eyes caught sight of the halter and bowed its head. Clearly, Wickham wanted to be out and free for a spell. Linc doubted Scout would mind. It would be another thing off her to-do list if he gave this antsy horse a bit of exercise.

As soon as the door to the stall opened, the seemingly charming horse reared up.

Linc knew better than to panic and try to pull down or step back. Instead, he loosened the reins and stood his ground. The blast from that fatal mission had left his brain foggy and unable to hold normal processes in his head. But when it came to horses, it was all instinctual.

He knew that Wickham was trying to show dominance. The horse was clearly an alpha male. But so was Linc.

After Wickham reared and his front hooves landed back on the ground, Linc pulled down on the ropes of the halter. With the horse's muzzle down, Linc advanced, causing the horse to take several steps back. It also established exactly which alpha was in control.

They stood there like that for several moments. Staring each other down. Once Linc was sure man and beast had an understanding, he led the horse out of the barn.

Wickham stayed in step with Linc as he took one turn around the enclosure. Satisfied by this behavior, Linc brought the horse over for a visit with the men. He could positively feel the horse's delight at being amongst the other males. Horses were, after all, herd animals. They didn't like to be separated from their pack. It was clear Wickham wanted to be apart of the President's Men.

"Stop what you're doing."

Lincoln gripped the reins tight as he turned to the sound of that voice. There was the timbre of her father in Scout Silver's voice. But just a timbre. There was still a healthy helping of the feminine in that sultry voice. It sent a shiver up and down Linc's spine until it came to settle somewhere in his chest.

"He's dangerous," said Scout.

"Who? Wickham?" Lincoln frowned. "Nah, he's pretty well behaved."

Of course, at that moment, Linc felt the horse's head preparing to jerk as though he was going to rear up again. Before Wickham could misbehave and prove him wrong, Linc gave a yank down on the ropes in his hand. The horse sighed in submission, like a child whose parent yanked his hand away from the cookie jar before he could reach in.

Scout pursed her lips at the two of them. Clearly, she'd seen the dominance play. Her gaze on the horse was one of disappointment. Wickham had the presence of mind to focus his large eyes down on the ground.

Scout's look at Linc was a cross between exasperation and bewilderment. He gathered the poor woman wasn't sure what to do with him.

"He's not usually good with people," she said, giving the horse another assessing glance.

"Neither am I these days," said Linc. "But I think we understand each other."

Now Scout's assessing gaze was back on Linc. Linc wanted to understand her. He wanted Scout to understand him.

"That's enough recreation for now," she said. "Mr. Wickham needs to be put up. He's on a schedule."

"Yes, ma'am."

Scout allowed Linc to lead Wickham back into the barn. She was close on their heels. So when she gasped, Linc heard the intake of breath.

"What have you done in here?" she asked, her eyes fixed on the tack wall.

"Just organized things," Linc said as he led Wickham back into his stall and shut the horse in. "Is it not to your liking? I can change it."

"No," she whispered, her hand grazing over the hanging saddles. "No, it's… perfect. It makes sense to have everything just as you've arranged it. It's exactly what I didn't know I needed."

Linc's chest puffed up at her praise. He wondered what else she didn't know she needed. He was determined to find out. That was still his mission. He wanted to pass Stonewall. He wanted to find out what she was hiding so that he could be the one to give her what she needed. Everything seemed clear when he was looking into her eyes. He wished he could do it every day for the rest of his life; have the clarity he saw when he looked at her.

"Why are you really here?" she said.

"I told you; your father sent me."

"What for?"

"For whatever you need."

Linc pushed off the door to Wickham's stall. He stepped toward Scout. He held out his hands, worried that she would rear back. She didn't. Like the alpha mare that she was, she held her ground.

"You really don't know?" she said. "Do you?"

He shook his head. But whatever it was, Linc wanted to know. Instead of asking, Linc held his tongue and remained silent. He found that often worked best when he wasn't certain what he should be doing or how he should be responding.

"This is my home," she said. "It's always been my home. I don't want to leave it."

"Why would you have to? Are you having money troubles? I can help—"

"No. I'm not...anymore. It was hard after my parent's second divorce. But my sisters and I turned this place around. It's not making a huge profit, but it's enough to pay the bills and send Brig to school."

"Then what? What do you need."

"Why did he send you?"

Now it was Linc who swallowed. Could she see through him? Did she know their failure to her father? The military had called them heroes, given them medals. But not a single man that served her father felt deserving of those honors.

"He sent me to take care of anything you need. Is there something you need, Scout?"

"Yeah." Her chin jutted up in the same way her father's would when his superiors questioned his strategy. "I need a husband."

The admission didn't shock him. It was kinda hard to shock a man whose brain fogged over most of the day. Somehow, Lincoln felt he'd known this all along. This had been his objective in coming here. He'd just passed Objective Stonewall.

"My dad put in his will that each of his daughters has to get married within the year, or the ranch goes to his remaining ex-wife. Cruella—I mean Catherine— hates this ranch and will sell it the first chance she gets."

Lincoln moved closer, the need to protect this woman over-whelming him. For some reason, the love story of George and Martha Washington came to his mind. The two had doted on one another and been nearly inseparable their whole marriage.

"With you all coming here, on the General's orders, so soon after his death, I just thought…"

Scout's gaze lifted to his. The blue was so vibrant that everything else around him paled to shades of dull gray. The idea of catching her, saddling her with a ring on her finger, and leading her through these pastures for the rest of his life was all his mind could wrap around.

"You think he sent me here to marry you?" said Linc.

Scout nodded.

The very thought of having a new person in his life, having to learn their patterns when his mind could barely hold onto the processes in his past, should've sent Linc into a panic. But the idea of marriage to this woman felt like the most natural thing in the world.

"Okay," he said.

Scout finally took a step back. "Okay?"

"Yes, okay." He took a step toward her. When she didn't rear back, he continued. "I'll marry you."

"You'll…marry…me?"

"If it will help you keep this place that you love, if it'll help keep you safe, then yes."

The mission specs were forming in Linc's mind. To fulfill the General's dying wish, he needed to protect his daughters. To do that, he needed to protect the ranch. To do that, he needed to marrying Scout.

He saw no hardship in this new objective, the Washington Objective.

"Yes?" Scout frowned. "Why?"

Because he felt grounded near her. Because he had already memorized every line of her face. Because the sound of her voice cleared the fog in his brain.

"Because I owe your father."

CHAPTER NINE

"You cannot marry him." Tilly threw her hands up. When she did, flakes of white flour rained down, mixing in with her blonde curls, making her look like a Christmas angel. "You just met him."

"I think it's romantic," said Brig, dipping a finger into the cake mix instead of the wooden stirring spoon. She brought her finger and the sweet batter into her mouth but still managed to clearly say, "Like something out of a Hallmark movie."

"I don't have many options," Scout said as she opened the oven door to check the roast. Just another minute and the meat would be ready to fall off the bones. "We're running out of time."

"I still think we can contest the general's will," said Saylor from the other end of the kitchen. Her back was against a wall as she tossed a bright salad of lettuce, tomatoes, and cucumbers.

They'd already been over the will with a lawyer and a fine-tooth comb. Granted, the lawyer they'd hired had been off a late-night TV ad. And he hadn't taken their call the first couple of times, thinking their case was a prank. And also that he'd laughed, rather unprofessionally, when he'd finally gone over the paperwork. Only to deliver the news that the document would hold up in a court of law.

Either each Silver sister gets married to retain her rights to the land, or the ranch goes to their stepmother.

Scout could still remember the first time Cruella had come to the ranch. Each of her footsteps had been light, careful, as though she were certain she'd step on horse droppings even when she stood in the family room. Her nose had been turned up at the same time her lips had been turned down, as though she smelled something foul as dinner roasted in the oven.

Catherine Chesterfield Silver had hated this place and wanted to leave the moment she came here. She hadn't come back, but she'd left her mark. She'd urged the General to turn the ranch into something useful, like an exclusive resort.

Just the thought made Scout shudder. The sound of her sisters' bickering brought her back to the present reality. Tilly swatted at Brig's hand as she tried to swipe another taste of cake mix. Saylor wiped at the flour on Brig's cheek before their youngest sister could get away from the maternal care.

This wasn't an exclusive resort for the rich and dainty. This was their home. And it would stay their home until her last breath. If it took marrying a stranger to keep it that way, then so be it.

Looking out the back window, Scout saw the man in question. Linc leaned against one of the fences outside of the cabins. The other five men were arrayed around him. They all listened intently as he spoke.

She could guess what that conversation was about. Their crazy idea to get married was the topic both in and out of doors. The thing was that it didn't feel crazy. It felt like the right decision.

Over the years, many people had brought their horses to Scout. They'd claimed the animals were broken, wounded beyond healing. Each time, Scout had looked into the horse's eyes and saw the truth; it wasn't the horse that was broken. Once she took the horse under her lead, the improvements were always dramatic.

Linc had that look of a wounded spirit in his dark eyes. All of the soldiers did. They all belonged here. She knew this place would heal whatever the General had put them through. In that way, the President's Men were just like her sisters. They needed a refuge to heal from his neglect and abandonment.

No, she wouldn't mind having them here at all. In fact, an even better idea would be to have her sisters each marry one of them. It didn't have to be forever. Marriage was a temporary promise if their father had taught them anything. Scout was liking this plan more and more.

"You do see that the general is meddling in our affairs from the grave," said Tilly.

The words were garbled, but Scout understood them. Scout looked up to see Tilly's mouth around a cakey mixing spoon.

"Yeah," agreed Scout. "He's still trying to get his little soldiers in formation. But this time with actual soldiers."

"I don't mind," said Brig, saddling up beside Scout to look at the men outside.

"I don't need a soldier," said Saylor. "Nick is the guy for me."

Scout didn't need to look over at Brig to see that she was sighing alongside her. All of the Silver girls agreed, even Mareen, that Nick was most definitely not the guy for Saylor. Just another reason to fall in line with the soldiers.

"How is Nick?" Brig asked, her voice pitched high with false interest. "It's been ages since we've seen him. Why don't you invite him over?"

Scout couldn't hide the wicked grin spreading across her face. From across the room, she saw Tilly's gaze narrowing in the same calculation.

"I don't think so," said Saylor. "You guys make him uncomfortable."

"Us?" said Tilly, in the same high pitch as Brig, but her tone was laced with false sincerity. "What have we done?"

"Well, there was the time you put nuts in his burger," Saylor said.

"I was trying out a new recipe."

"He's allergic to nuts."

Tilly shrugged. "It must've slipped my mind."

"Or the time you gave him Wickham to ride," Saylor turned to

Scout.

Scout held up her hands in self-defense. "Hey, he said he could handle any horse."

Saylor crossed her arms over her chest and frowned at each of her sisters. "Look, guys, I know he's not your favorite person. But he's my favorite person. He's the one for me. And we all need to get married to save this place, so…"

Saylor let that sentence trail off. Scout's gaze trailed out the window. She knew how she wanted that sentence to end. But first, she had to get her own marriage underway.

"All I know," said Scout, "is that we can't afford to lose this place. It's what holds us together."

"This place isn't what holds us together," said Tilly. "Our blood holds us together."

Scout's heart pounded in her chest at Tilly's words. She loved her sisters fiercely. Though Tilly only had half their blood, Scout had never looked at the twins as anything but all hers.

"Speaking of blood," said Scout. "I'm surprised Cruella hasn't been sniffing around."

"I don't think Mareen told her," said Saylor.

"You talked to her?" asked Scout, the prickles on the backs of her hands standing straight at the thought of the bond Saylor and Mareen shared.

"She's our sister."

"Half-sister," Scout corrected.

"She's the only other sister that's getting married."

"I bet she'll call it off to spite us. Definitely, if Cruella tells her to."

Saylor didn't stand up to that remark. From what Scout knew the marriage between Mareen and Sylvester Savino was not a love match. It was more of a society match. Didn't matter to Scout as long as the two tied the knot before the end of the year.

"I still say you can't marry a stranger, Scout," Saylor was saying.

"He's not a stranger. The General vetted him."

And besides, Scout liked Lincoln Rawlings. And so did her horses. That was a good enough character reference for her.

CHAPTER TEN

"One; we can stay here indefinitely." Linc held up the first post-it and pressed it to the fencing. The yellow patch of paper stuck there. He pulled off the second note from the post-it pad. "Two; we can work with the horses. Three..."

But the post-it he held in his hand said four. Linc shuffled them around, but he couldn't find number three. What had he written down as the third reason they should each consider marrying one of the Silver sisters for the Washington Objective?

"This is just crazy." Truman threw up his hands. It was hard to miss the wince as he did so. He hunched his injured shoulder to his ear but continued his tirade. "Didn't we just leave a ranch where soldiers had to get married in order to stay there? What is this? Some cosmic craziness to force all military personnel into holy matrimony?"

"I don't know? I wouldn't mind." Jefferson fastened the sling that cradled his limp arm. They were all about to head into polite company, and he liked to keep the limb out of the way and out of sight when around others.

"You think you're ready to twirl a bride around on the dance floor," said Truman.

"Hey." Jackson pointed a blunt thumb at Truman. "That was a low blow."

Truman huffed an apology, but he did not look cowed. "It's just that I'm not a charity case."

"None of us are," said Jefferson. "What if this was apart of the general's plan all along?"

Linc still couldn't find the third reason to commence Objective Washington, but he had found the final reason he'd written down on a post-it. He held that note up for all the men to see. "We owe it to the general."

The silence in the fields was deafening. Even the animals went mute at the sight of the writing Linc posted on the fence. Their last mission for the general had been total mission failure. Though the United States Military hadn't seen it that way.

The President's Men had saved the lives of twelve aid workers and civilians. But they'd lost their most precious asset; their leader.

"We pledged to him that we'd see that his daughters were taken care of," said Linc. "Well, this is what they need."

"But wait," said Truman. "You said he put this in his will, that his daughters had to get married to keep the ranch? And then, before he died, he made us pledge to come here."

Truman looked around the ranch. Then he looked at each man in turn. "It's a setup."

Linc shrugged. Maybe it was. Maybe this was the General's true dying wish, that his men and his daughters all become a new unit. Linc had no problem with those orders as long as he could be united with Scout.

He liked the way he felt when he was near Scout Silver. He liked gazing at her. He liked hearing her talk. Her voice rang so clearly in his head.

Linc's path was clear. Marry Scout. Make sure all of her sisters got married so they could save the ranch. Work on the ranch. Live happily ever after. He didn't even need to write that process down to remember it.

"Just have dinner with the girls," said Linc. "See if you hit it off with one of them."

"I'm keeping my mouth shut," said Truman.

"Thank God for small favors," said Jackson.

Linc turned on his heel and started for the house. As they'd done countless times before, the men all fell in line behind him. They walked into the main house, showered, and clean-shaven from the day's work on the ranch. What they saw inside the four walls of the dining room made each man groan in pure delight and hunger.

There was a veritable feast on the table. A roasted steak that was already carved sat at the center. Around the slices of meat were small potatoes whose herbaceous seasoning brought Linc closer to the table. Even the colorful salad that was off to the side of the main dish looked appetizing. There was the sweet smell of cake in the air, though unseen. Lincoln was certain the happy groans, and grumbling bellies were causing some minds to change about the mission objective he'd outlined.

"So, you're marrying my sister," said the youngest one just as Linc had lifted a healthy portion of the meal onto his plate.

What was her name again? He had it on a post-it. But he also had a knife in one hand and a fork in his other. He was not about to relinquish either to retrieve the note. So, he decided to chance it.

"Yes, Brenda-"

"It's Brig."

"Right. Sorry." Linc put down his knife. He itched to reach for the post it in his pocket, but he didn't think he could do it inconspicuously. So, he reached for the salt shaker instead.

"Not off to a good start, are you," said the blonde sister whose name Linc also couldn't remember.

Linc looked to Scout. She scowled at each sister and then turned an encouraging smile on him. Linc got lost in that smile. He forgot everyone at the table. He forgot the salt shaker in his left hand. He forgot the fork in his right.

All he saw was Scout. He wanted to impress her. He wracked his brain for the right word, the right name. And there it was. He had it.

"I'm sorry," Linc said, turning to the blonde. "I'm not so good with names. Got knocked on the head one too many times, Terry."

"It's Tilly."

Linc winced. He could feel the flush creeping up his neck and spreading across his cheeks. A bead of sweat formed on his brow. The moisture collected there, threatening to drop into his eyes. Again, his hand itched to go to the notes in his pocket.

But all eyes were on him. Instead of reaching into his pocket, he poised the salt shaker over his steak, sprinkling the crystals over the perfectly cooked meat. When he looked up to Scout, she was frowning at him this time. He was really blowing it.

"So, Brig," said Jackson. "What is it you're studying in school? I think your father mentioned equine therapy."

"My dad talked about me?" said Brig.

"Yeah," said Jefferson. "He talked about all of you. All the time."

"He never told us anything about you," said Brig. The young woman's attention stuck on Jackson. "He never told us anything about … anything."

"Most of it is classified," said Wilson. It was the first thing he'd said since sitting down at the table. Wilson didn't like to talk about any mission, but especially not the last one. More than any of the men, he blamed himself for the General's death.

"The General wasn't much of a talker when he was home," said Scout. "Except if it was to shout orders at us."

Linc didn't like the bitterness in her tone. He especially didn't like the hurt at the corner of her eyes. He didn't understand that. The General had loved each of his daughters fiercely. The pride in his blue eyes was clear to see each time he spoke of them.

"I'm sorry about that," said Linc. "But you should know he was very proud of each of you. He always said his daughter Scout could rehabilitate any horse you brought to her. He said Saylor could fix any broken bone on any animal. He talked about Mareen's awards in dressage. And the twins, Tilly and Gunnery, and how they'd taken the world of vaulting by storm when they were younger. And he had printouts of Brig's straight-A report cards at his desk."

Silence greeted Linc after he closed his mouth. Once again, he looked up to find all eyes on him. What had he said now? He couldn't remember. No sooner had the words left his mouth than they'd receded into the recesses of his brain.

"You got all our names right," said Brig. Her face split into a wide grin, her blue eyes shining at him.

For the first time in a long time, Linc allowed himself to grin back. He'd forgotten the pleasure of smiling at someone. He'd forgotten what it felt like to feel proud of himself.

He carved off a bite of the steak. He put it into his mouth. And he barely maintained his manners by not spitting it back out.

"Something wrong with my steak, soldier?" asked Scout.

"No, it's great." But Linc's words were choked around the salty bit of meat.

"Then why did you put a pound of salt on it?"

Linc's mind rewound back a few moments. He could remember picking up the salt shaker. And then he recalled shaking the small glass container not once, not twice, but three times.

A slight chill went through him. Again the hairs lifted on his forearms, as well as on the back of his neck. His scalp prickled with the awareness that everyone was looking at him.

"Easy now," whispered Jeff.

But Linc couldn't take it easy. He couldn't remember names. He couldn't remember handling a salt shaker. How did he think he could manage a marriage?

CHAPTER ELEVEN

*S*cout finished giving Bingley his morning rub down before she deposited the bale of hay in his stall. The horse let out a gust of air in thanks. Then he got to work on his breakfast.

The stalls on either side of Bingley's were empty. Both Heathcliff and Wickham were out in the corral having their breakfast with the other horses whose injuries were either healed or not pronounced enough to cause any issues. The wounded and still healing, like Bingley, remained in the barn, eating their breakfast in bed. They weren't ready for the morning meal games the others played in the corral.

Outside, three horses were snacking on three piles of hay. But after a few bites, Wickham decided he needed to try a different pile. Pinning his ears, he headed over to the next pile where Heathcliff had been happily munching. After being chased off his pile by Wickham, Heathcliff squealed at Tilney, running the gelding off to the next pile. After a few minutes of chewing, Wickham would decide he wanted some of what Heathcliff was having in the next pile, and the game of musical hay piles would start again.

The soldiers sitting around the fencing clearly found these antics amusing. Jackson slapped Wilson on the shoulder, eliciting the first grin Scout had seen from the man. Jefferson rubbed rapidly at his injured arm as he laughed alongside Carter and Truman.

Scout looked to the left and saw nothing but open pasture. She looked to the right and saw her sisters in the distance taking care of the mares' feeding in a separate pasture.

"Morning, Scout."

Scout looked up to see that Jefferson had made his way over to her. He'd captured his injured arm up in a sling.

"Morning," Scout said. "You all sleep okay?"

"Best bed I've been in in years."

"Good. Good." Scout nodded. "Breakfast should be ready soon. You all are welcome to join us."

"We appreciate that, but you know you don't have to cook for us every meal. We can take some of that work off your hands."

"Right. Sure, sure." After an awkward moment's silence, Scout cleared her throat and asked what she really wanted to know. "I haven't seen Lincoln around."

She aimed for casual, but her voice missed the mark. Whoever had just spoken sounded breathless and maybe a bit needy. Which she certainly wasn't. She was just curious.

Dinner last night had been a bust. They hadn't argued, not exactly. Could what happened even be called a disagreement?

So he hadn't liked the taste of her cooking. So he hadn't gotten the names of her sisters right the first time. Those flubs hadn't been enough to deter her. She still wanted to go forward with this marriage of convenience. The question was, did he?

"Linc went for a walk earlier to clear his head." Jeff looked off toward the western side of the property.

"Clear his head?" Each of those three words came out of her mouth with a question mark.

Jefferson sighed as he regarded her. He scratched at his chin before he spoke. "Look, you gotta give him some space from time to time. That last mission... it messed with all of us."

"Is he a danger to me?" Scout was desperate to save her ranch, but not desperate enough to put herself, her sisters, and her horses in any danger.

Jefferson's hand dropped from his chin, and his shoulders went erect, like a soldier standing at attention. "Lincoln Rawlings would never hurt you or any of your sisters. None of us would. We all pledged to your father that we would look after you. That's a promise none of us will ever break."

Scout thought over Jefferson's words. She believed him. But there was something still niggling at the back of her mind that she was missing something. "Is he a danger to himself?"

Jefferson's shoulders didn't relax into an at ease pose. They slumped in defeat. "Not in the way you think."

Jefferson pursed his lips. Indecision was clear on his face. Scout wasn't sure, but she thought she might've seen the pinky finger of his injured hand twitch.

"Despite our job, none of us are violent men. We're all still in recovery from our injuries, from the separation from the military, from trying to figure out what to do next."

"I understand," said Scout. And she did.

Though she'd never been in a war zone, her family had been through three divorces. The saying love is a battlefield was an apt one. Children of divorce have their own forms of PTSD that stay with them all their lives despite what the experts might say. And Scout would know; she'd been to her fair share of family counseling.

"Next to your father, Linc is the best man I know," said Jefferson. "I don't know why the General wrote his will the way he did. But we'd do anything to help you. We owe him that."

"So, you'll marry one of my sisters because you feel you owe our dad?"

"I'm at your service." Jeff didn't hesitate. He gave a sharp nod that felt like a salute. "It would be my honor."

His gaze lifted. Brig and Saylor were laughing as they made their way back to the house. It was good to hear Saylor laugh. She rarely did these last few years that she'd been in a relationship with The Boyfriend.

It was clear Jeff was eyeing one of her sisters. Scout just wasn't sure which one. If there could be one good thing that would come out of the General's insane will demands, it would be that The Boyfriend balked at marriage, forcing Saylor to marry one of these soldiers. Each and every one of them, even the scowling Truman would be better than Nick.

Scout grabbed a saddle from the barn and headed to the eastern pasture. Unlike the musical chairs of breakfast, Lizzie, Fanny, and Emma all ate from their own piles. No one shoved the other out of the way.

"Morning, Lizzie."

A chestnut brown head lifted from the bale of hay. The mare walked toward Scout, lowering her muzzle like a dog seeking a scratch. Scout obliged the horse, rubbing up and down the white stripe of her nose.

"Wanna go for a ride?"

Scout saddled up her horse and headed off in the direction Jeff had indicated Linc had wandered off. She passed by the old forts the Matthews and Silver kids had built when they pretended they were at war. She was happy to see that the Silver fort still looked sturdy while the Matthews structure leaned to the side.

It didn't take Scout long to find the man she was looking for. When she spotted him, she saw that he was standing in a place she didn't want to go.

Her father's stone was right next to her mother's. They were together again finally. Though Scout wouldn't have been surprised if she'd found her father's stone turned over all these months after being laid to rest. Her parents had loved hard, but they'd fought just as hard.

Lizzie must have felt Scout's agitation because the horse let out a low whinny.

Linc looked up. His gaze caught and held onto Scout's, but he reached for the horse.

"Whoa, girl," he crooned. "Whoa, now."

Lizzie listened to Linc's gentle voice and steadied. The wobbliness Scout had felt earlier, the uncertainty of what she was doing, that also steadied at his tone. How did this man have that effect on her?

"What are you doing out here?" Scout asked.

Linc turned away from her. He looked at the horse. Then around at his surroundings. Confusion marred his strong brows for a moment. Then he looked down at the headstone. His gaze cleared as though there had never been any fog there.

"I was paying my respects," he said finally. "But I'll go if you want some time..."

"No," Scout said, dismounting.

As she swung her leg over, Linc reached up to grasp her waist. Scout placed her hands on his shoulders as he brought her to the ground.

Scout Silver was not a slight thing. She was built sturdy, like all her sisters. But Linc had just handled her as though she weighed nothing. It made her feel dainty, like something precious.

"I was just..." She let the sentence trail off. She was just what? Stalking him? "I was just coming to find you for breakfast."

"I got up early and took a walk to clear my mind," he said. "I must've gotten turned around. I didn't realize the time."

Linc looked out at the vast fields. His hold was still on her waist. Scout felt no need to move out of his embrace.

"It's easy to lose your way out here if you don't know where you're going," she said.

"Hmmm." Linc turned back to gaze down at her. "I would've found my way back eventually."

He was a foot taller than her. That was a rare thing; for a man to have much or any height on her. Both her parents had been tall; the General over six feet. Her mom just under. Scout felt small as she tilted her head back and looked up at Linc—and she liked it.

"But you found me," he continued. "When I'm around you, things are so clear."

Scout was not the type of girl that boys wrote poetry for. But that had to be the most poetic, romantic thing anyone had ever said to her. If things kept going like this with this man, she might actually have to send up thanks to her father for depositing Lincoln Rawlings on her doorstep. That would be most annoying.

"So clear, in fact, that I've come to a decision." Linc finally let her go. He took a step back, folding his hands behind his back in that way of soldiers. "I can't marry you."

Scout blinked. Then she blinked again, this time leaving her eyes narrowed on him. "You what?"

"The last mission messed me up. It messed all of us up."

"Yeah, I heard." Scout couldn't help but look over his body. Lincoln Rawlings looked like a perfectly fit specimen, except for the scar on his forehead. But even that added to his handsomeness. "You said you'd help-"

"And I will," he interrupted. "But I promised your father that I'd do what's best for you. I believe you should marry Jackson."

Behind them, Lizzie let out a low whine. The horse backed up a few paces as though she could sense the oncoming storm.

"You're passing me off to one of your men?" said Scout.

"Jackson's a better fit for you than me," said Linc. "He's a better man than I am."

Linc ran his fingers through his hair. When he lifted his hand, a small, square piece of paper escaped his palm. The post-it sized note floated down and landed against Scout's chest.

Scout reached for the note. Flipping it over, she could barely make out the chicken scratch written there. Slowly, the squiggles and scratches began to make sense.

Reasons to let her go was written across the top. There was only one item on the list. And what she read there was unbelievable.

*L*inc's first instinct had been to grab for the post-it. Though his mind was prone to fog, he knew better than to grab where the parcel of paper had landed. His mind might be muddled, but his manners were intact. So he'd kept his hands off Scout, which meant he could do nothing when she retrieved the missive from the top of her blouse.

"Please give that here," he said.

But it was too late. She'd already seen the writing on the paper. Linc had no trouble remembering those words. He'd only written the note a few minutes ago when he'd been communing with the general.

Linc had taken the time to explain to his former commander that he wasn't fit for the mission the General had sent him on. Even though it was a job Linc desperately wanted.

Holding Scout to him a moment ago had felt like the rightest thing in the world. Letting her go so that she could stand on her own two feet, and aiming to send her in the direction of Jackson? Well, that had been the hardest thing he'd ever had to do. And he'd faced down insurgents in suicide vests.

"You don't think you're worthy of me?"

Linc closed his eyes as he heard his words come out of Scout's perfect mouth. Part of him reveled at the disbelief in her tone. His heart kicked against his chest as she narrowed her eyes in disbelief at him.

But there was still the truth in the words he'd written. And that truth stung.

"Says who?" Scout demanded. "Says him?" With the yellow post-it clutched in her palm, she pointed at her father's stone. "He barely even knew me."

That brought Linc's attention back around. "What are you talking about? He's the reason I know you."

Scout balled her fists as she glared at the gravesite. As she did so, the crinkle of the post-it note was loud in Linc's ears.

The horse walked up behind Scout. The mare nuzzled at Scout's arm. Absentmindedly, Scout reached behind and petted the horse's muzzle. Then she leaned into the mare as though seeking its comfort.

Linc wanted to be the one to wrap his arms around her. But he'd just given up that right. He wanted the best for this woman. He wished he was it, but he couldn't fool himself into being what she needed.

There were times his memories blurred. Times when he wasn't sure if he was remembering things as they were or things as he wished they were. But that hadn't been a memory. Those words were touching his ears for the first time.

"Scout, there are things you don't know about me."

"Well, there are things you don't know about me too. Like I'll do anything to save this ranch and keep my family together. My dad sent you to help, so help you will."

Now he stared at her, stunned.

"You'll marry me. Jeff is on board to marry one of my sisters. You seem to think Jackson will take the plunge, too. If Mareen keeps her wedding date, then we just have to convince one other Silver girl—hopefully, two, if we can get rid of Saylor's boyfriend."

She turned away from the gravestone then. She looked up into Linc's eyes. He swore he could see the General staring back at him.

Linc always followed the General's command. Those actions had always come out of a sense of duty, of loyalty. What he was feeling now, looking at General Silver's eldest daughter was pure, unadulterated desire.

Linc knew then and there that the mission plan he'd drawn up, the one where he stepped aside and allowed Jackson to marry Scout would've resulted in total mission failure. Scout had the better plan. He was going to marry this woman, and he was going to do his utmost to make her happy every day of his life. No post-it note would be required for this mission.

"Okay," he surrendered.

"Okay." Her voice was terse as she handed him back the crumpled sticky note.

Linc took the scrape of paper gingerly. He shoved it into his back pocket, out of sight, and already forgotten.

"You had to write that down to tell me?" she asked.

Linc fingered the pad of unused notes in his front pocket. "Sometimes, I have trouble remembering things or keeping them in the right sequence."

Scout nodded at his admission. Just a quick bob of the head, like it didn't trouble her at all. Maybe he could do this.

"Life on a ranch is pretty monotonous," she said, her tone all business. "With daily chores and the same schedule each day, you should be fine."

Linc doubted anything would be routine with this woman, but he was willing to give it his all.

"Come on." Scout climbed up on the horse. She motioned to Linc as though he should climb on the horse's back as well.

The thought of riding with his body pressed against hers overwhelmed his senses. "I can walk back to the ranch."

"We're not going back to Silver Star just yet. We're going to see my other father."

Linc looked back at the gravesites that held both of Scout's parents. Then he looked back at her, saddled high on her horse. "Your... come again?"

CHAPTER THIRTEEN

As the midday sun rose higher in the sky, Scout wondered if she'd miscalculated. Sweat trickled down the back collar of her shirt. It was instantly cooled by the steady exhale that beat out a sure rhythm.

Linc's breath.

The man surrounded her. The hard muscles at the front of his body pressed flush up against the soft curves of her back. Though she faced forward, she smelled the earthy musk of him. It was doing things to her brain, like making her wonder what his lips would taste like. It was doing things to her body, like making her tummy grumble with want.

Lizzie trotted along under the weight of the two of them. Scout held the reins in her hands, but she was no longer certain that she was the one in control. The sound of the horse's hooves beat in time with Linc's heart. Her body swayed in time to Lizzie's clomp-clomp. But Scout still had the sense that she was falling. It was a slow descent. The fall was to the tune of a strong and sure ba-bump. Linc's heartbeats.

The reins went slack in her hands as she became lost in the

sensation. It wasn't unpleasant—the falling. But it was a new experience. She'd never followed anyone else's lead but her own.

Suddenly the reins were being tugged from her hands. It was Linc. He'd taken the lead from Scout since she wasn't paying the best attention.

Scout should've demanded he give them back. But she remained mute. For the first time in her life, Scout let a man lead her. She felt safe in Linc's care, secure.

She didn't understand what he'd meant about not being the right man for her. If her body were to tell that story, it would shout that they were a perfect match.

They fit physically. They were in sync, internally. And he smelled freaking amazing.

So he was a bit forgetful. Who wasn't? She couldn't blame a man who had spent years in combat to not want to forget some part of that life.

Besides, he was guiding her and her horse perfectly fine today. They could work on him remembering her sisters' names. They could put those post-it notes to use.

The bronze crosses of the Flying Cross Ranch came into view. The metalwork on the gate showcased the emblem with pride. The five rays of the sun extended beyond a four-bladed propeller to form a square.

"When you said your other father..." Linc started and took in a breath. "Is this...? Are we at...?"

Before Linc could find the breath or the words to complete any of those sentences, Father Matthews came to the door.

"Scout is that you? What a lovely surprise."

Linc dismounted, then he reached back to help her down from the horse. His hands on her waist felt good. So good that she momentarily forgot they had an audience.

But Linc was very aware of their audience. The softness of his body was gone. He stood erect, like a soldier greeting a superior.

"Colonel Matthews, a pleasure to meet you, sir."

"At ease soldier," Father Matthews chuckled.

It took a moment, but Linc relaxed into a slightly less stiff stance. While Linc worked to ease into the command, Scout brought herself into the colonel's embrace. Her own father had never been big on affection. Whenever Scout needed a fatherly hug, she had to go next door to receive one from her father's best friend.

"Father, I'd like you to meet Lincoln Rawlings. My fiancé."

Father Matthews's dark brows lifted up to his hairline. But he didn't look surprised.

"Yes," Scout said in answer to the older man's unasked question, "this has to do with my father's will."

Father Matthews held Scout's gaze before turning those hazel eyes onto Linc. Father Matthew's eyes always reminded Scout of sunlight. But now they looked like the sole illumination in a dark room made up for interrogation.

Linc had a few inches over the retired airman. But Father Matthews somehow looked bigger. Under the fierce scrutiny, Linc with his large muscles and sure stride, gulped like a teenager come asking a father to take his daughter to prom.

"General Silver told us many stories about you, sir."

"I'm not *sir* in these parts, son. I laid down my wings and picked up the Good Book years ago. You can call me Father Matthews."

"Yes, sir. I mean—yes, Father. I mean, Father Matthews."

Father Matthews chuckled again as he turned into the house. Scout fell in step behind him, only to find that Linc was grinning like a kid about to enter the gates of Disney Land. When Scout motioned him to join, Linc picked up his steps.

"Do you know who that is," Linc whispered as they walked into the foyer. "Colonel Matthews is a legend in the Air Force. Did you know his father was a Tuskegee Airman.? And that his great grandfather was a Buffalo Soldier?"

Scout shrugged. Sure, she knew all those things. She'd grown up hearing the stories right alongside Father Matthews's own children.

"I feel like I'm walking into U.S. Military history right now," Linc said as they came into the office.

Though Scout had been in this room countless times over

her life, she always felt the same way. Linc's gaze bounced from portrait to picture to photograph on the wall. Scout's gaze lingered on the photo of the General and the Colonel standing together, grinning like they'd just gotten away with something.

"Lincoln Rawlings," said Father Matthews as he took a seat. "You're one of Abe's President's Men. He told me about you six."

Funny. The General hadn't told his daughters about the men.

The ease that had coursed through Linc's body only a moment ago appeared to seep out of him at the mention of the general. He sat at the edge of the chair before the massive oak desk. His erect back did not touch the back cushion.

"It was an honor to serve the general," said Linc.

"You're now separated?"

"Medical discharge, sir."

Father Matthews raised an eyebrow.

"I mean, Father Matthews."

"Yet somehow, I suspect you're here to continue your service to the man." Father Matthews's gaze came to rest on Scout.

Scout had years of practice being under that gaze. There were times she deserved the scrutiny, and times she didn't. In either case, she'd learned that the best thing to do was to come clean.

"We want you to marry us," said Scout.

"We do?" Linc's head whipped to Scout.

"We were thinking maybe this weekend?"

"So soon?"

Linc was all the way at the edge of his seat. One more word from her, and Scout was sure he might fall off.

"Are you changing your mind?" she asked.

"No, not at all," said Linc. "I'll do this."

"Because you owe her father?"

They both turned to look into the penetrating gaze of Father Matthews. His fingers were steepled. His mouth set in a firm line.

Linc's lips quivered. It looked as though he was about to press his teeth together to make the *yes* sound. But then he appeared to think better of that. He pressed his lips together, but when he opened them, no sound came out.

"The two of you are planning to marry to satisfy the demands of Abe's will," said Father Matthews. "I can't officiate such a pairing before the Lord."

"People around the world are forced into marriages every day," said Scout.

Father Matthews turned to Linc. "Are you being forced, son?"

"No, I want to marry her," said Linc.

Now it was Scout that was in danger of falling out of her chair. Those words came out easily. Not a single hesitation. Not forceful. Just facts.

"I know about the will," Linc continued. "And I do feel a certain sense of responsibility for the general's daughters after..."

Now he trailed away. His gaze went over Father Matthews's shoulder. Scout knew without following Linc's eye line which picture he was looking at.

She hadn't asked exactly what had happened in that last mission. She supposed she should. Though the look of pain that darkened Linc's handsome face made her not want to go down that road.

Linc's gaze shifted and focused back on Father Matthews. "Scout's a good woman. She is efficient. Gives good direction. And she's thorough in her instructions."

"That doesn't sound like a wife," said Father Matthews. "It sounds like a job description for a member of your team."

"In the military, we become brothers for life, you know that, sir. I think those are the perfect qualities for a life partner."

Father Matthews continued to look at Linc over his steepled fingers. Finally, he pressed his palms together and laced his fingers one over the other. "Tell me, son, is this going to be one of those fake marriages where you'll get divorced after the land is secured?"

Just the sound of the D-word had Scout squirming in her seat. She had decided on this marriage. But Father Matthews was right. This family had seen enough separation. She was only doing this once, and she expected it to last forever.

"I would never leave Scout. I gave her my word. I'm not a perfect man, but I am a man of my word."

A slow grin spread across Father Matthews's face. His gaze turned from Linc and fixed on her. "All right, then. I'll marry the two of you."

Somehow his words didn't sound like a blessing. They sounded like a threat.

CHAPTER FOURTEEN

*L*inc held Scout's back to his front as they rode back to Silver Star ranch. It was solidified. They were getting married. Colonel Matthews had given his blessing, along with an interrogation worthy of a CIA operative.

They'd spent a couple of hours in the man's office as he went through a slew of pre-marital counseling questions. Colonel -Father Matthews, because with the intimate questions the man asked, he might as well be Linc's confessor. Father Matthews had asked about his financial wherewithal, his family background. He'd even delved into Linc's military background.

Linc had answered all questions, even though the beads of sweat were clearly visible all around his neck. He'd been proud that he'd answered each question, each query clearly and without a mist of fog in his brain. It wasn't until Father Matthews had asked about children that Linc had fumbled.

Children. Children with Scout. Having children with Scout. Making children with Scout.

Why hadn't that particular process crossed his mind a single time over the past day? Sure he thought about kissing her. He thought about holding her, as he was doing now. But his thoughts hadn't gone beyond that.

Now, with her back pressed to his front, they did. Linc shifted in the saddle.

"You okay back there?" she asked.

"Yeah, great."

He was not great.

As he forced his addled brain to replay all the conversations he and Scout had had about their impending nuptials, there was not one instance where they'd discussed living arrangements, specifically sleeping arrangements.

Father Matthews hadn't brought it up either. Linc supposed the old man assumed they would be sleeping together. But was that Scout's assumption?

Everything she'd said to him had been about saving her family, preserving the ranch and the animals. There hadn't been any discussion of preserving her virtue?

And then, Linc realized, it didn't matter.

Holding her to him. Standing sentry at her back. Having her trust in his guidance as he led her horse back to her home, that was enough for him.

The sun had set by the time they arrived back at the cabins surrounding the big house. He could see the lights on in the big house. The others were likely in there having dinner. Linc was hungry, but not for food. He hadn't had his fill of Scout. He wanted any morsel she was willing to give him, even if it was just more conversation.

Linc dismounted as they came to the barn. He reached up to Scout. With his hands on her waist, he was slow to bring her to standing, letting her linger in the air as she came down his body.

Scout looked up at him. He looked down at her. Her lips were there for the taking. She didn't move away.

It wasn't the most romantic setting in the world. The sounds of horses pawing the ground as they settled in for the night. The smell of manure wafting in the air.

Lizzie bumped her rump into Linc's back, sending him careening into Scout. Scout caught him in her arms, just as he wrapped her up in his embrace. They stood like that for another long moment. Until Lizzie, tired of the waiting, let out a loud whine.

Scout disentangled herself from Linc and went to put her horse up for the night. With Lizzie in bed, Linc and Scout walked side by side in silence. The direction they took was back toward the living quarters. At the fork in the road, Scout continued right, which would lead them to the cabins. The cabin he was staying in was the first cabin on the path.

Linc knew it had been built for Scout. The General had told him that he'd had his daughters each build their own home with their own hands. Which was another reason the will made no sense. Why would he have these girls build something only to take it away from them?

"We said we'd have a platonic marriage," she said.

Had they said that? Linc could not remember that conversation. One of his doctors had pondered if his memory was selective. At this moment, Linc would've given the theory credence.

"Maybe we should discuss the pros and cons of such an arrangement," she continued. "To see if it suits us moving forward."

Linc straightened. His hand immediately itched for a post-it note to take down these new details. This was something he wanted to remember every detail of. But in his heart, he knew he would never forget the way her hair wafted in the breeze. The way her gaze was uncertain. The way her lips had a determined set to them.

Linc took the few steps to her. He wanted to kiss her, but he also didn't want to spook her with the force of his desire for her. So he held out his hand.

Scout looked at the offered appendage as though she'd never seen a man's hand before. She took it gingerly. Linc wondered if no one had ever held the woman's hand before. He gave it a reassuring squeeze and then tugged her into walking beside him.

"If I'm being honest," he began, "I never thought a platonic relationship would last between us."

Beside him, Scout stumbled. Her blue gaze went wide. Linc would've sworn he'd say the night's stars reflected in them.

"You're far too beautiful for me not to work out the process of how to kiss you."

Even in the darkness of the night, Linc could see her blush. "You don't have to say things like that to me."

"Things like what?" he asked.

"I know I'm no stunner."

"Then you know nothing. You're the most beautiful woman I've ever seen in my life. I can't believe you're going to be mine."

Scout stopped walking. They were just a few steps from her cabin, the one he was staying in. She turned to him. The next thing he knew, his head was being yanked down, and her lips were pressed against his.

Linc forgot. He forgot everything around him. He forgot everything except for her.

She tasted of the wind, sweetened by honey. She felt like fire, cooled by a meandering breeze. Her soft, contented sigh was a wave that went over his head and pulled him under.

When she broke the kiss, she mumbled against his lips, "Invite me inside."

Linc was already walking backward with the handful that was soon to be his bride. But his steps faltered as something tugged at his consciousness. With one hand, Scout was angling to get inside the cabin she'd built with her own hands. The door was open. None of his men felt any need to lock their doors here in this idyllic setting far from any combat zone. So why was he blocking the entryway with his body?

Linc should let her in. However, there was a reason he shouldn't. But he couldn't remember it.

His side brushed against the door frame. When it did so, he felt the indent of the square pad of paper in his pocket. Every desire in him went cold.

Linc released Scout as though her skin had burned him. She wobbled on unsteady feet. He did not reach out to steady her.

"You must be hungry," he said.

"I am, but I can eat whatever you have inside."

"No, I think we should go to the house to be with the others."

Confusion was at war with the desire in her eyes. "You don't...want to?"

Linc gulped, but it was the hardest truth he'd had to swallow since the blast that had altered his life. Because he wasn't ready to recount that life-changing event, and all the consequences that came with it, Linc told Scout a different truth.

"I think we should get to know each other more," he said.

Scout took a step back. Her proud head dropped, and she stared at the ground. "Right. Of course."

Linc got the sense she was answering a question he hadn't asked. One he would never ask. "Scout..."

But she was already turning away, marching like a soldier who'd been given their orders. "I'll see you in the morning."

Linc let her go. He couldn't chase after her. Not with the burden he had behind this door.

He turned the doorknob and stepped inside. The first post-it greeted him, reminding him to lock the door behind him. There were others. They were all around the cabin with the little reminders he needed to function.

What had Linc done agreeing to marry this woman when he didn't have this under control?

CHAPTER FIFTEEN

*S*he'd been too pushy. Scout had always been terrible with the opposite sex. With horses, she could get the animals to follow her lead. With boys or men, they often balked at her commands. Because men liked to be the ones giving the commands.

Growing up with a General for a father, she knew that lesson all too well. Still, it didn't translate in the classroom, or on the game fields, or at the local bar.

Once she opened her mouth, men would always take back their offer of a dance or a drink and turn to one of the bubbly girls in the corner. Scout didn't do bubbly. Her feet were planted too firmly on the ground.

Linc had swept her off her feet. Well, it had technically been off a horse. But she'd always climbed on and off a horse all by herself. She'd liked having a hand at the task. But then she'd pushed too hard.

Scout wasn't exactly sure what she'd done that had pushed him away. She often wasn't. But Linc had definitely turned away from her like all the other guys. Well, this fake marriage was off to a great start.

"Scoutie, pass me the eggs."

Scout pushed the carton toward Brig. Probably for the first time in her life, she didn't push hard enough. The carton teetered at the edge of the kitchen counter and smashed onto the floor.

From her place at the island, Tilly looked up from her open laptop. "What's gotten into you this morning?"

"The better question is what happened last night?" said Brig. "She and Linc were gone for hours."

"Really?" said Tilly closing her laptop.

"Yeah," said Saylor from the other end of the island where she was slicing oranges. "I don't think I heard you come in, Scout."

Scout had come inside the house last night. That was the problem. She'd come into the main house instead of into the cabin her soon-to-be-husband occupied. She'd gone alone into her bedroom. All because she'd pushed Linc too hard.

She didn't know how to be soft. At least not with humans. She had a gentle hand when it came to horses.

"We went and talked to Father Matthews," said Scout. "He said he'll marry us this weekend."

"So you're really doing this?" said Tilly.

Scout hoped she was really doing this. She hoped Linc wouldn't back out. Not just because she needed him to help fulfill the General's demands. But because she wanted him.

"I'm sorry about the eggs," Scout said, but even that came out gruff.

"It's no big deal." Brig's grin was completely unaffected. "I'll just go grab some more from the hen house. That's the beauty of living on a ranch. You have a built-in grocery store."

"No, I'll go," Scout said, already moving to the door.

Scout had to escape. Both Saylor and Tilly were slowly moving in toward her. She knew her sisters would ask a million questions about what had happened when she'd gone off with Linc yesterday. Scout didn't want to talk about it, especially the parts where she'd bumbled it. She certainly didn't want her younger sisters giving her advice about how to fix her love life. What really rubbed was that all of her sisters had more experience than she did in that arena.

Out in the circular arena of the ranch was the object of her bumbling ardor. Linc led two horses around the enclosure. Or at least he was trying to lead them.

Wickham was far more interested in trailing Anne-Elliot than following Linc's directions. For her part, Anne-Elliot was having none of either male. She pulled against her lead when Wickham fell back, trying to get a sniff of her.

Scout picked up her steps as she hurried inside the gate. Linc was managing the situation. The man worked well with the horses. The man simply worked well.

Scout loved seeing the powerful build of him. The strength in his hands. The problem was he had no idea what he was in the middle of with the two horses.

In fact, he didn't appear to notice any issue between the horses at all. Linc looked off in the distance. His gaze clouded over. He even slowed his pace, grinding both horses to a halt. That was all Wickham needed.

The horse broke free of Linc's hold. Wickham fell back, aiming to get around the inattentive human and at the buxom beauty on the other side. That's when Anne-Elliot broke free of Linc's hold as well. She trotted off, evading Wickham's attentions.

Scout took a step back toward the fence as the horses passed her. When she turned to find Linc, what she found were strong arms coming around her.

"Scout," Linc said, his hands running up and down her arms. "Are you hurt?"

"No, I'm fine."

She was more than fine. She was back in his arms. And Scout wasn't entirely sure her feet were on the ground.

"I don't know what happened?" said Linc, his gaze still hazy.

"We're having a baby."

He blinked, his eyes filling with clear alertness. "A baby?"

"Anne-Elliot, she's pregnant."

"Anne-Elliot?"

"The mare."

Linc looked over at the two horses. Wickham was walking with his head hung low after being rejected by the pregnant mare.

"You have to be careful with a pregnant mare, especially around males."

"I thought she was male," said Linc, his brows pinched in confusion.

"No, if you look hard enough, it's pretty obvious she's a girl."

Now Linc's lips pursed to match his brows. "I must not have been thinking clearly."

Linc rubbed at his head. Before Scout knew it, her hand was on his temple. It was a pushy move. But she couldn't find it in herself to regret the touch or pull her hand away.

Looked like she wouldn't need to. Linc turned his face into her palm. He nuzzled it as would one of her horses who wanted to be stroked.

Scout's fingers tingled as she touched him. Linc gave himself, well his head, completely over to her. She felt the same trust coming from him that she had with her horses.

"Hmmm," he sighed.

Or was that a groan? She wasn't good at reading the sounds of men.

"Is your head bothering you?" she asked.

Linc stepped closer to her. His strong chest came flush against hers. If he did answer, Scout couldn't hear him over the beat of her heart.

His hand rested on her hip. A moment later, he pulled her closer. "Everything feels so clear when I'm with you."

Linc's forehead came to rest against hers. Scout knew she should hold back. She should wait for him to make his move. But she'd never been good at standing by. She lifted her head and captured his lower lip.

Linc inhaled. Or was that a gasp? Just another male sound she wasn't sure how to categorize. When Linc's top lip took hold of hers, Scout decided it was a good sound.

He pulled her even closer, deepening the kiss. But as he did so, there was an unsteadiness to the hold. They broke the kiss, still clinging to one another. Scout wasn't sure who was holding whom up. She certainly felt dizzy. But there was a pained expression on Linc's face.

"Hey," she said.

He opened his eyes. His gaze was once more cloudy. It took him a minute to focus on her. "I'm sorry. I forgot myself there."

He stepped back, letting her go. But his steps were unsure, and he reached for the railing.

"Do you need an aspirin? There's some in your cabin in the first aid kit. I'll go grab it for you."

Linc's eyes flashed wide. Any trace of fog blew out the way. "No, I'm fine."

Scout swallowed. It was a hard maneuver with all the desire still stuck in her throat.

"I'm sorry," he said.

Scout didn't dare ask what he was sorry for. If he said he was sorry for that kiss they'd just shared, she would die of mortification. "I should put Anne-Elliot out to pasture with the other mares."

"What about the babies," he said, but then frowned. He pinched the bridge at his nose. "No, I mean eggs. You said you needed eggs, right?"

Scout nodded. She'd forgotten about the eggs.

"I can get those for you," he said.

"Thank you." The words sounded lame to her ears. She'd just been wrapped up in this man's embrace, pressing her body against his.

Linc nodded. He stuck his hand in his pocket and turned on his heel. As Scout watched him hesitate at the gate, he pulled out a square pad. He quickly jotted something down and then pushed out the gate.

It was likely another reason to let her go. All because she had pushed him again. When would she ever learn?

CHAPTER SIXTEEN

*L*inc stood in the middle of the hen house. He looked around. He couldn't remember what he was doing here. All he could remember was the feel of Scout's fingers rubbing against his temples. The soothing scent of her breath hitting his skin. The oblivion that took him when he claimed her mouth for his own.

Babies. She'd spoken of babies. That thought stuck in his head.

Could he be a father? What if he messed up a simple process like changing a diaper? What if one day he forgot some important detail about his child?

But that was his fear talking. His heart was beating loudly in his ears. His heart wanted to make a baby with Scout. His heart wanted to make a life with Scout.

She was his new mission in life, his sole purpose. That thought, he could keep straight. But no other sequence seemed to stick.

He looked down at his post-it note. His writing looked like chicken scratch. Soon he was able to decipher his hurried scrawl. *Get Scout babies.*

That could not be right. But he had flashes of memories of her saying something to him about babies. The horse, the mare, she was pregnant. Walking to them together had been a mistake he should've caught. If he'd just looked closely, he would've noticed the difference in the two horses he'd brought into the pen.

Linc was trying to develop a routine at the Silver Star Ranch. He thrived in monotony. But each day brought a new and exciting adventure with Scout.

He was having a hard time finding his way. What he needed to do was to sit down with Scout and tell her everything. Everything about that last mission. Everything about his injury. He'd have to eventually. They were going to be married soon. She would know. Especially if they were going to be married in the true way and share living space.

And man did Linc want to be married in the truest of ways. But he didn't want to share the extent of his condition with her. Not the memory fog. Not the confusion. Not the frustration of forgetting the simplest tasks, the request just made of him a moment ago that slipped through the cracks of his fractured brain.

Scout looked at him like he was a whole man. She looked at all the men as though they were abled bodies and not broken men. She treated her horses the same way, expecting them to perform -not regardless of their injuries- but in spite of them.

If any woman would understand what he was going through, maybe it would be her?

Back in the hen house, the rooster strutted his stuff amongst the hens. That had been Linc in the past. He'd had his choice of women. Had he looked that ridiculous? He couldn't remember, and that was likely for the best.

All he wanted to do now was to be the best man he could be for the woman he was going to spend the rest of his life with. Her father had seen excellence in him. But that excellence had fallen short when the general had needed it most. When The President's Men should have been protecting the General with their lives, it had been General Silver who had made the ultimate sacrifice to protect his men.

Linc tried not to dwell on that. He knew he couldn't change the past. That was something he tried to stress to his men. Wilson still had trouble with it. Because Wilson had been the closest to the General when it had happened.

"Oh, hey, good morning, Linc."

Linc turned to see the youngest Silver Sister. He wanted to reach into his pocket for the post-it he'd prepared on the sisters, but the chart he'd created flashed in his mind. Each of the Silver girls was named after a military rank or object.

"Good morning, Brigadear."

She gave him a nod, her features filled with what looked like respect. "You know I always wanted a brother. And now I'm getting six. Well, five if I can bag one of you for my own husband."

Linc may have been able to recall the girl's name, but he was having trouble following the line of conversation. Brig talked so fast and switched topics so fluidly that he was having trouble keeping pace. She might favor her older sister, but the younger version of Scout didn't help keep Linc's train of thought clear and in focus.

"I came to get some eggs for breakfast since Scout dropped the ones from earlier. But she didn't come back. Wait, is she in here with you? Were you guys making out?"

All Linc caught from that was Scout and eggs. She'd said something about babies and eggs. He put those two together and remembered why he was in here. He said he'd get the eggs for her. But he'd forgotten. Even his note to himself hadn't been clear.

Likely because his mind had been preoccupied with other thoughts.

"So tell me, did my dad, like, assign one of you guys for each of us?"

"What?" Linc turned his attention back to Brig.

"Because I think he did. And I think he got it right with you and Scout. You're perfect for each other."

"We are?"

"It's clear Saylor and Jeff would make a perfect match, too. But she's still stuck on that awful boyfriend of hers. We've been trying to break them up for years. Dad couldn't stand him either."

"Brig, can we go back to what you said about me and Scout-"

"I'm not sure who he would've picked for me? Who do you think? Wilson seems too severe. I bet he'd get along with Mareen. Too bad she's already getting married. Probably Carter? But I've seen him eyeing Tilly. That leaves Truman and Jackson. Exactly how old is Jackson?"

Linc had long since lost the thread of the conversation. The only thing he clung to was that the General thought he was the man for the job when it came to his eldest daughter. Linc might've messed up with the eggs and the horses. But maybe he could pull this mission—this marriage—off.

CHAPTER SEVENTEEN

*S*cout had to continually slow her steps as she led Anne-Elliott out to pasture. The broodmare was twenty-one years old, far past the age that a horse should be carrying. But her former owner had been a greedy, uncaring woman. She'd only looked at the horse as a cash cow, or rather cash horse. After the last pregnancy, the Animal Welfare League had stepped in. But it had been too late to prevent this pregnancy.

They'd brought Anne-Elliott to the Silver Star Ranch when they realized the mare was with her twelfth calf. It was going to be a rocky birth, but the horse had the two best women for the job. Scout and Saylor would help the old gal through the birth every step of the way. And the best part was that the former owner would see no profit from it.

Horses Scout didn't have to push. They naturally went where she wanted them to. Even the stubborn ones eventually caved to her demands. Why couldn't human males be the same?

Looking ahead, Scout saw a man in the pasture with the other mares. He had the same upright posture of all the soldiers. The only reason she could tell him from the others was by the way he held his arm.

Jefferson worked to roll out a bale of hay, one-handed. Her horses waited patiently for the man to perform the task. Once their breakfast was in place, the ladies gathered around. These mares weren't prone to shoving each other aside like some of her males in the other pasture.

Jefferson reached up and patted at Lizzie's muzzle. When he did so, Scout noticed the scrape on his limp arm. Blood trickled down from his elbow, likely a wound from the rough ties on the rope.

"Jefferson," she called out.

He lifted his head with a welcoming smile as she came into the gate. There was a sense of pride in the man's eyes. It was a look Scout knew well. It was the look her horses gave her when they accomplished a task she'd set them to.

Jefferson was out here on his own. She knew these men had all been separated from the military due to their injuries. She figured most of them weren't sure what to do with themselves if not on a mission. Scout was happy to allow them to find a new purpose on this ranch.

"Morning, Ms. Silver."

"Please, call me Scout. It looks like you've got yourself a minor wound there."

Jefferson pursed his lips as he looked down at his left arm. The look in his eyes said he wanted to brush it off as nothing. If he did, Scout would have to resort to her pushy ways.

It wasn't a minor wound. The blood continued to run freely. They had to get it bandaged soon.

"I should've put the sling on," Jeff said, sounding entirely reasonable. "You got a first aid kit nearby?"

"Yeah, come with me."

The closest place was the cabin where Linc was staying. She guided Jefferson the short distance there while he used the edge of his shirt to stave off much of the blood. When he looked up to see where they'd arrived, he got that pinched look on his face again.

"There's a first aid kit in my cabin," said Scout.

"No, wait," said Jefferson. He lifted his free hand to her but pulled it back before his bloodied fingers could touch her.

"Don't worry, Linc isn't in here. He's in the chicken coop gathering eggs for breakfast."

The door was unlocked, as always. It was dark inside, but she didn't need the light. She knew this cabin like the back of her hand. She'd helped build it. She'd helped build them all as the eldest. Hers had taken the longest since it had only been her and her dad when they'd started.

But Scout didn't like to think of those times. In the echo chamber in her mind, she could've sworn she heard a rumbling sound in those memories. Sometimes, she thought the sound was laughter. But that wasn't possible. It was just her and her dad.

Scout made her way past the sparse furniture until she was in the bathroom. She flicked the light on then and froze. There were post-it notes on the mirror above the sink.

Objective; Personal Grooming, was written in bold block letters. Beneath in a slimmer marker was written a list of tasks; *shave daily, brush teeth, floss*, and a few others.

She already recognized Linc's handwriting from the first post-it she'd seen of his. Scout touched the note. It felt intimate to see the inner workings of his mind.

Feeling as though she were intruding on his personal thoughts, she grabbed the first aid kit and turned. Before she turned out the light, something across the hall in the bedroom caught her attention.

The sheets on the four-poster bed were done with military precision, the way all the Silver girls had been taught in their youth. There were no clothes on the floor, nothing out of place. But that's not what caught her attention.

There was another array of post-its on the wall. This time *Night Routine* was written in bold as the Objective. Beneath the objective was a set of new tasks related to sleep preparation. Things like *make a to-do list for tomorrow, consult today's to-do list, mental exercises, check locks, and home security.*

Linc had said he had trouble remembering things. But he's said more. He'd said he had trouble keeping things in the right sequence. Is this how he was coping with that issue?

Stepping back into the hall, Scout flipped the light switch on for the main room. Post-it notes were on the small fridge about meal prepping and eating times

On the wall closest to the door was the most extensive array of post-its. The coordinated colors were a thing of beauty. But it was the mission objectives that set Scout back on her heel.

Primary Mission; Save Silver Star Ranch.

There was an array of tasks listed below. Things like *Assign men jobs. Improve working of the ranch.* And then, *select potential wives.*

Scout saw each of her sisters' names, filled with a few words about their personalities. Beneath those were the names of the soldiers and their listed character strengths. String dangled from the post-its, but only one string was attached.

Scout's pink post-it was attached to Linc's blue post-it.

It might have been romantic, but for the cold, calculating words surrounding the connection.

Acquire Scout's hand in marriage. Along with a *Task Complete* scrawled on the bottom. But that was not the end.

Beneath that was a new post-it. The first read *Deliverable; marriage.* Written beneath that was the date they'd agreed to have the ceremony.

"Scout..."

Scout whirled around to face Jeff, nearly dropping the collection of bandages she'd gathered from the bathroom. She'd forgotten he was here. He held his arm. Red seeped between his fingers. Right, that's why she was holding the First Aid Kit in her hand.

"You have to understand..." Jefferson was saying. "He's had a traumatic brain injury. We all have. It's affected us in different ways."

"He said he had trouble keeping things in order," Scout said as she turned away from the mission board.

"He has trouble sequencing events. It helps him to map out processes."

Scout nodded instead of speaking. Her head whirled. The words *mission* and *objective* and *tasks* kept playing in her head. Those were words her father always used.

The General was always away on a mission. He couldn't return until he'd met his objective. He'd always give the girls tasks to complete.

"It may sound clinical," said Jeff, "but it's how his brain works best."

"No, I get it. I'm a mission to complete."

Jeff winced. "That's not—"

"What are you doing in here?"

Both Scout and Jeff looked up to see Lincoln darkening the doorway. His eyes clear as he took the two of them in. His face was set in a grimace of anger.

CHAPTER EIGHTEEN

*L*inc had gone on high alert when he saw the door to his cabin open. His mind instantly cleared and told him that there had been a breach. His typical protocol would have been to lock the door. But after a couple of days on the ranch, he had come to know there were no enemies present. He'd felt safe and secure here. He was surrounded by his men.

But the open door was not something his men would do. They had had so little privacy in the service that they wouldn't dare intrude on another man's space. So it couldn't be one of his men.

That left one of the girls. This was their home, not his. They had every right to go in and out of the cabins.

But that wasn't the issue. If someone was inside, they were seeing things he didn't want to be shown. His post-its were on display. It was as though the entire contents of his mind were laid out in the open, making him vulnerable. His worst fears were realized when he heard the sultry voice from inside.

Scout was hunched over Jefferson. Jealousy, white and hot, briefly shoved aside Linc's shame at her nearness to Jeff. She was bent over him, too close for Linc's comfort. Then he saw the bandage in Scout's hand and the blood on Jeff's arm.

"I had a disagreement with a bale of hay," said Jeff, using his free hand to hold up his bleeding arm so that Linc could see."

But Linc had already come to that conclusion and moved past. His attention was focused on Scout, whose attention was focused on the process map on the wall of the main room. Lincoln felt lobotomized with both Scout's and Jeff's gaze on the array.

"I'll let you two talk," said Jeff. Before he went out the door, he laid a hand on Linc's shoulder. Linc's second in command gave him a meaningful look, one that said take it easy.

Lincoln took a deep breath, preparing to do just that. He'd already resolved to tell Scout about the extent of his brain injury. Looked like it was time to both tell as well as show.

"Task complete, huh?" said Scout, her gaze trained on the post-its on the wall.

Scout's voice sounded different to him. There was still the bossy edge that Linc liked. But he also heard a hint of hurt in her voice. Had she been hurt alongside Jeff? He hadn't even considered that.

Linc was in front of her in two strides. He looked her over. But all of her skin was intact. Nothing appeared out of order. She looked whole, but something told him that there was still something wrong. Maybe something internal?

"What is it?" he asked. "Are you hurt?"

Scout's eyes flashed to his. "Am I hurt? How can you ask me that?"

Scout had always made Linc's mind clear, but now things went hazy. She looked angry, and he couldn't understand why? She looked like she was in pain, but there were no open wounds.

"Tell me the truth," she said, finally turning her gaze away from the papers on the wall and onto him. "Did the general assign you to me?"

The General? Assignments? This harkened back to the conversation Linc had just had with Brig about their commander assigning a man to each of his daughters.

"No, General Silver didn't assign us to you. Like I said, he asked us to come and check on you in the case of his untimely death. That's why we're here."

"So you made me your objective?"

Yes, she was his objective. Securing Scout's hand, her happiness, that was Linc's new life mission. But how did he say that to her without sounding like a crazy person? It was too soon to feel what he was feeling.

"I don't know whether to be afraid of you or not," Scout said, confirming his fears. "This wall is what a serial killer would have in his place."

Linc tore his gaze away from her and looked at the wall. The wall looked the way they would organize most of their missions. Tasks, objectives, deliverables. He could see how it could be a little disconcerting when hers and her sisters' names were part of the mission.

"This was how your father always outlined our missions. Down to the last one. And just like now, that mission didn't go as expected."

Scout's shoulder's tensed at the mention of her father. He knew what the girls had been told, that their father had been killed in the line of duty. Families weren't often given the exact details as most of the unit's missions were classified.

Linc pinched the bridge of his nose as scenes from that fateful day flashed behind his closed eyes. His mind threatened to fog, but he had to stay clear on this. It was mission critical.

"We were sent to rescue an American diplomat and his family; a father and his two children who were trapped in an embassy. We made it in but got pinned down as the facility came under heavy fire."

Linc opened his eyes, but his gaze remained lowered. He felt if he lifted his head any higher, he would meet the sun's glare from the window, and the memories would burn away. He didn't want that. He owed it to the general to remember the truth of that day.

"They call us heroes, but we failed that mission. We lost a prized asset; your father."

The unit had completed each task. The objectives had been met. The mission had succeeded, even though the outcome had not been what they'd expected.

Linc had always trusted the general's planning. He'd never questioned the man's logic or motives. Not even when they'd failed them on that fateful day.

"I don't want to be your mission," Scout said, her voice sounding choked.

At the sound of those words, Linc's mind didn't fog. The world inside Linc began to darken. "You don't want to marry me?"

"I…" Scout's chin wobbled. And then… tears.

Lincoln was at a loss on what to do. He didn't have a process map for calming a crying woman. He held out his hands, but did she want to be held? Her hands were fluttering in front of her, sending a ripple through the post-its on the wall.

"Scout, I know I'm not a whole man with this…" Linc motioned to his head. There was no fog there now. His objective was clear. "But I swear I'll work my hardest to complete these tasks and make this mission a success. Failure is not an option."

Linc hoped those were the right words. He hoped that she would fling herself into his arms. He hoped they would end this debacle in a breathless kiss.

Instead, she let out an agonized cry and stormed out the front door, slamming it behind her. With the harsh wind from the door, some of his post-it notes fell from the wall.

CHAPTER NINETEEN

*S*cout paced the length of the barn. Luckily it was empty. Otherwise, the way her boots ate up the ground would've agitated the horses.

She didn't want to return to the house and face her sisters with her failure. She couldn't return to the cabin where the evidence was written on the walls. She'd been right all along.

They were nothing but a mission. The plan was written in colorful sticky notes on Linc's wall. She was an order for him to follow. An objective for him to accomplish. A task for him to execute.

She had to give it to him. It was a good plan. One she could've plotted herself. One she'd tried to plot herself in getting all of her sisters married so that she could save the ranch. What she couldn't abide was her father's hand in this mess.

Because it had his handiwork written all over it. Though it was Linc's handwriting on the walls. But he was just following orders.

He couldn't have any real feelings for her. Right?

"Can you feel that?"

The voice came from the other side of the barn walls. It was Saylor. It was her doctor's voice.

As a veterinarian, Saylor often talked to the animals in her care as though they could understand her. Scout knew that most of them could. Even more that sometimes they responded.

"Can't feel a thing," came a deep male voice.

Scout started. She knew that voice. She'd just left that voice.

"Well, I've got you bandaged up now," said Saylor.

Scout winced at that. She had been tasked with bandaging up Jefferson. But she'd been derelict on those duties once she saw the post-its.

"Thank you, Saylor."

"So, hey, tell me the truth. Did the General give you orders to marry us?"

"No. He told us about each of you. But before he… he made us pledge to come here and look after you all."

"Look after us?"

"Matrimony wasn't the mission, but if that's what you need…"

Scout chanced a glance around the corner in the ensuing silence. She might be upset about what she'd just seen on Linc's walls, but she'd put all her pride aside if a good man like Jefferson caught her sister's eye.

Saylor clearly didn't notice the interest in Jeff's voice. She wasn't even looking into his eyes, which were fixed on her. She was still checking out his wound.

A ringing phone cut through the silence. "That's my boyfriend. I'll need to get it. I've been waiting for his call since yesterday."

The disappointment that clouded Jeff's face at Saylor's departure mirrored Scout's. They both watched Saylor walk off to take the call. Scout wished her sister could see the man behind her who'd cared enough to offer his hand just a few days after knowing her to ensure her livelihood and wellbeing. Instead, Saylor was off kowtowing to a creep who barely acknowledged her existence.

But then again, who was she to talk. Scout had just stormed off from a man who had diagramed how to give her and her sisters what she needed.

She couldn't figure out what upset her most? The fact that Linc had his own plans to give her what she wanted? Or that he didn't have any actual feelings for her? She was only a mission objective he'd been tasked with.

Linc didn't care for her. He never could. Just like her father. At the end of the day, it was always about the mission.

"I don't suppose it went well back there?"

Scout looked up to see Jefferson approach, his one arm outstretched. The other arm at his side. The bandage in place.

"You think?" said Scout.

"Well, with the steam coming out of your ears, and the way you're pawing at the ground, I'd say you're ready to charge."

"Wouldn't you be if you realized the man you..." Scout swallowed. She couldn't believe she was about to admit that she was falling for Linc. But the truth was she had fallen for him.

"I know Linc's methods might be confusing-"

"You mean the serial killer wall of post-its?"

Jeff winced. "He's a meticulous man. He was always very detail-oriented. But he can't keep all the details straight in his head anymore. He writes them down, so he has a visual representation. That's how he organizes the things that are most important to him."

That called Scout up short. She kicked at the ground, but the rock was embedded in the earth, and she stubbed her toe. The things that are most important to him? She had been a fixture on Linc's wall. Did that mean that she was important to him?

"But he called me a mission? He put our marriage down as an objective. I was just a task on his list."

"Scout, that's just how soldiers speak," said Jeff. "He made you his mission, but you're missing the point. He made you his end game. Do you know what an end game is?"

Scout had heard her father talk about an elusive final mission. The last one he'd take, the one that would bring him home... someday. But someday had never happened.

"An end game is a final mission. Linc wants you to be his final mission, and he plotted out the best way to make that happen."

CHAPTER TWENTY

inc stayed inside, completely immobile after Scout had stormed off. For long moments, he simply stared at the wall of post-its. Though there was a clear plan of action outlined for him, he didn't know what to do next.

Should he go find her? Should he give her time? There was no game plan for that line of action. What he did know was that he could not stand still for the rest of the day. He was a man of action, and so he stepped outside.

The bright light of the sun hurt Linc's eyes when he stepped out of the cabin. He let the rays burn into his brain, hoping they would make his next action clear. But it was as though he walked through a cloud of steam.

His traumatic brain injury had robbed him of his dream to serve longer in the military. Just as soon as he was coming to accept his new fate, a life on this ranch with Scout in his arms, it looked that that would blow up in his face.

Maybe he'd been delusional to think that such a strong woman would take on a wounded man like him. He could no longer lead his men. Did he really think he could be the man she needed both in her work as well as in her heart?

By the way she'd walked off, he knew the answer was clearly no. But that was the only clarity he had. He didn't know what to do with himself now.

In the distance, he saw Wickham running around the pasture. The horse was making mischief this morning. He ran off Bingley, who was nibbling at a bale of hay. But no sooner had the blond horse moved onto a new bale did Wickham run him off again.

Linc made his way to the pasture. As he did so, he caught the dark horse's gaze. Wickham sauntered up to the gate and put his head over the fencing as though seeking a pat on the head. Clearly, the horse needed some extra attention. That Linc could handle.

Taking the horse by its lead, Linc walked into the barn. Wickham gave a tug of the reins. Linc held his ground, waiting until the horse settled down. Once Wickham calmed, Linc managed to fit the horse with a riding saddle. When the horse continued to behave, Linc mounted him.

Atop the horse, power surged through Linc's body. There was nothing like riding a horse to make a man feel in control. The horses at the Purple Heart Ranch had all been docile, gentle creatures. Wickham needed a strong hand. Though Linc's mind sometimes blurred, he still had strength in his hands.

Linc gave a gentle tug of the reins to get the horse's attention. Then giving a squeeze with his thighs, he urged the horse to walk on. Wickham obeyed without a single hesitation. Clearly, the horse needed to get the exercise as much as Linc wanted to give it.

The other horses lifted their heads as the two of them walked by. Once they were clear of the pastures where the mares were being fed, Linc found the trail he'd rode with Scout. He put Wickham on that path and let the horse pick up speed.

With the sun on his back and a little wind in his hair, the fog in Linc's mind began to dissipate. Scout's face was all he could see in his mind's eye.

He'd drawn out a process to win her. He'd almost accomplished that mission. But then she'd seen his process and walked away.

All Linc could think about was Scout's reaction to his post-its. If they were the problem, then he'd get rid of them. What he couldn't change was his end game.

Those pathways he'd strung with paper and string were, in reality, set in stone. Or rather in vessels and veins. Because Scout Silver was now in Linc's heart.

He loved her bossy attitude. She thought she was pushy? She had nothing on him when he set his mind to something. No matter which way he turned, no matter what direction he looked, he knew that from this moment onward it would always lead back to her.

Except, looking around, Linc wasn't sure where he was. They were no longer on any discernible path. He'd been so lost in his head that Wickham had led them astray.

He looked up to the sun to get his bearings, but the sky was cloudy. The sun hid hits locations.

He couldn't see the ranch house or the cabins. The skyline was uniform. All around him, everything looked the same. He might go one direction only to end up even further from his goal, which was to get back to Scout.

He hadn't bothered bringing his cell phone as service was spotty out here. So he couldn't call for help. He had a pad of post-its in his pocket, but all the square sheets were blank.

Linc didn't need to put pen to paper. He knew where he wanted to go. He'd simply have to pick his way back there. He'd muddle through the green monotony of the land until he was back to Scout. It might not be a straight shot. The process might not be pretty. But he knew whatever move he made would lead him back to her.

He gave a tug of the reins. Instead of heeding his command, Linc felt Wickham beginning to rear. His immediate reaction was to pull the horse tighter to assert his control. But as seemed the theme of the day, Linc had to admit he wasn't the one in control at this moment. And so he loosened the reins.

Dismounting was not an option. Linc aimed to stay centered in his saddle. He leaned forward, tipping his body toward Wickham's neck and waiting until the horse's feet were back on solid ground.

With Wickham's feet on the ground and Linc's hands still on the reins, Linc continued to lean forward. He kept his breathing and his emotions calm. There was no need to yell. The horse had tried him, as an alpha horse might be want to do. But Linc had kept his head. Now that the horse realized Linc couldn't be led, he walked on as though nothing had happened.

But for Linc, everything had changed. This little tug of war had shown him that his instincts never led him astray. That even in a fugue state where he was lost and unsure of his surroundings, he could always trust his gut, his intuition.

Now, if only his gut could point him in the right direction back to the woman he loved.

"Lost your way, son?"

Lincoln looked over to see a larger than life Black man on an Arabian. Father Matthews wore a dark cowboy hat, but there were no shadows cast on his serene face. His hazel eyes twinkled as he regarded Linc.

"Not at all, Father. I'm on my way back to her." Linc urged Wickham to turn right. Then left. He looked back up to Father Mathews. "But if you could point me in the right direction so I can get there faster?"

CHAPTER TWENTY-ONE

The last time anyone had seen Linc had been when he'd come out of the barn. Jackson had said he'd seen the man mounted atop Wickham. Scout's heart stopped. Wickham hadn't let a soul mount him since he'd come here.

Perhaps Jackson was wrong about which horse Linc had ridden out on. But no. Wickham's stall was empty. There was a saddle missing from the tack wall Linc and his men had organized the other day.

"Which way did he go?" Scout demanded.

She followed the direction of Jackson's finger. It was toward the Flying Cross Ranch. The path between the two ranches was well-tread. If Linc had ridden off on any other horse, Scout wouldn't worry. But that it was Wickham made her concerned.

"I'll round up the guys," said Jackson.

"No, I'll get there faster on my own."

"But you're not on your own, Scout. We were your father's unit. Now that you're with Linc, we're your family."

The corners of Scout's eyes pricked with tears. She didn't have time to let them fall. "I pushed him away. I've gotta bring him back."

As though Lizzie knew she was needed to save the day, she

trotted over to Scout as Scout came into the pasture with her saddle in hand. Once situated, Lizzie raced down the path the two of them had taken for years. If Wickham had misbehaved as Scout expected him to, then the horse and Linc wouldn't have gotten far. But she and Lizzie were pretty far along the path, and they hadn't come across the two.

Maybe there was nothing to fear after all? Wickham had taken to Linc. Perhaps the two were getting along just fine?

Even if that were true, Scout needed to find Linc. It was her mission. She didn't want there to be any more distance or misunderstandings between them. He was her end game. Whether it be her father's will or not.

And speak of the devil. The sight of her father's headstone caught Scout's eyes. Without even realizing she was doing it, she slowed Lizzie and urged her to the clearing of the family gravesite.

Her sense of urgency for Linc momentarily waylaid, Scout climbed down off her horse. With a pat, she allowed Lizzie to go and graze on the bright flowers poking up from the ground. Her mother had planted the horse-friendly flowers before she'd been laid to rest. Sarah Silver had wanted the beloved animals to visit her in death.

Scout ran her fingers over her mother's gravestone. Off to the side of her mother's final resting place sat another tombstone. It read *Roxanne Silver, loving wife, devoted mother until the day she died.*

Roxanne had been the General's third wife. Well, technically, his fourth since her parents had married and divorced again briefly. Scout had been determined to dislike the woman as much as she'd disliked Catherine the Cruel. But Roxanne had been diagnosed with cancer shortly after the twins were born, and everything changed. During those dark days, Scout had overheard the conversation between her mom and her second stepmom that had changed her and her sisters' lives.

"You're not on your own," Sarah had said to Roxanne. "Our girls are family." And then, after a deep breath and with a lift of her chin,

Sarah said three words that were rarely heard between two women who'd married the same man. "We're your family."

The words echoed what Jackson had just said to her. Scout's gaze swung to her father's stone. As per his wishes, there was no inscription on his stone save for the hard cold facts of his birth date and the day of his death.

How had this man brought together so many people while being apart from them at the same time? He was always ready to give an order. But Scout never knew what he was thinking. She never understood why he did what he did.

"You were a great leader," Scout said to the earth that cradled her father. "I just wish you'd let me in, that you'd talked to me more. Then maybe I wouldn't question your judgment so much."

The stone stared silently at her.

"If you did send him to me, if you made me Linc's mission—"

"He didn't."

Scout didn't turn to the sound of the deep voice coming from behind her. Her gaze stayed focused on her father's gravestone.

"I made you my mission," Linc continued. "You will always be my mission, even if I have to fight for you for the rest of my days."

Scout turned in time to see Linc dismount from Wickham. The horse turned its head to rub its muzzle against Linc's arm, as though nudging the man forward. Scout caught a glimpse of Father Matthews before he tipped his hat and walked off on his Arabian.

"I'll see you two this weekend," the older man muttered with a smile. "At your wedding ceremony."

Scout couldn't take her eyes off Linc as he marched toward her. He looked every bit the soldier striding forth to claim his victory. His purposeful strides were taking far too long for her, so she raced to him and leaped into his arms.

"I thought I lost you," she said into his neck as he wrapped her uptight.

"I was headed back to you. I just lost my way for a moment."

"I'll draw you a map. We can put it on a post-it, so it fits in your pocket."

Scout pressed her body into his, needing to get closer to this man. Linc might not always see the path clearly, but he had no problem in letting her take the lead in a process. Which was precisely why she would never have any trouble following behind him.

"About the mission wall," he said, pulling away from her. "I'll take it down if it upsets you."

"Don't," she said, running her fingers through his thick hair like she'd wanted to do since the moment she met him. "It freaked me out at first. But now that I'm seeing clearly, that wall, your process, it helped me to understand you better. It let me know what you're thinking."

"All I think about is you. How to win you. How to be the man you need."

"You are exactly what I need," she said. "And you've done it."

"Done what?"

"You've won me. I'm yours."

"What you're saying is mission accomplished?"

"Roger that."

"Permission to engage with friendly fire?"

"Permission granted."

Linc pressed his mouth to hers. With the first touch, Scout felt a spark light in her heart. With the second brush of his lips, she felt her soul ignite.

All the while, her soldier was there. Keeping her safe and secure. Making her feel wanted and adored. Letting her know that he would never lead her into harm's way. That with his kiss he pledged to honor her every day for the rest of their lives.

CHAPTER TWENTY-TWO

*L*inc pulled the last sticky note from the bathroom mirror. The adhesive gave without protest. It made a crackling sound as he crinkled it up in the palm of his hand. With a flick of his wrist, the wadded missive landed in the wastebasket with the others.

With the note gone, Linc got a clear view of his face. He was cleanly shaven. His hair trimmed. Stepping back to get more of a view, he could admit that he looked handsome in the suit he'd picked up from in town.

The town's folk had eyed him skeptically as he and his men did their shopping the other day. The six strangers had only been in town a week, and yet here they were shopping for wedding clothes. Outside of following them with their eyes, no one made a peep.

Outside the cabin, some of those same people were gathered. They awaited the main event. The wedding of Scout Silver and one of her father's soldiers.

A knock sounded at the bathroom door. Linc pulled it open to find Jeff leaning against the open door frame. His second in command looked dapper in a dark suit. His left arm was caught up in a matching sling.

"You take care of it?" Linc asked.

"Yeah," said Jeff. "I did what you asked. I still don't think it's a good idea."

"But you did it?"

"Yes, I did it," Jeff said as he backed away to allow Linc to pass. "You're really going through with this?"

"Of course," said Linc.

Linc knew Jeff wasn't referring to the wedding. Linc was itching to get out of the cabin and walked down the aisle. There was just one thing he had to do first. A critical task he had to accomplish before his mission was complete.

"What if the other girls don't get married and they wind up losing this place?" Jeff asked.

"I can't help that."

That was tough for Linc to admit. He didn't want to fail that broader mission. Just the week he'd spent on this ranch had given him a renewed purpose in life.

He loved working with the horses each day. He loved caring for the land. What he loved most was the woman who walked by his side each day, the woman with who he'd spend the rest of his life with, looking in Scout's crystal blue eyes and finding clarity and peace.

"If we lost the ranch," he said, "then we'll rebuild someplace new. In the meantime, we work the objective. Have you made any headway with your mission with your Silver sister?"

Jeff looked away. It didn't look like he'd answer. Finally, he opened his mouth… and a knock sounded at the front door.

"That'll be for you," Jeff said as he slipped past to go to the door. Jeff opened the door to an empty space.

"Is he in there?" came Linc's soon-to-be-wife's voice.

"Yeah," grinned Jeff.

"Well? What's so important that it couldn't wait until he sees me at the end of the aisle in twenty minutes?"

"You'll have to ask him yourself." Jeff stepped outside and marched away.

Scout didn't come into view. "Linc? What's going on?"

"I need you to come in here," he said.

"You can't see me before the wedding. It's bad luck."

"Do you really believe that there is any chance I'm not putting a ring on your finger today and spending the rest of my life with you?"

A pause. And then a vision of white stepped into the door frame. All rational thought left Linc's brain at the site of Scout.

She was a vision in a simple white sundress. White cowboy boots hugged her shapely calves. A bouquet of colorful flowers was held in her hands.

Linc stepped toward her. His arms ached to pull her close. His lips were itching to have a taste of her. But Scout wasn't stepping into his arms. She stepped around him.

"Linc…" she breathed. That was all she managed.

She stopped in the center of the room and stared, her jaw slack. Linc watched her expression as her eyes roved the expanse of the mission wall. He'd removed all the sticky notes from the cabin, except the new mission he'd posted to this wall.

Linc came to stand behind Scout. For a moment, he worried he'd gone too far. But the tears pricking at the corners of her eyes told him he'd gone just the right amount.

On the wall was a collage of sticky notes. He'd gone for pinks and purples because he supposed those were girly. Though his Scout was far from a girly girl. Still, he'd wanted it to be pretty. And those pastel colors were pretty as they formed the shape of a heart.

Scout stepped up to the wall. Her right hand shook as she raised it. With trembling fingers, she pulled at the center sticky note. On the piece of paper was written a single statement.

Be the best husband to my wife.

"This is my new mission," said Linc. "I have a number of objectives and tasks."

Scout replaced the mission statement. Her fingers were no longer shaking. She laid her flat palm over the square patch of paper and pressed it back into the wall.

Her attention turned to the next post-it. On varying shades of purple slips of paper were the first of Linc's objectives.

Be a helpmate. Be a good father. Show my love.

"I don't have all the tasks written out yet," he said. "There are some blanks that need to be filled in."

"I can help with that," she said. Scout reached to the side table where Linc had left his materials. She picked up a blank note, a light green color, and wrote. Once she was done, she turned back to the wall and pressed the note amongst the others.

Beneath the objective *Show my love,* Scout posted a note that read *Task: kiss your wife every day—a lot.*

Scout set the pad down. She recapped the pen and placed it beside the post-its. Then she straightened in her white dress, looking anything but innocent.

"Well, soldier? You have your orders. Are you up to the task?"

"Yes, ma'am," Linc grinned. "I think I'm up for that task."

Linc pulled his woman, his world, into his arms. His kiss wasn't an assault. There was no need for it to be. He'd laid down any arms he might've held the moment he saw this woman. She'd conquered him, body and soul.

"How'd I do?" he asked when he broke the kiss.

"You're going to get a very good performance report, soldier."

"I love you." Linc pressed his forehead to hers. "I may have forgotten to tell you that before. But I want you to know it's true now and will be true every day of our lives together."

"It's okay. I'll remind you." Scout lifted her head to gaze up at him. "I love you, too."

Linc kissed her again. Not only his heart but his mind felt in tune with her. This was a process he would not need prompts to remember.

When he broke this last kiss, he turned to look at the mass of sticky notes he'd compiled to please this woman. "I think it'll take me a lifetime to complete these loving tasks, but I'm up for it."

"Me, too."

"Then we should probably get started on the first task," he said. "The one where we get married."

Linc held out his hand. Scout placed her hand in his. Together they walked out of the cabin and toward the aisle. In the distance, the horses whinnied their approval.

EPILOGUE

*J*eff kept his eye trained on the cabin in the distance. The door still hadn't opened. Either Linc had failed in his clerically romantic notion, and they were taking the office stationery down off the walls. Or he had won Scout over with his post-it notes of love, and they were even now anticipating their vows. In either case, Jeff didn't mind the wait. Not when the view was so lovely.

Saylor Silver had her hair down around her shoulders. The lush strands fell like waves around her face. Jeff envied each tendril that had the right to kiss her flushed cheeks.

Jeff was able to look his fill at the second eldest Silver sister. Her attention was diverted elsewhere. Mostly her gaze was trained on the bouquet of colorful flowers in her hands. But every once in a while, she'd lift her head and look over at the bride's side of the aisle where guests were seated. Her blue eyes settled on one guest in particular.

A man sat with his arm drooped around the back of a pretty brown-skinned woman's chair. Brig had pointed the man out to Jeff earlier. The youngest Silver hadn't told Jeff the man's name, only his title. With a sneering lift to her lip, Brig had raised two fingers, as though in a curse, and labeled the man as The Boyfriend.

Jeff didn't need to ask whose boyfriend. Only one of the Silver sisters present was in a long term relationship. Though by looking at The Boyfriend's body language as he flirted with the woman seated next to him, it wasn't clear the man understood the term relationship or boyfriend.

The Boyfriend leaned in to whisper into his companion's ear. As the woman threw her head back and laughed, The Boyfriend blatantly looked down her top. Then he had the indecency to lick his lips.

Saylor fidgeted as the scene continued to play out under her nose. Under everyone's nose. Because they weren't the only ones looking at the two with open disdain. Some of those glances of the guests assembled traveled back to Saylor, which is when she would always drop her gaze to the ground.

Just as Jeff's mother always did.

Saylor had the same downcast eyes, as though she wasn't seeing the reality of her world, then it wasn't happening. She had the same helpless pinch to her lips, as though she were searching for the right words to make the man she loved only whisper sweet nothings for her ears alone. Her feet did the same restless tapping, as though she wanted to march over to The Boyfriend but knew it might end in her humiliation.

So she stayed still. She stayed quiet. She kept her gaze cast down.

Jeff felt a tingling in his palm. He wanted to ball his fingers into a fist and strike The Boyfriend. But it was his left hand that felt the tingle. The hand that had gone numb since he'd been caught in an explosion.

The doctors told him that from time to time, he might feel something there. The limb was numb, but it wasn't dead. This past week, Jeff had been feeling more and more sensations.

Like when he'd had his first glance of Saylor as she climbed out of the truck. Like when she'd passed him the salad at dinner, and her shoulder had brushed against his left side. Like when she'd bandaged him up in the barn, and her fingers had done quick, competent work of his injury.

His need to reach out to her, to offer her comfort. was overwhelming the thriving parts of him. So it was no wonder the sensation was seeping into his numb extremities.

"There they are," said Saylor. Her gaze was lifted to the cabin in the distance where Linc and Scout were making their way toward the outdoor ceremony. "You ready?"

Saylor slipped her hand through the crook of his left elbow. His left arm was done up in a sling that matched his suit so that it would look like he was leading her down the aisle like the others. When her fingers tucked into his side, Jeff felt an explosion of sensation at his ribs. The heat flooded his body, pooling in his heart and going up to his head.

The only thing he could think of was how to get her away from a man who clearly didn't know how to love this treasure in his keep. But was Jeff even qualified for the job?

His physical injury aside, there was still the case of his mental ones. This wasn't the first time he'd stood by in the face of such abuse. Could a man who witnessed his father hurt his mother emotionally, mentally, and physically every day of his young life truly be able to cherish a woman of his own?

It was a mission Jeff had to gather the courage to undertake. He'd made a pledge to the General. So, he was duty-bound to try.

But the question isn't will Jeff do everything in his heart to cherish Saylor, it's can Saylor find the strength and confidence in herself to believe she is worthy of such true and unconditional love?
Find out in "His Pledge to Cherish"
Book 2 in the Silver Star Ranch romances.

SHANAE JOHNSON

HIS Pledge TO Cherish

CHAPTER ONE

cool breeze swept a loose strand of hair across Saylor Silver's forehead. Her hair was normally pulled back from her head in a tight ponytail. The style was practical, allowing her a clear view to do her work with small and large animals.

She wasn't working in the barn this afternoon. There were no wounded animals about whinnying or squealing in pain. A joyous sound rang up as Saylor's older sister leaned forward to kiss her new husband.

Scout's grin was so big, her blue eyes so bright and filled with love, that Saylor felt the warmth even though it wasn't directed at her. Lincoln Rawlings, Saylor's new brother-in-law, smiled down at his bride as he met her lips. The crowd of family and friends cheered and whooped at the display of affection. When the couple broke the kiss, Linc looked at Scout in wonder, as though he still was in disbelief at his luck in finding the woman standing before him, accepting his vows to honor, protect, and cherish her until his last day.

More loose hair blew across Saylor's forehead. She swiped at it with her fingers, taking a moment to wipe the wetness from her eyes. When she did so, she saw the man standing behind Linc do the same.

Jefferson Moore was Linc's best man. Like most soldiers, his hair was cut close to his scalp. Meaning no strands of wayward hair blew into his face. Meaning there was no way he could brush the emotional movement off as moving his hair from his eyes. Unlike Saylor, Jeff didn't try to use his hair as a ruse.

With the index finger of his right hand, Jeff caught the moisture at his eyes. Then he caught her gaze. Saylor knew she should look away. Men didn't like women seeing them in times of weakness. Instead of frowning at the intrusion, Jeff offered her a grin.

It wasn't even a sheepish grin. It was a conspiratorial grin. As though he saw her tears as well and was standing beside her in solidarity.

Saylor liked that feeling, the feeling of standing united with someone. Too often, she felt alone in this world. Though she was always surrounded. By her sisters. By the animals she tended to as a veterinarian.

And by the man in her life. Her boyfriend, Nick. Who was seated not too far away. But when she looked for him in the small crowd of seated guests on the bride's side, she saw no hide nor hair of him.

Had he left? He'd told her he hated weddings. He'd told her that they were boring and self-indulgent and a waste of time. She'd begged him to come. It had taken days for him to relent and agree. And now he was gone.

No, wait. She caught sight of his red hair. He'd moved to the groom's side of the aisle. Perhaps he was making nice with Linc's soldier buddies over there.

But no. Nick wasn't rubbing elbows with straight-backed, broad-shouldered men with buzz cuts. A woman flipped her dark hair over her shoulder as she leaned into him. Another touched his forearm to bring his attention back around to her.

When Nick lifted his head, his gaze didn't connect with hers. When he lifted his hand to brush the strands of red hair out of his face, his eyes gleamed. Not with tears. Any moisture would evaporate in the heated gaze he split between the two women.

Saylor jerked her gaze from the scene. When she turned her head, her eyes landed on Jeff. His mouth was pressed in a firm line of displeasure. Saylor's immediate thought was to wonder what she'd done wrong to him? Following Jeff's eye line, she saw what upset him.

Saylor wanted to assure Jeff that Nick wasn't being unfaithful. He was just a flirt. All men flirted. All men looked at other women. It didn't mean anything.

Look at her own father. Abe Silver had had three wives in ten years. That was normal, at least in her world.

Nick was an attractive man. Women were bound to notice. She couldn't expect him not to look. But Nick's attention always turned back to her. Just like her father had always come back to her mother. That was the true test of love, that they came back.

The sound of the Wedding March brought Saylor's attention back to the happy event. It was time for Linc and Scout to begin their walk down the aisle as newlyweds. Saylor's oldest sister, who had been her first friend, was now walking away with the new most important person in her life. Saylor stood on the raised platform, feeling utterly alone.

To the side of her, Saylor felt Father Matthews's gaze on her. He'd just officiated one marriage. Saylor was hoping he might preside over hers and Nick's. If the pastor saw Nick getting cozy with those two women, he might get the wrong idea.

But Father Matthews wasn't looking at her. He wasn't looking at Nick. He was grinning at Jeff and clapping him on the shoulder.

"I suppose you'll be next?" said Father Matthews.

"If only I'm so lucky," was Jeff's answer.

With his right hand, Jeff rubbed at his left arm. The left one was cradled in a sling, injured and numb after his last mission in the military, the one that had taken her father's life and brought The President's Men here to the Silver Star Ranch.

Those six men from her father's unit had only been here on the

Silver Star Ranch for just over a week. And in that time, one of their own had met, fell in love with, and married the eldest daughter of their former commander.

It was General Abe Silver that had made his men promise to check on his six daughters just before he died. It was the General that had written in his will that in order for his daughters to keep the ranch, they each had to get married or the land and house they all had grown up in would go to their ex-step-mother who wouldn't hesitate to sell the land and pocket the profit. Catherine, or Cruella as the Silver sisters had taken to calling their step-mother, was still angry that her ex-husband had chosen to come back to his first wife.

That move hadn't surprised Saylor at all. First love never dies, her mother had told her. Nick was Saylor's first love. She would always come back to him.

Though he didn't rise to come to her now that the wedding was over.

Jeff held out his arm for Saylor. It was his right arm. Saylor hesitated but took his arm. As they began the walk down the aisle and toward the tables set out for the wedding reception, she didn't feel so alone anymore.

What she felt was tired. She wanted to close her eyes and follow Jeff's lead. She wanted to sink into the warm heat of him and fall asleep. She wanted to press her fingers into his hands and ask him to not let her go.

Saylor's eyes flashed open. She gave her head a shake to clear her mind. Where had those thoughts come from?

"You okay?" Jeff asked, his voice pitched low so that only she would hear.

"Of course," Saylor said. "Why wouldn't I be?"

"It's a big change. Your sister got married." Jeff gazed into her eyes, seeing more than she wanted him to. His smile was gentle. His features held no judgment of what she knew he'd seen. "Do you think you'll be next in line?"

Saylor wanted to laugh as much as she wanted to whimper. She wanted to be next in line. She'd wanted to be the first Silver sister to marry, ever since she was old enough to know what marriage meant.

She wanted a boy to look at her and choose her to be his wife, to be his love for the rest of their lives. "Yes, I do want to be next."

"Next for what?"

And just like that. The weariness she'd felt, the loneliness covering her shoulders, left her with the sound of his voice.

"Hey, Nick," Saylor said.

She let go of Jeff's arm and reached for her boyfriend's. Nick's hands were on his phone. His gaze as well. But he was here. He'd left those other women behind and come for her. He always came back to her.

"Next in line for marriage," said Jeff.

That brought Nick's gaze up. Saylor stood perfectly still in the silence. Another strand of her hair blew in front of her face, but her view was clear.

Instead of smiling at Saylor gently, Nick's brows shot up to his hairline. His lips turned down in a frown. His nose wrinkled as though he smelled something foul.

And then he burst out in laughter. "We're too young to get married. Personally, I don't plan to do that until I'm thirty-five at least. Gotta sow those oats, am I right?"

Nick lifted his hand for a fist bump.

Jeff did not raise his fist.

Nick looked down at Jeff's left hand, held securely in the sling. "Aw, sorry, man."

Nick didn't sound in the least bit sorry. Saylor's face burned at her boyfriend's manners. She wanted to explain to Jeff that Nick didn't always notice things. That he sometimes put his foot in his mouth. That he wasn't always mindful of other people's feelings.

She didn't have the opportunity.

Jeff turned his back on Nick. His gaze focused on her. He lifted his right hand to her shoulder and gave her a squeeze.

"Save me a dance?" Jeff said.

Again, warmth spread through her at his touch. It was a calming, soothing warmth, much like a heated blanket on a cold night. Saylor couldn't remember the last time she'd slept through the night. She bet she could if Jeff were her blanket.

Again, she had to blink and shake off that errant thought. The shake of her head looked like she was declining.

"Oh, no," she rushed to say. "I mean, you don't have to."

Jeff offered her a tight smile. With a slight bow like something out of a historical novel, he straightened and turned on his heel. Taking with him the warmth and comfort and leaving her standing alone with Nick.

CHAPTER TWO

*J*eff massaged the flesh of his left arm. His right hand squeezed and kneaded, but he felt nothing. He wished the rest of him was so lucky. He had feelings all over his body. Mostly in his heart.

Since the first day here, since the first time he'd seen her, it seemed his heart was auditioning for the role of acrobat in a circus. It had flipped the first time Saylor Silver's gaze had landed on him. It had swung high when she'd smiled so sweetly at him as she was introduced to the men in his unit. The smile was small as it had to stretch to greet all six of the President's Men. There hadn't been any interest in him in the curve of her lips. Just politeness.

Saylor was polite. She was kind. She was thoughtful.

When her gaze slipped to his limp arm, her brows had drawn. Not in morbid fascination like some. Or idol curiosity like others. Nor even wanton pity like a few women he'd meant in the past months. Lonely women who looked at him with a calculating gaze that they could nurse him and earn his undying love.

Jeff had no interest in such an exchange. For him, love was unconditional. Not transactional. There was no tit for tat. Only an open heart given freely with a no returns policy.

So when his gaze met Saylor Silver's and his heart dropped into his gut, he knew.

Saylor had looked at him and smiled. She'd looked at his arm and calculated. But those calculations weren't on how to indebt Jeff to her. Saylor saw an injury she wanted to heal because it was simply her nature.

Over the past week, he'd seen how she stayed up forty-eight hours straight with an elderly, pregnant mare. Soothing the old girl as she'd birthed her last foal. He'd watched from a distance as she'd splinted a chicken's broken foot. The other guys had been disappointed they wouldn't be having chicken salad for lunch.

Unfortunately, Saylor's healer's soul extended to the undeserving kind of animal as well.

Jeff spied The Boyfriend across the outside dance floor. The Boyfriend, that's what Saylor's sisters called him. Not one of the Silver sisters even deigned to use the man's name.

The Boyfriend's hand slid down a woman's forearm. It came to rest at her lower back. And then dipped farther.

None of that would be a problem. If the bottom in question where The Boyfriend's hand now rested belonged to his girlfriend.

It wasn't Saylor's bottom. Saylor was sitting down in a chair, not too far away from the display. She had a clear sight of what was going on. Instead of getting up and marching over to her boyfriend, she turned her back to the scene. Taking a deep breath, she plastered on a bright smile.

Even from across the space, Jeff could tell that the smile didn't reach her eyes. It was dull and heavy. It was fogged and unfocused, trying to erase what she'd just seen.

Jeff knew the look all too well. His mother had worn that look whenever they were out in public. Women in their small town had snickered behind their hands or looked at her pityingly.

Audrey Moore had worn a serene smile as though she were oblivious to her husband's indiscretions. But Jeff had seen what his father was up to. He'd also seen the bruises his mother tried to hide along with her heartbreak.

Saylor had no bruises that Jeff had seen. All of her hurts appeared to be internal. He knew for a fact that those hurt the worst.

He clenched his right fist, wishing he could shove it down The Boyfriend's throat. But then that would make him no better than his father. Even worse, he had a sinking suspicion that it wouldn't change Saylor's view of her cheating ex.

So instead of punching The Boyfriend, Jeff massaged his left forearm. The nerves there were frayed and not getting the signals. Just as his heart wasn't getting the signal that any pursuit of Saylor Silver was a fruitless endeavor.

"There you are."

Jeff looked up to see the bride walking toward him. The sun had set on Scout and Linc's wedding day, but the party was only just getting started.

"I was hoping you would dance with my sister," said Scout.

Jeff perked up at that. He'd asked Saylor to save him a dance. But he hadn't managed to make his way to her yet. He'd been far too busy watching the antics of her boyfriend, much like Saylor pretended she wasn't doing.

"You should dance with Brig." Scout shoved her youngest sister into Jeff's arms.

With his attention still on Saylor, Jeff nearly didn't catch Brig. Luckily, the young woman wore cowboy boots and not heels, so she was able to steady herself in his one-handed catch.

Brig turned to glare at her oldest sister. Scout winked at the youngest Silver before wrapping her arms around her husband and tugging him a short distance away. Linc shrugged apologetically at Jeff before following his wife's lead.

"Looks like you drew the short stick," said Brig.

"Pardon?" said Jeff.

"Scout wants you with me because she thinks you're the most harmless."

Jeff knew that Scout was trying to set up all of her single sisters in an effort to meet her father's deadline. If all six of the Silver sisters weren't married in three months, then the ranch would go to their stepmother, whom Jeff understood wanted to sell the ranch for a profit and kick them all off.

"Harmless?" Jeff parroted. "Me?"

"Yup."

Scout had no idea how wrong she was. Jeff had had a reputation of loving them and leaving them up until a year ago. All of the President's Men had a similar reputation before their separation from the military. They each had kept their lives small and contained enough to fit in a duffle bag. A woman couldn't fit in that baggage.

"I don't believe it, though," said Brig. "You're too quiet to be harmless. My dad said always watch out for the quiet ones."

"You're not quiet either," Jeff said as he gave Brig a twirl.

Brig's face split into a grin, confirming his suspicion. "I'm also not the Silver sister you've got your eye on, am I?"

Jeff couldn't help it. He lifted his gaze. He found her immediately. He always knew exactly where Saylor was. She was like a beacon for him.

She was standing now. Talking with an older lady. But Saylor's gaze kept dipping back to The Boyfriend.

The cheater was still in conversation with the brown-skinned woman. At least his hands weren't on her body. They were on his phone as he tapped at the keys. The woman tapped at her phone as well. Were they exchanging numbers?

"I think we could help each other," said Brig. "In fact, I think you can help us all."

"Help?" said Jeff, his mind not processing Brig's words as he watched Saylor's carefully blank features crumble. "How?"

"We need to get rid of him."

Jeff didn't need to ask who Brig meant by *him*. He also knew it was likely a fool's errand. Saylor clearly knew what was happening beneath her nose. Those in abusive relationships often did. Because make no mistake, cheating on one's partner was emotional abuse.

A woman's reasons for staying with a man who hit her or called her names wasn't often very different from staying with a man who betrayed her trust. Trying to separate an abuse victim from an abuser was a tricky mission. One Jeff had failed at before.

"We can't get rid of him," said Jeff, though it was a bitter pill to swallow. "She has to make that choice."

"Does she look like she's happy?"

The Boyfriend wasn't looking down at his phone any longer. He was on the dance floor. He pressed his body against the woman who was not his girlfriend as she shimmied in front of him.

The smile on Saylor's face slipped. She was clearly holding tears back. This time they weren't the joyful kind as when she'd watched her sister kiss her new husband. Jeff had let his own tears fall at that happy occasion.

No, Saylor did not look happy now.

"Why is she even with him?" asked Jeff.

"He was her first boyfriend. She keeps going back to him. Just like mom did with our dad. In case you haven't noticed, we all have daddy issues."

Jeff couldn't understand why? He would've killed to be raised by a man like the General. Instead, he was raised by a monster who liked to put his hands on his mother.

Jeff felt a tingle in the palm of his left hand. From time to time, the numbness receded, leaving him with a shock of sensation. He no longer had hope that he would get the full use of his arm back. But if he could use it just once more, he knew exactly what he'd do with it.

No, he wouldn't use it to commit violence. He would use it to sweep Saylor Silver off her feet and carry her away from that poor excuse of a man. Then he'd wrap her up tight and never let her go.

But that was just a dream. She stood immobile, unreachable on the other side of the dance floor. He stood numb, watching her.

CHAPTER THREE

aylor's face was tired. Her vision blurred with the strain of staying open. Her lips split with a dry crackling sound under the pressure of the fake smile she'd been holding on to all throughout her sister's wedding reception. Her forehead ached from the pressure of projecting the pretense that she was perfectly happy and content with her lot in life.

She wasn't. But it was fine. She would manage.

Saylor sat off to the side of her mother's garden, alone and unnoticed. Meanwhile, Linc spun Scout around and around in dizzying circles that made her older, no-nonsense sister giggle. Saylor couldn't remember the last time she'd heard Scout giggle. She couldn't remember the last time her own lips stretched so far in a smile of complete happiness. But she supposed the love of a good man would do that to a girl.

Saylor's gaze skated to the other side of the make-shift dance floor. It looked like her own man was having a good time now. Saylor watched him move and shake his body in time to the beat.

Nick was a great dancer. He had a natural rhythm and grace. The first and only time Saylor had tried to match his moves, he'd laughed at her.

Which had been fine since he hadn't been the only one. Everyone around them at the high school dance had laughed at her. Saylor had feigned a twisted ankle and sat the rest of the song out. She never got up to grace a dance floor again.

Which was why her boyfriend was dancing with his ex Holly Marks and his other ex Kellie Dustin. The two women moved their hips and shimmied their shoulders on either side of him. Nick spun first Holly, who he'd dated in junior year, and then Kellie, who Saylor was certain she'd seen him out with in their junior year as well.

They were all still friends even after the drama of high school. They still hung out from time to time. Even a couple of overnight trips to beaches and ski resorts.

Saylor bet they were fun. She wouldn't know. She hadn't been invited. Nick thought she'd feel awkward around the group she'd never been part of. Which had been fine because Saylor always had tons of work to do at the ranch and tending to the injuries of other animals in the county as a veterinarian.

Nick pulled Holly close and dipped her in a move Saylor had always wanted to try. But with her two left feet, she was sure she'd take both herself and her partner crashing down to the dance floor. Nick and Holly managed the steps, their bodies pressed so tight together that she couldn't get a dime between them.

Which was fine. Just fine.

It was good for him to get out and socialize now that he was unemployed. It wouldn't do either of them any good if he were up under her every day seeking attention. It was good for him to seek attention elsewhere. When people clung in relationships, it tended to suffocate them.

Saylor let out the breath she was holding as Nick held Holly close as the two of them slowly swayed to the beat of the fast-paced song. Nick whispered something in Holly's ear, and she grinned. The music was too loud, which explained why they were dancing so close. So that they could hear each other.

Which was fine.

Because any minute now, Nick would come back to her. Likely after this song played. Then a dance hit from when they were all in school came on. Everyone threw up their hands and started a choreographed series of movements.

Saylor stayed in her seat, tapping her foot in time to the rhythm. She licked at her bottom lip, trying to keep it from cracking under the pressure of her smile. And then, just as she'd predicted, Nick made his way over to her at the end of the song.

"You look tired, babe." Nick reached his hand out to her cheek.

Saylor rested her cheek in his palm. His hand was sweaty and smelled of two different brands of perfume that clashed with each other and turned her stomach. But she didn't turn her head away from the man she loved.

"Those bags under your eyes are not cute," said Nick, tilting his head to the side and regarding her. "You should call it a night."

"Sure," said Saylor as she rose. "Just let me say good night to my sisters. I'll meet you at the car, and we can head to your place."

"Oh, no-no." Nick held up his hands. "No need for you to drive back into the city. Why not stay here with your family tonight?"

"Because I'm sure my sister, the newlywed, wants some privacy with her new husband."

Nick scratched at his chin. "Well, it's just that I'm not ready to call it a night yet. And I don't want to drag you out."

"I'll come out with you. I'll just grab a cup of coffee. Besides, there's something I wanted to talk with you about."

Nick bit at the inside of his lip. His gaze was over Saylor's shoulder. When she turned, she saw Holly and Kellie waiting against the back gate. Their grins were tilted up, their eyes cast down in that way of the two gossiping girls Saylor remembered from high school.

"It was a nice ceremony, wasn't it?" said Saylor.

"Hmm?" Nick brought his gaze back to her. "Oh, yeah."

"It made me think about what I might want for my own ceremony."

Nick frowned down at her as though she were speaking in an alien tongue. "Your ceremony?"

Saylor swallowed. There was a fluttery feeling in her stomach. She and Nick had been dating for three years. Well, they had gone on their first date three years ago. Then he'd called her up three months after that. Then two months after that. It had taken a little over a year, but soon they were going out on a regular basis of a handful of times each month.

It wasn't the regularity that had sealed the deal. In Saylor's purse, she held what no other woman in his life had; a key to his apartment. He'd given it to her last winter when he'd come down with a nasty case of the flu. Saylor had dropped everything and nursed the man she loved back to health. When he was all better, he hadn't asked for the key back.

That had to be a sign.

She'd wanted to give it a few more months, maybe another year. But she no longer had the luxury of time. If she wanted to keep the ranch, and her job, and the horses she'd cared for since she was a girl, and her sisters with a roof over their heads, she had to get her boyfriend to marry her.

"Nick, you remember what I told you about my dad's will?"

He frowned again. His brows drawing in that cute V of confusion he'd always get when she'd tried to tutor him in math back in high school. That look that said he did not remember what she'd said to him just a minute ago.

"We all need to get married to save the ranch."

The V in his brow sprung upward into a flat line. Nick stepped back. "Look, Saylor, you know how I feel about you... But marriage? At my age?"

Well, at least he remembered their conversation. That was a good start. She just wished they were having this conversation out of earshot of two of his exes.

"Look, babe, you know I'm going to marry you."

The world stopped. Time stopped. Saylor's heart stopped.

It wasn't exactly a proposal because he didn't form it in a question. But that was fine. In fact, it was even better. To Nick, their marriage was a foregone conclusion, so he didn't need to ask.

"You know," he continued, "...someday."

"Well, the thing is, we all have to be married by the end of the year."

This time his brows scrunched together, in the way they did when he was trying to calculate a simple math problem.

"That's only three months away," Saylor supplied the answer for him.

Nick scrunched his lips together in the way he did when he got the answer wrong. "I tell you what; if it's really that important to you, and all of your sisters get married in time, then we'll be the last ones to go. How's that?"

Again, it wasn't the most romantic of overtures, but Nick wasn't a romance kind of guy. He'd had difficulty spelling that word all the way back in elementary school. Roman, he could spell as it referred to soldiers. But he always added an S instead of the C and E.

Still, this was exactly what Saylor wanted. The guy she'd had a crush on since kindergarten, the guy she'd pined after all through middle school, the man she'd dreamed of all through high school was finally agreeing to spend the rest of his life with her.

It was too much. It was everything. Saylor couldn't form words. And so she nodded.

Nick pressed a soft kiss to her mouth. His lips tasted of cherry lip bomb, the kind Kellie was wearing. The sweet flavor was bitter on Saylor's tongue. She swallowed it down regardless.

"Why don't you go get some rest," Nick said after he pulled away from her. "You look dead on your feet."

Saylor looked over at Kellie and Holly, who were moving toward the cars parked out back. "Where are you guys headed?"

Nick shrugged. "Just to catch up. Reminisce about old times. Stuff you weren't there for, so you'd be bored to tears."

Because Saylor hadn't run with the popular crowd back in high school. Or in college. Or, as it would have it, now.

"I'll call you, okay."

"Yeah, okay."

Nick turned and headed to his car with Holly and Kellie each taking one of his arms. They were already laughing and giggling as they left her behind.

Which was fine. Because Saylor actually was tired. She rubbed at her lower eyelids. She couldn't feel any bags there, but she did sense a wellspring of tears ready to spill over with any more pressure.

Saylor turned from the reception area. She didn't want to go into the house to the bedroom there. She wanted a few moments alone to gather herself. So, she headed to her cabin at the back of the house.

She should be happy. Nick was going to marry her. Her dreams were coming true. Everything was well and truly fine.

The sounds of her sister's wedding reception died down as Saylor reached the cabin's door. The sky was clear overhead, but Saylor felt drops running down her cheeks. She had to hurry inside before the deluge started.

She turned the knob and walked inside just in time. Tears poured from her eyes. Her sobs sounded like thunder in her ears. Luckily, she walked into a darkened area. But something moved in the darkness.

"Saylor?"

Lights came on, and she saw Jeff. He stood in the middle of the room. His jacket was off. His shirt open. His gaze wide and trained on her.

Saylor had thought her sobs sounded thunderous. They were nothing to the growl that escaped Jeff's clenched jaw. And then she was against his chest. A strong arm and two warm lips pressed to her forehead.

All of a sudden, Saylor didn't want to be anywhere but right where she was.

CHAPTER FOUR

*J*eff pulled Saylor tightly into his chest. His right forearm fit snuggly around her slight shoulders. His hand skated up to squeeze her shoulder cap. He felt a tingle in his left palm. The same tingle he'd felt the first time he'd seen her. The same tingle he'd felt when she'd tended to his slight wound last week. The same tingle that arose each time he saw her face, heard her voice, or simply thought about her.

Because, yes, just the mere thought of Saylor Silver could bring feeling to every part of him. Including the part that had been ravaged by an explosion. Jeff closed his eyes as he held this burst of sunlight to him. Behind his eyelids, he would've sworn he saw stars.

She sniffled against his chest. Her hands were balled into fists that lay at his sides. But she didn't appear to be pushing him away. That was a good sign because he wasn't sure he could've let her go. Instead of moving away from him, Saylor turned her head and buried herself more deeply into his chest.

Her breaths against his bare skin should've heated him through. Her soft cheek on his beating heart should've made his desire spike. Instead, all Jeff could feel was white, hot anger coursing through his veins.

He was going to kill Nick.

Yes, Nick and not The Boyfriend. Jeff was using the man's name. Most of the casualties of war were nameless bodies left behind as the spoils of battle. But not this one. For this traitorous villain, Jeff would look directly into his eyes just before he wrung his neck.

The desire to do violence caused the pinky of his left hand to twitch. Not even his feelings for Saylor had brought that much feeling in him. But the thought of doing harm to Nick did. With that thought, Jeff's ire instantly cooled.

For most of his life, he'd been an angry kid. Needing to put his fists against anything and anyone who moved against him. Because he could not protect himself or his mother at home.

It wasn't until he'd joined the Armed Forces that he'd learned to put that anger, that pain to use. General Abe Silver trained him as a soldier, ready and willing to take orders to combat the enemy the commander pointed at. Jeff learned to never raise his hand in anger, but only in a calculated plan sanctioned by his betters.

He was under no orders to attack The Boyfriend. The General had sent him here for one purpose. To make sure his daughters wanted for nothing. Saylor's tears told him that she ached for something she did not have. Jeff pledged he would do all he could to fill that need.

The anguish in Saylor's sobs gutted Jeff. He wanted to be able to wrap both arms around her and hold her securely. His left arm hung limp at his side, numb from the blast that had taken her father from both their lives.

Slowly by bits, Saylor's sobs tapered off until only her even breathing remained. As she quieted, she didn't let Jeff go. At some point, her fingers had unballed from fists. They now wrapped around his back. Her hands clasped in a deadlock at the base of his spine.

Jeff knew he should say something comforting. But for the life of him, he didn't know what those words might be. He wasn't the best with words. A map and coordinates, certainly. But with the lines and curves that made up words instead of topography, he was left directionless. And so he asked the stupidest question on the face of the earth.

"Are you all right?"

Of course, she wasn't all right. Jeff had seen that loser neglecting her all night. He'd watched as The Boyfriend had danced with not one but two other women, getting inappropriately close for someone in a committed relationship. All the while, Saylor had sat off to the side looking so lost.

Jeff had wanted to go to her, but he didn't have that right. And he knew any of the words he had for her would not be appreciated. Words like; *you need to leave him*, or *you deserve better than this.*

She did deserve better. But he knew that she wouldn't believe it. His mother never believed it. But Jeff wasn't sure if he could ever muster the strength to walk away from another victim of abuse.

At the sound of his voice, Saylor seemed to snap out of her fugue state.

"It's fine," she said. "I'm fine."

She unlocked her hands from his back. Her arms came from around him and snapped back to her sides.

"I'm sorry," she said, wiping at her eyes. "You must think I'm a complete basket case."

Jeff wanted to tell her he thought she was perfect. He wanted to bring her back into his arms. He wanted to kiss the dark bags under her eyes and hold her as she slept, taking all of her old baggage away from her.

"It's just the wedding was so beautiful… That's why I was crying. I got emotional."

Jeff nodded his head at her obvious lie.

"I wanted to give Scout and Linc their privacy, so I came to my cabin. I forgot you were staying here."

"It's fine," said Jeff. "You can stay here. I'll go next door to Scout's cabin."

He took a step and then froze. Saylor looked so lost standing in the middle of the room. Jeff wanted to reach for her, to pull her back to him. But he had no valid reason to. She was trying desperately to hide her pain.

He wanted her to know that she could never hide it from him. He knew that pain all too well. But because he knew the taste and texture of it, he knew that it did not want to be seen. And so he turned away, but not in the direction of the door.

"I was going to make a cup of hot tea with milk first. Do you mind? I could make you a cup as well."

In his peripheral vision, Jeff saw Saylor's shoulders relax. Just a bit. She didn't quite look up at him. But she nodded. And so Jeff put the kettle on.

CHAPTER FIVE

*S*aylor scrubbed at her face. The woman staring back at her in the bathroom mirror was unrecognizable. No, that wasn't true. She recognized herself all too well.

The make-up she'd carefully painted on her face to hide the blemishes had sweated off. Her hair, which normally was pulled back to show off the angles in her face, hung limp, making her face look fat and chubby. The bags under her eyes were so dark she looked like she'd been slapped in the face.

This was her. Saylor Silver. Second sister of the Silver girls. Second best beside her near-twin Mareen. It all added up to never being first. Not just in her family, but also in her lovelife.

Her own boyfriend, her first love, rarely put her first. Which was fine. She wasn't begrudging Nick his friendships. She just wished he'd hang out with guy friends instead of two of his ex-girlfriends. Women who had been his loves before he'd even noticed Saylor.

"Saylor, do you want honey or sugar?"

And there was that. Saylor couldn't' believe she'd just cried in front of Jeff. Now, like the rest of the town who'd watched her boyfriend dance attention on two of his exes, Jeff knew how pathetic she was.

"Um, you decide," Saylor called out to him.

Because she knew better than to tell a man her desires. She'd already tried to get her boyfriend to consider marriage to her. At least Nick hadn't shot her down like she'd feared he would. He'd considered it. He'd even made it a possibility. Which meant she had no reason to be crying in another man's bathroom.

Saylor gave herself another glance in the mirror. There wasn't much she could do about her appearance. It wasn't like she was trying to impress Jeff. She had a boyfriend who would consider asking her to marry him in a few months.

Maybe.

If all her sisters got married first.

Which even she had to admit to herself was a long shot.

Mareen was engaged, so that was a done deal.

Brig was chomping at the bit to pick one of the soldiers.

Tilly was on board but going about it in a way that made Saylor cringe. If her younger sister wasn't careful, she would end up with a Russian mobster as a husband.

Not to mention Gunnery, who wasn't even on this continent and had no plans to return any time soon.

There was no way they could pull this off in three months. Meaning they were going to lose the ranch. And Saylor was likely to lose her chance at a husband.

"Tea's ready," called Jeff.

Saylor wiped at her face one last time. She left her hair dangling around her shoulders since she had no hair tie. It was the best she could do. Not that Jeff was in any way interested in her. He was just a kind man who was eager to help.

And so, Saylor trudged into the main room of the cabin she had built with her father, Scout, and Mareen. Mareen had hated every second of the exercise. She'd complained with each smudge of dirt she'd gotten on her clothing. Saylor hadn't been thrilled at the building project either. She'd much rather tend to the animals. But like good soldiers, the girls had done as the General commanded.

The cabins had gone up and then been left empty at the back of the main house. Until these six soldiers came to stay.

Saylor found Jeff holding two mugs in one hand. He was on his way to the table Mareen had built. The piece of furniture was surprisingly sturdy for being built by a young girl who hated wielding a hammer.

"Let me help you with that." Saylor reached for the mugs, but Jeff had already set them down. Instead of meeting cool ceramic, Saylor's fingers brushed the warm mound of Jeff's bicep.

"I've got it," he said, giving her a smile.

The smile was simply a lift of one side of his mouth accompanied by a flash of straight white teeth. It should have brought to mind a predator. Perhaps a wolf, toying with its prey before sinking its teeth in.

Not for one moment did Saylor feel that Jeff was a threat. She felt safe. She felt protected. Which was odd since there was no danger in her life.

For his part, Jeff watched her. A wary expression in his gaze. He glanced downward. Saylor was embarrassed to see that her hand still rested on his bicep. She was mortified to see that it lay on his left arm, the one he often carried in a sling.

"I'm so sorry," Saylor yanked her hand away. "That was so rude."

Her fingers felt branded, as though she'd just yanked them away from fire. Jeff's arm had been warm under her touch. She had expected the limb to be cold to the touch since he'd lost feeling in it. However, it had felt alive and vibrant.

"I would have considered it rude," he said. "If you were getting fresh with me."

Saylor looked up, mortified until she saw Jeff's grin. He was playing with her. Joking as she did with her sisters. Nick was never playful or jokey with her.

Jeff scooted back into the couch. His hand on the back would've brushed her shoulder if she leaned over. She had the urge to curl up next to him and enjoy the warmth of the sweet tea.

"Cold?" Jeff reached for a blanket.

Before Saylor could say anything, he'd flung it over her legs. She felt overheated, but not by the blanket. She wasn't used to having a man anticipate her needs, much less take care of them.

She spent her days looking after Nick, trying to anticipate his needs. She also spent much of her free time cleaning his apartment. Nick was often careless about his things. Looking around the cabin, it looked spotless and tidy. There wasn't a thing for her to straighten up.

"I feel like I just lost you," said Jeff.

Saylor blinked until Jeff came into focus. His light brown eyes were focused on her face. That was another thing she wasn't used to. Nick often had his face buried in his phone, on the television, or looking at his surroundings when they were out. Saylor often caught him looking at the backside of a pretty woman as she walked by.

"Wanna tell me where you just went?"

"It's Nick." His name popped out of her mouth, unbidden.

"The Boyfriend."

"You say that like my sisters. They don't like him very much."

"I gathered that." Jeff took a sip of his tea.

"It's just because they haven't taken the time to get to know him."

Jeff nodded, his gaze thoughtful as he looked into his mug. "How long have you guys been dating?"

"Three years."

Jeff lifted an eyebrow. "That's a long time."

"You've never dated anyone that long?" If her tone was defensive, Jeff didn't appear to react to it.

"If I had," he said, "we'd be married with a child starting to walk and one on the way."

"You want children?"

"I want it all," he sighed, setting down his mug. "A house, a picket fence, a dog. A woman who'll stand by my side. Who's a partner to me. Who has my back and knows I have hers. That's my dream."

It was Saylor's dream too. Though Nick had got impatient when she'd taken him to look at houses. He once shouted at a child who'd spilled a drink on his shoes when they'd gone to the county fair. And he didn't like dogs, or really any animals.

"Scout is pushing me and Brig together," said Jeff.

Saylor's mouth fell open. Then shut. Then opened again. "No, Brig is all wrong for you."

"Who would you suggest?" Jeff's face split into that toothsome grin once more.

Saylor didn't want that sharp smile near any of her sisters. Not because she feared for her sisters' well-being. No, any of them might rip Jeff to pieces. All the men in town knew that to date a Silver sister was to go on a wild ride where they wouldn't have access to the controls.

Except Saylor had never lived up to that reputation. In fact, she'd tried to live it down in her relationship with Nick. But it was her who was left feeling she didn't have the controls of her life in her hands.

Jeff gazed at her, waiting patiently for her answer. "Too bad your hand in marriage isn't on the table. We get along so well."

"Yeah... I mean, right. I mean, Nick said he'd marry me."

"He did?" Jeff's smile lowered a bit, covering the gleam from his teeth.

"Well, he said he'd consider it."

"Yeah?"

"For the ranch."

"Okay."

"But not until all of my other sisters got married first."

Jeff's jaw seemed to harden at those words. Instead of saying anything, he took a sip of his tea. When he finished, he looked her dead in the eye. The smile was back, but this time Saylor swore she saw a predator gleaming in his soft brown eyes.

"Well, he'd better hurry up. A woman like you won't stay single forever. Someone is going to come in and swoop you up when he's not looking."

CHAPTER SIX

he Boyfriend was a lucky man. Not because the scoundrel had a beautiful, kind, trusting woman at his beck and call. Not because the lowlife somehow inspired Saylor's undying devotion. No, the creep was lucky that he wasn't in a combat zone and that Jeff could no longer handle the high-powered rifle he'd favored during his time in service. Otherwise, Jeff would be on an unsanctioned mission tonight.

Instead, Jeff stayed right where he was, on the couch next to Saylor.

"Marriage is a strange thing," Saylor was saying.

"How so?" Jeff asked, placing his empty mug on the wood table.

"Most animals don't mate for life, you know."

Jeff did know. Humans were a part of an elite group of lifeforms on this planet who remained with a partner for more than a reproductive reason. Though the divorce and infidelity rate would decry the notion.

"This animal will," Jeff said, his gaze intent on Saylor.

He could easily see spending the rest of his life with her. Trying to catch that shy smile. Whispering sweet nothings to make those beautiful blue eyes widen. Running his fingers through those lush brown strands and tangled up.

Saylor's hair moved from her shoulder as she turned to face him. Her gaze was wide with surprise. Had she heard his thoughts?

No, she wasn't stunned at the words he hadn't said. She was surprised by the words he had. That angered Jeff. A woman as desirable as Saylor Silver shouldn't be surprised that a man would want to spend the rest of his life with her, and only her.

His left palm tingled, missing the weight of a weapon in his hand. With his right hand, he pressed into his left palm, brushing the thought away. Tamping down on that side of himself.

Growing up in a household of abuse, Jeff had often worried he would do the same to his loved one. When he looked in the mirror, he saw his father's judgmental brown eyes. He knew his mouth pinched in distaste when things didn't go the way he wanted. His hands naturally hung in fists instead of open palms, even at rest.

Jeff knew he had his father inside him. He'd been trained by the General to only let that side out on command. With the General gone, Jeff worked even harder to tamp down his violent nature.

"You're a rare bird, then," Saylor said.

One of her perfectly plucked brows rose. The movement made Jeff think of a bird whose feathers had been ruffled.

"Most birds mate for life. Like swans." Jeff's gaze dipped to Saylor's elegant neck. A picture of two swans linking necks into a heart shape came to mind. The urge to bend his head to hers and kiss her slender neck made his blood pulse.

"Yes, they do." Saylor nodded. "Not ducks, though. Ducks practice seasonal monogamy."

"I don't see why that would matter to a swan, like you."

"Me? A swan?" She giggled. "If anything, I'm an ugly duckling."

Jeff sat up straight, his body poised for retaliation. "Who told you that lie?"

Saylor swallowed. Her body angled away from his. She broke eye contact and shrugged. "No one needed to. I looked in the mirror."

Jeff wasn't sure if she was fishing for a compliment? But he knew she believed what she was saying. Which only served to make him angrier.

He inhaled, bringing in more of her sweet scent. That helped to cool him down. He needed to get himself and his anger under control.

The last thing he wanted was for her to have even an ounce of fear of him. He would never hurt her. His ire was not directed at her. Only at the man who was hurting her even in his absence.

Jeff reached out and took her chin between his fingers. "You're a swan, Saylor. From the long, elegance of your limbs, to the graceful way you move, to the strength with which you carry yourself."

She held still for a long moment. There was something in her eyes, something urgent that wanted to believe him. But then she blinked and turned away.

Jeff wanted to reach out to her, but he knew better. He hadn't known better as a child. So when he reached out to his mother trying to tend to her wounds, she had always brushed him away as though her injuries were nothing. She'd cover them with makeup and was beautiful again in no time. Until her husband's feathers were ruffled again for some new, unpredictable reason. Then the makeup case came out again.

"My dad had three wives," Saylor said. "Technically five because he married my mother three times in total. He always came back to her, even after he went away."

Jeff wasn't sure what Saylor was trying to tell him? But he sensed it was important. So, he listened.

"My mother never took another lover. Because she always knew he would come back. They were each other's first loves. She said you never forget your first love."

And now he understood. The Boyfriend was Saylor's first love. By the looks of him, definitely by his actions, Jeff doubted Nick knew what the word love even meant. So, Jeff doubted Saylor was Nick's first love.

He knew better than to tell her so. When Jeff had tried to tell his own mother that love shouldn't hurt, she had stopped talking to him for weeks.

"I haven't been in love yet," he told her. "But I do believe in forever. When I find that woman, when I find my swan, I'm going to hold her tight forever."

"She's going to be one lucky woman."

"Yes, she will."

Saylor smiled, but the movement didn't reach her eyes. Because her eyes were heavy-lidded. She was clearly tired if the dark bruises under her eyes were any indication.

Jeff kept speaking, keeping his voice low and lulling. Between the hot tea and milk, his voice, and her heavy lids, Saylor was quietly dozing in a matter of minutes.

Jeff lifted his hand to run his fingertips down her temple. The heat that flared throughout his body, including a touch in his numb limb made him know that it wouldn't be the last time he did this. He would fight for the right to hold this swan in his arms for the rest of both of their lives.

CHAPTER SEVEN

Saylor was slow to wake. Slow, likely because it was the best night of sleep she'd had in days. Maybe weeks. Possibly months.

She hadn't woken a single time during the night and checked the nightstand's clock to see that the hour was late and she was still alone. She hadn't been awoken by the slam of the front door, alerting her to Nick's arrival back at his apartment only hours before her day was to begin. She hadn't awakened to the smell of cheap women's perfume that she couldn't hold her breath to.

Where Saylor now slept, she inhaled the smell of cedar and chamomile. She exhaled a sigh of peace and tranquility. She wasn't alone. She was wrapped up in a warm embrace. Her head rested against a strong beating heart.

But wait? That couldn't be right. Nick did not like to hold her or be touched when she was beside him.

She often awakened in the night with a chill all over her body as the covers had been yanked off her and wrapped around him. Which was fine as he had low iron, and his blood didn't circulate well, leaving his extremities cold.

Or she woke up disoriented because Nick, if he had come home, was sleeping on the couch with the television blaring.

It all was silent this morning. Because she wasn't at Nick's apartment. She wasn't in her bed. She was on a couch, but the cushions were the softest and warmest Saylor had ever felt. Because the cushions were male flesh.

Saylor lifted her head to find Jeff sleeping peacefully beneath her. She should've scrambled off this man's chest. She should've dashed out of the cabin.

She did neither of those things. She simply stared down at him as he continued to hold her with only one hand pressed to her lower back. She could've easily disentangled herself from his one-armed hold, but her body seized.

She was caught, mesmerized by the peace in his features. Jeff looked almost childlike in his repose. Almost. Jefferson Moore was definitely all male.

That thought unlocked her limbs. Looking at him sleeping peacefully was one thing. Thinking of him as anything other than a friend who'd been there for her during her time of need was something else entirely.

Saylor pressed her hand into the cushion to lift up. When she did, Jeff's arm tightened his hold on her. His fingers dug into the flesh at her low back, as though he didn't want her to go.

Again her limbs locked up, disabling any escape. Saylor had never had a man hold onto her. Nick was always turning away from her. She was always the one to reach out to him, never the other way around.

Nick had never rested his hand at her back. He'd never pulled her to him as though he didn't want her to go. Saylor had to go. Because Jeff wasn't Nick.

Saylor balled her hand into a fist and pushed. As she lifted off Jeff, he sighed. As his lips parted and the small breath escaped, he didn't open his eyes. Neither did he reach for her. He reached for his other arm, the one that hung limp at his side.

It was nippy inside the cabin in the early morning. None of the structures had been built with the modern conveniences of air and heating units. Just the bare necessities.

Saylor covered Jeff with a thick blanket. It was one she'd made when she was younger, when her mother had taught her to crochet. It covered this powerful soldier making him look as though he was covered in down.

Jeff had called her a swan last night. All her life Saylor had felt like an ugly duckling. With an older sister who never tried to be beautiful but still managed it. And a sister who was her twin in age, but her opposite when it came to looks.

Scout and Mareen were swans. Saylor was the duck in the family. Definitely this morning with a rumpled sundress, a rat's nest of hair, and smeared makeup. If Jeff could see her now, he'd see the truth. Which was why she dashed out of the cabin before Jeff could wake up and take in her true state.

When she turned after quietly closing the door, she ran smack dab into Wilson. He reached out to steady her. Once she had her balance, the dark-haired soldier lowered his hands but not his eyebrows. His thoughts were written clearly on his furrowed brows.

"It's not what you think."

Saylor had to pause after saying those words. She had heard them more times than she cared to count coming from her boyfriend's lips. Another reason she should keep giving Nick the benefit of the doubt. What had just transpired between herself and Jeff as they slept in the same space all night was not what Wilson was thinking.

"We were just talking," Scout said.

Wilson said nothing.

"And then, I fell asleep."

Still, Wilson remained mute.

"Nothing happened."

"Wouldn't think so," Wilson finally piped up. "Jefferson is a gentleman."

Saylor's lips pressed together. She wasn't sure if Wilson implied that she wasn't a lady? In any case, the presumption was awful. She finally understood how poor Nick must feel when people made assumptions about him and his behavior.

"You know how his arm injury came about?" Wilson continued. "He saved a kid in our last mission. Grabbed him just before the blast. Jeff was thrown into a wall, shoulder first. The kid walked away without a scratch."

Jeff hadn't told her that. But Saylor could easily imagine it. He'd stayed up all night with her when he could've shown her to the door, or walked out himself. A woman he barely knew. He hadn't thrown himself over her to protect her from an explosion, but he had let her break down in front of him. Yes, Jefferson was a gentleman.

"But that's Jeff, always putting others before himself, even if he's the one that gets hurt."

The look Wilson gave her was meaningful. Too bad Saylor wasn't clear on his meaning? She wouldn't have the chance to ask him because Wilson turned on his heel and marched away from her.

Saylor didn't have time to ponder the cryptic message the soldier had tried to deliver. She had animals to tend to. So she headed in the other direction to get to work. Before heading inside the house, she grabbed one of the honeysuckles from the bushes at the back of the house.

Tugging at the stamen, she found the prize; a dollop of nectar. It was only a taste. But that's what she was used to getting out of life. And like everything else, she made the most of it.

CHAPTER EIGHT

*J*eff woke. Not with a start. The passage from the dream world to awake was smooth. No nightmares, no sleep paralysis. Just ease. He hadn't woken like this in years.

The lingering scent of honeysuckles filled the air. When he was a kid, there were bushes of the fragrant blooms in his backyard. Whenever things heated up in his household, he'd escape out the back door to the smell of citrus and honey.

It surrounded him now, so strong he could taste it on his tongue. He felt he could reach out and touch it. So he did.

His hand filled with softness. He brought it to his lips, and sure enough, there it was. When he opened his eyes, he saw that he clutched a blanket in his hands.

Looking down at the blanket, he saw a pattern of horses woven into tightly knitted fabrics. At the bottom of the blanket was the name of the garment's creator.

Saylor.

Last night he'd had Saylor in his arms. She had let him in to see her hurts and wounds. She'd trusted him enough to fall asleep in his care. It was a start, but he still cursed himself for falling asleep.

He hadn't intended to. When she'd fallen asleep in his arms last night, he'd been content to look his fill at her heart-shaped face. Saylor had felt more than right in his arms. She'd felt inevitable. There had even been a few instances where Jeff thought he could feel her silky skin against the lifeless fingers of his left hand. Those fingers tingled beneath the warm blanket made by her hands. His right hand clenched with want that she had covered him with her sweet scent before she left him this morning.

Jeff allowed himself one more moment to bask in the heady smell of her. Then he tossed the blanket off, ready to head into battle. Jefferson Moore was ready to report for duty. He had officially signed on to Mission Terminate The Boyfriend.

In his military career, he'd assisted in helping to fell corrupt leadership. He would use those tactics now. But this wouldn't be a simple in and out mission. This would be a coup because Jeff fully intended to install himself as Saylor's new boyfriend. No, not her boyfriend. He wanted to become her husband.

He wouldn't waste three years leading her around. He didn't even want to waste three minutes. The problem was Jeff was sure Saylor had left him this morning to go back to her boyfriend.

Jeff couldn't say that he didn't understand why a woman would go back to a man who neglected her and abused her trust. He'd seen it happen over and over again with his mother. It was lucky for The Boyfriend that the cheater hadn't laid a hand on Saylor. If he ever did, Jeff wouldn't hesitate to take the man down with his good hand tied behind his back.

While showering and dressing for the day, Jeff began to formulate a mission plan in his mind. He'd always been great with maps. He could easily find the best routes on their missions, the ones that kept them out of danger or got them to their location the fastest.

He needed to find a route to Saylor's heart. From the glimpse he'd gotten last night, he knew the terrain was ravaged and war-torn. He'd have to overcome the treachery Saylor had endured to penetrate all her defenses. Jeff knew exactly where to start.

All cleaned up, Jeff made a beeline for the barn. Even though it was Sunday, there was still work to be done on the ranch. Horses didn't care or even know about weekends. The mares were already out in the pastures munching at the bales of hay laid there.

"Oh, I thought you were Jackson." Brig's posture slumped at the sight of Jeff.

Jeff couldn't help but hide his grin. Brig was trailing after a lost cause. She'd said the Silver sisters had daddy issues. Jackson wasn't old enough to be Brig's father by decades, but the coed was still a touch on the younger side of Jackson's taste.

"I noticed Saylor didn't come home last night," said Brig, her brows drawn together as though in conspiracy with one another. "Last I saw of her, she was headed toward her cabin… where you're staying."

"We were together," Jeff confirmed.

"Dude!" Brig raised her hand in a high five.

"It's not what you think."

"There's something to think about? Yes!"

Jeff tried and failed to hide his grin. There was something to think about. He had to think about how to wedge even more cracks in Saylor's relationship than were already there. And he had to do it before her sisters all married and The Boyfriend had a chance to make good on his promise of marrying Saylor last. Just the thought of putting her last made bile rise in Jeff's throat.

"So, what's the plan?" asked Brig.

The plan was to first get some of the responsibilities off of Saylor's plate. The woman looked like she hadn't rested in weeks. Maybe even months by the heavy circles under her eyes. Jeff wanted to get her well-rested so that she could start to think clearly, see things with fresh eyes. So he was going to step up his assistance around here.

"You finish getting the mares out," he said. "I'll take care of the stallions."

"Are you sure?"

Jeff didn't miss the quick glance Brig shot to his left arm. "I've got this. If I can't help with the horses, she won't even look at me twice."

Brig considered that and then shrugged. She made a clicking sound in her throat, and the two mares she had on leads fell into step with her.

Jeff went into the barn and loosed one of the haystacks. The bale was big and cumbersome. Luckily, it was also a circle, and like a wheel, it just needed a push to gain momentum.

Once four bales were out, he went back for the horses. Thanks to Linc's organizational skills, the tack on the wall was easy to reach. Jeff grabbed a halter. The blond horse, Bingley, was patient as Jeff slid it over the horse's head. The two of them had developed a rapport since Jeff's first day here. But when Jeff made the same sound as Brig for the horse to move forward, Bingley lowered his head.

"It's breakfast time, buddy. You hungry?"

The horse still did not move forward.

Jeff gave a tug on the lead.

Bingley stepped back. He pawed at the ground.

"Easy," Jeff crooned.

Instead of taking it easy, Bingley turned his head. He opened his mouth, and his large teeth bit at his flank.

"I'll bet the hay tastes better than your hide. Come on, fella."

Finally, the horse allowed Jeff to lead him out of the stall. But it was slow going getting the horse to walk forward out of the barn. Jeff was sure once the horse saw the food he'd get with the program. But once they were out of the barn, Bingley still wasn't cooperating.

As they approached the hay, Bingley tugged again on the lead. Before Jeff could get the horse under control, it reared. The movement caught Jeff unawares, and he fell onto his back, just out of reach of the horse's hooves.

Jeff scrambled back as he heard someone shout in the distance. It was Saylor. He'd recognize her voice in a wind tunnel.

He had to get back on his feet. He had to show Saylor that he could manage the horse. But by the time Jeff got to his feet, he looked over to find that the horse was lying on the ground and whining pitifully.

When he looked up, he saw Saylor racing toward him. So much for showing her that he could be a helpmate to her. Shame burned him as he scrambled to his feet. Instead of stopping to check on him, Saylor bypassed Jeff and went directly for the horse.

CHAPTER NINE

"What is it, boy?" Saylor asked Bingley as she came to kneel by the blond Sorrel's head.

In response, Bingley waved his head from side to side. The horse let out a pitiful breath and then laid flat. Saylor had an idea of what was wrong with the horse, but she needed some more information.

"You okay over there?" Saylor asked without looking up at Jeff.

She'd seen the soldier take that fall just before the horse laid itself out on the ground. Saylor had made the calculated move to tend to the horse before tending to the man. Men didn't like it when women noticed any of their weaknesses. She probably shouldn't have even asked Jeff that question. He was sure to go off in a huff, just like Nick did whenever she caught him in a weak moment.

The thought of Jeff walking off in a huff made Saylor incredibly sad. The idea of him huffing seemed wrong in her mind. It belied that even demeanor of his. But she knew that all men had tempers, and she couldn't deal with the man's tantrum right now. She had a sick horse to tend to.

"What do you need me to do?"

Saylor glanced up. She was sure there was utter shock in her gaze.

Jeff was back on his feet. He was standing close to her, but not too close. Just close enough to her to swoop in if she needed. But far back enough as though he trusted her to handle this matter.

What did she need him to do? Had she heard that right? Not *It wasn't my fault.* Or *You should've known what would happen.* Was Jeff trying to be of assistance?

It was a sight Saylor had never seen before. She had to blink a few times to be sure she wasn't hallucinating. Then she had to clear her throat before her words were intelligible.

"Just tell me what was going on before he dropped," she finally managed.

"I was leading him out of the barn to have his meal," said Jeff. "He was antsy in his stall. He kept turning his head when I tried to put on his halter. But I knew he had to be hungry since he kept biting at his flank."

That confirmed what Saylor had been thinking. "It's likely colic."

"Colic?" Jeff said. "Like a baby?"

"Something like that." Saylor managed to bring the horse back to standing. "It's a bad tummy ache. Eating is probably the last thing he wants to do."

She ran her hand over the horse's side. Leaning in, she pressed her ear to his belly to listen. Sure enough, she heard the grumbling there.

"What's there to do?" asked Jeff.

"It doesn't sound like a serious case, just a mild bout. So, I'm going to work his pressure points first."

Saylor was already moving into position. She reached down the horse's leg, squeezing at the spot above his hoof. She rotated the joint she found there, giving it a good amount of direct pressure.

Bingley looked back at her. The horse let out a low whine that sounded like a sigh of relief.

"There, there," she said. "It's already getting better, isn't it?"

"Should I hold him still? He could kick you."

Jeff was just behind her. She felt the sigh of heat from his breath against the cone of her ear. She almost shivered. What made her warm through was the worry and protectiveness in Jeff's voice.

"He's not gonna kick," she said, her voice a low and rumbly ache like the sounds coming from Bingley's belly. "This is helping it feel better. So, he'll hold still."

Saylor couldn't hold still with Jeff beside her. There was a part of her that wanted to turn around and find her way back into that space at the center of his chest. That space where she had found her own relief just hours ago. An ache rose low in her stomach.

"Have you eaten this morning?" Jeff asked.

Saylor flushed that he'd heard her want. "I will. Once I finish soothing Bingley."

"You have a habit of doing that."

"Doing what?"

"Putting others before you."

Saylor frowned at that. "Well, this poor horse can't soothe himself."

"I could take over if you showed me what to do. Then you could go grab a bite to eat."

What was he trying to say? That she was too thin? Too fat? Saylor wasn't sure where the dig on her was coming from, so she rounded the horse and went to his tail.

"Let me give you a hand," said Jeff.

"I'll need two hands for this part." The moment the words were out of her mouth, Saylor grimaced. "That's not what I meant."

She turned to Jeff, expecting anger, or at least withdrawal. There was neither on his face. He stood by her, steady and calm.

Saylor was anything but. Her fingers shook as she grasped the strands of Bingley's tail. There were some of his vertebrae in the hair there. Saylor pulled down on it with tight pressure.

All the while, she watched the horse. The horse watched her. Jeff watched them both, but she noticed that Jeff's gaze lingered mostly on her.

She must still look a fright. She had just hopped out of the shower. She hadn't had time to put on any makeup or fix her hair.

"He didn't hurt you, did he?" she asked.

"No," said Jeff. "I thought I was helping."

"No, you were. You did. How were you to know Bingley was sick?"

"Yeah, I guess."

"Listen, about last night…I'm so sorry for overstaying my welcome and falling asleep on you like I did. And then waking up and leaving without saying goodbye."

The words all came out in a huge gush. They weren't the only thing that came out in a gush. Saylor let go of Bingley's tale just in time. She only just managed to leap out of the way as the horse dropped proof that his belly was starting to feel better.

Before Saylor could wobble, she was encased in a strong arm. A strong arm that felt familiar. Jeff had one arm around her, but she felt engulfed by him.

"You don't have to apologize for anything," he said. "I'm here for you, whatever you need."

Saylor couldn't take her gaze from his mouth. Or the words he'd just said. As Jeff held her to his chest, her own belly stopped its grumbling as she let out a sigh of contented relief.

"Morning," called Brig.

As though she'd been caught, Saylor sprung herself out of Jeff's arms. She felt the instant loss of his warmth. Her insides went to mush. Or rather, that was how her foot felt as she stepped right into Bingley's heaping gift of wellness.

That was also the moment her cell phone decided to ring.

CHAPTER TEN

*J*eff watched as Saylor slipped out of his hold. It wasn't a hard thing to do as one arm hung uselessly at his side. If it had been working, he might've been able to lock her down. Instead, she was sliding her boots against the grass, trying to remove as much manure as possible as she answered her cell phone.

He knew without seeing the caller ID who was on the other end of that line. The Boyfriend. *She keeps going back to him*, her sister had said. Well, Jeff was here to interrupt that script. He just had to figure out how.

"Looks like you're making progress." Brig grinned at him from the fencing. With ease, the young woman hopped over the fence, deftly avoiding the little gifts dropped by the horse. Bingley was up and moving about once more. He came to Brig, lowering his head for a pat.

"Aw, did you have a bellyache, Bingley Wingley?" crooned Brig.

Jeff's attention couldn't be moved from Saylor. She moved farther away from him, away from the barn, and farther out to pasture. He couldn't hear what she was saying, but he saw that she wasn't smiling as she talked on the phone.

Was Nick saying something to upset her? Was the man she had chosen taking another crack at her?

Jeff hadn't missed Nick's disparaging remarks about her at the reception, as The Boyfriend prepared to leave with not one but two other women. Neither had Jeff missed the slight fall of Saylor's smile. That dip in her perfect lips had appeared to Jeff an avalanche of hurt.

Jeff felt a tingle in his left hand. Was it a tingle to cuff Nick? Or a tingle to reach for Saylor. He knew that if given the chance, he would choose comforting Saylor. But he was already having a hard time getting her to accept his care. It was clear she was unused to a man looking after her.

"I saw you two in what looked like a pretty intimate moment," said Brig.

"She came into my arms to avoid falling into manure," Jeff said.

"If that isn't a metaphor, then I don't know what is." Brig sent Bingley off into the round pen with a pat on the rear. The horse walked on, still ignoring the hay that Jeff had laid out.

"Nick was the first guy to tell Saylor she was pretty."

"The first guy? You can't be serious. She's gorgeous."

"I know. But she doesn't believe that. You haven't seen Mareen. Saylor and Mareen are the same age, just a few months apart. Irish twins."

Jeff frowned at the term. The General had told his men that he'd come from a Germanic heritage.

"My mom found out she was pregnant on the day of my dad's wedding to Mareen's mom, Catherine the Cruel."

Jeff cringed. He'd had no idea what a soap opera the general's life had been outside of the military. The man ran everything by the book. His movements were precise and regimented. But Jeff knew all too well that love was a messy affair.

His father had heated on his mom numerous times. Cheated wasn't the best word. It implied a trick or dishonesty. Patrick Moore had no problems telling his wife the truth, and watching the pain crease her features.

And still, Audrey Moore had stayed with her sadistic husband. Stayed to endure the harsh words, brutal caresses, and the constant infidelity.

Jeff had heard Nick's harsh words to Saylor. He suspected the man was relaying more to her over a cell tower. Jeff also suspected the infidelity. But he'd seen Saylor physically turn away from potential evidence the other night.

"I've tried everything I can think of to break the two of them up," Brig was saying.

When he was a teen, Jeff had tried everything he could think of to get his mother to leave. He'd shown her evidence of the cheating, but she had only turned away. He'd run away, but she hadn't followed. He'd shouted that his father would be the death of her, but she'd turned up the sound on the television.

"Telling her he's a worthless scumbag doesn't work," Brig was saying. "She just makes excuses for him. I've tried spreading gossip so that it reaches her ears through others. But everyone knows how he is. I've even tried throwing his ex-girlfriends at him, like at the wedding."

"That was you?"

"Yup, I invited them. And the idiot took the bait. Problem is, Saylor didn't let him off the hook."

That indeed was the problem. Again, Jeff got that fleeting feeling in the palm of his hand, an itching feeling that made him want to ball his fist. But when he looked down, his fingers hung limply at his side.

"His exes will dance and dally with him," Brig continued. "But none of them want to keep him. Surprisingly, they're actually smart. If total dishonest, traitors to their gender."

Jeff's father was the same. The women he brought into his life had no shame as they pranced on his arm for a few days or weeks. They allowed him to drip them in cheap jewels and two-star restaurant meals while his family scraped by. But none of them wanted to stay with a man who had a wife and child.

"My old college roommate befriended her bestie's cheating

boyfriend and then sabotaged him from the other side," Brig said with a gleam to her blue eyes. "It was the most brilliant espionage I've ever witnessed. Too bad I can't pull that off in this case. I tried to have a pleasant conversation with The Boyfriend, but it turned my stomach."

"I could do that." It was a tactic Jeff had never tried when he was trying to split his parents up. Mainly because he'd been far too young to manage or even consider it.

"Yeah?" said Brig.

"Infiltrate behind enemy lines? I've done it before."

That had been part of his job in the military, turning assets against the bad guys. It was intel he'd gathered that led them to their last mission. The intel had been good. They'd gotten the bad guy and saved many lives. Even though they'd lost the one life they held dear.

It would be nothing to Jeff to befriend this particular enemy if only to take Nick down and save this most precious asset. He owed it to the general, he told himself. But it was his heart that was in charge of this particular decision.

His mother had chosen time and again to stay with his father. But Jeff was determined to rescue Saylor from this particular villain. Even if Jeff didn't wind up the hero.

"I have to go into the city," Saylor said as she walked back to them.

"What does he need now?" asked Brig. "His pancakes cut in bite-sized pieces?"

"That wasn't Nick." Saylor scowled at her sister. "It was his dry cleaner. They're closing up early and wanted him to pick up his suit. He's not answering his phone, so they called me."

"You're going to run all the way to town to pick up his dry cleaning?" said Brig, lifting an eyebrow.

"But Nick still has my car," Saylor said as though she hadn't heard her sister or seen the raised brow of disbelief.

"He always has your car," Brig murmured.

"I'll drive you," said Jeff.

Saylor blinked up at him. Then she shook her head. "You don't have to do that."

"I need to pick up some things anyway." The lie was smooth coming from Jeff's lips. He'd twisted more flimsy truths to get people to turn on corrupt leaders. "You'd do me a favor by providing the company."

"If you're sure I'm not putting you out?"

Jeff offered Saylor a pleasant grin in answer. The only person he was focused on putting out was that boyfriend of hers. As he and Saylor walked off, Jeff turned back to Brig, who winked at him, throwing two large thumbs up.

The plan was in motion.

CHAPTER ELEVEN

Saylor pulled the strands of her hair back and away from her face. She chided herself for letting her hair down for so long. Scout had insisted that her younger sister let her tresses flow free yesterday, and Saylor had acquiesced because she knew better than to argue with a bride on her wedding day.

Now, she gathered the strands into a tight queue at the back of her head. Nick often told her with her hair down, it made her face look fat. Pleasing her sister for one day was fine. Now Saylor was back to her normal routine, and at the top of that routine was being pleasing to the eyes of her boyfriend.

Although with her hair now in its customary ponytail, she was uncomfortable sitting in the passenger seat. She turned her head left, then right, trying to find the best angle on the headrest.

"Is my driving making you nervous?" asked Jeff.

Saylor glanced up and at his profile. His gaze was on the road, but she could feel all of his attention on her. She'd never had someone focus like this on her. Well, she'd never had a man focus so much of his attention on her.

"I do still have a driver's license," he said when she didn't answer. "I was cleared by the DMV to drive even though one-handed."

Now Saylor's glance fell down to the hand he held in his lap. His left hand was caught up in its sling as his right hand maneuvered on the steering wheel. Saylor blushed again to be caught staring so openly at the man's lap.

"I'm not clear to operate military-grade heavy equipment, but I can manage a car."

"I wasn't thinking about your abilities," she said. "I know you're perfectly capable. I trust that you wouldn't do anything to put me in danger."

"You do?" he said, a note of disbelief in his voice.

With that note of uncertainty, she thought she should be nervous. But she wasn't. The week she'd known Jefferson Moore, he had shown at every turn that he was an able-bodied man despite his injury. Even after the mishap this morning with Bingley, Jeff hadn't shied away from doing what had to be done.

Their gazes locked as they ambled down the deserted road that led to town. Jeff's light brown eyes skated from her eyes to her hairline.

"What?" Saylor asked, patting at her hair, searching for any wayward strands that may have escaped her elastic band.

"Nothing," he said in that tone that belied there was something. "It's just, you look different with your hair up."

Saylor's fingers trailed down the mane of hair that hung over her shoulder. "Nick likes it up."

From the corner of her eye, she saw Jeff's jaw tense. She braced herself for a crack about her boyfriend. Nick didn't have many guy friends. In fact, he didn't have any. It was because he was so misunderstood, was all.

"Nick's a lucky guy," said Jeff. "To have a woman who is beautiful no matter her hairstyle."

Saylor could only stare. She felt a tendril escape her ponytail at the back. She did not reach to press the loose strand back into place.

Jeff glanced at her again, this time flashing her that genial smile he had last night when he'd asked her to stay for warm tea. He should've had his eyes on the road. She should've felt unsafe. But the truth was, this man made her feel safe. Why else would she spend the night in his arms?

Her cheeks heated at the thought of last night. She waited for the guilt, for the shame to assault her. It never came.

Saylor's mind thought back to waking up in Jeff's arms. She'd never felt such peace as in those few moments. The residual peace left no room for guilt or shame.

Nick never held her. He rarely hugged her. Wait? Had he ever embraced her with the intention to offer comfort?

She and Jeff were cruising down the main street now. Honor Valley had a colonial feel to it, with red brick shops lining the street. Wooden placards hung over doors announcing the family name first and then the type of business.

"It's just over there." Saylor pointed to Cohen's Dry Cleaner's Shop.

The Cohens had already put up a closed for business sign. Everyone knew their oldest granddaughter was expecting her first child. They had announced they would be closing for a couple of weeks at the beginning of the month to be there for the happy occasion. Though it was Nick's dry cleaning she was picking up, a pang of guilt still washed over Saylor that she was holding them up. She should've anticipated this.

Jeff parked the car in front of the shop. Before he could unfasten his seat belt, Saylor stopped him.

"Don't trouble yourself," she said. "I'll just run in and get it."

"I'm going to get out to open your door for you."

"I can open my own door, Jeff." She grinned, pleased by the old world chivalry at the same time that she was unsure what to do with it. "I mean, I know you can open it for me. But there's no need to—"

"Saylor?"

"Yes, Jeff?"

"Stay where you are," he said pointedly. "I'll be around to open your door like the gentleman your father trained me to be."

Saylor pressed her back into the seat. The place at the back of her head where her ponytail was gathered found the right spot at that moment.

Jeff undid his seatbelt and opened the door. He walked around the truck with sure strides. He arrived at the passenger door and pulled the door open wide. Then reached for her.

Saylor reached for his hand, but she was held back. She'd forgotten to take off her own seat belt. Seeing the problem, Jeff reached across her body.

That peace that had lulled her to sleep in another man's arms woke inside her. But it was no longer calm and quiet. The head of it seemed to perk up, look around, and settle on Jeff. As it did so, heat bloomed somewhere in Saylor's middle, making her breath catch.

Jeff lifted his head. They were eye to eye, only a few inches apart. She could lean forward and be right back in that space at the center of his chest. There was a part of her, the warm awakened part, that wanted to reach for that spot.

A click cut through the imagined tension she felt. The strap let her go, giving her the space to move. Saylor hesitated.

Jeff backed up, giving her the space she needed to climb out of the car. In the gulf between them, he held out his hand once more. Saylor had to take a breath to regain her composure. Her fingers trembled as she put her hand in his. The instant she felt the coolness of his palm, her fingers stopped shaking.

Jeff wrapped his fingers around hers. And there it was again, that feeling of safety and peace. Only it was a few degrees warmer now.

"You good?" asked Jeff.

Yes, she was good. She had never felt so good. She felt so good that she didn't let go of Jeff's hand as they walked into the shop to pick up her boyfriend's dry cleaning.

CHAPTER TWELVE

Saylor's hand in his felt good. It felt right. It felt perfect.

Jeff had lied to her earlier before he'd climbed out of the car to come around and hand her out. A gentleman would not be holding the hand of an unavailable woman. A gentleman would keep his distance.

Jeff was not a gentleman.

General Silver may have chastised the men when it came to their manners. But the man had also trained them to be merciless when it came to winning battles. This wasn't a battle Jeff was fighting. He was waging full out war.

It was a war for Saylor's heart, and Jeff was all in. He was prepared to use any and all tactics to press his advantage. So far, he wasn't meeting with any resistance.

Part of Jeff knew that that was because his target had never received an actual full-court press. He doubted Nick had ever had to press his suit at all. It was written all over her face. And it was criminal.

Jeff wanted to pummel The Boyfriend for the neglect. But had Nick not neglected Saylor, then it would've been all the more harder for Jeff to move forward with this sneak attack.

Walking a few steps away from the car, Jeff reveled in the feel of Saylor at his side. There was space between them, but he knew that if he pulled her closer, she'd fit right into his side. He already knew that she fit against his chest like a puzzle piece he'd been searching for all his life.

Jeff was sure no one else would fit his hard edges as smoothly as Saylor Silver. Which was why this wasn't a game for him. He was in this to win it.

He rubbed the back of her knuckles lightly as they walked into the dry cleaner's shop. The bell overhead dinged as if to signal that this round was up. Saylor was here to collect her boyfriend's things. However, Jeff didn't let go of Saylor's hand. And she didn't tug free of his hold.

"Thank you for coming in, you two," said the small woman behind the counter. She had a cloud of gray hair and the type of crow's feet at the corners of her eyes and mouth, the kind that told she was prone to laughing and smiling a lot. Which made it odd that a second later, she was frowning.

"Oh?" The woman, who Jeff assumed was Mrs. Cohen, looked between them at their clasped hands. "I didn't realize you had a new beau, Saylor. I wouldn't have called you for Nick's things if I had known."

That's when Saylor dropped Jeff's hand. It took everything in him to let her go. She even stepped away from him, putting a foot of distance between them. Instead of stepping forward and back into her personal space, Jeff decided to keep sentry at her back.

"Oh no, Jeff isn't my beau. He's my…"

Jeff's blood heated that Saylor hesitated on their relationship status. The word *friend* should've rolled off her tongue with ease. Could that pause mean that she was already warming up to the idea that they could be more?

He wanted to wait until Saylor filled in that blank. Instead, he dipped his head to the woman in greeting. "Jefferson Moore, ma'am. Pleased to meet you."

"Such nice manners," said Mrs. Cohen. "I always said you could do better than Nick Murphy. No one thought he was good enough for you."

Saylor's cheeks heated. Her head lowered as she spoke. "I'm still with Nick, Mrs. Cohen."

"Oh." That oh was not a sound made in embarrassment. It was not a question mark as though Mrs. Cohen had misheard. It was the sound of weary disappointment.

"Jeff just gave me a ride," said Saylor. "I'll just grab Nick's things and get out of your way so you can get out of here and see your great-grandbaby."

Mrs. Cohen nodded and disappeared around a divider. "I wasn't able to get the lipstick stain off the collar. It was a pretty dark shade of red."

From his vantage point behind her, Jeff saw Saylor's shoulders tense. He balled his right hand in a fist, aching to step forward and soothe her. Again there was that tingle in his left palm, as though it wanted a part in the war effort.

Mrs. Cohen came from behind the divider with a plastic bag in one hand and a scrap of paper in the other. "I found this in the back pants pocket. There's a phone number on it. It looked important, so I kept it."

The woman's face was impassive, but Jeff saw the challenge there. Unfortunately, Saylor didn't rise to the occasion. Her face was implacable. But Jeff saw cracks. Fine little fissures that he knew he could use against Nick. But he hesitated.

Jeff had gathered mountains of evidence against his father's infidelity. And still, his mother never left. Not for any of the lipstick stains she'd laundered herself. Not for the blocked numbers that called their residence. Not for the couple of women who showed up at her doorstep.

Audrey Moore had not left her husband. She had not strayed from her vows. Not the times her husband raised a hand to her for insinuating that he'd done something wrong.

Jeff had held his mother's hand many a night. He'd tended to the wounds both internal and external. But every time he tried to tug her away, she would not budge. In the end, it was Jeff who'd left.

Leaving his mother behind had devastated him. Even to this day, he still held out hope that one day she would leave. Looking at Saylor's stiff upper lip, Jeff knew he could not walk away from her.

"I gather you're settling Nick's bill for the month as well, dear?" asked Mrs. Cohen.

"Of course." Saylor reached for her pocketbook. After a few moments of rummaging through the bag, her cheeks were even redder than the lipstick stain. "I left my wallet at the ranch."

"Don't worry," said Jeff. "I'll get it."

For the first time that he'd known her, Jeff saw Saylor's brows raise in alarm. "You don't have…"

But Jeff ignored her protests. He exchanged a look with Mrs. Cohen. It was the same look that Brig gave him when they were concocting a plan to break the couple up. It appeared everyone had that look when it came to Saylor and The Boyfriend. Clearly, Mrs. Cohen wanted him gone as much as the other Silver sisters.

Jeff winked at her after she handed him the receipt. Mrs. Cohen gave him an encouraging smile, a smile that said bring out the heavy weaponry if you have to. Jeff intended to.

"I'm sorry about that," said Saylor once they were out of the store. "I'll pay you back."

"Don't worry about it," said Jeff. "I'm sure Nick would do the same for me if I forgot my wallet."

Saylor chewed at her lower lip, not meeting Jeff's gaze. "Well, thank you again for the ride. I can walk to Nick's apartment from here."

"Not on my watch. I'll deliver you safely to your destination."

Jeff held out his hand for her. Her moment's hesitation was only a second this time. Saylor took his hand as he helped her into the car. But her eyes weren't on him. They were on the faint stain of red on the collar of her boyfriend's suit.

CHAPTER THIRTEEN

Before getting into the car, Saylor let the slip of paper found in Nick's suit fall to the ground. She should feel guilty over littering, but she doubted anyone would pay much mind to the scrap. The slip of paper was no longer with her, but the numbers were burned into her mind. Because Saylor knew to whom that sequence of numbers belonged.

Holly Marks had given Saylor her number once in middle school when they'd been paired up on a class project. Holly had been the most popular girl all throughout middle and high school. Next to Mareen, of course. But unlike Mareen, who had never wanted the attention her good looks brought, Holly wanted all eyes on her at all times.

She got the attention she craved because of her on-again, off-again, tumultuous gossip-worthy relationship with Nick. Their arguments in the lunchroom were the stuff of legend. Their makeup make-out sessions behind the bleachers were more instructive than the Judy Blume novels in the library. Nick would often emerge with Holly's devil-red lipstick stained on his lips and shirt collar.

They were forever breaking up, dating each others' friends, getting back together again, only to break up again. It was dizzying to pay attention to. Saylor had followed every twist and turn of the high school drama.

By the time high school was over, so were Nick and Holly. Or so she had thought.

"Where do you want to go, Saylor?"

The sound of Jeff's voice brought her back to the present. His voice was gentle but strong. Coaxing, yet insistent.

Saylor wanted to wrap herself up in the warm comfort of Jeff's voice. No, she wanted to wrap herself up in his arms and not deal with any of the past protruding into her present. Not the phone number. Not the red shade of lipstick Holly Marks had been wearing at the wedding yesterday.

Even though she closed her eyes, Saylor still couldn't block any of it out. She just wanted the world to stop for a moment. And then it did.

A large hand came to rest on her knee. That hand grounded her. It gave her an ounce of strength. She just wasn't sure what to do with the boost of power.

"Tell me what you need?"

Saylor wanted to laugh. She had no idea what she needed. She had been so busy tending to the needs of others that it never occurred to her that she might have any of her own.

What Saylor needed was just to sit still at this moment with this man who gave her strength, who gave her peace, and asked nothing of her in return. Jeff had driven a few blocks down. The next block over was Nick's apartment building.

Saylor turned from the brownstone and faced Jeff. She expected to see pity on the handsome soldier's features. Jeff had to be thinking the worst of Nick. If she were honest with herself, she'd admit she was more concerned with what Jeff was thinking of her.

"The phone number belongs to his first girlfriend. She was at the wedding."

Jeff said nothing. He only turned his torso in the driver's seat and waited. His gaze landed softly on her with not a single ounce of judgment.

She had a boyfriend with a wandering eye. All men had wandering eyes. Look at her father. But even with Abe Silver's wandering eye, he always came back to his first wife. Holly had been back in town for over two years now, but Nick hadn't dumped Saylor to get back together with her. Though Saylor had seen this shade of lipstick on more than one of his shirt collars recently.

Her gaze couldn't hold Jeff's. Her head dipped, and her eyes fell on Jeff's collar. There were no stains there from a woman's cosmetics. When she looked back up, Jeff's eyes weren't wandering. They were fixed on her. Like there was no one else in the world. Like he had nothing to do but sit here with his hand on her knee, grounding her into a reality she wasn't sure she was ready to face.

"You love him."

Saylor wasn't sure if she heard a question mark on the end of Jeff's statement? Or a period? So she wasn't sure how to respond.

"I'm going to drop his suit off," she said in response.

Jeff didn't argue with her. He simply nodded. Then he reached for the driver's side door.

"No, you don't have to come with me."

He turned back, his gaze now hard. "Didn't we already establish this? I am a gentleman. A gentleman always opens the door for a lady. You're the lady in this scenario."

Saylor sat obediently while she waited for Jeff to round the car. She looked down at the suit in her lap. That red lipstick stain glared back at her, accusingly.

As though she were the one who had done something wrong. Obviously, she had. If she couldn't keep her boyfriend satisfied.

It wasn't the first time she'd seen lipstick stains on his clothing, in a different shade. There had been business cards and napkins with scribbled numbers in his pockets before. Random texts, a little too personal to be work-related, popped up on his cell phone at late hours in the night when he left it unguarded.

Day in and day out, Saylor had tried to push those memories aside. When they wouldn't go, she would try to explain them away.

All her excuses flew out of the window as Jeff opened the passenger door.

Jeff held his hand out to her. Saylor took the offered hand and immediately felt grounded again. None of the thoughts surrounding her boyfriend's infidelity plagued her as Jeff's fingers gripped hers. Saylor didn't want to let go. So she didn't.

She allowed Jeff to hold her hand as they walked around to the front of Nick's apartment building. She didn't let go as they climbed the stairs together, side by side, to the second floor. She didn't let go until she had to fumble with the keys to the front door.

"Thanks for the ride," she said.

Jeff's right arm tensed beside her. "You sure you want to stay here? I could wait and drive you back to the ranch."

It was a simple question. All it needed was a yes or no answer. Somehow it wasn't so simple.

Did she want to stay here with her boyfriend and his lipstick-stained clothing?

Did she want to go back to the ranch with Jeff, who would open the door for her and leave her feeling grounded and peaceful?

The key was in the door. Her fingers turned it as she turned to Jeff to give him an answer. The door should've opened with her movement. It did, just a bit. Until the top chain stopped her entry.

Inside Saylor heard muffled voices. One of the voices was low and masculine. The other high and feminine. At the sound of the chain stopping the door's opening, the voices stopped.

Again Saylor closed her eyes, trying to shut out the world. She wanted to use her body to block Jeff's vision, his hearing. She didn't want him to see this.

From the crack in the door, Nick appeared. He was in boxers that were askew. His hair was mussed. "Saylor? What are you doing here?"

Saylor stepped back from the door, letting it shut in her face. It was a childish move. She knew Nick had seen her. When she stepped back, she stepped right against Jeff's chest. The urge to turn her head and bury her face there was overwhelming.

The chain rattled at the door. It flung open and Nick appeared. The guilty look on his face rearranged itself when he saw Jeff. "What's going on here?"

Nick reached for her. Instead of going to him, like she always did, she handed him his dry cleaning.

"I'm sorry," Saylor said. "But they couldn't get Holly's lipstick stain out."

Nick blanched at Holly's name on Saylor's lips. Then a bright color, similar to the shade of lipstick still staining his shirt, warmed his cheeks. Nick's lips sputtered a few times before coherent words formed.

"What are you talking about? I haven't seen her since..."

"Last night at the wedding," Saylor supplied. "When you two left together to catch up."

"Right," he agreed. "So, this couldn't be hers."

"Kellie's, maybe?"

Nick cocked his head, as though in thought. He realized his mistake a few seconds too late. When he opened his mouth again, a bump sounded from the bedroom.

"A book must've fallen," said Nick.

Saylor nodded. Something had fallen. The scales from her eyes.

"You were never going to marry me, were you?" she said.

"Is that what this is about?" He sounded relieved. As though she hadn't just caught him red-collared for the umpteenth time. As though she wasn't aware that there was someone else in the apartment. As though she was going to come back into his arms again, pretending that he'd done nothing wrong.

That's when Saylor realized. Nick never came back to her. He was always flitting off to flirt and step outside of their relationship. It was Saylor who always came back to him.

"I'm never going to be enough for you, am I?" she said.

Nick's gaze cut from Saylor to Jeff, who still stood firm at her back. "Exactly what's going on here? You stepping out on me with this cripple?"

Saylor expected Jeff to lash out. Another man would have. Jeff was no ordinary man. Instead of lashing out at Nick, Jeff wrapped his strong arm around Saylor and pulled her against him. It was that last ounce of strength she needed to do what she had to do.

It was the hardest thing she had to do, but Saylor stepped out of Jeff's embrace. She stepped toward Nick. With her foot just over the threshold of the apartment, she reached around to the wall until she felt what she was looking for; her car keys.

Without another word, she turned on her heel and walked away.

CHAPTER FOURTEEN

The moment Saylor stepped away from him, Jeff wanted to pull her back into his embrace. It was enough to watch her walk away from the cheat standing in the door. He had to quickstep it to keep up with her now.

Saylor tore down the stairs and flew out the door of the apartment building. Jeff wasn't surprised to see that The Boyfriend didn't follow behind her. He didn't even call out to her.

Was he The Ex-Boyfriend now? He had to be. She'd caught him red-handed. Red lip-sticked. Red-penned phone numbered. And red boxer shorted.

Though Jeff was sure this couldn't have been the first time. It just so happened that this was the time she wasn't making any excuses for him. This was the time she'd had enough.

The analytical part of Jeff wanted to stop Saylor and ask what had changed? He needed to know so that he could keep those parameters engaged. Brig had said Saylor always went back to Nick. Jeff wouldn't have been able to stand by in that hallway if she'd stepped through that apartment door and gone back to a man who would treat her so callously.

If Saylor hadn't been running away from him, Jeff would've

stayed behind and given the cheater a piece of his mind using his fist. Nick was lucky Jeff was only working with one arm. Otherwise, it would be a bloodbath.

That thought made Jeff slow his pace. Ever since he'd joined the military, he'd slowly gained control over the anger that lived inside of him. The part of him that had come from his father. He never attacked without orders.

He had no orders to attack anyone. His final order from the general had been to protect his daughters. Jeff wouldn't want to disappoint the man who had given him so much. With a deep calming breath, Jeff pushed the anger and frustration he wanted to direct at Nick out of his body until none of it was left.

When he finally caught up to Saylor, she stood staring at a car. Looking into the driver's side, Jeff could see what she was staring at. A woman's jacket was casually slung on the passenger seat. It was the same shade of red as the stain on the suit from the dry cleaners.

"I can't drive," she said, not looking at him. "Can you take me home, please?"

"Of course."

He expected her to move away from his touch. She didn't. She allowed him to guide her back to his vehicle. There was tension in her walk, in the way she held her shoulders, in the way she looked blankly at the world around her.

Jeff handed her inside the truck. She sat looking out the window, her eyes unfocused. He reached across her and pulled her seat belt on. The click of the buckle into its slot roused her. Their gazes locked.

The light blue of Saylor Silver's eyes darkened. The circles beneath her lids had grown heavier on the short walk. Her lower lip trembled.

"You think I'm stupid, don't you?" she asked.

"No," Jeff said, holding her heavy gaze and not flinching from the weight of it. "Not even slightly."

Jeff did not move his hand from the seat belt's lock. He held it in place. He hadn't been able to get his mother to leave his father, but he was sure he would not allow Saylor any space or quarter to go back up those stairs.

"I think you're one of the smartest women I have ever met. You are trusting and filled with optimism. You simply misplaced your loyalty. It happens."

Saylor winced. At the crinkle of her eyelids, tears pricked at the corners. Jeff ached to rub his fingers there. To capture all of her hurts and take them away.

And so he did. He lifted his hand from the belt to her face. He caught the tears before they could fall and leave any trace.

"My mom stayed with my dad, even after he beat her," he confessed.

Jeff had never admitted that to anyone. The general had guessed. But Jeff had never confirmed it.

Saylor's next tears didn't fall. They stayed at the edge of her eyelids as she peered down at him. Jeff didn't remove his hand from her face, just in case. He didn't want her to cry for him. He wanted to bring her joy. He also wanted her to understand that he knew her pain.

"She stayed and took all of his anger, his frustrations, his shame. She stayed until he raised his hand to me."

Saylor closed her eyes in relief. He hated to tell her that that wasn't the end of the story. So, he pushed on.

"When I joined the military, she went back to him."

Saylor's eyes flashed open. "Did he...? Had he changed?"

"For a while. But old habits..."

"Nick never..."

"Even if the abuse isn't physical, it still scars."

Pain crumpled her features. Jeff brought her into his arms. He held her as the tears left her. He held her as he tried in vain to soak up every ounce of hurt this woman had ever felt. He felt the phantom ache in his left arm that wanted to press her more fully to him.

"What am I going to do?"

It was a whisper, so he almost didn't hear it. He pulled back slightly, not letting her go so that he could look into her face as she spoke.

"We're going to lose the ranch because of me," Saylor sniffled. "Scout's married. Mareen will be married soon. Tilly's got prospects. I know Scout is trying to pair you and Brig. And Gunny—" Saylor let out a humorless chuckle. "She won't have any problems getting a guy to marry her. People tend to do what she tells them. But what about me?"

With the humor gone, Saylor sniffled again. Her beautiful features crumpled into a mask of misery. Her head fell, but Jeff's hands were there, not letting her get too down on herself.

"What do you mean, what about you?" he said.

"No other man besides Nick has ever shown interest in me. And now my only prospect—"

"He was not your only prospect," said Jeff. "And I highly doubt no other man has ever shown interest in you. You must not be paying close attention."

Her head tilted back under her own strength. Those blue eyes brightened hesitantly, as though there were more clouds just outside her vision.

"You're beautiful, Saylor. I told you before, you're a swan. Not the duckling you pretend to be."

Jeff held still as Saylor searched his gaze. The clouds still threatened in the blue, but he saw a small ray of hope.

"Jefferson?"

"Yes, Saylor?"

"I know Scout thinks you and Brig are a match, but..."

"Brig and I don't think we're a match."

"You don't?" Saylor's brows lifted. All traces of clouds fled. "Do you think... Would you consider marrying me? Not for real, of course. Just so we could save the ranch. I wouldn't make any demands. You could still date and live on the ranch and—"

"Saylor?"

She closed her eyes and took a deep breath. "I'm sorry for asking. It was a stupid idea—"

"I'll marry you."

Her eyes flashed open. "You will?"

"It would be my honor."

It would be more than honor. It would be more than duty. Jeff's new mission was clear. For the rest of his days, he would show this woman what it meant to be cherished.

CHAPTER FIFTEEN

"Y ou said yes?"

Saylor opened her mouth to respond to her older sister. But the words caught in her throat as she looked down at the spice rack. She picked up the glass jar that held the vanilla, only to see that it was an imitation of the seasoning rather than the real thing.

During the lean times, their mother had begun buying bargain brands of everything. Dollar Store seasonings that often had a grain of sand in the salt. A peppermill that only had a few good cranks in it before the peppercorns spilled out.

It was no longer a lean time in the Silver household. Saylor and her sisters had turned the ranch around. They were making a profit off the rehab of racehorses, the veterinarian care Saylor gave to the surrounding ranches, and the lessons Tilly gave. Even Gunny's research on rare horse breeds brought in money for the ranch. All meaning there was no need for the fake stuff on the spice rack.

"Where's the real vanilla?" Saylor asked, shifting the Lazy Susan around. "This imitation stuff makes my sugar cookies taste like they came out of a package. And besides, do you know how they make this stuff?"

"I do," said Brig. "It's disgusting."

"How do they make imitation vanilla?" asked Scout.

"Google it," grinned Brig.

"Do not google that," said Saylor. "Trust me."

Having seen the process for herself on the Science Channel, Saylor threw the imitation bottle out. But she was still having trouble finding the real deal. She wanted this meal to be perfect. Everything needed to be perfect for tonight.

"Forget the vanilla," said Scout. "You said yes to Jeff's proposal."

"Actually, no."

Two pairs of blue eyes narrowed on her.

"What I mean is; *I* asked *him*. He said yes to me."

Now those blue gazes widened.

"And…Nick knows?" said Scout.

"Nick and I broke up."

There was an exchange of doubtful looks that passed between her sisters. Saylor usually got this treatment from Scout and the twins. Brig was the youngest. What was she doing exchanging looks with Scout? Brig hadn't even had her first boyfriend yet, just a series of crushes on her male teachers and soccer coaches.

"What happened?" asked Scout.

Saylor did not want to rehash what had happened earlier at Nick's apartment. It wouldn't be the first time she'd told her sisters about her suspicions of Nick's infidelities. By the next look her sisters exchanged, Saylor knew that they were guessing the truth.

As per her usual, Saylor opened her mouth to defend Nick. Only this time, nothing came out. There was nothing to say. She'd caught him cheating. Again.

Saylor leaned against the counter, waiting for the pain in her chest. Like her mouth, her heart was silent. There was nothing left to break. He'd hurt her callously. Again.

Only this time, he hadn't come after her. He hadn't called to explain away what she'd seen. He hadn't texted to rewrite the history she'd witnessed.

"So, you and Jeff?" said Brig.

"It's not real." Saylor found her voice and straightened. When she turned, her gaze met her youngest sister. "Oh Brig, were you interested in him?"

The thought of that made Saylor's heart hurt. The pain wasn't at the thought of hurting her sister. The pain was at the thought of releasing Jeff to her sister.

"Not at all." Brig emphasized each word through her huge grin. "I think you two make the perfect couple."

"It's not real," Saylor repeated. She felt a cool balm of relief now that she knew she wouldn't have to hand Jeff over.

Saylor turned her attention back to the search for the real vanilla. She finally found it in the back of the cabinets. There was just enough in the small glass vial for one batch of cookies.

"We're just doing this so that we can save the ranch," said Saylor. "I'm done with men."

Saylor didn't need to turn around to know that her sisters were sharing another look. Instead, she scooped the dough out of the bowl and began spreading it on the baking sheet, concentrating on making perfect circles. A hand came on her shoulder.

"I think you made the right decision," said Scout. "Jeff is a good man. He's going to be good to you."

The words weren't an imitation. They were real. Saylor could feel the truth of them seeping into the cracks of her heart. Just as she had felt the warmth of Jeff when she'd rested her head against his chest the other night.

Ever since they'd pulled away from the apartment, Saylor had felt as though something was shifting inside her. She and Jeff hadn't talked much on the car ride. If that had been Nick, she'd have tried hard to fill the silence. But sitting with Jeff, she hadn't felt the need to say or do anything.

Saylor had just had one of the most embarrassing things in her life happen. Jeff had witnessed it all. Instead of dragging her over it and telling her what he thought she should do, he'd exposed his secret pain.

At the thought of Jeff in pain, Saylor felt pinpricks in her heart.

Not the stabbing wounds she felt every time Nick disappointed her. Or any of the times he implied she was lacking in some area, which was why he had to go outside of their relationship to have his needs met.

The back door opened. And there he was. Not Nick. He wouldn't come to the ranch unless he was dragged, which would happen if any of her sisters got a hand on him. It was Jeff who stood in the backdoor alongside Jackson.

"Hey," said Jeff, his gaze finding and holding hers.

"Hi," said Saylor.

"I was just coming to check on you."

The warmth wasn't seeping through the cracks of her heart any longer. It spread uniformly through her as if her heart had never been broken in the first place.

Had Nick ever come to check on her? Had he ever come after her? She had always been the one to seek out and chase after him.

"Nice work, bro," said Brig.

"They know?" asked Jeff, coming to stand beside her.

Saylor was so focused on the feeling in her heart that her mouth refused to work. So, she simply nodded.

"How are you holding up?" asked Jeff.

Wait? Wasn't that her job? To check on him? To ask after him?

"Come walk with me." Jeff held out his right arm. His left was caught up in the sling.

Saylor took Jeff's arm. She wrapped her left arm around his. And then, for good measure, she rested her right hand in the crook of his elbow.

The sun was lower in the sky. A cool breeze blew as they walked away from the house. Saylor was so warm where her body contacted Jeff's that she shivered at the contrast.

Jeff dropped his hold on her. Saylor wanted to protest. A moment later, he shrugged out of his coat. It looked to be a chore with only one arm operable.

Saylor reached to help him rid himself of the jacket. But by then, he was already done. And then she was being encased in his warmth.

Not just his heat, but his scent. Spice and earth and Jeff. Saylor was at a loss for words. Mainly because every time she breathed in, she got a strong whiff of him. She closed her eyes and soaked him in. When she opened her eyes, she saw him looking at her.

"I told them it wasn't real," Saylor rushed to assure him. "That this was all fake. I won't be a bother."

She wanted to chide herself for being caught in such a silly fantasy. Nick would've never stood for such a reaction as sniffing his coat. Wait? Had Nick ever given Saylor his coat when he thought she was cold?

"You do realize I'm getting the best part of this deal," said Jeff, looping up her arm to rest inside the crook of his. "A beautiful wife on my arm. Who is one of the kindest, most capable women I've ever met."

"I..." Saylor didn't know how to complete that sentence. "You don't have to say things like that."

"What? The truth? Has no one ever told you that you are beautiful, Saylor?"

"Well, my mom. But she's supposed to say things like that."

"Saylor, you're breathtaking."

She shook her head. "You've never seen my sister, Mareen. We could've been twins, even though we have different mothers. But she got all the best features."

"I've never met Mareen. I've only met you, and I stand by what I said. I never lie."

Saylor wanted to believe that. She'd made excuse after excuse for Nick, who never proved her right. Not even once.

Jeff had never once proven her wrong. Maybe she should believe him?

"Come." Jeff tugged her toward the cabin. "I think you should rest. I don't like those bags under your eyes."

Jeff's hand moved to the small of her back. But the warmth was gone in light of that last comment.

I don't like those bags under your eyes.

Saylor had known it was too good to be true. He'd already found something wrong with her. Less than a day into this new relationship and she already wasn't good enough.

CHAPTER SIXTEEN

They weren't married yet. Still, Jeff wished he could lift Saylor in his arms and carry her over the threshold of the cabin. He'd have to settle for holding her hand as he led her through the front door.

Jeff had only been in the cabin a week. But from the first day he'd set his foot in here, it had felt like home. Now he knew it had everything to do with the woman beside him whose hands had helped build this place.

He wanted to start his life with her here. Maybe they could add on to the structure in the coming years. This time they would build it together.

At the thought of the work, Jeff felt another tingle of sensation in his left arm. He wanted to get an appointment with the VA clinic soon. Perhaps this increased neurological activity spelled something good for him?

He'd long since given up hope that he'd ever had the complete use of his left arm again. With Saylor now in his life, he was experiencing more and more sensations on a daily basis. Maybe it was his arm that had different ideas about its prognosis now that the woman of his dreams was within reach.

"I was making you my famous sugar cookies," Saylor said as Jeff shut the door behind them. "They're always a big hit at gatherings."

"I can't wait to try them later. Right now, you need to rest."

"I still have chores to tend to," Saylor protested as he led her into the bedroom. "And I need to check on horses."

"I'll take care of that," he said.

Jeff got the impression that Saylor was always on call, especially with that ex who couldn't seem to do anything for himself. Those times were over. He was going to look after her, starting with her health and well-being. Then he'd move on to see if she could let him into her heart.

For now, he turned her around to face him. Saylor looked flustered. But she wasn't fighting him, which let him see just how tired she was.

"If there's an emergency or something I can't handle in the next couple of hours, I'll come wake you. But for now, I want you to get some rest."

Saylor lowered her head so that all he saw of her was the top of the hairband that gathered her brown locks into a ponytail. Jeff itched to wrestle the tie away so that her hair would fall around her shoulders. But that was not his place. Not yet.

"I have eye make up," she said.

He frowned. He must have been so caught up thinking about her hair that he'd missed part of the conversation.

"To cover the bags under my eyes." Saylor waved in the vicinity of her eyes even though her head was still down.

With his index finger, Jeff lifted Saylor's chin until she met his gaze. "I don't want you to hide anything anymore."

By the time he was done showing this woman all the care in his heart, she wouldn't have a single load to carry. Not under her eyes. Not on her back. And certainly, not in her heart.

"We're partners now," he continued. "We're going to share our load."

Saylor's brows pulled together. The move made the dark circles under her beautiful blues look as though they were bruised. Jeff couldn't stand it any longer.

"Lie back," he said, and she did. "I'll take care of it."

As Saylor slipped out of her shoes and gathered her legs onto the mattress, Jeff pulled the sheets up to her chin. Then, because he couldn't help himself, he pressed a kiss to her forehead. It was just a light press, a whisper of the affection he truly wanted to give to her.

Though it was a whisper, he let the soft caress linger. He wasn't sure how long he held there. When he pulled away, Saylor's eyes were already closed.

Jeff pressed a kiss to each of her eyelids in turn. "I'll take care of everything."

He stayed and stared at her for long moments. She was his. They only had the words between them. Soon it would be legal. She could call it fake all she wanted, but he was going to prove to her that his feelings were real.

Jeff had accomplished his mission. He'd gotten Saylor away from Nick.

No, actually, he hadn't. Saylor had done that herself. Which was why this time, the break up would last.

"You did it," Brig said when he shut the front door of the cabin. "How did you do it? Is Nick still alive? Because if he's not, I won't mind."

"I didn't do anything," said Jeff. "Saylor decided."

Brig's frown was doubtful. As though she suspected Jeff was holding out on her.

"Really, she did it all herself. I was simply there to pick up the pieces."

"She doesn't know, does she?" asked Brig.

"Know what?" said Jeff.

"That you're in love with her."

Jeff didn't correct the youngest Silver sister. He was in love with Saylor. Had been since the first moment he'd seen her from a distance. Had known it to be true the first time he saw her with a horse and saw the gentle spirit who wanted to heal wounds. Now he was going to be her protector. He was going to help her heal from the years of emotional and mental abuse she'd suffered.

"Just marry her quick," said Brig as they walked along. "I'm sure Nick will come sniffing around here soon. Likely when his clean laundry runs out."

"She's not going back this time." Jeff was sure of it.

Out in the pastures, they saw Bingley ambling along. The horse wasn't running or eating with the other horses, but he was upright.

Saylor had said the colicky horse might not want to eat for a few days while his stomach calmed down. It was clear that whatever parasites that had invaded Bingley's body were making their way out.

The horse was in much better spirits this morning. He made his way over to Jeff. Bingley placed his muzzle over the fence in a clear sign that he wanted a pat.

Jeff obliged the animal. He looked into the blond horse's deep, soulful eyes. Just the other day, the horse had writhed in agony, searching for relief. Now, with the attention and care he was receiving, Bingley was on the mend.

"It's all gonna be fine, buddy," Jeff soothed. "You just gotta be patient while it works its way out of your system."

That's exactly what he'd be while Saylor worked The Ex out of her system. Jeff was going to hold her, feed her, pet her, and anything else Saylor allowed him to do until she was a brand-new woman. His brand-new woman.

CHAPTER SEVENTEEN

or the second night in a row, Saylor woke easily from sleep. Her toes were toasty under the covers, not exposed to the cold night air. Her body was cradled in the soft, pillow-top mattress, not the firm brick that Nick had at his apartment. But she knew she was not in her own bed. She smelled the heady musk of man on the pillowcase.

With that thought, Saylor bolted upright. She was in a man's bed. Laying under sheets that smelled like him. Awareness brightened all around her as the sun set out the window.

She'd slept the day away. In Jeff's bed.

Instead of feeling panicked, Saylor felt a sense of calm wash over her. Instead of feeling shame at being in another man's bed, she felt a sense of rightness. Jeff wasn't some other man. He was her fiancé. He'd only known her for a week, and he'd agreed to marry her.

Very soon, waking up in his bed could be her life. Climbing into the bed with Jeff tucking her in. Falling asleep against Jeff's chest. Waking up with Jeff's scent all around her. The only thing that was missing was him.

The sun was low in the sky outside the window. It looked more like the evening was approaching than a new morning. Looking over at the clock on the table beside the bed, she saw that it was only early evening.

She hadn't slept the day away. She'd only taken a nap. Just that slight bit of rest had made her feel renewed.

A beep sounded from the table beside the bed. There was a phone lying there. Unlike her phone that was wrapped in a pastel covering, this phone was black with no case. It had to be Jeff's phone.

There had been many times when Nick would leave his phone out. Saylor had gotten in the habit of looking away from the messages that would pop up. She'd learned her lesson when a casual glance would shatter her heart at the sight of an inappropriate emoji sent to a man who had a girlfriend.

So, Saylor had gotten in the habit of only reaching out to turn the phone over so that she didn't see the women texting her boyfriend, making demands on his time, his attention, his body. Demands that Nick was always more than happy to fill. Demands he'd cater to when he could never keep his promises to her. Not even the basic, unwritten one of fidelity.

Saylor wasn't with Nick any longer. She was now with Jeff. A man who listened when she talked. A man who sought her out for her company. A man who offered her his hand not only in her work on the ranch but because he was a gentleman and insisted on treating her like a lady.

Jeff's phone beeped again. Saylor glanced over. And then wished she hadn't.

A message popped up on the rectangular face of the cellphone. Saylor was just far enough away that the letters were unclear. She had no need to look closely.

Jeff wasn't Nick. This relationship would be different. In fact, she should find Jeff and give him his phone. Which would mean getting nearer to the device and risk making sense of the words there.

The door to the bedroom opened. Saylor snatched her hand

back. Jeff filled the doorway. His smile was the brightest thing she'd seen this day.

"You're awake," he said, coming to the edge of the bed. "How do you feel?"

"Fine." Saylor took a deep breath. Clucking that word off her tongue, she tried again. "I mean, good. I'm good."

"That rest did you good. Your eyes are shining bright again."

Jeff tilted his head as he gazed down at her. There was no judgment in his gaze. No, that looked like satisfaction and a touch of delight in his light brown eyes.

The phone on the bedside table chirped again. Both of their gazes went to it. Now that she was sitting up, Saylor could see the letters stringing together. They formed words in her mind.

Call me back. I need you.

Saylor blinked, but the words wouldn't go away. She tried to pull up the list of what that could mean, like all the times she'd done when she'd seen similar messages on Nick's phone. But none of the excuses of the past were within her mental reach.

Jeff reached for the phone. He sat down on the edge of the bed as he swiped up to unlock the device. He didn't slip the phone into his pocket. He held it in the palm of his hands where she could clearly see the message.

Instead of looking at the message, Saylor chose to look at his face. Jeff didn't seem pleased at the message. He appeared weary.

Saylor wanted to reach out to him. She wanted to offer him comfort for whatever hurt this woman was bringing into his world. And yes, it was a woman's name at the top of the message.

"It's my mom," said Jeff.

It took Saylor's fogged brain long moments to understand the meaning of his words. It was his mother asking him to call her back. It was his mother telling her son that she needed him.

"She only ever calls when my dad needs something."

Right. His dad. The one who abused his mom.

Jeff let out a weary sigh as he placed the phone back on the bedside table. Saylor reached for his arm, only to find that she held the left arm, which was in the sling.

Jeff looked down at her hand. Saylor made a move to yank her hands from him, but he covered her hand with his right one, ensuring her hold on him.

"People always ask; why doesn't she leave."

Jeff didn't meet her gaze. He kept his eyes on her hand. His thumb rubbed over her knuckles as she ran her own thumb in a circular motion on his forearm. She knew he couldn't feel it, but she had a suspicion that watching the motion soothed him nonetheless.

"No one ever asks what's wrong with him. They always blame the victim."

Jeff lifted his head to her then. His gaze penetrated hers, letting her see a vulnerable side she'd never been privy to with any male on less than four feet.

"The physical violence stopped about a year ago when he became sick. But the mental violence, the emotional violence continues. I think it's worse now that he can't raise his fist. I know she needs help, but whenever I reach out, I get pulled into that hurt as well."

Saylor pulled him to her. She worried she'd overstepped after a second when he didn't hold her back. His left arm rested between them. But he didn't place his right hand around her.

Instead, he buried his nose in her neck. The deep inhale he took sent a shiver down her spine. The exhale a moment later brought her closer to him than she'd ever been to anyone in her life.

They stayed like that for long moments. Possibly an hour. When he finally pulled away, the sun had set.

"Come on," he said. "Let's go get you fed."

CHAPTER EIGHTEEN

The bounty of food before him was a feast for the eyes and nose. A roast ham covered in pineapple slices pinned with cloves promised dessert as the main course. Collard greens marinated in the leftover pieces of the hog, like the ham's hock, guaranteed that the sweet tooth would be satisfied.

Jeff's fork remained where it had been placed next to his plate over twenty minutes ago. Not a morsel of the dishes touched his mouth. It was very likely that he was going to starve, and he had no qualms about it.

There was a grumbling of need in his gut. It wasn't his stomach. Jeff's hunger was for the woman at his side.

His right arm was wrapped around the top of Saylor's chair. Every time she leaned back to put her fork in her mouth, her nape brushed the fleshy part at the back of his thumb and set off fireworks at his fingertips. Her soft hair tickled his palm, urging him to capture the strands in his fingers. With his right hand so occupied with being close to Saylor, it had no interest in going near his own cutlery.

Jeff's left arm was in his sling. Though it was captured and held, he swore he felt twinges of sensation every now and again. The twinges happened each and every time Saylor's skin brushed against his. It was as though he wanted to reach out and pull her to him with that arm that hadn't felt much since the blast destroyed his nerve endings.

"You're not hungry?" Saylor asked, her fork paused at her mouth.

Jeff had to take a deep breath before he could tear his gaze away from those lush lips. Oh, how he envied that fork.

"I can get you something else if you don't like it."

Jeff was still staring at her lips, which was why he caught the slight tremble there. Saylor bit her lip as though she were uncertain. Her gaze cast downward at his untouched plate.

With the greatest of reluctance, Jeff slipped his arm from around her shoulders. He picked up his fork and shoveled a heaping helping in his mouth. He'd made the move to stave off her worry that he didn't like her cooking. The moment the food hit his tongue, Jeff's eyes went to his hairline. He couldn't help his grin of pure bliss as he swallowed the bite.

That grin spread even wider when he saw Saylor watching him. Her lips still trembled. Though this time, they shook with a small laugh of delight.

Jeff watched Saylor move through opposing expressions. If just the simple act of showing his enjoyment of a meal she helped prepare for him made her happy, then he'd have this woman on Cloud Nine for the rest of her days now that he'd be by her side.

Something flared in Saylor's blue gaze. The delight shifted into something that looked like sparks of interest, of want, of desire. Jeff had every intention of fanning those flames into something as close to love as he could get them. Because that was what was in his heart.

Saylor was so easy to love. Her every thought was to be of aid to others. Her every move was to be a comforting light. That light had been smothered for years.

No longer. Jeff was prepared to turn himself into kindling if that's what she needed to stay bright. He would shine his light of love so fiercely upon this woman until she knew what it meant to be cherished.

"When's the big day for you two?"

Saylor blinked at the sound of Linc's voice. It took her another second to tear her gaze away from Jeff's. Jeff allowed his eyes to linger on her beautiful profile.

"We have a couple of months," said Saylor.

"Why wait?" said Jeff.

Saylor blinked again when her gaze connected once more with his. Her lashes fluttered over her baby blues like she was a bird feeling the warmth of the sun on its face for the first time.

"A-are you sure?" she stammered.

"About spending the rest of my life with you?"

The blush that pinkened her cheeks was endearing. Jeff couldn't wait until he had the right to lay featherlight kisses on those cheeks.

"Yes, Saylor, I'm sure."

Saylor brushed a stray hair from her temple. That strand had escaped the ponytail she'd gathered her tresses back into. Unlike her normal style, this queue was loose, allowing many of her strands to rest around her face. Jeff couldn't wait until he had the right to rip the band off and let her hair flow free every day.

"I vote for sooner," Brig piped in. "Everything from Scout's wedding is still here, including the flowers."

"Well," said Tilly, "looks like you'll be able to schedule it soon. Here comes the man who could make it happen."

All eyes around the dinner table went to the back door where Father Matthews was striding up to the porch. No one rose to open the door for him. This hadn't been the first time their next-door neighbor had stopped in at the ranch. Aside from being General Silver's lifelong best friend, Father Matthews was like a second father to the Silver sisters, and this house was like a second home for him.

"Evening, hellions," Father Matthews said with a jovial grin on his face.

"Evening, Father," the four girls all said in their faux angelic voices.

"Pull up a chair," said Scout rising from her place. "I'll fix you a plate."

"This is actually more than a social call," said Father Matthews. "I came to see Saylor."

"Is something wrong with one of your horses?" said Saylor, her body already tensing to rise and jump into action.

"No." Father Matthews shook his head. His head tilted as he looked at Jeff's arm strewn across the back of the chair. His brow raised when he met Jeff's gaze. "The horses are fine. I was in town, and I ran into Nick Murphy."

A cold wind breezed through the dining room at the name of The Ex-Boyfriend. It was as though the holy man had spoken a curse.

Under Jeff's arm, Saylor stiffened. He cupped her shoulder cap, trying to let her know he was here. If he was being honest with himself, he'd admit that the move was more of a staking claim. Saylor was his. Nothing The Ex-Boyfriend could say or do would change that.

Father Matthews' gaze narrowed, as though he could hear Jeff's thoughts. There was a slight upturn to his mustached mouth. Jeff couldn't tell if it was amusement or disapproval. For all Father Matthews knew, Jeff was the interloper in Saylor's relationship.

It didn't matter. Jeff would've wanted the man's approval. But he was moving forward with this marriage regardless of what Father Matthews thought of him.

"Nick was asking about your father's will and the marriage clause," said Father Matthews. "When I asked why he wanted to know, he said it was because he was thinking about marrying you."

The slight intake of breath that gushed from Saylor's lips was enough to knock Jeff down. He knew he wasn't mistaken that he'd heard the tiniest sliver of hope in that inhale. Jeff had to stop his nails from digging into Saylor's shoulder to hold her in place.

Saylor sat forward. She didn't rise. However, it was just far enough forward that she was no longer within Jeff's reach as his right arm now hung limp on the back of the chair.

CHAPTER NINETEEN

ecause he was thinking about marrying you.

Father Matthews' words kept swirling around in Saylor's head. What had Nick been thinking seeking out the pastor? Why hadn't he called her himself? Would she have even answered the phone if he had? Where was her phone?

Those thoughts were soon drowned by the conversation all around Saylor. The voices in the kitchen sounded like the hum of a Charlie Brown cartoon. Fog moved into her brain. Her temples were pounding, begging for the press of her thumbs to ease the ache. Her ears demanded her palms cover them, so they stopped the ringing she heard.

"You caught him with another woman."

"You're not going back to him this time."

"He is the worst man in the world. You deserve better."

Her sisters all spoke at once, so Saylor didn't know who said what. The cacophony of sounds harmonized into a needle scratching on vinyl. With a repeated chorus of nails screeching down the world's longest chalkboard.

A brush of warmth cleared all thoughts and sounds away. Like the sun drying up an errant puddle on the floor, Jeff's fingertips brushed against the exposed skin of her shoulder. At his touch, all Saylor could think about was turning her head into his chest and resting.

Her sisters' voices made her feel heavy with shame and self-doubt. Her thoughts of Nick made her feel weary and tired. The feel of Jeff? That refreshed her, drowning the others out with his calming reassurance.

Jeff said nothing to her. He only looked her over. His gaze skated over the tension of her tight shoulders. They took in the indecision on her furrowed brow. They rested a moment on her quivering lips as they vacillated on her response.

"Would you all excuse us," Jeff said. His words were firm. Not a question.

With a scrape of wooden legs against the floor, he scooted his chair back and stood. Then he offered his hand to Saylor. She stared at it before placing her hand in his. When he tugged, she came willingly, as though this man would lead her toward salvation.

All around them, the room fell into a hushed silence. That was a neat trick. Not even their parents could ever get the Silver sisters to quiet down all at once.

Jeff's gaze was intent on hers as they left the dining room. Saylor wanted nothing more than to go back to the cabin and lay down inside the cradle of his strong chest. She wanted to rest her cheek against there and listen only to his heartbeat.

Jeff had never once made her feel that there was something wrong with her for staying with Nick. He'd never made any comments about her choices in partners that reflected badly on the woman she was. He'd only ever offered his compassion and understanding and his kindness.

This man was going to marry her. True, it was going to be a fake relationship. But Jeff would never lie to her, or question her decisions like her sisters, or make her feel like someone who would never be enough like Nick had done for the duration of their relationship.

"Are you gonna reach out to him?" Jeff asked as they began to climb the stairs.

It took Saylor a moment to answer. She was more focused on lifting her legs to conquer the stairs. She had expected that she and Jeff would leave the house and head back to the cabins. Instead, they were headed to the second floor of the house where the bedrooms were.

Saylor opened her mouth to say no in response to Jeff's question. The word wouldn't come out. There was some part of her that held back.

Nick had reached out to her. Well, not exactly out to her. But he had metaphorically lifted a finger. In the past, it was always Saylor who made the first move when he'd had an indiscretion. He'd take his time in responding, but he always responded. He always came back to her, just as true loves did.

Jeff's sigh was nearly soundless, but Saylor felt the slight slump in his tall frame. His gaze shuttered, but only for a second. He pursed his lips as though he wanted to keep words in. Unlike her, he let them out.

"He was with another woman." Jeff's words were terse. "You know that. You saw it."

Technically, she hadn't seen it. Just the evidence that pointed to it. But she hadn't actually seen Holly inside that apartment.

"You deserve better."

Saylor tried not to flinch as he threw her sister's words back at her. There was that implication again that she was settling when she had done her best in this relationship. She had fought for what she wanted. Though all the fight was gone out of her now.

Saylor was tired. All she wanted was to be held. But Jeff was barely touching her. And then he was.

Jeff pressed his lips to her forehead. It was a chaste kiss, confirming what she already knew. He was only doing this, offering to marry her, out of a sense of duty. It would never be love.

Still, her heart raced. It ached to have him feel something in return. Her heart ached for him to yearn for her as she was doing for him.

"Which one is yours?" Jeff asked as he pulled away from her.

Saylor pointed wordlessly to her bedroom door. Even though her finger wanted to riot and point back down the stairs and across the way to the cabin where he would be sleeping.

They walked the few steps to her door together, side by side. Jeff wasn't touching her, and she wanted him to. She just wasn't sure how to ask for it.

She opened her mouth. But once again, no words came out. Saylor choked as indecision obstructed her throat.

Jeff stepped back at her silence. Before she'd even turned the knob, he'd already disappeared down the steps. Saylor closed her door behind her and sank down on her bed.

She had already slept a few hours, but she felt as though she hadn't slept in weeks. Her head aimed for her pillow, but before it made it there, she saw her phone charging on her nightstand.

Glancing at it, she saw that there were ten missed calls from Nick. Beneath the calls flashed an alert for unread text messages. Swiping her thumb over her phone, she read the missives.

Give me another chance.

I need you.

That had been the wrong thing to say. But it had been the truth. Saylor did deserve better.

Jeff had known better than to push her. All the years of watching his mother endure the violence of his father, he'd read enough pamphlets from women's shelters, watched enough online intervention videos, and spoken to enough school counselors and social workers to know.

He knew the script that he was supposed to follow. He knew he was supposed to make Saylor feel heard, not judged. He knew his words should aim to validate her feelings, not blame or shame her for how she had reacted in the past. Because, in truth, Saylor had done nothing wrong.

She had trusted someone who was a liar. She had loved someone who was unworthy. She had stayed with someone who was disloyal.

None of that was her fault.

Jeff had slipped up with his last words to her. Because his words were also true. Saylor did deserve better.

Jeff wanted to punch a wall. Not with his right hand. He felt the tingles in his left palm, which was cradled in a sling. Instead of being joyful at the sensations there, he wanted to use that energy to commit violence.

Walking out of the front door, Jeff stopped as he came to the fencing that separated the front yard from the first pasture. He inhaled deeply, trying to calm the ire inside him. It took all the fresh air of the night to get his wayward emotions under control.

He hadn't felt this out of control since he was a teenager wanting to throw his fists at any and everyone who dared cross him. He'd grown up helpless to stop the violence against his mother. Helpless to get her to see the wrongness of it.

Jeff had joined the military because he'd had rage in him. His commanders always pointed him in the direction of the true bad guys, the ones who committed heinous acts against the innocent. Jeff had never felt an iota of remorse when he took down an insurgent.

And wasn't that what Nick was, an insurgent? The villain committed heinous acts against Saylor. Acts that had crumbled her infrastructure and weakened her spirit.

Saylor didn't have a physical mark on her from Nick's attention. It was his lack of attention that had left the woman bruised and blackened. And for that, Jeff wanted to wring the man's neck.

Just like that, all of the control he'd fought for with those deep breaths left him on an exhale. Jeff unwrapped his left arm from the sling. Instead of the arm remaining cocked or his fingers clenching into a fist, the arm slumped to his side.

"You look ready for a fight."

Jeff didn't turn to see Wilson come up behind him. He knew one of his brothers would be tracking his movements and keeping watch. Not that any of them suspected the anger he was now trying to keep under wraps. He'd always been cool while in combat.

"Did she call the wedding off?" asked Wilson.

"No, she didn't," said Jeff.

"But your trigger finger is still itching for a fight." Wilson was looking at the prone fingers of his left hand.

"She might call it off," Jeff admitted. "She might go back to him."

Wilson whistled low. "Then she's not the girl for you. If she does go back to him, then she'll only get what she deserves."

Jeff wheeled on his friend. "You think she deserves to be treated like that? To be cheated on? To be someone's doormat?"

"If that's what she wants."

Jeff was close to punching out one of his closest friends. He might have if Wilson's chin was high and tilted to the left. Just the perfect angle for Jeff to connect with a right hook.

They all had long suspected that Wilson had a death wish. He blamed himself for the General's death. After all, the General had shoved Wilson out of the way just before the bomb went off. Had Wilson still been standing in that space, it would've been his funeral months ago, and the general would be here with his daughters.

When Jeff's fists failed to connect to Wilson's chin, the man lowered his head and went on.

"She's not a stupid woman. None of these Silver women are. They had the General for a father. She can get out if she wants. Maybe she doesn't want to."

Jeff tried to swallow, but he couldn't get that lump down his throat. His mother could've left his father. Years ago, Jeff had provided her with the financial means to do so. But she'd funneled the money to pay off his father's debts. Meanwhile, they continued to live in squalor. Because she didn't want to leave. Because she claimed she loved him. That he was her world.

For all of his life, Jeff had never understood that sentiment. Now he did. In just a week, Saylor had captured his heart, his body, his soul.

He didn't want to leave.

Because he loved her.

She had become his world.

Jeff needed to go back into the house. He needed to go back up the stairs. He needed to go back to the script.

Tell Saylor that he was sorry for what had happened to her.

That she wasn't to blame for what Nick had done to her.

That he couldn't pass judgment on her decisions of the past.

That she'd had her reasons for staying.

True, Jeff believed all those reasons were false. Saylor didn't believe she was beautiful. She believed men needed a long leash. But neither of those were true.

Saylor was beautiful and desirable. All men did not cheat. Just the ones who were too weak to stand next to a good woman.

Jeff was that man. He would stand next to Saylor. He would tell her she took his breath away every day. She would see his desire for her in his every look, in his every touch. He would never even think of straying.

He looked down at his phone. The message his mother had sent him earlier was still on the face of his phone, left unanswered. His mother had made a choice. She knew her options, but she wanted to stay with her husband.

Saylor had never believed she had a choice. He'd just given her one upstairs. Now he just needed her to choose him.

Before he could take a step back toward the house, he heard footsteps coming down the front porch. In the moonlight, Jeff saw a woman's figure rushing to the parked cars. All of the Silver sisters favored one another. But he could tell Saylor's frame from a mile away.

Jeff wasn't a mile away. Saylor was climbing into a car. Jeff's heart sank that he knew where she was headed to at this time of night. It looked like she had made her choice, and she was headed back to The Boyfriend.

CHAPTER TWENTY-ONE

*S*aylor paralleled parked in front of the building. It was rare at this time of night that there was a space available, especially one right in front of Nick's apartment building.

She looked down at her phone before she reached to unbuckle her belt. Her mind went to Jeff as she clicked the red button. She sat forward a little, feeling the strap's hold on her.

The seatbelt was there to protect her from harm. It offered a sense of security in the world that whizzed by her. Much like being held in Jeff's caress. Though the seatbelt wasn't as warm as Jeff. Still, the belt let her go after she clicked the release. Much like Jeff had let her go once he'd delivered her safely to her bedroom.

Saylor had expected him to argue with her. She'd expected Jeff to rail against Nick like her sisters had done at dinner. She'd expected him to fight with her over her decisions to remain in her relationship with Nick. She'd hoped Jeff would fight for her. Instead, he'd walked away from her.

You deserve better.

Did she? She certainly hoped so. She stepped out of the car, prepared to get the better she was due.

Looking down at her phone, Saylor saw the unanswered text

messages from Nick. Even his words were all about him, asking her to do things for him.

Give me another chance. Not even a please. *I need you.* What about her needs?

Nick had never given a care to her. He hadn't even come after her directly. He'd sent Father Matthews to fetch her. Well, that type of behavior was stopping right here and right now.

All these years, she'd given so much of herself to this man when he never gave her a single thing. Except for a set of his house keys.

Saylor had treasured having this single key added to her key chain. Though Nick had only given her the bottom lock. Not the top one. So that if he was home, she still needed his permission to enter.

Saylor didn't use the key as she came to Nick's door. She knocked. It took a moment for a response. As Nick came to the locked door, Saylor heard the rattling of locks. Not just of the bottom lock, but the top one as well. Clearly, Nick wasn't alone.

That was confirmed when the door was flung open. Nick stood there, shirtless. Hair mussed. A twenty-dollar bill in his hand.

"Saylor!"

The color drained from his face. He shifted from barefoot to barefoot. Beads of sweat appeared between his two perfectly manicured brows.

How many times had she seen this exact same scenario? Her supposed boyfriend, blocking a scene he didn't want her to see. His mouth working to weave a story that was too flimsy to be considered for a doily.

What was different this time was that instead of looking away, Saylor stared openly at the mussed pillows on the sofa and the discarded high heels on the rug. Instead of searching for comforting, compliant words, she lifted a brow of her own and watched him squirm.

"What are you doing here?" said Nick, angling his body so that Saylor couldn't see any further into the apartment.

Before Saylor could respond with the rehearsed speech she'd made, a feminine voice beat her to it.

"She's back? Really?" Holly Marks came into view. She wore Nick's old football jersey and nothing else. "Girl, have you no self-respect?"

"I do, actually," said Saylor, pressing her hand to her chest. "Do you?"

Holly smirked at that, cocking a hip. "My boyfriend isn't community property."

"Well, he's not my boyfriend anymore. I broke up with him last night when he was with you. Which means the chain of custody passes to you."

All color leached from Holly's face. She straightened, shifting from foot to foot as Nick had done when he'd seen Saylor standing on the threshold.

"Look, Saylor," Nick said, using his soothing voice. "There's nothing going on between her and me. Just two old friends hanging out."

Holly's features contorted with disgust. She turned on her heel, grabbed a rumpled dress from the back of the couch, and headed for the bathroom.

"It's fine," said Saylor.

Nick's brows rose in suspicion. Then they lowered, all perspiration sliding away and drying up.

"It's my fault," Saylor continued. "I should've assumed you would have company. I just came to return your keys."

Saylor reached for Nick's hand. She dropped the solitary key in his palm. Then she turned and walked down the steps.

With each step away from him, Saylor felt a load lift from her shoulders. There was only a small part of her that protested. The part of her that believed that if you loved someone, you came back.

Nick had never come after her. Not once. She'd always chased after him. This would be the last time.

Before she got out the outer door of the apartment building, someone grabbed her arm. Saylor turned to find Nick behind her.

"Saylor, I told you, she doesn't mean anything to me."

"That's the problem." Saylor yanked her arm, but he didn't let go. "Women should mean something to you. I should've meant something. But no one means anything to you, except you."

"Saylor, we can work on this."

What he meant was that she could do all the work. She didn't want that. She wanted someone to look after her as much as she looked after him. She wanted someone who made her feel strong, not tired. She didn't want someone who came back to her. She wanted someone who would never let her go in the first place.

She wanted Jeff.

"Let me go," she said to Nick.

Saylor yanked her arm again, but Nick wouldn't let go. Then with a high-pitched cry, he was flying through the air. When she looked up, Jeff stood between the two of them.

CHAPTER TWENTY-TWO

*J*eff had had no orders to engage The Ex. But the second he'd seen his hands-on Saylor, he'd lost it. Nick was lucky he'd been shoved away. Jeff's right fist was cocked, ready to do serious damage to the man's face. His left hand was itching to get into the fight. His boots ached to dance a tune on the man's chest. But something held him back.

Saylor.

She held onto his left arm. He shouldn't have felt it. But he did.

He felt the imprint of her thumb on his bicep. He felt the heat of her chest against the back of his forearm. He felt the tug of her plea louder than any words she might say.

"Jeff?"

All Jeff could see was red. Nick was the enemy, and Jeff had to take him down before he could do any more destruction to the woman he loved.

Only, Jeff didn't want Saylor to see him like this. Like his father, standing in a rage over his mother, who was cowering on the floor. Begging, pleading. Insisting that she loved him even while she took his abuse as her due.

"Jeff?"

The sound of Saylor's voice broke him. Slowly, the red haze began to clear as Jeff came back to the present.

Nick was down on the ground. The pitiful excuse for a man crabbed walked backward, trying to put distance between himself and Jeff. His face was a dark mask of fear.

And wasn't that the irony. Having let go of his temper, Jeff had turned into the villain. He could never face Saylor again now that she knew that this was in him. Which was why he resisted when she tried to turn his face to meet hers.

"Jeff, look at me."

He couldn't. It was going to kill him to hear her take up for Nick. It was going to stop his heart to watch her go back into his arms.

Why wasn't she back in Nick's arms? Nick had managed to scramble to his feet. He was tripping up the steps of the apartment building. His arms were flung out, as though trying to protect himself from blows that weren't coming his way.

He wasn't even reaching out for Saylor. He wasn't even waiting for her. He was running away and leaving her behind.

The red haze threatened to come back to Jeff's eyes. Until bright blue blinded him.

"Are you okay?"

Jeff heard Saylor's words, but he had trouble deciphering them. She wasn't looking at Nick's retreating form. She wasn't looking into Jeff's confused gaze. Saylor held onto his right arm. She was checking on his hand, his fingers. Then she switched to his left hand.

"Did you hurt anything? Can you move your fingers?"

Still stunned, Jeff did as the veterinarian told him to. He was just a beast, after all. After years of training and careful control over his base instincts, he'd become what he feared. He'd become his father.

"Nothing's broken," Saylor said. Cradling his bruised knuckles to her chest, she finally looked up into his eyes. "You came for me."

"Of course, I came for you."

With her free hand, Saylor brushed her fingers across his cheek.

With the soft caress, something broke inside of Jeff. He turned his face into her hand and let out a shaky sigh.

Jeff inhaled the sweet scent of her. He had no idea how she was still here, in his arms? He fought to keep his hold loose. It was another battle he lost this night.

Once again, his right fist clenched. But this time, it wasn't to commit violence. It was an act of love. He wouldn't be able to hide it any longer. Nor would he be able to follow the script to help an abuse victim find the inner courage to leave her abuser.

"You thought I was going back to him," she said. "Didn't you?"

In response, Jeff pulled her closer. She didn't resist. She came to him willingly, resting both her hands against his chest. His heart leaped in response.

"I came to give him his keys. I was on my way back to you."

Jeff had to close his eyes again. The brightness of the light blue eyes gazing into his was overwhelming. Saylor hid nothing from him now. Not her vulnerability, nor her strength. She was both at the same time. And she trusted him to see it shining through.

"I want to marry you. Not because of the will and the ranch. I want to marry you because I want to be your wife. I want to take care of you and have you take care of me. I want to be your swan."

Jeff didn't need to hear anymore. He stopped her with a kiss. Not needing to open his eyes, his mouth found hers. He was a heat-seeking missile. He zeroed in on his target, and all around him, the world exploded.

He was blasted apart. Then flung back together. When his soul reknit itself, he felt an extra weight added to it. He felt a part of Saylor now living inside of him.

"I love you," he said when the fires inside him were cool enough to allow him to form words. "I felt something for you the first time you touched me."

"I want to say those words back to you," she said. "But I won't yet. For years, my definition of love was wrong. When I do tell you that I love you, I want you to know by my actions that I mean it."

Jeff pressed his lips to hers again. "I'll wait. I'll wait forever for you."

"I don't want you to wait. I want you always by my side."

"I will never leave it."

And with that, he twined their fingers together. Saylor rested her head in the crook of his neck. Jeff leaned his cheek on her forehead. To those walking by on the street, the two of them looked as though they were two swans entwined in a kiss.

EPILOGUE

"Wilson, you're not coming in for lunch?" asked Scout from the back porch of the big house.

Wilson gaze was on the horizon instead of the woman offering him an invitation. The sky was the same blue as Scout's eyes. Which were the same blue as her father's had been.

A blue so clear Wilson could see his own reflection and everything he'd done wrong that fateful day with General Abraham Silver. That clear blue was the last thing Wilson had seen right before the general lost his life.

Even from the distance Wilson had been from the man, Wilson had seen directly into the general's eyes. In that typically stern blue gaze, Wilson had seen a flash of fear, then resignation, then … something Wilson hadn't been sure of. But the look was always near the forefront of Wilson's mind.

The shame at his failure to act was the only thing Wilson saw in his reflection these days. So he avoided mirrors, water, reflective surfaces, and every Silver girl whose eyes were just like her father's. Because Wilson knew he should've been the one who'd lost his life that day, not the old man. General Silver was far more valuable a man than Wilson Michaels could ever hope to be.

But here Wilson was, alive and well. Standing in the man's kitchen while his daughter filled his plate with food. Wilson sat the plate on the counter and turned to the back door.

"Where are you going?" called Scout.

"I've still got work to do," Wilson said to the floor.

Whatever words she said afterward were swallowed up by his boots crunching over hard earth. Wilson quick-marched it away from the main house. He bypassed the stables, the barn, and the trails. He walked directly into the woods on an untrod path.

He kept his head low, unwilling to even look at the blue of the sky. He'd taken to getting up at night as the night's sky was dark and didn't remind him of that clear blue day when a blue-eyed man sacrificed his life for someone so unworthy.

Wilson should not be here. He did not why he was here. All he wanted to do was get lost and be alone.

Unfortunately, it sounded like he wouldn't get his wish today. A feminine yelp reached his eardrums. There was a woman out here and she was in danger.

Wilson picked up his pace in the once peaceful wooded area. He'd been one of the best trackers in his unit. So it took him no time at all to zero in on the location of the sound.

It came from a treehouse that looked like it had seen better days. The cracking and splintering of wood let him know someone was up there. Before he could think of how to climb up and get the woman down safely, a splintering sound boomed through the air.

The sound sent him back to that fateful day when the bomb had exploded. Wilson had seen blue eyes, then red flames, and finally black smoke.

When he looked up now, he saw a flash of ice, like a large snowflake. Or maybe a diamond. Was that a ring? It clunked to the ground at his feet. Before he could reach down and investigate there was something red falling.

A woman in a red dress. Her limbs flailing as gravity turned on her. Wilson didn't hesitate. He scrambled into place to catch her before she hit the ground. She landed safely, and securely in his arms.

Her hair was a deep chestnut brown with honey highlights. Her nose was high and pert as though it was often tilted up towards the sun. Her lips were shaped like a bowstring; a perfect sideways heart that he felt the urge to tug at with his fingers to see if they would give.

Wilson's entire body warmed and came to life with this creature in his arms. It was the shock of awareness that nearly knocked him off his feet, not her weight. She was well built. Long legs, strong arms, and womanly curves. But her weight was slight. He could hold her for days. He wanted to hold her for days.

The warmth and the desire rattled him. It had been so long since he'd felt anything. Since he'd desired anyone.

More pieces of wood rained down on them. Wilson looked up. The treehouse was about twenty feet off the ground. If he hadn't been there to catch her, she definitely would've injured herself. Maybe even fatally.

A small cry left her lips as though she could sense her potential fate. He felt her cry like an arrow to his heart.

"It's all right," he said. "I've got you."

Slowly, her eyelids opened. The shock of blue behind her lids was a punch to Wilson's gut. He swore he saw the general peaking out from that blue reflection. His hands nearly dropped her then.

She was a Silver. She had to be. If not for that special brand of blue eyes, then just the fact that she was out here on the land.

Wilson had no desire to entangle himself in the fool plan of the general's daughters to get married to save the ranch. He of all men didn't deserve such happiness when he was at fault for the general's death.

He should be setting the general's daughter on her feet.

Instead, he cradled her to him as he looked into those reflective blue eyes.

"You saved me," she said.

"I did," was his reply.

He had.

Maybe this is why he was here?

Maybe the general had saved him so that he could save his daughter?

If so, then Wilson's debt was paid. So he should set this Silver girl down and walk away.

As though she sensed his intentions, she wrapped her arms around his neck. He could've easily broken her hold. Instead, he pulled her closer.

That's when Wilson knew that he was good and trapped.

~

Want to know who this mysterious Silver sister
who just fell into her true love's arms is?
You'll find out in "His Pledge to Protect,"
the third book in The Silver Star Ranch romances!

His Pledge to Protect

SHANAE JOHNSON

A SILVER STAR RANCH ROMANCE

CHAPTER ONE

The sound of the loud, bursting pop didn't make Mareen Silver jerk with surprise. She had expected the small explosion. Maybe even hoped for it?

It happened while she was on a dirt road that was more sharp-edged rocks than paved concrete. A road made for tractor trailers, all-wheel-drive vehicles, and horses. Not for a luxury town car that was tricked out with all the modern computerized conveniences for city living. In all honesty, Mareen was surprised the car had made it this far on her journey without blowing a tire.

The back tire of her car threw up the white flag now. The car limped on three wheels instead of four as she came to a crossroads in Honor Valley. To the left lay the Silver Star Ranch, the home that had been her father's when he was alive. Mareen had spent the years of her youthful summers running wild and free on that land.

Metaphorically speaking. The daughter of Catherine Chesterfield Silver would never do something as unladylike as running. At least not out in the open where her mother could see.

Young women should step lightly on the ground so as not to disturb a blade of grass or overturn a stone. Or so Mareen's mother had drummed in her head. Catherine's words were gospel.

No, really, it was gospel. Catherine had gone up to the societal equivalent of a pulpit—the head table of Sunday brunch with the elite ladies of the capital city of Helena—and decreed it so. It might not have been written in scripture or on a stone tablet, but it was indelibly etched in each young lady's mind that day.

So Mareen had stopped running before she'd reached double digits in age. Now, at twenty-five, she found herself running for the first time in decades. Though she wasn't exactly breaking any of her mother's rules. Her feet weren't even touching the ground.

When she pushed the pedal of the gas, gravel spewed from the ruined tire. The sound was another assault on the ears. She might not have been turning any blades of grass, but she was making a mess of the stones in the road.

Mareen didn't let up on the gas. It wasn't her soul she feared for. She had to do this now, or her sisters would face the wrath of who they had determined was the devil. Unless Mareen picked up the pace, her sisters would have to face her mother. Though Mareen and her sisters rarely saw eye to eye, she wouldn't wish her mother's wrath on her worst enemy. Never mind that Scout, Mareen's eldest sister, thought the worst of her.

Mareen steered her limp, luxury car away from her childhood home. At the fork in the road, she went to the left. At least there, she knew she would be welcomed. There she might even find an ally.

In the late morning sunlight, Father Matthews sat on his front porch. A pipe was between his mustached lips. A cowboy hat sat low on his head, casting a soft shadow on his elderly features. His long legs were stretched out before him as he rocked back and forth.

He didn't rise to greet her when she stepped out of her car. His gaze traveled to her busted tire. One of his bushy brows lifted.

He didn't offer to help her change the tire. He knew she was capable of doing it herself. Another secret she kept from her mother, who would've sent a car service all the way from Helena to these country roads to perform the simple service.

Mareen didn't want that service. She didn't care to have the town car fixed. She didn't care to go back into town anytime soon.

Instead, she shut the car door behind her and stood tall. Her first step was a tricky one. The gravel of the Flying Heart Ranch's driveway was treacherous on her six-inch heels. She wobbled as she picked over the rocks. One false move and her ankle would be the next blowout.

The man on the porch watched her silently. Well, his mouth didn't move, but his brows drew together. Mareen knew from years of knowing the man that it was his touch-the-fire look.

Father Matthews believed in experiential teaching. He could tell a child what to do and what not to do. However, the lesson was cemented when said child would defy his advice and subsequently yank their burned finger back from the flame.

Mareen knew better than to have worn these shoes. The designer heels were entirely impractical on a ranch. Just like the luxury car that had already bitten the dust. Though she knew better than to try to walk in heels on gravel, she stepped into the flame. Luckily, she didn't get burned. She managed to climb the porch without incident and took a seat next to the old man.

Sitting poised, just as her society mother had taught her, Mareen arranged herself as elegantly as possible. She crossed her hands in her lap. She held her head high as she waited for Father Matthews to say something. If she didn't have him on her side, then her plan was destined to fail.

Father Matthews stretched his sturdy legs out. The movement caused the porch swing to rock backward. When it did, Mareen lost her composure. She slumped back onto the swing. Her back didn't meet the hard wood of the bench. Her shoulder landed on the cushion of Father Matthew's barreled chest.

She didn't bother to try to straighten. She let herself crumple into the person she trusted most in the world. Mareen rested her head on the old man's shoulder, taking in the sweet-smelling smoke, the woodsy scent of straw, and a hint of horse manure. It brought back memories of racing through fields on horses, rolling down hills of grass, laughing so hard that tears pricked her eyes.

Mareen couldn't remember the last time she'd laughed. Smiled, yes. She smiled all the time. It was part of her work uniform, how she presented herself to the world in city life. Like the shoes and the car.

Mareen looked down at Father Matthews's cowboy boots. She felt the ache in her instep from the high arch of her heels. She felt the pinch in her toes of the narrow front of the shoe.

Off in the distance, she heard the whinny of one of the horses. Then the answering call of one of its friends. Her hands itched to squeeze the leather of a lead.

"I don't think it's going to work, soldier."

Mareen sighed at Father Matthews's words. Deep down, she knew that would be his verdict on her plan.

"Scout's too proud," Father Matthews continued. "Your other sisters will fall in line behind her out of loyalty."

"Then they'll lose the ranch." Mareen sat up. She planted her feet firmly on the ground. But she didn't rise.

She did note Father Matthews's raised brow at her statement. She could guess exactly which word had caused that lift. She'd said *they* instead of including herself in *we*. It had always been them and not her.

"Why don't you go talk to them," said Father Matthews.

Mareen snorted at that, a very unladylike sound she was thankful her mother wasn't around to hear.

"That's the problem with you Silvers, you don't talk to one another. Your father was the same way."

Mareen couldn't disagree there. General Abraham Silver was not one for talking. He hadn't spoken to Mareen in nearly a year before she got word he'd been killed in the line of duty. His last words to her weren't even addressed to her. They were written down in his will and addressed to all his daughters. Either each of them find a husband before the year was out, or the ranch would go to his second wife, Mareen's mother.

When that part of the will had been read aloud, each of her sisters had turned accusing eyes on her. As though she'd written the words of their father's will. As though she wanted her mother to take ownership of the ranch.

She didn't.

Catherine hated Silver Star Ranch. If Mareen's mother ever learned what was in the will, then she would descend upon the valley like the Wicked Witch the other Silver sisters believed her to be. She'd kick them all out and sell the ranch for profit, just to spite them all. But mainly to spite Sarah Silver for always holding a piece of her ex-husband's heart.

"Your sister's wedding was lovely," said Father Matthews.

Mareen wouldn't know. She hadn't been invited to Scout's wedding just a week ago. "I hear Saylor's engaged."

"The wedding's this weekend."

Mareen knew that. Saylor had sent her a message inviting her. Mareen hadn't responded.

"You'll be wed soon," Father Matthews continued.

Mareen didn't look down at the rock on her finger. She didn't have to see it to be reminded it was there. It was heavy enough that she often had trouble balancing while standing.

"Maybe one day I'll get to meet this Stephen?"

"It's Stephán," she corrected. "There's an accent on the A."

Father Matthews raised one of his bushy brows. It reminded her of her father's expression when she'd told him about her new boyfriend. Mareen and Stephán had only just started dating when she'd talked to her dad over a bad cellphone connection. In the poor reception, her father hadn't gotten Stephán's name right either. Mareen had assumed she'd have time to correct the mistake. She'd been wrong.

"It looks like you girls are halfway there to meeting the demands of your father's will." Father Matthews stretched his legs out to rock the porch swing back again.

"You really think Gunny, Tilly, and Brig will get married in a couple of months?"

In answer, Father Matthews bent his legs and let the swing waft forward.

"It won't work." Mareen stuck the heels of her shoes in the ground to stop the rocking motion of the swing. "Gunny isn't even in the country. My plan is the only real chance to save the ranch. If you would just talk them into it."

Father Matthews shook his head slowly. "I've already played my part as messenger for my best friend."

Abraham Silver and Haran Matthews had been best friends since their time in the service together. Then they'd raised their families next door to each other. In his will, General Silver had tasked his best friend and neighbor with delivering his final order to his six daughters; to get married or lose their home.

It been hard for the girls to hear. Mareen was certain it had to have been just as hard for Father Matthews to say it to the girls he'd helped raise.

Father Matthews snuffed out his pipe and stood. "Go talk to your sisters."

Mareen was used to getting orders. If not from her military father, then from her image-conscious mother. But hearing this from Father Matthews stung. It was a mission she knew she was ill-equipped to take on.

Father Matthews reached down and gave her shoulder a squeeze. He lifted that bushy brow in a manner that gave her permission to reach out and touch the fire. Problem was, Mareen knew it would burn. A small smile played at the corner of Father Matthew's mouth, as though he was well aware of the price. And still, he wanted her to pay it.

After he walked into his house, Mareen sat on the porch, looking off into the distance. She could just see the boundary of Silver Star Ranch from her perch. She tried to tell herself it wasn't like walking into a firing squad. The little pep talk failed to work because though she and her sisters weren't close, she knew they all knew how to shoot. Herself included.

This was going to be a bloodbath.

Well, if she was going into war, she might as well be properly attired. She was already dressed in red. Her red sundress molded to her form, exposing her bare arms and calves.

Mareen rose in her heels and came down the steps. She rounded to the nearest barn. Inside, she found an old pair of cowboy boots. She slipped out of the heels and into the old boots.

The boots were a size too small, but her arches relaxed into the soles. The heels of her feet settled into the cramped space at the back, and her toes spread in the excess place in the front.

Coming out of the barn, the sun was at its pinnacle in the sky. It would be lunchtime on the Silver Star ranch. Her sisters would all be in the big kitchen, sitting down for a meal and talking about their day. Tactically speaking, it would be the best time to ambush them, catch them unawares, and present her peace treaty to allow them to keep the ranch.

Mareen took a deep breath. She put one foot in front of the other. Instead of heading for the boundary line of the Silver Star Ranch, she turned tail and headed into the woods.

CHAPTER TWO

"Wilson, you're not coming in for lunch?" asked Scout from the back porch of the big house.

Wilson's gaze was on the horizon instead of the woman offering him an invitation. The sky was the same blue as Scout's eyes. Which was the same blue as her father's had been. A blue so clear, Wilson could see his own reflection and everything he'd done wrong that fateful day with General Abraham Silver. That clear blue was the last thing Wilson had seen right before the general had saved Wilson's life and lost his own.

Even from the distance Wilson had been from the man, Wilson had seen directly into the general's eyes. In that typically stern blue gaze, Wilson had seen a flash of fear, then resignation, then… something Wilson hadn't been sure of. The look was always near the forefront of Wilson's mind.

The shame at his failure to act was the only thing Wilson saw in his reflection these days. So he avoided mirrors, water, reflective surfaces, and every Silver girl whose eyes were just like her father's. Because Wilson knew he should've been the one who'd lost his life that day, not the old man. General Silver was far more valuable a man than Wilson Michaels could ever hope to be.

But here Wilson was, alive and well. Standing in the man's kitchen while his eldest daughter filled his plate with food. Wilson sat the plate on the counter and turned to the back door.

"Where are you going?" called Scout.

"I've still got work to do," Wilson said to the ground.

Whatever words she said afterward were swallowed up by his boots crunching over hard earth. Wilson quick-marched it away from the main house. He bypassed the stables, the barn, and the trails. He needed to find a place where he wouldn't be found.

The four Silver sisters -Scout, Saylor, Tilly, and Brig- all had perfect radar when it came to anything and anyone in the vicinity of their property. In the few weeks he'd been on the Silver Star Ranch, he'd learned pretty quickly that there was no place he could hide from the Silver sisters.

They'd find him in the hayloft when he wanted peace and quiet. They'd find him in the worn-down barn when he wanted to be alone. They'd find him on the trail when he wanted to get away.

If the United States military had had even one of these sisters on their payroll, all combat the world over would have ceased a decade ago. Instead, Wilson got their attention now when all he wanted was to sink down into a hole and be forgotten.

He walked directly into the woods on an untrod path. Surely they wouldn't find him out here -though he wouldn't put it past them. He kept his head low, unwilling to even look at the blue of the sky. He'd taken to getting up at night as the night's sky was dark and didn't remind him of that clear blue day when a blue-eyed man sacrificed his life for someone so unworthy.

Wilson should not be here. He did not know why he was here. All he wanted was to find a new purpose, a new command. A reason as to why he—a man abandoned in the hospital after his birth—was spared when an important man like the General had been taken too soon.

Wilson wished he could go back into the military under someone else's command. He'd been discharged from the military due to his injuries. They weren't severe enough to end his life. They were damaging enough to end his life of service. Unless he could strengthen his body and get it back in shape to ship out.

With that thought in mind, he picked up his pace. He pushed himself to go faster over the uneven terrain. Even before he'd run a mile, he was already out of breath. His knees were protesting. His shoulders were aching.

Wilson stopped and hit a tree. There was that saying about the bark being worse than the bite. Wilson's knuckles disagreed as the bark of the tree bit into his flesh.

He cradled his injured hand in his lap as he sank to the ground. Even when he tried to better himself, he wound up hurting himself more. At this rate, he'd never get his weary body into shape to re-enlist.

He was done. He was washed up. The general had sacrificed himself for this.

Why?

If it had been Linc that the general had pushed out of the way or Jefferson, no one would've given it a second thought to either man's survival. Linc was a leader. Jefferson was a talented tracker. All Wilson had was a brute force that leaders pointed in a direction for him to Hulk Smash. Wilson looked down at his bruised fists. Now even that superpower eluded him.

Nearly a year after the incident and Wilson still had no answers and no purpose. He'd hoped coming to the general's ranch and working the man's land would provide him with a new lease on life. Every time he looked at one of the man's daughters, nothing but guilt ran through his veins. He couldn't even contemplate what they all suspected was the general's latest mission.

Before his death, General Silver had made his unit, The President's Men, pledge to come to his home in the event of his death. Their said mission was to look in on his daughters. But when the six men got to Silver Star, they came to suspect that looking-in-on might mean marriage.

Already Linc and the general's eldest daughter Scout were married. Jeff and Saylor were engaged. Jackson and Carter were willing to take the plunge in holy matrimony with one of the girls, too.

But Wilson?

There was simply no way he'd ever even consider. Not after being the cause of their father's death. He felt like an interloper.

Wilson decided here and now that he was leaving this place. Leaving it for what, he didn't know? He wasn't sure it mattered any longer. If he was not to have absolution from the general, if he was not going to have a new mission from the military, then all he wanted was peace.

Unfortunately, it sounded like Wilson wouldn't get his wish today. A feminine yelp reached his eardrums from where he sat against the tree. There was a woman out here, and she was in danger. This he knew how to handle.

Wilson picked up his pace in the once peaceful wooded area. She was easy to track as this part of the land looked as though it had been undisturbed for years. It took him no time at all to zero in on the location of the sound.

It came from a treehouse that looked like it had seen better days. The cracking and splintering of wood let him know someone was up there. Before he could think of how to climb up and get the woman down safely, a splintering sound boomed through the air.

The sound sent him back to that fateful day when the bomb had exploded. It had shoved Wilson farther out of the way while at the same time engulfing Wilson's savior. Wilson had seen blue eyes, then red flames, and finally black smoke.

When he looked up now, he saw a flash of ice, like a large snowflake. Or maybe a diamond. Was that a ring? It clunked to the ground at his feet. Before he could reach down and investigate, there was something red falling.

A woman in a red dress. Her limbs flailing as gravity turned on her. Wilson didn't hesitate. He scrambled into place to catch her.

A vine caught at his boot. He yanked it free, trying to make it in time as the red-clad body fell hard and fast toward the ground.

CHAPTER THREE

These boots were made for walking. So that's what Mareen did. She walked a familiar trail that hugged the boundaries of the Flying Cross and the Silver Star ranches.

Her father and Father Matthews had named the ranches after they each earned their first medals. As a former pilot, Father Matthews had earned a Flying Cross, which was an honor given to pilots for heroism and extraordinary achievement during aerial flights that were not routine. Abe Silver had earned his first of many medals before his first wedding. The man who would be general earned his first Silver Star for gallantry in action while facing an enemy during a military operation.

The difference between the two heroes was that after earning his medal, Father Matthews came home and stayed to raise his boys into manhood. While General Silver had six girls, three wives, and five weddings—because he'd remarried his first wife, Sarah Silver, twice. The General mostly passed through the ranch, rarely staying for too long. Where he did stay was in active duty until his untimely death.

Mareen and her sisters had learned at a young age that if they wanted fatherly advice, they had to go next door to get it. Since

Mareen had never lived full time on the Silver Star ranch, Father Matthews's number had been the first number programmed in speed dial on her cell phone. It had the prime spot of Number One on her contacts lists. Though she always punched in the ten-digit code since she knew it by heart.

Looking down at her cell now, she saw she had an unanswered message. Her fiancé Stephán wished her well on her mission. He even used the term *mission*. Though Stephán had never met the general, he'd always got a kick out of knowing his prim and proper fiancée was, for all intents and purposes, an army brat.

Mareen snorted at the thought. Then she immediately covered her mouth at the unladylike sound. She'd never been one to misbehave, overindulge, or act entitled.

Though to have her oldest sister Scout tell it, that description fit Mareen to a T. Which was why Mareen knew she would be met with resistance when she actually began her mission and presented her plan to her sisters. Scout would just have to get over her prejudices about Mareen because if she didn't, she was going to lose everything.

Mareen took a deep inhale and sighed as she looked out at the view. The lush greenery of the Silver Star Ranch always took her breath away. She loved nothing more than saddling up and getting lost on the winding trails. Or hiding inside the husk of an old tree. Or laying in the field of fragrant blooms.

The lands of the Silver Star Ranch were magical. Because outside of the house, when she and her sisters would get lost on the land, there was no fighting. There was only laughter.

Mareen knew she wouldn't likely get to run and laugh with her sisters after all these years. What she did know was if they didn't fulfill the demands of their father's decree, then this magical land would be lost to them forever, and she would certainly never get the chance to even walk with her sisters again. They would have nothing connecting them any longer.

With that thought, Mareen picked up her pace. She marched on in borrowed boots, determined to present her plan and get her sisters in line. But the light breeze in the air slowed her advance. Because despite her father's drilling, Mareen had never taken to soldiering.

She had no idea how to marshal troops. She wasn't overly confident of the plans she'd drawn up. It could all fail, and then everyone would blame her. Again.

Mareen knew she was the reason for so much strife in the family. After Abe and Sarah filed for divorce the first time, Sarah found out she was pregnant with Saylor. It also happened to be the day of Catherine and Abe's wedding. Mareen's conception was announced a month later. Thus began the divide of the Silvers.

Sides were drawn. Boundaries staked out. Mareen was the only one forced to go back and forth across enemy lines between her father's ranch and her mother's townhouse.

Now, instead of stepping onto her father's lands and possibly bringing an end to this decades-long cold war, Mareen continued to hug the borderline. Her destination was in sight. The Silver-Matthews Fort came into view.

Though the Matthews boys had done most of the work, Scout had demanded that their last name go first on the treehouse. Even though all the Matthews boys were bigger and older, no one argued with Scout Silver. Not if they wanted to keep their heads on straight. Mareen remembered that Scout had knocked around one of the boys, but Saylor had been there to nurse him back to a smile.

That was the dynamic between her two oldest sisters. Scout was demanding where Saylor was accommodating. Mareen? Well, she just preferred to stay out of any conflicts.

Looking up at the old fort, Mareen had the notion to climb the structure. She'd sat by when it was being built all those years ago. She had never gone inside. It would've gotten her clothes dirty, and her mother would've silently raged. Because a lady never raised her voice above a whisper. Though Mareen had heard her parents arguing enough to doubt that edict.

A speck of dirt fell down onto her red dress. It left a brown smudge on the crimson. Mareen snorted at the discoloration. Then she outright laughed. Well, she was already dirty. She might as well climb and see what she'd been missing.

Her first step on the ladder brought a storm of dirt down onto her head. If her mother could see her now. But her mother wasn't there. No one was there. And so Mareen climbed higher.

Inside the fort, there were pieces of wood missing from the four walls. The floor creaked as she stepped inside. Now that she'd accomplished the feat, it didn't feel like such a great accomplishment. Mareen was pretty high off the ground, and she didn't like the way the wood swayed.

She turned to head back down. When she did, her ring slipped off her finger. The large rock rolled to the center of the fort.

"Oh, no!"

Mareen took a step to retrieve it. The floor creaked. Then splintered.

She had to get down. She had to get down now. Every time she shifted her weight, she heard another creak. Another splinter. Then a crack.

The wood split in two, and Mareen was falling.

Miraculously, she didn't hit the ground. She fell into brawny arms. When she opened her eyes, she was staring into eyes the color of the green grass she loved to run free through. Those eyes belonged to a man. A handsome man if the high cheekbones, and angular nose, and firm jaw were to tell her anything.

As Mareen stared, a peculiar thing happened. Her heart skipped a beat, and the sound plummeted into her belly. Then her belly grumbled with want.

CHAPTER FOUR

The sound of the wood splintering and then the scream brought Wilson back to that fateful day in a combat zone. Gone was the peaceful wood he'd walked through. Gone was the smell of flowers. He expected to smell the harsh chemicals of the blast. He expected to feel the burn of splintering wood and hot shrapnel.

That had been Wilson's life in combat. That had been his life from an early age. Having been abandoned at birth, he'd never rested easy. He, of all people, knew that his place in the world was never secure. That was until he'd been selected by General Silver to be a part of The President's Men.

It had taken months, but somehow, someway, he'd found his place in the unit. A place where he was respected, where he was expected. Respect was easy to gain for someone of his size and strength. All his life, he simply needed to raise his fists, and others would get in line or get out of his way.

The men of General Silver's unit were all skilled and had undeniable strengths of their own. Not one of them cowered at Wilson's size, but each and every one of them had his back. Moreover, they expected him to have theirs. And so, for the first time in his life, Wilson had expectations of himself.

It was no wonder he took the general's death so hard. He hadn't been in the place he was supposed to. If he had been, then the general would still be with them today. Wilson would give anything to go back and trade places with the man.

Now, in the present, as the wood rained down on his head, he thought he might finally get that wish. But the splintering bark was not metallic shrapnel. It wasn't hot. Instead of being shoved out of the way by a burly general, a warm bundle landed in Wilson's arms.

The delicate impact knocked him off his center, and the loss of gravity made him lightheaded. None of that brought Wilson to his knees, though. What almost brought him down was the blue eyes looking back at him.

Back on that fateful day when they'd lost the general, the last thing Wilson had felt was the man shove him out of the way. Wilson had tumbled forward. It took one second too long for his training to kick in. Wilson had scrambled to his feet to take his position, but it was too late. He turned to reach for the general when the bomb went off.

There had been a crash. A flash of red. A flash of blue. And then nothing as Wilson blacked out.

Even in his dreams, he'd remembered that flash of blue. It had been General Silver's eyes. Wilson had seen a flash of fear, then resignation, then… something. It was that something that woke Wilson up every night. It was that something that invaded his thoughts during his waking hours.

That something was in the eyes looking back at him now.

Wilson realized he held a woman in his arms. Her hair was a deep chestnut brown with honey highlights. Her nose was prominent and pert, as though it was often tilted up toward the sun. Her lips were shaped like a bowstring; a perfect sideways heart that he felt the urge to tug at with his fingers to see if they would give.

Wilson's entire body warmed and came to life with this creature in his arms. It was the shock of awareness that nearly knocked him off his feet. Not her weight. She was well built. Long legs, toned arms, and womanly curves. Her weight was slight. He could hold her for days. He wanted to hold her for days.

The warmth and the desire rattled him. It had been so long since he'd felt anything. Since he'd desired anyone.

More pieces of wood rained down on them. Wilson looked up. The treehouse was about twenty feet off the ground. If he hadn't been there to catch her, she definitely would've injured herself. Maybe even fatally.

A small cry left her lips, as though she could sense her potential fate. He felt her cry like a shot to his heart.

"It's all right," he said. "I've got you."

She'd closed her eyes when she cried. Slowly, her eyelids reopened. Seeing the shock of blue behind her lids again was another punch to Wilson's gut. He swore he saw the general peeking out from that blue reflection. His hands nearly dropped her then.

She was a Silver. She had to be. If not for that special brand of blue eyes, then just the fact that she was out here on the land.

Wilson had no desire to entangle himself in the fool plan of the general's daughters to get married to save the ranch. He, of all men, didn't deserve such happiness when he was at fault for the general's death.

He should be setting the general's daughter on her feet. Instead, he cradled her to him as he looked into those reflective blue eyes.

"You saved me," she said.

"I did," was his reply.

He had.

Maybe this was why he was here?

Maybe the general had saved him so that he could save his daughter?

If so, then Wilson's debt was paid. So he should set this Silver girl down and walk away.

As though she sensed his intentions, she wrapped her arms

around his neck. He could've easily broken her hold. Instead, he pulled her closer.

That's when Wilson knew that he was good and trapped.

CHAPTER FIVE

hat was she doing?

Well, it was clear to see what she was doing. Mareen was out in the middle of nowhere, in another man's arms. If anyone saw her—an engaged woman—that wouldn't only be the end of her relationship with Stephán, it would be the end of her arrangement with him.

Mareen wasn't sure what troubled her most? That she worried over the agreement she had with Stephán about the ranch? Or the fact that she worried more about messing up that agreement than she did their relationship.

It wasn't as though her and Stephán's relationship was one of passion. The two of them were well matched in all areas of their lives. That's what mattered most. Mareen had never bothered with things like love and the such. She knew firsthand that that emotion between two people could bring a person up high one moment and send them crashing down in the next.

Crashing was the last thing on Mareen's mind right now. She had just fallen. Nearly to her death. But she was still up high, held high in muscular arms.

It was a warm and cuddly embrace, like a teddy bear. Which was an inane thought because Mareen had never been a stuffed animal kind of girl. She was more of a porcelain doll kind of girl. A look, but don't touch kind of girl. She played with priceless dolls that were put up on a shelf and admired, not brought down and cradled.

All of a sudden, Mareen felt bad for the dolls back on her shelf collecting dust. It was really nice being held in someone's arms. Especially if that someone had green eyes, whose color mimicked the rolling pastures she loved to ride over. Especially if their lips looked pillow-soft even when drawn into a hard line.

Mareen had the strangest desire. She wanted to fall into his mouth and have his lips cradle hers. She wanted to lower her bottom lip and find out what it would be like to have his bottom lip catch hers.

This man, this stranger, was certainly looking at her. She must look a fright. The walk in the afternoon sun had more than likely melted her layers of makeup away. Tendrils of her hair were plastered to her forehead. And her dress still had that god awful smudge that was so unladylike.

She needed to get down and straighten her dress. She needed to turn away and fix her hair and makeup. But instead of running her hands through her hair or smoothing her clothing, Mareen found her hands circling around the man's neck.

She stared at her hands as they moved, as though they didn't belong to her. She had never wrapped them around a man's neck before. Not even around her fiancé's neck.

Her fiancé. She had a fiancé. What was his name again?

Something starting with an S. It was a little girly sounding, but that was because he was of European descent. France or something.

"Stephanie?"

"Is that your name?" His voice sounded like he'd swallowed a bear, and it spoke for him. It was part growl, part grunt, all grumpy.

Mareen shook her head back and forth slowly. She could tell that green gaze tracked her movement, but his eyes never left hers. He'd asked her a question. She should answer it. "No, that's my fiancé's name."

"Your fiancé's name is Stephanie?"

One of his bushy eyebrows rose. She'd never met a man with such unkempt facial hair. Mareen wondered if the hair there was soft.

"Hmmm? No. It's Stephán."

Mareen's focus was still on this man's facial hair. She routinely had every excess strand of hair lasered, waxed, or plucked from her body. Not this man.

The excessive dark hair didn't just sit above his cocked brow. There was a slight mustache above his lips. A beard sprouted from his chin and cheeks. The dark tendrils of hair appeared downy, like feathers. She wondered if they would feel that way?

Unbidden, her hand rose and reached out to him. She pulled it back at the last second.

"Where's the ring?" she gasped.

Mareen's left hand was inches away from this stranger's chin when she noticed her ring finger was entirely naked. Because her engagement ring had fallen through the floorboards of the treehouse.

"The ring?" he asked in that bear man's voice.

Mareen had to stop and focus. Though he had only said a few words, every time he spoke, his deep baritone sent shivers across her shoulders and down her spine. When he said the word ring, it resonated in her head and made her heart flutter as though it had been struck like a bell.

The sound of those two words on his lips made Mareen's belly grumble with want. A buzzing sounded in her ears, making it hard to concentrate. It was as though he was offering her honey.

Mareen wanted to gobble his offering down. But he wasn't offering her a sweet, golden treat. He didn't have a ring to give her. He was asking for clarity about what she'd just said to him.

Mareen already had a ring. From another man. And she needed to find it.

"My engagement ring," said Mareen.

No sooner had the words left her mouth did her feet hit the

ground. He'd put her down quickly, instantly. As though she were a buzzing bee and her stinger had just come out.

Her arms were still around his neck, but he stepped away, breaking her hold on him. Not that she should have a hold on this man. He was a stranger. But for a moment, while he'd held her close, she'd felt closer to him than any other person in the world.

"You're engaged?" he asked.

There was a simple answer to that question. It was just a single syllable. Mareen's mouth wouldn't open. So, she nodded.

"Good," he said the word with a bitter distaste in his tone. "I'll help you."

"You will?"

"Find the ring."

"Oh, right. The ring."

He nodded his head. Sharp and succinct, as though he'd been given orders. Though he had copious amounts of facial hair, the hair on his head was closely cut, like a soldier's. He even had the countenance of a soldier; straight spine, shoulders back, head high. Mareen would know since her father had been one. Maybe this was one of the soldiers staying on the ranch?

"I'm Mareen. Mareen Silver."

"Wilson," he said. Not lifting his gaze to hers. His eyes remained on the ground, searching.

Wilson was a strong name. It had been the name of one of the U.S. Presidents. She knew her father had had a unit of men who all shared a name with the leaders of this country.

"You knew my father?"

Wilson's jaw tightened, but he nodded. His gaze remained firmly locked down in its search.

"Are you one of his men?"

"Found it."

Wilson dropped to one knee. He brushed aside some of the grass. The gem gleamed under the sunlight. Its glare was harsh enough to cause both Mareen and Wilson to wince under its shine.

Wilson picked it up. Brushed off some of the dirt. Then he handed it to Mareen.

Mareen stared at the gem in his hand. Her heart fluttered wildly in her chest as Wilson held it out for her. Her breath went shallow as she gazed down at Wilson on bended knee with a ring presented to her.

A butterfly fluttered out of the grass and circled around them. Up above, birds chirped a sweet melody. The sun broke through the clouds and cast its brilliant light on the spot around them.

When Stephán had proposed in a room full of their friends and associates at the country club, Mareen had stood poised as her mother had taught her. She's smiled blandly, not showing any teeth because she was not a horse or a dog. She'd been calm and cool as she'd given her answer to Stephán's proposal.

Now with Wilson on his knee, holding the ring up to her, Mareen felt the world going a bit off kilter. She felt faint as she held her hand out for Wilson to place the ring on her finger.

Wilson reached up for her hand. He grabbed her fingers roughly. With a twist of his wrist, he turned her hand over, palm up, and unceremoniously dropped the rock into her hand.

CHAPTER SIX

 S he was engaged. That was good. More proof that Wilson had done his duty and he could prepare to leave this place. Because he had no place here. And now, having met Mareen Silver - the engaged Mareen Silver, the very engaged Mareen Silver if the size of that rock told him anything- Wilson was more certain he didn't belong here on the ranch.

"You probably should avoid that treehouse from now on," he said. "It's not stable."

If he hadn't been here, she would've fallen and broken something. Or worse. The thought sent a rage through Wilson.

He stood up and paced away from her. Then he paced back. Only to pace away again.

"What were you doing up there, anyway?" He demanded when he was a good ten feet away from her. He didn't like the distance between them, but he held himself still. Only to steadily make his way back to her.

There were still falling twigs and leaves. One might not clunk her in the head, but it could get in her eye and blind her. Or something.

"I wanted a walk down memory lane," was her answer.

"That way seems treacherous." Wilson pointed up to the decrepit treehouse. They could now look through the floor and see directly to the roof of the structure. If he had been a few seconds too late…

Wilson walked past her. He clenched and unclenched his fists as he did so. A few seconds was all it had taken to lose her father. Why was he going through this again? Once through the nightmare was enough.

"Yeah," Mareen was nodding when he turned back.

She placed the ring back on her left hand. Her fingers shook as she did so. Then trembled when she was done. That rock looked like it made more than she did.

"Well, I'm done with the memories," she continued. "Time to face the future. You ready?"

She marched up to him. Light blue eyes pierced into green. But in those blue eyes, Wilson saw something he recognized.

Fear.

He'd seen that look before. He'd seen it the last time he'd seen the general.

A flash of fear. Then resignation. Then… something Wilson still wasn't sure of.

But the fear, he knew. Mareen Silver was afraid of something. And just like her father, she was resigned to do what she must.

There was a determined lift to her proud chin. Wilson felt the urge to tuck her head against his chest and kiss her temple. He wanted to tell her that there was no need for her to face whatever she was marching toward. He would stand in front of her and protect her from whatever may come.

Only he'd failed at doing that when it came to her father. Wilson crossed his arms over his chest. He looked away from Mareen Silver, lest she see the shame of his failure.

"I need you to escort me to the house."

Wilson looked back at her. This time he really looked at her. She had the same features as Scout and Saylor with her dark hair and light eyes. Unlike the older two, Mareen Silver's skin wasn't kissed by the sun. She was far paler, as though she didn't get out much. Her arms were toned, but from the definition that came from yoga or Pilates, not work in the fields or with animals.

She didn't look helpless. There was some fight in her. It simply looked as though she hadn't had to face any adversity in a long time.

"I'm walking you to the house?" Wilson asked, more to clarify than anything.

Mareen nodded. "It's what a gentleman would do."

"I'm not a gentleman," Wilson scoffed. "I'm a soldier."

"Same difference." Mareen shrugged and then brushed past him.

Wilson watched her for a few seconds, then he followed in her wake. After a few steps where the sweet scent of her expensive perfume wafted over him, he decided to step up beside her.

That was a mistake. Now he was right in the midst of that heady aroma. It was going straight to his head. He needed a dose of reality, and he needed it now.

"I didn't see you or your fiancé at breakfast this morning." The word fiancé was acid on Wilson's tongue.

"I came to the Flying Cross Ranch first to talk to Father Matthews. My sisters don't know I'm here."

Wilson noticed two things. Mareen's shoulders slumped when she brought up her sisters. And she didn't bring up her fiancé at all.

"I didn't see you at Scout's wedding either," he said.

"I wasn't invited."

Definite bitterness in her tone there. Wilson didn't have any sisters. At least, not that he knew of. But he knew women. They could argue and hold grudges with the best of them. It couldn't have been easy with six young women under one roof.

Wilson and Mareen walked off the beaten path. In fact, the path they were on seemed to be beaten up. Tree stumps came out of nowhere. Large rocks laced a crisscrossed path. The scurrying of creatures great and small went on nonstop in, over, and around the underbrush. He was on constant alert in this natural battlefield.

"So you're here for Saylor's wedding?" he asked as he kicked a fallen tree branch out of the way.

"I won't be staying that long," Mareen said as she stepped around the branch. "I just have a proposition to offer my sisters."

"A proposition?" He steered her clear of an anthill. Not by touching her, just standing between Mareen and the raised dirt.

"Yes, a proposition." Mareen heeded his direction and gave the mound a wide berth. "One that will allow them to keep the ranch but not have to get married."

That piqued Wilson's interest. He had no plans to marry any of the general's daughters. Though something had prickled his flesh when he'd held Mareen's engagement ring in his hands. The cold ice had felt hot in his hand. Wilson was sure it was because the rock had sat out in the sun.

"I just hope they go for it," Mareen was saying.

"Why wouldn't they?"

"Scout probably won't because it's my idea."

"Since I've known her, Scout seems to be a level-headed woman."

Mareen rounded on him, fire in those blue eyes. "So she's got you wrapped around her finger, huh?"

Yep. Women and their grudges. Wasn't there some saying about holding a grudge was like holding onto a hot rock? It would probably be better if Mareen took that iced rock off her finger, then she'd probably let go of the past.

But he wasn't one to talk. Not with how tightly he was holding onto his recent past.

"Everyone always takes her side," said Mareen.

"I'm not on anyone's side."

She wasn't listening to him. Mareen marched in a circle around him. She didn't have Wilson cornered. He could easily get out of her path. He just didn't want to.

There was some color to her cheeks now. Her hands were gathered into fists, which showed off the cute muscle-bumps of her forearms.

"Everyone's always been scared of her. Even boys. Even a big soldier, like you."

"I'm not afraid of your sister."

"No?" Mareen stopped her circular marching and stormed up to him. "Then prove it."

Wilson couldn't decide whether to laugh at the fierce kitten poking him in the chest or cuddle her.

No. Scratch that. There would be no cuddling with her. Wilson stepped back, increasing the perimeter between himself and his adversary.

Because make no mistake, Mareen Silver was his opponent at the moment. Somehow she'd ended up in his arms when he'd kept her sisters at bay. Somehow he'd presented her with a ring when he'd vowed not to take any part of this fool marriage of convenience scheme. Somehow he was watching her back when he swore he never wanted that responsibility for another person again.

But here he was with her. In a matter of a quarter-hour, she had him doing everything he said he wouldn't. And she was still pushing for more.

"You present my idea to her," said Mareen.

"Me? Even if I did, she has no reason to listen to me."

"Well, I know she's not going to listen to me. And if you tell her, then that shows you're not wrapped around her finger."

"I'm not—I don't—wait—what?"

Wilson was rattled at the turn of events. He'd just been outmaneuvered, and he hadn't realized he was in combat. He was so rattled by this spitfire of a princess that he missed the signs of impending danger.

It was the actual sound of rattling that got his attention. Then the sight of pebbles turning. The grass moved as Mareen stepped toward him, and that's when Wilson saw it.

He reached for her, pulling her into his arms, into his protection. But he was too late. The rattlesnake had already sunk his fangs into the back of her calf.

CHAPTER SEVEN

The dolls sat in perfectly straight lines on the shelf. Their legs dangled over the sides. A light breeze wafted into the room, and the delicate figurines' legs swayed back and forth, like soldiers marching from their seated position.

"Let's play with them."

Mareen's back went straight at the command in her older sister's voice. Even in the nursery, and only at the age of ten, Scout sounded like a drill sergeant.

"We can't play with them," Mareen said calmly. "They're antiques."

"They look like toys to me." Scout stood in front of the shelf. Her fists on her hips, her nose in line with one of the dolls, staring it down as though daring it to disagree with her.

Mareen worried less that her sister might break a doll and more that the perpetual dirt under Scout's fingernails would smudge one. She'd learned that word *perpetual* from her mother. Mareen had to deduce the meaning all by herself.

Her mother would say things like *The General is perpetually deployed. That ex-wife of his is perpetually perfumed by horse manure. That poor excuse of a woman perpetually takes him back.*

"They are toys," Mareen patiently explained. "They're expensive. So, we can't touch them."

"What's the purpose of a toy you can't touch?" Scout's tone was superior, as always. "Your mom won't know."

"Scouttie, if she doesn't want to play with the dolls, we can do something else." That was Saylor's voice. Saylor always tried to play the peacemaker between the two of them. Not that Mareen ever tried to start any fights.

"It's boring here." Scout flounced back on the lacy covers of the divan. The white fabric took on a streak of the dirt from Scout's nails. At least her nails were cleaner. So if she did touch the dolls, they wouldn't get dirty.

Mareen worried a speck of dirt would land on her white cloth, but she didn't say anything to her older sister. She'd just make sure to point out the spot to the maid after Scout and Saylor left. Their father was visiting town, so he'd brought her half-sisters for Mareen to play with.

All they'd been doing for the last thirty minutes of this visit was staring out the window to the garden they couldn't go into. Then staring at the black screen of the television set they weren't allowed to turn on because it wasn't Mareen's normal screen time. Mareen wasn't sure what else to do with her sisters. She had learned well to sit still and mind her manners. She knew Scout and Saylor had not had those lessons.

A crash brought Mareen's attention back around. Scout had vacated the divan and was standing at the shelf. One of the antique dolls was on the floor. On its porcelain face was an unfashionable crack.

Mareen gasped, half rising. Then she sank back down onto the divan in utter silence. Saylor's arms came around Mareen. Mareen sat stiffly in the embrace.

"There's no need to fuss," said Scout, failing to hide the panic in her voice. "I can fix it with some glue."

And she had done it. By the time they'd left, Scout had fixed the doll with a bit of craft glue. Later that evening, Mareen's mother had seen the smudge on the couch. Catherine knew the dirt had to have come from her half-sisters, but Mareen had gotten in trouble.

Catherine had insisted that Mareen should've come to tell her mother immediately. Those two little girls were the enemy -not her sisters. Mareen should not take up for their failings. They would never do the same for her.

Catherine never saw the crack in the doll's face. Mareen never told. Neither did her sisters.

"Don't fuss over her, Saylor."

Scout's voice was much deeper than the one in Mareen's memory. Mareen wasn't sure if she was still dreaming the old memory or if she was finally awake. She felt as though she'd been asleep for days. She may have still been asleep. She wasn't sure.

Her body felt heavy. Her mind was hazy. She knew her eyes were still closed because shadows moved in light. Mareen was certain that wasn't how images behaved when she was awake.

"It was just a rattler bite. It's not like she's going to die. I've been bitten many times before."

"Scout, you are so mean," someone slurred from somewhere above her, but Mareen heard them perfectly.

Whoever said that Mareen wanted to be their best friend. Her oldest sister could be as mean as a snake. Mareen wondered if it had been Scout who had bitten her leg out in the woods.

"Sounds like that venom is still in her system," said Saylor in her pacifist way.

"Yeah, because Scout slithered up and bit me," slurred Mareen's hero.

Mareen remembered being bitten. She remembered the pain at the back of her calf. Then she remembered being wrapped up in big, strong arms. Mareen urged her mind to go back to that part of the dream, the part where a soldier with haunted green eyes held her tightly.

But she couldn't focus on that part of the dream. The bright shadows around her were being too loud. A chorus of snorts sounded around Mareen. And then a haughty huff.

Mareen knew that sound. It was the sound Scout made when someone got the best of her. It was rare to hear that sound because Scout Silver rarely let anyone get in front of her. Mareen was liking this dream more and more.

"Good one, Mo."

Mo? No one had called her that in a long time. No one except the Matthews boys and...

Mareen tried again to pry her eyes open. Slowly the shadows began to coalesce. But Mareen still wasn't sure if she was dreaming or awake. A younger version of herself peered down at her.

"Briga... Brigadahhh... Gosh, someone should've taken our dad out and shook him when he named you."

A grin broke across Brig's face. "I like her like this. She needs to get bitten by a snake more often."

"Give her some space, Brig." That came from Saylor.

Saylor placed her hand on Mareen's head. Saylor's hand was cool to the touch. It reminded Mareen of her mother, Sarah. Sarah had always been warm and kind to Mareen.

Even though she smelled like horses. Mareen had never cared. She loved horses.

Her stepmother had not been any of the unkind words that Mareen's own mother had called her. It was no wonder the general kept going back to her. If Mareen had had the choice, she would've come to live with Sarah Silver, too.

"How are you feeling, sis?" asked Saylor.

"Me? I'm fine. But you're not. Your boyfriend is awful, Saylor. He uses and abuses you. You deserve better. You need to stop being a doormat."

That hadn't been what Mareen had planned to say. She'd only meant to say fine and then clam up. But something had loosened up her tongue, and everything in her head, everything she'd ever dreamed of saying to Saylor, if they had been true sisters, had spilled out. And it would seem that Mareen wasn't done.

"Don't marry him."

"I'm not marrying him," Saylor said with a grin. "I dumped him. You can meet my fiancé when you feel better."

"I feel fantastic. Like I'm flying." Mareen spread her hands like a starfish.

"Do you think it's the venom?" said another voice from the doorway. This voice had a halo of bright, yellow light around her face.

"Oh, Tilly! And Gunny! You're both here." Mareen had to blink because her twin sisters kept merging into one and then separating like they were dancing in a hall of mirrors. "Good, there's something I need to tell all of you. You don't have to get married."

Tilly and Gunny pushed off the doorjamb. They became one person again as they came closer. Their single face looked concerned as they peered down at Mareen.

"See," said Scout. "I told you that's why she's here. The truth comes out with the snakebite."

"You're so suspicious, Scout. It's not attractive. It makes your brows come together until it's almost a unibrow."

Tilly and Gunny separated again as they turned and tried to hide a very unladylike snort. Brig giggled openly, not bothering to cover her mouth. Saylor couldn't hide her smile as she pressed a cool cloth to Mareen's forehead. Scout shot her daggers.

"It's fine." Mareen tried to lift her hand and wave Scout's eye-daggers away. "My fiancé will buy the land and give it to you as my wedding present. Ta-dah!"

There was silence. Tilly and Gunny became one again as they stared down at Mareen. Brig pursed her lips. Saylor brought the cloth away so that she could peer into Mareen's eyes.

Wow, that was easier than Mareen had expected. Looks like Father Matthews had been right to send her over to deliver the message herself. There was no arguing, only silence. It was a rare sound when there was more than one Silver sister in the same room.

Scout put her fists on her hips. Much like she had done when she wanted to get her hands on the delicate dolls in Mareen's nursery. "I'm sure you want us to believe that because then Cruella-"

Saylor elbowed Scout.

"Because then your mother will get the land," Scout finished.

"My mother doesn't know about the will. I didn't tell her."

Again silence. This time Tilly and Gunny became one and stayed that way. Mareen noted it was only Tilly standing there. Gunny, who preferred to sleep in a tent rather than on a mattress, never wore sundresses or sandals.

"I haven't told my mother about the will." Mareen pressed her hand to her head. The delineation from the dream world and the real world was still crystalizing, but she knew where she was. She was in her cabin, the one she'd built with her father and sisters.

"But you will tell her," said Scout. She came up to the edge of the bed, getting in Mareen's face.

Mareen wasn't some porcelain doll. She wasn't going to crack if her sister rubbed her the wrong way. And with Mareen's plan, no one would get into trouble at the end of the day.

"It doesn't matter whether she knows or not. Mother wants me to marry Stephán, so I wouldn't be the one who doesn't fulfill Father's stipulations. But there's no guarantee that Brig, Tilly, and Gunny will get married."

Brig's lips were still pursed. It wasn't a natural look for their youngest sister. Mischief and cunning was her natural state of being. She clearly didn't like Mareen's plan. But it was the only way to keep this roof over her head. Brig was too young to get married. She had her entire life ahead of her.

"The plan is I marry Stephán. Stephán buys the ranch from Mother when the deed passes to her. Then Stephán signs it over to Scout. Everyone gets what they want."

It was the perfect plan. So why wasn't anyone smiling? Likely because it was Mareen's plan and not Scout's.

"Do you love him?" asked Saylor.

That question surprised Mareen. It was the one query she hadn't expected to get. No one had ever asked it of her.

Mareen looked up then. Another shadow appeared in the doorway. This shadow was familiar to her. It had brought butterflies to her belly. It had awakened a burning in her chest.

"There's my hero."

Wilson's broad shoulders blocked out the setting sun and beckoned to her. But she couldn't go to him. He wasn't part of her plan.

"I'm feeling a little nauseous," said Mareen. "I think I need to lie down some more."

And so she did. As soon as her head hit the pillow, she felt drawn back into the dreamworld where she was free to rest her head against the chest of the big bear of a man who'd rescued her not once, but twice today.

CHAPTER EIGHT

ilson had tried to stay away from the cabin. He'd tried to stay out of the Silver sisters' business and let Mareen's family handle everything. But when he'd heard the raised voices coming from the cabin he'd been staying in the past couple of weeks, he went in. The moment he stepped across the threshold, he realized his mistake.

Mareen Silver laid in his bed. Technically, it wasn't his bed. It was her bed.

This was the cabin she had built with her father and sisters. Looking at the porcelain princess propped up on pillows, it was clear to see why. Inside Scout's cabin, where Linc had stayed when they'd first arrived, it was completely utilitarian and sparse. Much like its builder. Next door in the cabin where Jeff was staying until his wedding to Saylor, there were more creature comforts like woven blankets and comfortable pillows.

Wilson hadn't chosen this cabin. It had been the one none of the other men had wanted to stay in. He'd understood why when he'd come inside. The cabin was dainty and impractical. On first glance, it resembled more of a dollhouse where everything looked delicate enough to break. On second glance, Wilson had seen that everything inside might look pretty and breakable, but it was all strong and sturdy.

Much like the woman who had built it. The woman who lay in the bed where he'd been resting every night. The woman whose lovely head snuggled into the pillow where he'd been sleeping.

After Mareen had been bitten and Wilson had disposed of the snake, he'd run back to the ranch with her in his arms. Her weight was slight in comparison to the heavy pack he'd worn during missions. The cabin wasn't the closest place for him to take her, but some part of him demanded she be placed inside of the place where he'd come to rest each night. So he shouted to all who could hear as he came into the cabin's door.

Luckily, Saylor and Jeff had been near. Saylor had medical training. After Wilson described the snake to her, she eased his worries that the bite wasn't deadly but did come with some side effects. Namely pain, swelling, nausea, and lethargy.

"There's my hero," said Mareen again. Her eyes were closed. She sounded drunk. The sleepy smile on her face punched him in the chest.

For the last few months, people had been calling him a hero for his actions overseas. They'd even pinned a medal on his chest for his valor. Wilson had wanted to shout each time he heard anyone utter the word hero at him.

Until now.

That word sounded right on Mareen Silver's lips. It sounded like his calling in life; to be her hero. Especially when he couldn't be that for her father.

"Nevermind him," said Scout, blocking Wilson's view of Mareen. "What's this about the deal between you and your fiancé? How can we trust you won't double-cross us?"

Mareen sighed, but it sounded like she was blowing a raspberry. "You always think the worst of me. Even though I have never done anything to deserve it."

Scout's posture stiffened, and her jaw clenched. Wilson had half a mind to march over to the woman and put himself between Scout and Mareen. A hand at his shoulder held him back.

"You don't want to get in the middle of these women when they fight," said Linc. "Trust me. Let them work it out amongst themselves."

"You broke my doll, and I never told," said Mareen. Her eyes were still closed. She tugged at the sheets, bringing them up and around her shoulders. Then she inhaled and hummed.

Something tightened in Wilson's chest. He'd been sleeping in those sheets every night. Was it his scent that made her hum with pleasure?

"What doll?" huffed Scout.

"I don't want my mother to have this place. She'll sell it." Mareen's eyes were open now, but her gaze was unfocused. "Won't it be better if she sells it to my fiancé instead of some big corporation that will break it up into housing or a mall? Or worse, turn it into a dude ranch."

All the Silver sisters grimaced at the possibility of that fate. The shiver that went over Scout's shoulders appeared to relax her defensive posture. With the eldest sister out of attack mode, Wilson let his guard down a fraction. But he didn't move from his post in the doorway.

"I think she's right, Scout," said Saylor.

"Thank you, Saylor." Mareen reached up and patted her sister's cheek but missed and got her ear. "You were always my favorite."

"Hey," said Brig, indignation in her tone.

"I agree," said Tilly. "This is the only way, since Brig's not getting married anytime soon."

"Hey," Brig cried again.

"We all know you'd agree, Tilly," said Scout. "Since you're not done sowing your wild oats."

"Hey," protested Tilly. "I like to go out and have fun."

"And Gunny isn't even in the country," Saylor continued as though she didn't hear either of her sister's protests.

"This way, only I have to bite the bullet of matrimony," said

Mareen, her eyes once again closed. Her nose turned to the pillow as she breathed evenly.

"Bite the bullet?" said Saylor. "Mareen? Mareen, you are in love with your fiancé? Aren't you?"

Wilson watched as Mareen peeled her long lashes open. She frowned down at the pillow and then the comforter. Then she narrowed her gaze as though she was trying to focus on her sister.

She raised her hand as though to reach for Saylor. But then her gaze seemed to get distracted by the rock on her finger. She looked at it as though she didn't know where it had come from.

Wilson remembered that she hadn't been wearing it when he'd rescued her. He also remembered what she'd felt like in his arms. He remembered what her breath tasted like as she'd sighed when he held her close.

Mareen Silver's gaze slid past her sister's and landed on him. Gone was the haze from her blue eyes. Mareen looked at Wilson with a clarity that belied the toxins she'd been assaulted with by that reptile's sneak attack.

He should've seen the snake coming. But he'd been caught off guard. Just like with her father.

He'd saved her twice. That would have to be enough. He couldn't be her hero, not when she was planning to marry another man. Not when she loved another man.

Mareen Silver was engaged. Her marriage would cement the ownership of this ranch, which would keep the general's daughters safe. That had been his mission. It would be accomplished as long as Wilson stayed out of the way. The best thing for him to do was to leave the ranch like he'd planned.

CHAPTER NINE

areen would've sworn she was on a stage. The spotlight blared in her eyes. The orchestra played in all the wrong keys. The audience talked over the music.

But she wasn't at a theater. That was the morning sun shining its light on her. Birds tweeted in high-pitched notes. Horses whinnied their conversations outside her window.

She was in a bed. It was her old bed. Well, it had been her old bed when she'd spent summers here on the ranch as a teen. Though the bed didn't smell like the flowers she would lie out in the room.

The sheets were warm and smelled of spice. Not the spice of apple cider. The spice she'd find out in the fields beyond the flower patches. The herbs that looked edible but could possibly prove dangerous.

Man, that had been some dream she'd had. Mareen didn't typically have vivid dreams. In fact, she rarely had any dreams at all. When she was younger, and she'd told her mother that she didn't dream like the other kids in her class, Catherine had nodded in approval.

"Dreams are for silly girls with cotton for brains and stars in their eyes," her mother had said. "Don't fantasize about any prince sweeping you off your feet, or one day you'll have a rude awakening when he drops you."

Mareen had disobeyed her mother last night. She'd dreamed of being swept off her feet. She'd dreamed of being cradled into a sturdy chest. Her memory was fuzzy, but she knew those things had happened. Wilson had lifted her and carried her back to her childhood bed. Her feet hadn't once touched the ground. He'd laid her down and tucked her in.

Mareen nuzzled her nose into the pillows. She burrowed deeper into the blankets. As she did so, she was hit with more of that strong, masculine scent. And she knew who it belonged to.

Of the six large grizzly bears of soldiers, she knew which one had been sleeping in her bed. And he smelled just right.

With that thought, Mareen threw off the covers. She should not be having thoughts like that about another man. She was engaged to… what was his name.

Her hand went to her throbbing head. She felt like she had a hangover. Even though she'd never drunk anything harder than wine, and she'd never finished a full glass.

Mareen's head felt like it was full of cotton. Stars danced behind her eyes every time she blinked. She felt like she'd been dropped on the ground -hard.

That was probably just as well. The rattling in her brain helped her remember more details of the other day. She'd been bitten by a snake. Wilson had rescued her. Then it all went fuzzy again.

She knew there was more. The only clear parts seemed to be the parts with a handsome green-eyed soldier in the mix. That was fine with Mareen because she liked her memories of that man.

She would have to keep that to herself. Any thoughts of Wilson, any memories of the other day, would have to remain in her dreams. The reason it would have to be that way weighed heavily on her left hand.

Stephán. Her fiancé.

Stephán Bushnell was a good man. Well, he was highly favored by the local society papers, which counted for a lot in Mareen's world.

He was kind. Well, he was polite. He had perfect manners, which was important in society.

He was strong. Well, he didn't have a barrel chest. But he worked out playing squash most mornings and golf in the afternoons, which was important for the connections he needed to make in his business.

He was handsome. Well, not the rugged kind of handsome where he had a little bit of scruff on his face. His beard was conditioned and trimmed each week at a high price salon for men, which was important to keep up appearances.

Mareen ran her hands through her own hair. Her fingers got tangled in the rat's nest. She was sure a rodent was living in her tresses after being out of doors all afternoon. Or at least a few bugs. She'd have to make a trip to the salon as soon as she returned to the city.

"You're awake."

Mareen winced at Brig's chipper voice. Her stomach grumbled at the smell of lard coming from the plate her youngest sister held out to her.

"I brought you breakfast."

Said breakfast was eggs sitting in a pool of butter. Buttered toast. Greasy bacon. And a single strawberry for decoration. None of it was on Mareen's diet if she wanted to look good in the designer wedding dress her mother had picked out for her.

Mareen's hands reached for the plate. She'd been bitten by a snake, for goodness' sake. Which was the excuse she would give her mother if they had to make an emergency trip to the seamstress before her wedding day.

"Last night was epic," Brig said as she bounced down onto the bed. "Scout's still red behind the ears after what you said."

"I didn't say anything to Scout," Mareen said after swallowing down the last bite.

"You don't remember, do you?"

That last bite got wedged in Mareen's throat as parts of the dream came back to her. They were hazy in her mind. They couldn't have been real. Could they?

"Listen, Mo, I don't want you to marry this Steve guy—"

"Stephán."

"—if you don't love him. It's not worth it. We have a plan to keep the ranch."

"How do you know about the plan?"

Brig's brows lifted, along with her grin. "Man, you really were out of it yesterday, weren't you?"

Mareen wasn't out of it anymore. None of that had been a dream. She had told off Scout. She had presented her plan to them. Had she told her sisters she didn't love Stephán?

The butter in Mareen's stomach churned as she thought about what else she might have said. She remembered one of her sisters talking of love. Then she'd seen Wilson standing in the doorway.

Her heart had sped up. The butterflies had danced in her belly. Had any words spewed from her mouth? She couldn't remember.

"Where's Wilson?" Mareen asked.

Brig's grin spread wider.

"I just—" Mareen stood, wobbling a bit as she did so. "I wanted to thank him before I go."

"He was getting ready to leave."

"Leave? You mean go to town?"

"Nope. I mean leave-leave. He's leaving the ranch. For good."

Mareen heard a crashing sound. When she looked down, nothing was out of place. Inside her mind, inside her body, she felt like she'd just been dropped splat on the hardwood floors.

"Mareen, wait. Maybe you want to get dressed before marching outside?"

Mareen looked down at herself. She was wearing only a camisole that came down to her upper thighs.

"Your old clothes are in the closet."

Inside the bedroom closet, Mareen found jeans and flannel. None of these articles of clothing were in her closet back in the city.

She didn't even own a pair of yoga pants. It was all dresses for her, like a proper lady.

Mareen stepped into a pair of jeans that molded to her form. The flannel felt warm on her skin. Suddenly she had the urge to do something she hadn't in a long time. She wanted to ride.

But that would have to wait until later. First thing was first. She had to find her soldier.

Wait. Not *her* soldier. Just the man who had likely saved her life.

Because she had manners. She had to thank him before he left. It was the civilized thing to do.

CHAPTER TEN

Wilson watched the girls as they walked toward the stables. If he were being honest with himself, the only girl he watched was Mareen. Brig chattered on, as she often did. Mareen nodded at intervals and made noncommittal noises that seemed wholly unnecessary as Brig went on.

Of all the Silver sisters, the youngest had been the one Wilson had avoided the most. Brig appeared to know that people didn't want to talk. She just didn't seem to care and sidled up to everyone in her path to get their life story out of them.

Wilson was sure Brig didn't want to know the most recent part of his life story, the part where he was responsible for her father's death. So he always steered clear of her, as he was doing now. He'd diverted his path, but he didn't do a full about-face. He stood in the shadows and watched Mareen endure her sister's chatter.

Mareen looked even lovelier dressed in jeans. In fact, she looked like a different person. The woman he saw today looked as though the girl in yesterday's dress had been playing dress-up. The person he saw in the jeans was the real woman.

The denim molded to curves Wilson hadn't seen in the dress. The dress had made Mareen look like she was model thin, like something from one of those thick magazines with the hefty price tags. When she'd fallen into Wilson's arms, he'd known there was more to her. That had been confirmed when he'd taken her into his arms and held her close as he ran through the fields with her.

Wilson balled his fists at the flashes of memory, at the tingles of feeling in his extremities, at the spark of desire in his gut. These were thoughts he shouldn't be thinking. He was leaving this place. Leaving all of this behind, and that included the reactions he had to this woman, this Silver woman. He'd just been waiting for Mareen to leave the cabin so that he could go in and gather the rest of his things.

Last night, he'd slept in Scout's old cabin, the one Linc had stayed in when they'd first arrived. Wilson had had an uncomfortable night of it in the sparsely decorated space. As a soldier, Wilson had slept in hovels, in dirt huts, and on concrete floors. His one night in the utilitarian cabin had left a crick in his neck. He'd missed the lace and frills of Mareen's cabin. Had he grown soft? Or maybe he was just soft for her.

Once he was inside the cabin, the smell of Mareen's perfume nearly knocked him over. She was everywhere. Her scent so permeated the air that she was on the tip of his tongue. Wilson couldn't help himself. He swallowed her down.

It was a mistake. A big mistake. Now, he didn't just have the memories of the way she looked, the way she sounded, the way she felt. He also knew the way she tasted.

He blew out a forceful sigh. Not that it did anything to erase her from his mind or his mouth. When he came near the bed, he was hit with an even stronger whiff of her.

Wilson had trained to hold his breath for over two minutes. It would take him less than that to clear out of this place. He gave in after thirty seconds.

Never had there been an enemy he wanted to be invaded by. He opened his mouth and breathed her in. His nostrils flared to gather more of her inside him. He picked up the pillow and caught a strong whiff. It was all he was going to get.

He tossed the pillow back on the bed and went to the closet. He gathered his things and prepared to leave the ranch forever, or at least until after Mareen's wedding. His brothers were his only family. He could leave them for some time, but not for the rest of his life.

He'd yearned for a connection all his life. The ties he had to the other five men were strong knots. He'd be back. But only after he was certain he wouldn't run into the one bind he could never forge.

The thoughts he'd had about Mareen Silver last night would've turned her porcelain skin pink. At least he'd thought about something other than those last few minutes with her father. Instead of seeing the look in the general's eyes, he'd seen Mareen's eyes. They'd looked directly at him when she'd said, "There's my hero."

The desire to be just that was strong inside him. He'd had to save her twice yesterday. What if she needed him again today, or tomorrow, or sometime in the future?

Another man would have that right. Her fiancé. The one with the feminized name. What father let his son go out with an accent over his name? Surely this Stephán got beat up a lot as a kid. He couldn't be qualified to take care of Mareen.

Then again, neither was Wilson. He had no right to marry. Not when he was responsible for the loss of a good man. Especially when that good man was her father.

Wilson stormed out of the cabin. Off in the distance, he saw Mareen atop a horse. Her slim body was the picture of elegance as she rode the magnificent beast.

Great, another picture of her to take with him for the rest of his days. Wilson tried to look away, but he was drawn to her. She was riding the horse unlike anything he'd ever seen. It looked as though the two were dancing.

The joy on her face drew his steps forward. He wanted to catch her flowing hair. He wanted to taste that smile on her lips. He wanted the light in her eyes to shine on him.

The horse patted its hooves to a beat. It pranced in the circular enclosure, coming close to the fencing without ever touching the siding. In fact, it sidestepped, moving back toward the center of the pen. It turned its big body as if on a dime, its knees marching high like a soldier.

All the while, Mareen smiled big as she guided the beast. Wilson matched her smile. He hadn't noticed his feet moving closer and closer to her until she looked up and caught his gaze.

Her smile dropped. Not into a frown. He saw as she inhaled a sharp breath. Her nostrils flared as she did so like she was scenting him.

With her attention taken off the horse, the horse stepped right, but Mareen's balance was still seated left. She wobbled in the saddle.

Wilson dropped his duffle and took off at a run. By the time he got there, Mareen was already dismounted. Her feet were planted on the ground, as were the horse's.

It hadn't reared. She hadn't been in danger. She had no need of a hero.

"I hear you're leaving," she said to him.

Wilson couldn't find his breath, let alone his words. His hands itched to bring her in close, to hold her firmly to him. But there was no reason to.

Mareen might have finished her dancing, but the horse appeared still raring to go. It bumped past Mareen as though it was shimmying. The bump sent her flying into Wilson's arms.

Mareen's breathing was harsh. Her lips parted. Her hands around his neck again, like a lover's embrace.

Her eyes shone brightly on him. Her hair tangled in his fingers. Wilson only needed to lean down, and he would taste her lips.

"What's going on?"

The sound of Linc's voice broke the spell. Wilson let Mareen go. When he turned, they were both met with Linc's and Scout's glare.

CHAPTER ELEVEN

"I knew it," huffed Scout. "You're trying to sabotage us, aren't you?"

Mareen heard her sister's words. How couldn't she? Scout was right in her face. But still the woman's words sounded far away.

Mareen's mind was still back a few seconds ago. She was back inside Wilson's arms. Back in the feel of his heart beating in time with hers. Back in the feeling of his breath settling onto her cheeks, her upper lip, her lower lip. Back to that look in his eyes.

That look that had tried to shutter, but she had been too close. She had seen inside of him. What she had seen was hunger, heat, desire.

Many men had looked at Mareen with that look. From the first day of her life, her mother had dolled her up to be a prize-worthy possession. Mareen had expected to be settled on a wealthy, influential man's shelf. She had not expected to want to come down and play.

Wilson had wanted to kiss her. Mareen was sure of it. And if he had, if he had bent his head just an inch lower, if he had just moved his lips a millimeter to the right, Mareen had no doubt that she would've let him.

"Do you even have a fiancé? Or is that part of your scheme as well?"

Scout's words knocked around in Mareen's head, rattling the few brain cells that were still present there and hadn't migrated south to her chest.

"What?" Mareen jerked her gaze to her older sister.

Scout was right in her face. Just an inch closer, and they would knock heads. Mareen was under no illusion that her sister would offer her a kiss. Scout would likely crack her skull like she had the antique doll all those years ago.

"Of course, I have a fiancé," Mareen said, taking a step out of striking distance.

She didn't think Scout would hurt her physically. They were blood, after all. There's was the type of family where no outsiders were allowed to pick on any one of the sisters. But all bets were off when it was sister against sister.

"Didn't look like it back there." Scout chucked her head to where Wilson stood huddled with Scout's new husband.

Wilson looked as though he was being chastised as well. What did he have to be chastised for? Mareen was the engaged woman who couldn't stop thinking about kissing a man who wasn't her fiancé.

She was still thinking about it.

She was still wondering how that dark beard would feel against her skin? Would he growl if he pressed his lips to her? Would she feel it all the way in her belly?

"I got bumped by the horse," Mareen managed to get out at the same time as she tamped down on the rampaging images in her mind.

"You expect me to believe that?" Scout swept a doubtful blue gaze up and down Mareen's body. "You've always had horses dancing to your own tune. Men, too."

"What's that supposed to mean?"

"Dad always treated you like you were delicate, but I know you."

That was a lot to unpack. First the part about their father, who Scout never called dad. It was always the General.

Mareen decided to ignore the *delicate* part. Everyone treated her like she was some soft, shattery thing. That was by her mother's design. Mareen never had any choice but to play along.

"You don't know me." That was what Mareen decided to focus on. "You never took the chance to get to know me. You just made up your mind that I was the enemy. And that was it."

Scout opened her mouth. Then closed it. She pressed her lips together as her gaze softened.

Mareen held very still. She'd never seen her oldest sister in a moment of indecision. Scout came, saw, and conquered. There were no in-betweens.

Except now Mareen was standing here. In the in-between. With her sister.

The moment broke. The only warning Mareen had was a tiny crinkling sound, like a delicate piece of glass cracking down the center.

"Tell me the truth," Scout finally said. "Is this all just a ploy to get the land from us?"

There was no anger in her voice. No accusation. It sounded as though she was pleading.

But, no. That couldn't be right. Scout was a Silver. Silvers never appealed. They crushed.

"I'm not a cheat." Mareen ground each word out as she stared into blue eyes just like her own. "I'm not our dad."

In a flash, the steel returned to Scout's gaze. "Our dad didn't cheat on my mom."

"No, he just made her so unhappy that she filed for divorce. Twice."

"Just like he was the one to file when it came to your mom," Scout bit out. "Only took him one time to get it right there."

Mareen bristled. Not at Scout's words. Her sister was right; her mother was a hard woman to live with. As her one and only child, Mareen knew that better than anybody. The reason Mareen bristled was because she couldn't disagree with her sister, but she didn't want Scout to know that.

Scout always thought she was right. Often she was. This was not that instance.

It wasn't the only thing Scout may be right about in this instance. Mareen was cheating. She would never cheat her sisters. Because despite what Scout thought, Mareen loved her sisters and didn't want any harm to come to them. Which was why she'd never told her mother about the priceless doll that still had a hairline crack in her porcelain face.

It was her fiancé that Mareen was cheating on. Her gaze swept once more to Wilson. At that moment, his head lifted, and she felt the heat of those green eyes.

Mareen had never swooned at the thought of kissing Stephán. Her blood didn't come to a simmer when his skin brushed hers. Her heart had never once skipped a beat when he looked at her. Not even when he asked her to marry him.

Mareen had known the proposal was coming. She'd been angling for it for a year. Well, her mother had. Mareen had simply allowed her mother to dress her up, prop her up, and place her where Catherine thought she'd look the best.

She didn't love Stephán, and thank goodness for that. Mareen knew that all love was good for was the breaking of hearts. She liked Stephán. She knew they would be good together. They were completely compatible, which was what a marriage should be. There would be no divorce in this marriage. Because there would be nothing to break.

Mareen looked down, breaking the gaze she shared with Wilson. She felt instantly cold without the warmth of those green eyes on hers. Then she gave herself a shake. She wasn't cold. This was her normal body temperature. This was the condition in which she'd chosen to live for the rest of her life. She could weather this, especially if it meant saving the ranch she secretly loved so dearly.

"Mo?"

Mareen's head shot up. Scout never called her that. Not even when they were young.

"Do you love him?"

Mareen truly wasn't sure which *him* her sister meant. She couldn't answer *no* with regards to Stephán. Her lips wouldn't form the word *no* with regards to Wilson. So, she gave the only answer she could.

"Wilson probably saved my life."

Scout said nothing. But those blue eyes bored into Mareen. The bully weight of them pushed past most of her defenses. But not all. There was a surefire weapon in her arsenal, and Mareen pulled the trigger.

"I'm getting married to Stephán. If I don't, you have no hope of keeping this land."

"I don't understand why you're doing this, Mareen."

"Despite what you might think about me, I do care about this place. My mother doesn't. I know what she would do if she got that deed."

"I'll believe it when I see you walk down the aisle," said Scout. "Too bad I'm not invited to your wedding."

For a moment, Mareen wondered if that was her older sister's way of hedging for an invite. But then Scout turned on her heel and walked into the barn. So, that was a loud no. Some things never changed.

CHAPTER TWELVE

"Are you trying to sabotage this operation?"

Linc was in Wilson's face, his dark gaze intent on him. His former leader poked him in his chest to emphasize his point. Wilson ignored all that. What angered him about Linc's posture was that his shoulders blocked his view of Mareen.

Wilson didn't like having the woman out of his sight. What if she stepped on an ant mount next? Or a bird flew into her face. Or a butterfly whizzed by and caused her to stumble. Any number of things could happen that would put her in danger, and he couldn't see her, so he'd know when to step in and yank her out of harm's way.

Deep down, Wilson knew the woman was made of strong stuff. She was a Silver sister. She was the daughter of a general. But trouble appeared attached to her heels these days. He needed to be near her to bat it away.

"This isn't an operation, Lincoln."

Wilson kept his voice low. He'd already seen Scout's reaction when she'd thought Linc's courtship of her was nothing more than a military operation set up by her father. Wilson wasn't entirely sure that the men's presence on this ranch wasn't an elaborate scheme of the general's. The man had been one of the most brilliant tacticians the military ever raised. This whole situation on the ranch had his signature written all over it. Complete with sneak attacks, evasive maneuvers, and ambushes.

But was Wilson the type of man that General Silver would've wanted for one of his daughters? He'd come from nothing. The military hadn't just been the best option for him. It had been his only option.

He'd spent the first years of his life in an orphanage before they found his birth mother. She was in his life for only a heartbeat, and that had been too long.

To put it kindly, his biological mother had been a product of the streets. She'd been born there, was raised there, and she'd worked there. He'd been born when she'd only turned sixteen. Figuring out who his father was would be harder than looking for a needle in a haystack.

The first eighteen years of his life had been a fight. It made sense to keep fighting for the rest of his life. But this time with a purpose.

He'd had his enlistment papers ready months before and was in line for his birthday. The duffel bag he'd been issued during Basic Training was the closest thing he'd ever had to a home of his own. Basic Training had been a cakewalk for him. He couldn't understand the crybabies and complainers in the ranks. If this was all he'd had to do to keep a roof over his head and three square meals a day, it was nothing. And then he'd been picked by General Silver to join his President's Men team.

For a time, Wilson had wondered if it was just his name that got him that golden ticket. He'd never told the general his mother had chosen the name based on the hospital street sign where she'd delivered him.

He'd worked hard to earn his place. But he'd never been sure he belonged. Because he had never belonged.

"Mareen's engagement is what could save this place."

Linc's words were a cold bucket of water to Wilson's face. He might not know where he belonged, but something inside of him told him that Mareen Silver belonged near him, next to him, protected inside his arms.

"If you keep dallying with her, it could ruin that."

"Dallying?" Wilson growled. "I'm not dallying. She got bumped by a horse. I caught her."

"She's an accomplished horsewoman. They all are. So are we. The general taught us all. You think a little bump was gonna knock her down?"

The mention of the general's name added ice to the bucket of water now dripping down Wilson's shoulders. He shrugged away from Linc's accusing thumb. Then he gave the man his back for good measure. But it was too late.

Already, that last scene, the last moments of the general's life played in Wilson's mind. That look in those blue eyes. That bright flash of fear. The dark glare of resignation. Followed by that *something*, that look that Wilson had never been able to decipher. It was that look that kept him up at night, not the fire and blackness that came after it.

All of the President's Men knew that they might pay the ultimate sacrifice when they signed up. They all went into every mission with their eyes wide open. Wilson desperately wanted to know what the general had been trying to communicate to him the last time he'd seen the man's eyes wide open.

"Wilson," Linc's voice softened. "Look, I didn't—"

"I heard you the first time. I didn't follow orders with the general. I'm not going to make the same mistake again. I'm shipping out."

"We don't want you to leave."

"It's for the best. There's nothing I can do here."

Maybe the reason Mareen kept getting into scrapes was because of him. That fort had stood for years until he'd wondered near it. That snake had been minding its own business until he stepped in its path. And Mareen was an accomplished rider. She'd been around horses longer than he had. A little bump was nothing to her. It was likely Wilson stepping in that caused that as well.

It was him. He was the problem. If he didn't get out of here soon, she might end up just like her father. And it would all be because of him.

CHAPTER THIRTEEN

*M*areen leaned over the fencing. Her upper body felt heavy and tired, but her legs were restless. They wanted to move. She just didn't know where to go.

Colonel Brandon trotted over to her side of the fencing. The horse lifted his knees in accented flexion in the dressage dance move known as The Passage. Clearly, he wasn't done dancing. Mareen wasn't surprised. None of her sisters had taken to the sport of dressage, so she knew that poor Colonel Brandon wasn't routinely exercised in the way she'd worked him out when she'd spent more time on the ranch.

It was yet another reason why she didn't want her mother getting her hands on this place. Catherine had balked when Mareen took to riding. When she saw the type of men who gathered at tournaments -men from wealthy families of good names- she quickly backtracked, doing a passage of her own.

Now the Mareen was engaged to one of the most upper-crust men in the city, Catherine saw no need to keep a horse. Much less for Mareen to continue with her horse dancing or even keep her horse. Saylor hadn't hesitated when Mareen asked to board Colonel Brandon on the ranch. She knew that if her mother got that deed, not only would her sisters go, but she'd never see her equine friend again.

"You okay, Mo?"

Brig walked toward Mareen, leading a horse Mareen didn't know. He was a beautiful blond horse. But there were wicked scars along his coat. Mareen instantly reached out to the horse. But he shied away from her touch.

"It's okay, Bingley. She's a friend. She won't hurt you."

Bingley appeared to heed Brig's words. He took a tentative step forward. He lowered his beautiful head. Soulful eyes watched Mareen wearily as her hand came to rest lightly on his muzzle.

"Bingley came to us a few months ago. He got caught in a fence wire. His human miscreants felt he wasn't beautiful anymore and therefore of no value."

Mareen felt tears prick her eyes at the utter baseness of some of humanity. To neglect such a beautiful creature. And then cast it off when they no longer wanted to look at it.

"If we lose this place, no one will take him. No one will take any of these horses because they won't see the value."

"You're not losing this place," Mareen said. "You have to trust me that my plan will work."

Mareen was so used to seeing her baby sister with mischief in those wide blue eyes. Her heart stuttered when Brig's brows drew close, and doubt radiated from beneath her lashes.

"You don't trust me?" It pained Mareen more than she knew to say the words.

"I trust you," Brig said. "I don't think *you* trust you."

Now it was Mareen's brows that drew together.

"Marriage is a big deal, Mo. No one knows that better than the six of us. If we've learned anything from our parents' mistakes, it's that when we get married, it should be to the right person, for the right reasons."

"It is," said Mareen. "I am."

But Brig shook her head, her gaze sad. There was still no hint of mischief in those blue eyes. Instead, they were clear with a wisdom the twenty-year-old should not possess.

"If you get married to save us and in the process lose yourself, I will never forgive you. None of us will."

"So what? You all can marry these strangers to save the ranch, but I can't?"

They hadn't even told Mareen of their plan. She'd only figured it out after Scout's impromptu wedding. They were leaving her out. Setting her aside as though she wasn't truly one of them.

"Scout and Saylor are in love."

"Are you in love?"

Brig didn't answer. She smiled a secret smile and looked off in the distance. In the direction of her gaze walked two soldiers. A dark-haired man with over styled hair that somehow worked for him. And a brown-skinned man with a touch of gray at his temples. Both men looked too old for her coed sister.

"You're too young to get married." For a second, Mareen was ready to whirl around, certain she'd heard the scolding tone of her oldest sister. But that hadn't been Scout admonishing the baby of the family. It had been her. "You have your whole life ahead of you, Brigadear."

"So do you. Especially if you're planning to have a loveless marriage. Or tell me I'm wrong. Do you love your fiancé?"

Mareen opened her mouth. Then closed it. Only to scoff at her sister. "You're being a child."

"Hmmm," Brig said with all the superiority of someone three times her age. Her gaze wasn't on Mareen. It was on the two men who were off in the distance but closer now.

Now that they were closer, Mareen saw that she'd been mistaken. There weren't two men walking. There were three. She knew without needing to see his features that the third man was Wilson.

Mareen was holding her breath with each step he took. Her head felt like stars were spinning around inside. Something was fluttering around in her stomach.

Not butterflies. Maybe a bird? Or two?

She took a step but stopped. Something told her to look down. When she did, she saw a rake lying on the ground. One more step and she would've stepped directly on it, and it would've clocked her in the head.

Was that a sign? It had to be a sign. A sign to stay away from that man. Whenever the two of them were in proximity of one another, danger was always near.

When she looked back up, she noted that Wilson was looking directly at her. Their eyes locked. She would've sworn his gaze was asking her if she was okay.

She didn't feel okay. She felt like she had been knocked on the head. She also felt certain that the only way to make it right was to snuggle deep inside his arms.

Wilson took a step toward her as though hearing her silent plea. A chiming sounded in the distance. The ringing grew louder.

Mareen realized the sound was coming from her pocket. It was her cell phone. She looked down at the device and saw her fiancé's name on the caller ID.

Wilson must have read something on her face. His lips pinched together. His brows drew. And he turned and walked away.

Mareen looked at her sister. Brig's eyes were no longer drawn in doubt. Now they were wide with mischief. She turned on her heel and led Bingley away.

"Hello, Stephán. How are you?"

"Ah, there you are, dear. I'm between meetings and wanted to give you a call."

"Checking up on me?"

There was a pause on the phone, as though Stephán covered the speaker so that he could talk with someone else.

Mareen waited patiently. Stephán Bushnell was a busy man. Most of their courtship had been done during business lunches or cocktail parties or evening fundraisers.

"Sorry about that, dear."

"It's fine."

"Are you still on your family farm?"

"Ranch," Mareen corrected. "It's a ranch."

"Is there a difference?"

Mareen took a deep breath and let that slide. She had to remind herself that Stephán's ownership would be better than her mother's because her mother would likely turn the ranch into a farm.

"How much longer will you be there? We have a cocktail party for the new Granger building this weekend."

"I'll be back in time for it."

"Good. I find that I'm missing you." His voice sounded quizzical. As though he'd found a misplaced file he'd long forgotten about.

"You could come out here," she heard herself saying. "See the place you'll be buying for yourself."

"Me? On a farm?" Stephán laughed.

"I thought you might like to meet my family."

"I have met your family. I met your mother."

"You haven't met my sisters."

"I thought you didn't get along with your sisters."

"I'm working on that."

That was another of the reasons Mareen wanted to strike this deal. If she could save the ranch, maybe it would get her into the good graces of her sisters. Not that she needed grace for four of her sisters. It was only one where the fences between them needed mending. Or maybe some fresh paint. Or probably brand new wood and nails.

"It's near impossible. I'm too busy." And then he sighed. "But for you, dear, I'll see if I can move some things around."

"Really?" Mareen hadn't expected him to actually try.

Now she wasn't sure about having her big city fiancé on the ranch. But she had to convince her sisters she was serious about this plan. Or maybe she just had to convince herself?

CHAPTER FOURTEEN

ilson put the tractor in gear. He'd dropped his duffle bag back in Scout's old bunk. He'd be living there from here on out. Jackson and Carter had found him after Linc's impassioned speech. They'd cornered him and fairly twisted his arm to stay.

It hadn't taken much twisting, to be honest. Wilson had no place else to go, and there was no place else he'd rather be. The men here wanted him to stay. That was a big deal to a man who had never belonged. Like it or not, these guys were his family. And like true family, the blood that stained their uniforms was thicker than water.

Besides, Wilson wouldn't have Mareen Silver to worry about much longer. She was getting married and would be beyond his reach. She already wasn't within his reach. She was so far out of his league that it was laughable. The only reasons he'd been anywhere near her were all due to freak accidents.

He'd saved her life, which he had assumed was why he'd been spared in that last mission. If he couldn't go back into the military, then he'd spend the rest of his life tending to the land the general loved. It would only be Mareen's for a few days before her future husband sold it to her sisters. Then he'd likely never see her again.

She and her sisters didn't get along so well, and by the looks of Mareen's frosty relationship with Scout, that didn't look like it would change anytime soon.

So, it was all over. It had never begun. Which was why he walked farther away from her. He needed something to do, something to keep him occupied until she left. She couldn't be staying much longer. She was a city girl. She'd be going back any moment now.

Wilson climbed into the tractor in a distant pasture. Like his own hair, the pasture was overgrown and needed a good trim. Scout had asked him to tend to it a couple of days ago, but he'd been busy with other chores.

He set the ancient vehicle into motion. It sputtered and protested. But only for a moment. Then it kicked into gear and headed up the hill. He might be staying, but he needed to be away from everyone else. He still preferred his solitude. Survivor's guilt wasn't going to let him go that easily.

It looked as though his connection to Mareen wasn't going to let him go either. Wilson spotted her at the bottom of the hill. She walked with the horse she'd been dancing with earlier. Her lips moved as though she talked to the animal. Its head bobbed up and down as though it responded to her.

A small smile played on Wilson's lips. At least she couldn't get into any harm out this far. No rickety treehouses in sight. Too much activity for snakes to want to roam about. And no rakes were underfoot -at least he hoped not.

The only danger to Mareen Silver out here was him. But he was too far up the hill to cause any commotion. He didn't plan to go back down until she was good and out of his sight.

The tractor came to a stop on its amble up the hill. Wilson stepped on the gas pedal. For a second, the vehicle obeyed. It rolled forward and then came to another dead stop. Before the stop, Wilson had heard the distinct sound of a crack. Like an egg, only bigger and denser.

He put the vehicle in park and hopped out. Looking down, he

saw he'd hit a rock. The large stone had indeed split its middle like a cracked egg.

Before he could hop back in the tractor to back it up, it rolled a few feet away. Then another few feet backward. At this angle on the hill, the tractor was liable to keep heading downwards unless Wilson could stop its momentum.

He grabbed for the broken rock. But by the time he had the makeshift brake in hand, the tractor had rolled a few more feet. Even worse, it was picking up momentum. Wilson's heart pumped hard in his chest as he took off after it.

The tractor came to a stop. He wasn't fooled. If the last two days had taught him anything, he knew the possibilities that lay before him. Or rather, lay down that slope.

A fall from a treehouse. A snake bite. A near rake to the forehead. It all pointed to one inevitability. Mareen was at the bottom of this hill. Even if it killed him, Wilson swore that tractor would never reach her.

He tossed away the rock and kept running. Just as he passed the stalled vehicle, it began moving again. But he was already ahead of it.

Wilson called out to Mareen. She looked up, her head bobbing like a bird's searching for the source of the sound. She caught his gaze for a second and then looked past him. Her eyes went wide.

She gave the horse a slap on its hindquarters. The animal took off running at a clip. But Mareen didn't follow suit. Instead, she ran toward Wilson.

A look over his shoulder told Wilson that the tractor was now aiming for him. That didn't kick his heart beat up any faster. It could crash into him, and the world wouldn't miss a beat. As long as it didn't—

The tractor slid off its current path. Its new path was in alignment with Mareen, who was making her way up the hill. Wilson picked up his speed.

He and Mareen reached each other just in time. Wilson tackled her to the ground, rolling on top of her in the tall reeds of grass. A loud booming crash sounded in his ears.

When he opened his eyes, the tractor was at the bottom of the hill. He and Mareen were off to the side. But that wasn't all.

Wilson was on top of Mareen. True, his body sheltered hers. His body also felt every one of her lush curves.

He should be glad that her body wasn't broken or flattened by the runaway vehicle. He should be glad that he'd gotten to her in time. None of that mattered.

All he could think about was her soft, sweet breaths hitting his lips. All he could feel was her racing pulse as he cradled her face in his hands. All he could see was the blue in her eyes.

For the first time, that particular shade of color didn't make him feel guilt or remorse. It lit Wilson with a desire that would not be contained. Before he could think better of it, his mouth was against hers.

CHAPTER FIFTEEN

Contrary to what some might believe, which were beliefs solely based on her looks and her social status, Mareen Silver hadn't been kissed a lot. There were, of course, the awkward pecks of her paramours at the ends of dates arranged between her mother and other society matrons. There were the French greetings where men kissed both sides of her cheek -some a little too close to her mouth for her comfort. And there were the few kisses she'd exchanged with her fiancé where she'd had to begrudgingly open her mouth to let him in.

Mareen had never understood the preoccupation with kissing. She had been a picky eater all of her life. So it followed that she didn't want someone else's lips against hers. Forget about having their tongue in her mouth.

That lifelong aversion changed the moment Wilson's mouth met hers.

At the first brush of his lips, a hunger flared deep within her belly. It grumbled so loudly she was certain they could hear it back at the house. Possibly even as far as Father Matthews's land.

On the second brush of Wilson's lips against hers, a loud thudding sound came from her chest. It felt as though her heart had crashed. First against her rib cage. Then down into the pit of her stomach.

She knew what this was. She had fallen. Mareen had fallen so hard for this man that she knew she would never stand on her own again unless he was beside her.

The grumbling in her belly increased. The thudding of her heart beat double time. Mareen would've been embarrassed with all the ruckus her body was making, except she was too consumed with desire. She tilted her head up to give Wilson better access to her mouth, to her heart, to her whole being.

When she let out a sigh, she felt the velvet of his tongue snake against her bottom lip. Mareen had been bitten by a snake, but she felt rattled at that. Her lips parted and allowed Wilson inside to deepen the kiss.

Wilson took what she gave him, but it was Mareen who demanded more. Her arms wrapped around him, and she clung for dear life. Because it was her life at stake.

"Sweetheart," Wilson moaned against her parted lips, "we can't."

Can't? They already had. The only can't that was going to happen was that no one be able to take these feelings, these sensations, this desire away from her.

"You're engaged." Wilson's words were spoken breathlessly, as though he were presently fighting an arduous battle. He didn't let her go as he spoke the single truth that should keep them apart. He pressed his forehead to hers and sighed.

Mareen didn't want his forehead pressed against hers. She wanted his lips back. She even wanted his tongue.

"I can't do it," she said. "I can't marry him."

Wilson's lips trembled as they brushed against her forehead. It wasn't enough. She needed those lips trembling against her lips.

"I always thought it would be better to marry a man that I didn't have feelings for," she continued. "That way I wouldn't get hurt."

Wilson cupped her cheek in his palm. He tilted her head so that he could gaze directly into her eyes. Without any words, Mareen saw clearly that there were just as many feelings in that gaze as she had inside of her.

Her hand rested against his chest. His heart beat just as strongly and loudly as hers. The trembling wasn't only on his lips. She heard it lower with the rumbling of his belly. Wilson was feeling exactly what she was feeling.

Staring into his vulnerable gaze, feeling the shivers in his big body, any hint of fear at the emotions swirling between them fled Mareen's every thought. She'd learned to be afraid of love at a young age. What was happening to her was also happening to him. They were in this together. Wilson didn't look afraid. He looked determined. It gave her the strength she needed to take the next step.

"I'm going to call off the wedding."

Wilson let out a low sigh. The side of his lips pulled together in a pinch of what looked like distaste. He looked away from her then. When he did, Mareen's heart fell again. Only this time, there was nothing to cushion the blow. This time it hurt.

Had she read him wrong? Was Wilson not experiencing the same emotions that were wreaking havoc on her body and clouding her cool judgment? Maybe all he wanted was a roll in the hay they were currently laying in? This was only their first kiss. It didn't mean they would get married. Even if the idea of not spending every day of her life from this moment forward with him felt like a dagger twisting in Mareen's heart.

So this was what it was like to fall in love? To be flying high one moment. Only to be flung low the next. Love sucked.

Mareen needed to pull on her facade of cool nonchalance. To do that, she needed to put distance between her and Wilson. But his arms were still wrapped tightly around her. In fact, they pulled her closer and locked even more securely around her.

Wilson's shoulders had gone soldier rigid. His gaze was locked on something in the distance. He was using his body to block Mareen from whatever danger was near.

When Mareen saw the trouble headed their way, she was glad for Wilson's protective armor around her. Even if he didn't have feelings for her, she wouldn't shy away from using him as a shield. Though she was sure they both were about to be eviscerated.

Scout ran toward them. Her steps slowed after she passed the toppled tractor. Her gaze narrowed as she took in the two of them, still caught up in a lover's embrace.

Mareen's heart took another tumbling plummet. This fall was familiar. All her life, all Mareen wanted was to fit in with her sister. To come and visit the ranch whenever she wanted and not just on holidays. She wanted this to be a home for her. She might've had that if she'd stuck to her plan. But now that her desire for Wilson was clear for all eyes to see, she realized she might lose the man her heart wanted. But she knew for certain she'd lost the fragile shred of trust of the sister whose love she'd so desperately wanted all her life.

CHAPTER SIXTEEN

*W*ilson stood, pulling Mareen against his chest as he did so. She came willingly, as though she wasn't able to stand without him. As though she was permanently attached to him. He liked that feeling.

She was inside his arms, safe and sound. That had been his initial goal. And now the dream he dared not dream was coming true.

She was his.

She wasn't going to get married to the fiancé with the girl's name. She'd told him so. Now they just had to tell everyone else.

Starting with the woman glaring at them. Scout Silver was a force to be reckoned with. If she had joined the military, she would've felled enemy combatants with just that glare. World peace would've commenced a decade ago and held fast because no one would've dared crossed the woman.

"What happened?" Scout demanded.

Mareen's fingers clutched at the material of his shirt. He felt the heat of her through the fabric and momentarily forgot the threat they were facing. All Wilson wanted to do was get Mareen alone and continue the kiss they'd started. Continue and never, ever let it end. First, they had to face the firing squad.

"The tractor came down the hill," Wilson said in response to Scout. "It nearly crashed into her."

There was a brief silence. Then Scout gave a barely perceptible nod. In her hooded blue eyes, Wilson saw a familiar flash of emotions; fear, resignation, then… Then Mareen was being pulled from his arms. Wilson nearly didn't let go.

"Oh my gosh, Mo." Scout crushed her sister to her chest.

Mareen couldn't answer. Her eyes were wide, her cheeks pink from the force of the impact.

"Are you okay?" Scout pulled away from her sister but didn't let go. She patted Mareen's cheeks, ran her fingers through her hair, peered into her eyes. "Are you hurt?"

"I'm okay." Mareen stared in clear bewilderment at her older sister as Scout looked her over for bumps and bruises.

"What are you even doing out here?" Scout demanded. "You were bitten by a snake the other day."

"I just—"

"You're coming back to the house and laying down. Have you eaten? Do you have a fever?"

"I—no." Mareen brushed Scout's hand from her forehead. "Scout, wait."

Scout stopped and stared at her sister. "Can you walk? Do you need to be carried?" She snapped her fingers at Wilson. "Pick her up and carry her."

Wilson hopped into action. It was a command he would more than enjoy performing. But Mareen stayed him with her hand.

"Scout, wait," Mareen said again.

When Scout finally held still and gave Mareen her full attention, Mareen seemed at a loss for words. She turned to Wilson. He wasn't sure where she was going, but he stepped up to her side, letting her know he had her back.

"Aren't you angry?" Mareen finally got out.

"Look, I'm sorry." Scout's lip curled as she tossed a glance to the side. "I should've gotten rid of that old tractor. It's definitely going to the scrap heap now."

"No, not about the tractor," said Mareen. Then she stopped and looked back at Wilson. "About us?"

Scout looked between them. She waited as her head swiveled back and forth once, twice. "What about you two?"

Wilson wanted to answer for Mareen, but he somehow knew she had to do this on her own.

"We're..." Mareen began and stopped. Her cheeks were completely red now.

Wilson found the blush lovely, but he wasn't sure why it was there? Was she ashamed of what was between them? Did she regret it?

No, he didn't think so. That was shyness in her gaze. Doubt.

What did she have to doubt? Certainly not him. He took her hand in his, feeling his entire body come to life as her fingers entwined with his.

"We're together." It came out of Mareen's mouth like a question. She even looked to Wilson for confirmation.

In answer, Wilson draped his arm around her shoulder and pulled her in close. For good measure, he planted a kiss to her temple, just because he now had the right to do so. Exercising that right made him feel stronger than he had in months, probably years.

In his arms, he felt Mareen brace for Scout's blowup. Her shoulders tensed as she looked back at her sister. Scout's blowup came out in a snort.

"Yeah, I figured," said Scout. "Like we all haven't seen the two of you making gooey eyes at each other for the past two days."

"You have?" asked Mareen.

"Gooey eyes?" objected Wilson.

"But the deal with Stephán," said Mareen. "It'll fall through."

"I never thought you'd marry him to begin with." Scout shrugged. "Then when I saw the way you looked at Wilson, I knew it wasn't going to happen at all."

"B-but..." Mareen stammered. "But you'll lose the ranch."

Scout turned to face Wilson. Those piercing blue eyes were like lasers on him. He felt it wasn't just her glaring at him but her father from above. "What are your intentions with my sister, soldier?"

"To care for and protect her for the rest of our lives," Wilson answered immediately.

"Does that include a ring?"

"If she'll have one."

Scout nodded. "Three down. Three to go. Now carry her back to the house, would you? I don't want her fainting."

"I wouldn't faint," Mareen protested.

But Scout was already marching away.

Mareen turned back Wilson. Indignation was written all across her face. "Do you see what I mean? She doesn't listen to anybody. She thinks she's always right."

In this case, Scout was right. But Wilson wasn't fool enough to press his luck. Instead, he did as his leader ordered him. Wilson scooped Mareen into his arms and began in the direction of the house.

"So…" he said.

"So?"

"So, will you marry me?" he asked.

"You don't think it's too soon? I mean, we only just met."

Wilson let his gaze rest on Mareen's beautiful face. It felt right. He felt right. It was the right place, the right time.

"You're just doing this to help save the ranch, right? It's not… it doesn't…" Mareen ducked her head as she spoke.

Wilson waited patiently for her to lift her head and meet his eyes. When Mareen's blue gaze met his, he saw the general reflected back at him. This time he realized what that unnameable emotion in the man's eyes had been; hope.

"I'll marry you to save the ranch," he said.

That hoped flared and fizzled in Mareen's gaze, pushing him to finish the true part of the deal he wanted to strike.

"But you'll have to promise to stay with me for the rest of your life."

Mareen lifted her gaze once more. The hope there was a delicate flicker.

"It'll be easier on my nerves if I can keep an eye on you for forever," he went on. "I have a fierce need to protect you, Mareen Silver. I want to keep you safe. I also want to hold you close."

"You do?"

Wilson nodded. He wanted to tell her that there was more. He wanted to tell her that he'd fallen hard for her. But Wilson had never loved anyone in his life. Having been discarded by the one person who was supposed to love him unconditionally, he wasn't quite sure how these things would go. If Mareen agreed to spend a lifetime with him, he would figure it out.

"So, is it a deal? Will you marry me?"

"Yes," said Mareen. "Yes, I will."

The flicker in her eyes was now a spark; a spark of… something. Wilson wasn't sure what it was. But he'd be happy to dream of it for the rest of his days.

CHAPTER SEVENTEEN

Mareen felt warmth coursing up and down her forearm. It started when Wilson had reached for her hand after she'd agreed to marry him. She was getting married. To Wilson.

When she'd accepted Stephán's proposal, it had been to raucous applause in the formal dining area of their club. And by raucous, Mareen meant that the clapping had light taps against palms accompanied by murmurs of appreciation and jealousy.

Out in the fields, crickets strummed their hind legs together in blaring serenade. Butterflies flapped their wings, making Mareen think she heard the chiming of windpipes. Birds lent their voices in a chorus of sincere congratulations.

She was losing her mind. She didn't care. She was getting married. To Wilson.

Wilson Michaels.

Mareen Michaels.

Yes, she liked the ring it had to it.

As Mareen and Wilson walked side-by-side back to the house, he laced his fingers with hers. His fingers were blunt objects with calluses and ragged nails. Where her manicure was still in place, though now tipped with dirt from her fall. Mareen decided she liked the dirt tips, but not nearly as much as she liked the heat coming off her new fiancé. The feeling was so strong, so powerful that it made her shiver.

"You cold?" Wilson asked, his breath whooshed against her temple as he spoke.

She was having sensory overload just from standing next to this man. Mareen gazed up into his eyes. A stupid smile spread across her face as she looked at the rugged angles of him, freely for once, and not sneaking glances. Wilson let go of her hand and draped his forearm over her shoulder.

Now engulfed inside his body heat, Mareen shivered again. Not because she was overly warm. She shivered because the realization hit her that she would get to experience these sensations for the rest of her life, starting from this moment.

The warmth all through her body when Wilson touched her, the goofy looks when their gazes met, the foggy head when his lips brushed against hers, these were all the signs her mother warned her about. Mareen had done the one thing she'd sworn she'd never do. She'd fallen in love with a man. She'd fallen hard, so hard that she'd lost her good sense and was about to make a bad business decision.

Mareen reached down to her left ring finger and tugged at the rock weighing her down. With Stephán's ring gone, Mareen felt entirely untethered to her old life. She felt free. She was floating, but she knew she wouldn't go far. Wilson had a hold on her, and Mareen wanted nothing more than to be tied to this man in every way possible.

Not just in name, but in body, in soul, in spirit. And yes, in her heart.

"Told you so," said Brig. "Pay up, Tilly."

Mareen looked up to see that her sisters lounged on the porch at the front of the house. Brig sat with her feet up on the wooden fence, a huge grin on her face. Tilly leaned against a post, a scowl as she dug into her back pocket. Saylor and her fiancé Jeff swung slightly on the porch swing. Scout took the steps two at a time to come into her husband's arms.

"You, too, Truman."

Truman wore the same scowl as Tilly. He glared at Wilson as he opened his wallet and pulled out a bill.

"Never bet against a Silver sister," said Brig as she held the two bills up in triumph and began a shimmying dance.

Tilly and Truman continued their salty glares. In a corner, the older soldier, Jackson, failed to hide a grin as he watched Brig dance around. Jackson turned away when Wilson sent the man a questioning smirk.

"So," said Tilly. "Looks like the easy way of keeping this place is off the table now that you've hitched your ride to this soldier."

"I'm sorry," said Mareen.

She might be getting the guy that she'd never dared to dream about, but her sisters would suffer for it. It was the divorce all over again. Sides were about to be drawn, and Mareen would be left on the outside again.

In fact, the sides were already apparent. Mareen stood on the ground, looking up at her sisters. All of them were on the porch, looking down on her.

"Sorry for what?" said Saylor, coming down the porch steps. She held her arms open and embraced Mareen.

"Because..." Mareen had to stop speaking. Her words were muffled with her head pressed against Saylor's chest. "I had it all planned out, and I went AWOL."

"You found love," Saylor smiled at her. "You're happy."

Both of those statements were true. None of her sisters scowled at her. Even Tilly's frown was gone now.

"You guys aren't mad?" Mareen held her breath as she waited for the response.

"It wouldn't have been right if you'd married someone you didn't love just for us," said Brig, bringing up the next hug.

"But now we'll all lose the ranch," said Mareen. "My mother-"

"We're not losing the ranch," said Scout. "The same plan is in place. Tilly's got some prospects with her online dating. Jackson and Carter are on board. One of them will marry Brig and the other Gunny -if we can just get Gunny back to this side of the world in time."

"But they'll be marrying for convenience," said Mareen. "Why is that okay for them?"

"Because those will be a temporary agreement," said Scout. "Not a real marriage."

Mareen looked at Brig, she caught her little sister sneaking a glance at Jackson. It was a glance that said Brig was in for a different type of agreement.

"So, really the only wild card is Tilly," said Scout.

"Thanks, sis," huffed Tilly. "Do not underestimate my ability to wrap a man around my finger."

Tilly held up her index finger as case in point. Coiffed-hair Carter snorted. When Tilly turned to glare at him, he shrugged in nonchalance.

Before any words could be exchanged, a car kicked up rocks on its way down the gravel road. It was a luxury car that had no business being in this part of the country. It was a car that was familiar to Mareen.

"Uh no," sighed Mareen. "I forgot I'd called him."

"Called who?" asked Wilson.

"It's my fiancé."

"Steven?" asked Scout.

Mareen didn't bother correcting her sister. It didn't matter any longer. Stephán wasn't going to be part of the family.

Wilson squeezed Mareen's hand, letting her know they would face him together. But when the car came to a stop, Mareen saw another woman in the passenger seat.

"It's my mother."

CHAPTER EIGHTEEN

Wilson eyed Stephán with an accent as the man climbed out of the luxury car. That vehicle likely cost a soldier's annual salary. No, scratch that. The price tag on that car was probably double what the military had paid Wilson to risk his life for this nation. Meanwhile, this man in a suit sat back in a cushy office off Wilson's and his brothers' blood and sweat.

Wilson hated him on sight. Stephán had an easy smile that said the world owed him everything. His suit was tailored to fit his lean form. A speck of dust dared to land on the toe of his expensive shoes. Stephán glared down at it, and the speck fell away.

Then he looked up, reaching out his hands for Mareen. Was that polish glistening off his fingernails? Really? A manicure? And Wilson wasn't supposed to make fun of him?

Mareen must've felt the tension running through him. She squeezed her hand around his bicep. Wilson pulled her close. With his gaze locked on her former fiancé, he planted a kiss at her temple.

Stephán stumbled. A few more specks covered his once glistening shoes, now dulling their shine. Stephán's amiable smile turned into a grimace of clear disapproval.

Wilson tensed for an attack. He would welcome one. But the

missile launched at him came from a place where he could not retaliate.

"I'll thank you to get your filthy hands off my daughter."

The older woman was beautiful, stunning even. If she was what Wilson had to look forward to as Mareen aged, he was a lucky man indeed. Catherine Chesterfield Silver was beauty personified. Except in the eyes.

Her eyes were dark, almost black. Though the rest of her skin was smooth, the wrinkles gathered at her eyes told all for miles that she was not someone to be trifled with. And those black eyes were on Wilson. He very nearly backed away from Mareen under that commanding glare, except for the fact that the woman he loved clung to him.

Wilson had faced down armed insurgents. He'd survived an ambush with low ammo. He'd even walked away from a bomb blast.

But the bravest thing he'd ever done in his life was to pull Mareen close instead of following the command of her mother. The woman who would be his mother-in-law, heaven help him. When Wilson didn't budge, Catherine turned her attention to her daughter.

"I had to learn from your fiancé," —and yes, Catherine emphasized the word fiancé along with a head jerk toward Stephán— "that not only were you out of town but that you were here on this godforsaken dirt mound."

Wilson heard a scuffle behind him. From the corner of his eyes, he saw Linc holding Scout back with one hand, followed by a double-armed bear hug.

"Mareen," said Stephán, "what's going on?"

It was clear the man was indicating the way she stood shoulder to shoulder with Wilson. Probably he was also referring to how they were hand in hand. And Wilson knew Stephán hadn't missed that kiss to her temple.

They were all lucky that Wilson didn't dip Mareen back and claim her mouth the way he wanted to, the way he—and he alone—

now had the right to. With just the first glance, it was clear to Wilson that this man would've never matched Mareen.

Stephán's tailoring was too close-cut for the woman whom Wilson had met dressed in scuffed cowboy boots. He was too stiff for the woman who taught horses to dance. He was too clean for the woman Wilson had rolled in the hay with. Even now, there were still a few twigs and weeds in Mareen's loose hairdo.

"Is this one of the childhood friends you told me about?" Stephán tried, but there was a tremor of doubt in the man's cultured tones that broadcast that he didn't believe it. "One of the Matthews boys?"

"No, Stephán. And I'm sorry, but this is the man I'm going to marry."

There was a moment of silence. The insects creeping around in the grass held their breath. The birds above silenced their songs.

Once again, Wilson braced himself for a battle. Of course, he was expecting one. Mareen was a war prize if ever there was one.

Unlike the accent in his name, Stephán didn't raise his voice. He didn't even raise his head. His lips pursed, and he nodded in what looked like easy acceptance.

Now Wilson was definitely ready to strike. Did the man not think Mareen was worth fighting over? That was insult enough for him.

"Are you out of your mind?"

The screech of Catherine's voice delayed any plan of attack that flitted through Wilson's head. Unlike Stephán, Catherine's brows were drawn up in marks that indicated something needed to be stressed.

"Mother, this doesn't concern you," Mareen said quietly.

"It is my concern if my only daughter is about to throw her life away on some-" Catherine's head whipped back to Wilson. "I bet you're a soldier, aren't you? One of Abraham's men?"

Catherine's head swiveled, taking in each of the men gathered around the porch. Her brows remained high. Yet somehow, she got her lips to curl downward in complete and utter distaste.

"His president's men. The men he took on dangerous missions.

Including the one that got him killed. Which one of you was it?" She looked at each man in turn. "Which one is the one that got him killed?"

True to their breed, every soldier stood with his shoulders straight and his spine stiff. All their mouths set in hard, impenetrable lines. All but Wilson's. For the first time in nearly a year, his body sagged with the accusation. It had never once been leveled at him. He felt the weight of it now.

"Mother, how dare you," said Mareen.

"No, she's right." Wilson uncurled his fingers from the woman he'd fallen hard for. Without her hand in his, Wilson felt all of his strength leave him. "It was my fault. I'm the reason your father is dead."

Mareen had been in the process of reaching for his hand, but her fingers recoiled at his last words. Five pairs of crystal blue eyes looked at him. With the General's daughters' gazes trained on him, Wilson felt like he was standing in the middle of a bomb that he'd detonated himself.

CHAPTER NINETEEN

Mareen's heart ached for Wilson. She had only known him for two days and... Wow, had it only been two rises of the sun? The moon had yet to set on her second day of knowing this man. Yet, she couldn't imagine spending another day without him by her side. So when his strong body bowed at the impact of her mother's words, Mareen felt the pain reverberate through her.

She wanted to wrap her arms around Wilson's drooping shoulders. She wanted to tilt up that proud chin that now angled toward the ground. She wanted to light a match to rekindle the spark that left his eyes.

Wilson blamed himself for her father's death? He'd never mentioned that to her. Though she could imagine it being true with the intense need he seemed to have to keep an eye on her. Was he fearful of her ultimate demise?

Made sense with the near-death experiences she'd had these past two days. But Wilson had to know he had nothing to do with that. Just as she was certain he had nothing to do with her father's death. If there was one lesson the general had drilled into her, had drilled into each of his daughters, it was this; that death would come for him when it was ready.

That's why there hadn't been any tears from his daughters at his funeral. They'd known the cost of what their father had signed up for. The Silver girls may have had problems with their father on the home front, but not one of them took for granted what he did to keep them safe. They all knew the price of the ultimate sacrifice, and they honored it.

Looking around at her sisters, Mareen knew without any of them saying that they each felt the same. Looking at the soldiers who had instinctively come to Wilson's back, she knew they believed it too. The only one who was in doubt was Wilson.

"He pushed me out of the way," Wilson said. His gaze was foggy, as though he were looking at the ghost of her father. "It should've been me, not him."

"Wilson, no—"

But the man Mareen had come to love in so short a time jerked his hand away from her. Mareen cradled her rejected hand as though Wilson had slapped it away. The horror in Wilson's gaze told her that that was what he feared he'd done.

Wilson cursed under his breath. After a harsh exhale, he lifted his head and looked at her. Shame mingled with an emotion Mareen had never had shone upon her. She knew the light in Wilson's gaze was love.

The soft light of love dimmed in a blink. It was replaced with the glare of guilt, of remorse, of anguish.

"I thought I saved you," he said.

"You did save me," she insisted.

"Or maybe I'm the cause of all the bad things."

Mareen opened her mouth to tell him that he'd misunderstood her. She wasn't talking about the fort, or the snake, or the tractor. Wilson had saved her from a life without love. If she had married Stephán, she would've lived a life where she would've been dead inside.

Her voice caught in her throat when Wilson reached for her

hand. Mareen gave it to him willingly, hoping that they were going to get beyond his guilt over her father and the nonsense idea that Wilson didn't deserve her. She felt something cold and sharp land in her palm. Her body iced over when she opened her hand and saw her engagement ring.

"I can't marry you," Wilson said. "If I do, I'll take even more away from your family."

Wilson lifted his head and looked around. Looking in his eyes, Mareen saw that he was taking in all of the ranch. She wanted to shout that she didn't care about the ranch, that she didn't care about any of it. All she cared about was him.

But that wasn't true. There were people on this ranch that they both cared about. There were the memories of Mareen's past that she wanted to hold on to, as well as the memories she'd just made with Wilson that she would never let go of.

Wilson met her gaze again. Mareen felt her heart breaking under the vulnerability this strong man allowed her to witness. He didn't say the words, but Mareen knew them to be true. Wilson loved her.

It looked like he loved her enough to let her go. And so Mareen held onto his hands. Unfortunately, her strength was no match for his. Slowly, Wilson disengaged her fingers from his. When he was done, all that was left was the cold rock.

The ring rooted her in place as she watched Wilson walk away. She could hear her mother's voice behind her, but Mareen couldn't make out any of the words. Instead, Stephán's face filled her vision.

Stephán looked down at the engagement ring in Mareen's palm and then back in her eyes. Mareen noted for the first time that his gaze was green, just a shade lighter than Wilson's. How had she not known that before about the man she had been planning to marry? She'd known Stephán for nearly a year, and she'd missed that detail. She'd known Wilson for just a matter of days and had seen the man's soul.

"Looks like we need to talk," said Stephán.

CHAPTER TWENTY

$\mathcal{M}$arching was one of the first things a soldier learned in boot camp. The repetitive motions were a coordinated effort, but the process became ingrained with how many times the unit performed it.

As Wilson marched away from the one thing that gave him a reason for living, his brain couldn't parse out his right foot from his left. His knees refused to bend to garner any distance. His toes became confused with his heels, and he stumbled more than once.

"Easy there."

Wilson was having a hard enough time on his own trying to get away. He was gutted that Mareen had to watch him. He didn't want any more company.

He wanted to turn and rail at the men in his unit. From the even strides, he could tell there was only one man. And it was the one who was just as stubborn as he was.

"Not now, Jackson."

"No, now is the perfect time." Jackson's even-tone kept the same pace as his measured footfalls. "In fact, this matter is past due."

Wilson stopped. He had to. His feet couldn't carry him any further, especially if he had to turn and fight one of his best friends.

When he did turn, he was surprised to see exactly how much distance he'd put between himself and Mareen. He could barely make her out in the distance. What he did see was that fiancé move in on her like an accent trying to come in for a landing over her head.

Wilson's fists clenched to see another man touching what was his. But he had that wrong. Mareen wasn't his. He'd just given her up so that she could have what she truly wanted, her family back.

He'd seen it in her eyes. He'd heard it in her voice when she'd talked about her sisters. It wasn't just the ranch she wanted. She wanted to be a family with her sisters.

How could he take that from her as well? He, who had never truly belonged to anyone or anywhere. He was not that cruel. Even if he felt nothing but darkness inside him now.

That's where he should go. Find some dark place and stay there. Because he certainly couldn't go march down the hill and take all of that away from her. Not when he'd taken her father away.

"I knew you felt guilty for what happened in that last mission, but I had no idea it ran this deep."

Wilson refused to look at Jackson. He couldn't take his eyes off Mareen. Her fiancé was now holding her hand. Wilson's mind wanted to scream at him that that wasn't her fiancé. He was.

"It wasn't your fault," Jackson was saying.

"The general sacrificed his life for me. For me." Wilson waved his hands up and down his body as though Jackson could see the unworthiness of him.

"We were all following orders. We did what he ordered. You dishonor that if you question him now."

"It should've been me. Not him. He was the best of us."

"And if it had been you, then Mareen would be marrying that guy." Jackson chucked a thumb over his shoulder. "Or maybe she wouldn't be because she would've broken her neck after falling from an old treehouse. Or she would've been trampled by a runaway tractor. Or maybe another snake would've gotten her."

Wilson's body jerked with each of those maybes. His feet ached to march into action. His hands itched to pull her close, to use his body to keep her safe. He had to be there to keep her safe.

"Or any number of things," Jackson went on. "When it's your time, it's your time. We have no say in it. Us more than others because we sign up to be put in harm's way to protect others."

Wilson shut his eyes. He knew the words to be true. Which made him know that he didn't want to spend another day where he wasn't by Mareen Silver's side. Not just for her protection but for his livelihood. She had his heart. A man couldn't live without his heart.

"I believe the general had this plan to get us out here before he died," Jackson continued. "I think putting it in his will was his contingency plan because he knew these girls needed us just as much as we need them."

Wilson looked back down the hill. Stephán was now embracing Mareen. His heart squeezed at the sight. And then he saw red. That is until he realized that Mareen wasn't hugging Stephán back.

"She's about to put herself in harm's way by marrying a man she doesn't love," said Jackson. "You can save her. So, the question is are you going—"

Wilson didn't stick around to hear the end of Jackson's rallying speech. The troops were already in motion. Wilson's right knee bent, and he strode forward. Left, right, left, he marched his way back down the hill, readying to throw himself into the explosive situation no matter what came.

CHAPTER TWENTY-ONE

Mareen looked up into Stephán's eyes and... she wasn't sure what she saw there? Just green balls staring back at her. Was that a question in his eyes? Was it surprise? Maybe anger? She had no idea?

She'd grown so used to looking into Wilson's eyes. In his green gaze, Mareen saw everything. She saw what he felt, what was on his mind, what was in his heart. Even if he was trying to hide from her.

She couldn't see into Wilson's gaze right now. He'd walked away from her. But she could still see him. He hadn't gone far. She didn't plan for this distance between them to last. She was going after him.

Mareen knew that in her parents' marriage, it was her mother who had walked away. Catherine had expected Abe to chase after her, just like all the other times she'd left him. Though she'd never gone very far while she waited for him to come for her. Until the day he didn't.

Mareen was determined that that day would never come for her and Wilson. Because she wasn't leaving. And she wouldn't let him go.

So why was she having trouble taking the first step toward him?

Oh, that's why. Stephán had a hold on her arm.

"I'm really sorry I dragged you into this," she said. "This isn't what I planned when I came here. I didn't plan to fall in love."

"You're in love?" Stephán said, his perfectly plucked brows rising to his styled hairline. That was surprise there.

"Yes," Mareen confirmed.

Stephán's gaze hooded. The emotions that reflected back were muted. Not that they had been strong to begin with. Because neither of their feelings for each other had run any deeper than surface level.

Breaking off the engagement was the right thing to do. Mareen doubted they would've made each other miserable. She knew for certain they would've never made each other happy.

"Don't be childish, Mareen," said her mother. "How many times have I told you that men aren't capable of love? You shouldn't make decisions that will affect your life based on something as flimsy as your feelings."

Stephán's head jerked back as he stared at her mother. It was more emotion than Mareen had ever seen out of him. Definitely more than he'd ever shown her when they'd kissed. Then he turned his attention back to her. He put both hands on her shoulders and squeezed.

Mareen didn't shrug him off. The movement didn't feel possessive. It was protective. They might not be in love, but they had cared for one another. The gesture brought a smile to Mareen's face.

If it were Wilson holding her, she would've felt engulfed by him. She would've felt both supported and strong enough to move a mountain. Which is what she would have to do once her mother found out about the will and got her hands on the ranch.

It was inevitable now. But it couldn't be Mareen's first concern. She needed to go find Wilson.

"I didn't think you loved me," Stephán said, loosening his hold on her. "But I thought we made a good team."

"We did make a good team. But I want more than that. And we can't give that to each other."

Stephán nodded, then he wrapped his arms around her in a stiff hug. "I'll be sorry to lose you."

He looked sorry. The kind of sorry when a boss lost his best employee. Mareen dropped the heavy engagement ring into Stephán's hand. She was glad to be free of its weight.

She wanted to be free of Stephán, but he was still lingering. He stared down at the ring. Then he lifted his gaze to her, as though doing a final assessment.

It took everything in Mareen to mind her manners and not tell him to hop back in his car and start the long drive back to the city. She didn't say any of that. She did look up in the direction Wilson had stormed off.

Her heart did its fluttering dance. Butterflies flitted in her belly. Wilson was coming back toward her.

The clouds parted overhead. The sun chose that moment to shine golden lights down on them. Birds were chirping a love song.

Her mother could naysay love all she wanted. Mareen wanted to pirouette in these emotions. She wanted to lift her knees and high-step it in a passage to the man she loved. She knew she would never leave Wilson. She didn't have an ounce of fear that love would throw her off, not with him.

"This place looks like a good investment. If you still want me to buy it, give me a call."

Mareen's eyes were still glued to the approaching soldier. The sound of a record scratching filled her ears. She was going to have the man she loved, but at what cost.

"Buy the ranch?" That scoff came from her mother. "As if Scout would ever sell it."

Scout's breath hitched as she turned to Mareen. "You really didn't tell her?"

There was a part of Mareen that wanted to stick out her chin and say no, she really hadn't told her mother. Just like she hadn't told her mother about the broken doll all those years ago. Instead, Mareen said nothing.

She didn't move an inch as Scout came toward her. Though they were eye level, her older sister gazed down at Mareen. Scout's blue eyes widened a fraction as though they were seeing something familiar.

"Tell me what?" demanded Catherine.

Mareen kept her mouth shut. She couldn't have spoken if she'd wanted to. She was so captivated by her sister's gaze.

"The general left a will," said Scout. She about-faced, standing beside Mareen and facing Catherine. "In it, he said all six of his daughters need to get married in order to keep control of this place. If we don't marry by the end of the year, Silver Star goes to you."

For the first few seconds after Scout's explanation, Catherine looked dazed. Then a slow, wicked smile spread across her porcelain-pale face. She reminded Mareen of the dolls on the shelf; glassy eyes and frozen smiles. It sent a shiver down Mareen's spine.

Warm arms came around Mareen. It wasn't Stephán. It wasn't Wilson. It was Scout.

Mareen felt a tingling of warmth spread from her middle. It took a slow route to her heart. Then it burst into pure joy as her sister gave her a reassuring squeeze.

Catherine turned her nose up as she looked at the two sisters. Then she smiled at her daughter. Her mother's expression pushed at the glow of affection passing from Scout to Mareen.

"Marry Stephán, and I'll sell the ranch to Scout when this whole scheme fails. I'll even give her a reasonable interest rate."

Mareen looked into her mother's eyes. Catherine's eyes were brown. Not a fire roasting brown. They were a hard, glassy brown. No emotions. No warmth. Nothing but hard brittleness.

"She is getting married," said Scout. "Mareen's going to marry the man she loves."

"And we'll be standing by her when she does," said Saylor, coming to stand at her other side.

"We sure will." Brig set her hand at Mareen's low back. "We got your back. Even when you want us out of your business, we'll be right here looking over your shoulder."

"Cause that's what family does," said Tilly. "They stick together."

Mareen was overheated from all the warmth suddenly surrounding her. Her legs were jelly, but she was in no danger of falling with the strength around her. She was close to tears, but there were plenty of shoulders for her to cry on.

Mareen looked to her mother. There was room enough in this tight circle for one more. But Catherine took a step back.

"Stephán, drive me home. I have wedding plans to cancel and developers to call."

Stephán looked weary as he handed Catherine into the car. Mareen nearly asked him to stay to avoid the drive. But she was better off with both of them on their way and off the ranch.

The luxury car kicked up a cloud of dirt as it pulled out of the drive. When the smoke cleared, Wilson stood there.

CHAPTER TWENTY-TWO

Once again, Wilson didn't make it in time to save the life of a Silver. His boots hit the gravel in time to see the Silver sisters close ranks. Scout looked up at him. Those blue eyes flashed at him, telling him to stay back. It took everything in Wilson to hold his place. Unlike with the general, he knew this was the best play.

Mareen had a wound that he couldn't heal, no matter how much he loved her. No matter how much he wanted to take the pain away from her and stab it into his heart and bear the brunt. Instead, Wilson held still while her sisters caught her. He held still while they soothed the sting of her mother's biting words.

The ex-fiancé and the woman who would be his future mother-in-law disappeared into the distance. When the dust of their departure settled, Mareen stood there with her sisters as a strong force at her back.

Mareen's blue gaze found his. In them, Wilson saw wariness and doubt. Those emotions reflecting back at him were a sucker punch to his gut. He was before her in two strides. But he only had to take one because she took a step and met him halfway.

"I'm sorry," they both said at the same time.

"I should've come after you," Mareen said as she placed her hands on his chest.

Wilson's heart pounded in response to her touch. He wrapped his arms around her and pulled her close. "I shouldn't have left your side."

"Promise me you'll never do it again."

"I'll never want to," he said with his lips pressed against her temple. "You have my heart. A man's nothing without his heart."

He felt her body shudder as though an explosion had gone off inside of her. Or maybe that was his own desire boiling over. Funny though, he didn't feel as though he'd been blown to pieces. For the first time in his life, Wilson felt whole.

He had a purpose to last him a lifetime. He had a home he was prepared to fight to keep. He had a family who would never let him stray too far -if they let him have any space at all.

Wilson lifted his head to peer around at them all. He was stopped short by a harsh glare. The look the elder Silver daughter gave him was pure censure. Wilson was man enough to wince. He nodded, letting Scout know without words that this would be his one and only misstep with her sister. That must have assured her because Scout turned on her heel to find her husband. Linc winked at Wilson, giving him a you're-in-for-it-now grin.

Wilson was in for it. He was in, and he was never getting out. He pulled the woman of his dreams into his arms. He felt his whole body, his entire being shiver and shake, and then settle into place.

"I can't give you any of the things that he could," said Wilson, inclining his head to where the luxury car took off down the road. "I'm not rich. I'm crashing in a house you built as a kid."

"I've had those things all my life," Mareen said. "They've never made me happy. You make me happy."

"What I do have to offer you is my beating heart, my strong hands, and my arms that will catch you every time you falter."

"That is exactly what I want."

Wilson looked into her eyes. What he saw reflected back at him were the two things he'd never thought he'd have in this life; forgiveness and love.

He sealed his lips over Mareen's. Ignoring the whoops and catcalls, he pulled her closer and deepened the kiss. He might have been the one to save her time and again over the past couple of days. But the truth was, she'd saved his life by giving him a purpose again, by giving him something and someone to protect.

EPILOGUE

"J Wilson Michaels..."

"I Jefferson Moore..."

"... take thee as my wedded wife..." Even though both men had joined voices, each of their strong baritones sounded raspy as they said the words to the women who held their hearts.

Also in unison, Wilson and Jeff cleared their throats. The emotions may have left their mouths, but they all migrated to each man's face as he looked down with a depth of love that made Jackson feel like a voyeur watching the dual wedding ceremony.

"For better or worse, for richer or poor, to have and to hold, to protect and provide, to love, to cherish, and to obey 'til death do us part."

Jackson felt a drop of water splash down atop his eyelid. He looked up, only to have another drop splash down directly into his eye. The sun shone brightly down on all who had gathered. The puffy clouds above wept a few more tears at the happy occasion.

"You know what they say about rain on your wedding day," said the brown-skinned man of the cloth who presided over the event. Father Matthews grinned at the two couples. "It's good luck. But go on and kiss these girls so we can get inside."

A cheer rang up through the crowd as Wilson and Mareen and Jeff and Saylor exchanged their first kisses as husband and wife, and husband and wife. With the deal sealed, the skies opened up and poured down droplets of water atop all who'd gathered.

Rice packets were forgotten in chairs as the bridal party and guests made a mad dash for the main house. Jackson hung back. Rain had never bothered him, so he didn't mind getting a little wet. What he did mind was people watching him possibly trip and fall in an attempt to move quickly.

He couldn't trust his bum knee. Even before the last mission, the joint had been giving him problems. It was a wonder he'd been cleared for duty.

He'd known that mission would be his last. Well, he'd known it physically. He still wasn't ready to give in in his mind. He was only twenty-nine. He should have more operating days ahead of him. But if he wanted that, he'd likely need an operation. And still, after that, there were no guarantees he'd be cleared to go back.

Another form hung back in the rain shower. Though this form didn't sulk in a corner like he was doing. She danced in front of the abandoned altar. Twirling in her skirts as the raindrops continued to fall.

The fabric of her skirt lifted, giving Jackson an eyeful of shapely calf. A tinkle of her laughter reached his ears. The light in her eye reached him, making him catch his breath.

"Brig, stop behaving like a child and get in her before you catch a cold!"

Jackson wasn't sure which of her sisters had admonished Brigadear Silver. But he felt the censure all the way down into his achy bones. Brig gave one last delighted twirl before skipping into the house, her dark hair falling down either side of her face like pigtails.

Because she was a child. And Jackson had to keep reminding himself of that. He should've had that thought in his head when he'd first seen her dancing in the rain like a little girl. Instead, he'd gotten a vision of her long legs, her perfectly shaped ankles, and those rounded knees that could easily allow her to dance round in circles.

Jackson hadn't been on a dance floor for over a year. He didn't trust that his knee would hold him, much less carry someone else's weight. Definitely not a young, spry woman of twenty.

"Three down, three to go."

Jackson jerked as Carter clapped him on his back. The sudden movement made his knee buckle. But he caught himself before his weakness became noticeable.

"You two are really sticking with this plan?" asked Truman, his perpetual scowl in place.

Besides Jackson, Truman was the only other man in this unit who'd prefer to be back in a combat zone. It was the former sniper's shoulder injury that had benched him.

"It's what we have to do if we want to stay here," Jackson answered.

The ranch was his only option now. He couldn't handle a desk job. It would kill what was left of his spirit. Working the land, tending the animals, helping General Silver's daughters, this felt like work that mattered.

"Tilly's got some poor chumps on the hook in that online dating app," said Carter. "So, that just leaves me marrying Brig, and Jackson marrying the other one -what's her name?"

Jackson knew the other one's name. But he balked at the idea of Carter and Brig. True, Carter was closer to Brig in age at twenty-five, but the man had his own dark problems. He didn't like the idea of Carter's habits in close proximity to Brig. She was still young and impressionable.

The fact that she was young and impressionable, and also vibrant and funny, with an intelligence in those blue eyes that often outshined the mischief...

Jackson couldn't remember where his thoughts were going? He just knew that he had to get his mind off Brig. A young woman like that, with all of her life ahead of her, had no business being with a washed-up, broken-down old man like him. And so, he resigned himself to marrying the other one.

❧

If Brig has anything to say about this
... and you know she does...
then she's going to manipulate Jackson to right where she wants him.
And that's holding her in his arms.

Stay tuned for this epic battle of wills in
"His Pledge to Obey,"
Book 4 of the Silver Star Ranch romances.

SHANAE JOHNSON

HIS Pledge TO Obey

A SILVER STAR RANCH ROMANCE

CHAPTER ONE

"Wow, soldier, you sure do put the fox in foxhole."

Jackson Bennett's brow furrowed in a wince. He was sure the woman aimed for a sexy purr with her voice. What came out was more of a wet cat's screech. Along with the assault on his ears, Jackson's nose wrinkled in distaste at the rancid smell of alcohol wafting from her parted lips. He wouldn't have been surprised if that foul tongue of hers couldn't hold up against the rag the bartender was using to wipe down the greasy bar.

"Do you even know what a foxhole is?" he found himself asking before he could think better of it.

The Screecher grinned. Or at least Jackson thought that was a grin. To him, it looked like a crooked slash across the bottom of her face.

Instead of waiting for her answer, which Jackson knew would be both wrong and inappropriate, he answered his own question. "It's a hole in the ground where soldiers seek shelter from enemy fire."

"Hmmm." Her next purr attempt sounded like a yowl. "I'd like to crawl into a hole with you."

"Yeah, well, this fox is spoken for." Jackson gave her his back as he took the drinks offered up by the bartender.

When he turned to head back to his table, there was still an irate feline blocking his way. He should've known better. Cats moved when they wanted, not when they were dismissed.

"I don't see a ring," she said, eyes peering at the two mugs in his hand.

Jackson held the two tumblers away from the Screecher in case she tried the age-old tomcat retaliation of knocking a drink over with her claws. In doing so, the bare skin below the knuckle of his left hand was clearly on display, showing its ringless state.

Nobody had put a ring on it yet. Because his fiancée hadn't said she liked him yet. But they were getting married. It was just that he and the woman he had promised to marry hadn't met face to face yet.

"Oh, you're just engaged."

The Screecher came dangerously close to Jackson's drinks. He pulled them back to his chest defensively. His eyes narrowed on her long, painted nails.

"Want a fling before you tie that knot?"

Jackson had had enough. He'd had enough of women giving him unwanted attention. This was the fourth one tonight. He'd thought he'd affected a stay-back kind of attitude, but he guessed the women in town took that as a challenge.

Jackson turned and slammed his drinks down on the bar. The impact of the thick glasses coming down on the hardwood reverberated up and down his arms. The sensation wasn't painful. However, it was enough to wake up the other aches and pains in his body. There were many.

"Did you just feel the earth move?" said the Screecher. "I imagine you'll be just like a surprise earthquake when I get you back to my place."

Somehow her hands were headed straight for his belt buckle. In the middle of a crowded bar, no less. Jackson was done with this outing. He'd had his arm twisted into this sociable excursion, and now he was being attacked by this wildcat. This was why he was a dog person.

With a flick of his wrist, Jackson disarmed the hellion and ducked out of harm's way. Once out of the foxhole of the bar, he stepped right into enemy fire.

Bodies marched left, right, then swiveled around in an about-face to repeat the moves again. The formation and synchronized steps reminded him of his time in the military. Though there wasn't that much shimmying and shaking in Boot Camp.

Jackson didn't know the moves of the line dancing that had most of the patrons up and on their feet. Even if he did, he wouldn't have joined in. The mere thought of moving so quickly made his knee ache.

He hadn't moved that fast in over a year. He might not ever be able to move that fast again. Not with the injuries he'd sustained during his time in the Armed Forces.

Jackson didn't begrudge a single ache or pain. He'd saved countless innocent lives and served with honors. Had a Silver Star medal to prove it.

What did bother him was that his injuries prevented him from going back and serving the greater good. The shrapnel that had lodged into his right knee on his last mission had left a lasting impression, one of constant aches and pain.

He wasn't quite thirty years old, yet he was already washed up. Ready to be set out to pasture like many of the horses on the Silver Star Ranch. There was more in him, more he could do for his country. But his body just wasn't up for the task. Not on the battlefield and not on the dance floor.

Jackson skirted around the quick-stepping bodies and made his way over to the table of his friends. Though he could hardly see his buddies. Wilson had his arms wrapped around his new wife, Mareen. Their dark heads were together as they alternately spoke into each other's ears and stole lingering kisses.

Beside them, his former team leader Linc and his wife, Scout, shared one chair. The newlyweds also spoke to each other as though no one else in the world existed. Their words were also interrupted by lingering kisses to the mouth.

This was why Jackson had gone to the bar. He was surrounded day in and out by happy couples trying to sneak off for privacy, which was near impossible when nearly a dozen people lived on the Silver Star Ranch. Sure, the ranch was sprawling with enough space. But the living quarters were simply too close for comfort now that there were three sets of newlyweds to contend with.

Jackson would be one of those newlyweds. Hopefully, soon. But he doubted he and Gunnery Silver would share the same chair, much less the same country. The sigh that escaped his mouth didn't sound like hope. It was a sigh of resignation.

This was the decision he'd made. It was all that was open to him now. He couldn't go back into the military. Not with his bum knee. He couldn't stand sitting at a desk and working the intel channels. Though he could no longer jump out of a plane, or swim for miles, or trek through a jungle, Jackson Bennett was still a man of action.

Much slower action, maybe. Action on even ground, probably. And no sudden movements, definitely.

The only action left to him was to marry a woman he'd never met. A woman he'd never even spoken to. All so that he could have a place on the Silver Star Ranch where he at least felt of use. The arranged marriages had worked out well for three of his buddies. Odds were it would work out for him too.

"What about this guy?" Carter Shane brushed his overly styled hair away from his brows.

It was a move Jackson had seen Korean pop stars effect that would make teenyboppers lose their minds. The woman sitting beside Carter, in her own chair, didn't notice. Artillery Silver's head was focused on the phone she held between them.

"Are you kidding?" said Tilly. "He's wearing a Hawaiian shirt. I wouldn't be caught dead with an 80s reject."

"Not everything in the eighties was bad," said Carter.

Tilly's blonde head shot up as she looked at him in shock.

Carter held his look of nonchalance for one second longer. Then he grinned and chuckled.

Tilly shoved him in the shoulder. "I almost believed you."

"Get real," Carter scoffed. "As if I'd let you marry a fashion-don't."

Carter bumped Tilly's shoulder as his gaze returned to the phone. Tilly bumped his back as her attention returned to her phone's display. Jackson caught the tilt of Carter's head and the flare of his nostrils as he leaned just an inch too close to the woman.

"Where's Brig?" asked Jackson. When Carter didn't raise his head, Jackson repeated the question, his voice an octave higher.

"Who?" said Carter, gaze still on Tilly's phone.

"Your fiancée," ground out Jackson.

Carter looked up then, but he didn't move away from Tilly. "Oh, right. She's..."

Jackson spotted her before Carter found her. Brigadear Silver was on the dance floor. She stepped in time to the beat, following the formation of the line dancing. She swiveled her hips and flipped her hair in a move that made Jackson swallow hard.

The impact of his gulp landed with such a resounding thud in his gut that he felt it in his kneecap. That was nothing to the jolt that registered when Brig caught Jackson's gaze. That mischievous grin that was always near her lips spread wide. She raised a hand and crooked a finger at him.

Jackson felt his body move unbidden. His legs straightened, a near-impossible feat with his injury. His toes spread in his boots. His heels flexed as though he was already marching toward the dance floor, toward her.

Something in his mind told him to stop, to halt, to about-face. That way lay a minefield. But like always, he couldn't help himself when it came to the youngest Silver Sister. Something about Brig drew him near.

Luckily, when Jackson looked down, he saw that his body hadn't moved from the chair. He still sat in it alone. Which was how he was going to stay.

Brig was off-limits to him. Not just because he would be marrying her sister in a matter of weeks. Because he had nearly ten years on her.

That became even more evident when Jackson saw a young man

move in front of Brig. She placed her hand on his shoulder and swayed with him. It had been the young man she'd been calling. The man without a touch of premature gray in his hair. The man without a knee problem that kept him from being able to dance those quick steps. The man who wasn't washed out of the only career he'd known just before his thirtieth birthday. Jackson turned away from her.

Brig wasn't meant for Jackson. She was meant for Carter. Carter, who was closer to her age. Carter, who didn't have a physical injury, though he still had issues of his own. Carter, who should be doing something about that young buck who was dancing with his fiancée while moving his hands into enemy territory at Brig's low back.

But Carter wasn't paying attention, so Jackson would have to step in.

CHAPTER TWO

"Thanks for the dance, Barry."

Brigadear Silver shoved the roving hands off her bottom as she watched Jackson turn away from her. What did she have to do to get the man's attention? She was in her best dress. This dress had gotten her out of a speeding ticket, a C on her last history exam, and drinks at the bar from the bartender who knew she was underage.

But apparently it had no effect on the one man she wanted to notice her. Anytime Jackson saw her coming, he turned the other way. Whenever she spoke, he always looked down. She didn't think he disliked her. She caught the grin each time she told a joke or made a witty comment that made others pause and repeat in their heads what she said before they got the joke.

Those witticisms often made others stare at her quizzically. Not Jackson. His brow always lifted when she said the unexpected. So much so that she expected he was the only person who actually understood her.

As the baby of the Silver sisters, no one listened closely to Brig. Most times, her sisters gave her a pat on her head when she offered any advice. Only to turn around moments or days later, relaying what she'd initially suggested to them as though it was their own idea. It had stopped bothering Brig, who never cared about the credit.

Until Jackson showed up.

Brig didn't want him to look at her as though she were a child. She didn't want him to think she didn't have the brilliant mind that put her first in her Occupational Therapy classes. She was the youngest person in the Master's level courses, having finished her four-year Bachelor's in three years.

She was used to hitting the books hard. She always found the answers either in the text or at the back of the book. She wasn't having such luck trying to crack Jackson Bennett's code.

Her fiancé was worthless in getting any information out of. All Carter cared about was what he put in his hair, or the clothes on his body, or making fun of guys on dating apps with Tilly. Which was likely what he was doing now.

Tilly and Carter had their heads together. The two had grown as thick as thieves as they ran a commentary on the men Tilly measured for marriage in her app.

Carter wasn't a bad guy. He was actually pretty cool. That is, when he paid attention to Brig instead of her sister. Brig had never fought for Carter's attention, not like she was fighting for Jackson's.

How could she not fight for Jackson's attention? He had the kind of eyes that bored into a girl. His muscles were more like a bear's than a man's. And that touch of gray at his temples made Brig shiver even when she wasn't on the dance floor. There was something about gray-haired men that did it for her.

Brig had a type. And that type was older men. She knew she had issues. She'd studied psychology as a minor, after all.

"Ah, come on, Brig, let me buy you a drink."

Brig's attention fell back to the young man in front of her. She'd forgotten Barry was even there. "I'm too young to drink."

She'd be twenty-one in just a matter of months, but she'd already tried plenty of alcoholic beverages. She didn't like most. Beer tasted like potatoes to her. Wine tasted like rubbing alcohol. She'd never understood the draw.

When she was just a girl, her sisters had ordered her a Shirley Temple. That fruity, fizzy concoction had remained her drink of choice to this date. She had no qualms about ordering it in a bar. She just preferred a tall drink of something else right now.

"One more dance," said Barry.

His hand was on her hip. Low on her hip. Brig did not like the grip. It was far too possessive for her. This was another reason Brig didn't like to date boys her age. They were still learning manners.

"Come on," Barry said. "You know you want to."

Those were five of Brig's least favorite words; *you know you want to*. Being the youngest of six sisters, everyone thought they knew better than her. Most of the time, Brig went along because she was often the one who planted the idea to begin with.

Take tonight, for example. She'd casually mentioned how hard they'd all been working all week to Scout when they were re-shoeing a horse, which was Scout's least favorite job on the ranch. Then she'd brought up how none of the now married men had had a bachelor party, and wasn't that a shame, while the guys were mucking out stalls. Finally, she'd hung up the flyer of the town's most popular -and only- bar on the fridge before dinner last night.

And here they all were. Except, the actual plan had been to get Jackson to dance with her. Unfortunately, he hadn't ventured anywhere near the dance floor all night long.

Brig had been throwing down a lot of her best moves on the hardwood. The DJ had started the night playing Hannah Montana's *Best of Both Worlds* and just finished up with Miley Cyrus's *Party in the USA*.

Now playing was *Blurred Lines,* the song Miley made famous with a certain dance move on a music awards show. But Brig was not in the mood to twerk. And certainly not with Barry.

"Good night, Barry."

Brig made to shove past the man. Boy, really. Barry couldn't have weighed much more than her. In fact, she probably had a few pounds on him. She had half an inch on him, and she was wearing boots, not six-inch heels.

Instead of letting her pass, Barry grabbed her arm. Brig whirled, preparing to throw a punch. She was too late.

Barry was already backing up with his hands raised. Fear in his wide gaze. An apology spewing from his lips.

Brig turned, expecting to see a big, brown bear of a man coming to her rescue. Instead of tall, dark, and handsome, she was met with four women with blue eyes blazing.

"I know you did not just try to force yourself on my baby sister," growled Scout.

Brig wanted to argue that she wasn't a baby. But she knew they wouldn't hear her. Even though the music had come to an abrupt halt.

"Sorry, sorry." Barry backed up at the same time as he looked for backup.

The crowd of men looked away or shook their heads sadly. This was one of the reasons that Brig and her sisters had had trouble finding husbands, even boyfriends, before the President's Men had come along. Her family had a bit of a reputation. No one messed with the Silver sisters without taking their lives into their own hands. And that included dating one of them.

Carter stood with Tilly's phone in his hand. His body angled toward hers as though ready to throw himself into harm's way to protect her and not his fiancée. That didn't bother Brig one iota. Something else caught her attention.

Jackson hung on the sidelines, watching it all go down. She saw that his hands were clenched into fists. Linc had a hand on his shoulder as though holding him back. So, tonight hadn't been a complete bust after all. Jackson did feel something for her, as evidenced by his stance and fists.

The seed she'd painstakingly planted had taken root. Now Brig just had to fan that seedling by throwing fire on it to make it grow. Water was for the faint of heart.

It was a start. This, coupled with what she had planned for Monday morning, should get her closer to her goal.

CHAPTER THREE

It felt like a tank was sitting on his legs. The pressure weighed Jackson down, making him want to stay in bed long after the sun rose. At the first light of day, he hefted himself out of bed.

His knees made popping sounds as he bent them to throw his legs over the side of the mattress. He let his right leg hang off the side for a moment. The joint creaked and groaned as it swung like a door, unsure whether it wanted to be open or shut. If only a bit of oil would quiet this ball and socket.

Jackson reached for the medication on the side table. With a shake, two pills popped out of the bottle and into his palm. Two was the recommended dose. Jackson put one pill back in the container and popped the remaining one in his mouth.

The aches and pains were manageable today. The thought of becoming addicted to the pain meds was not. He'd seen far too many hardened soldiers bend the knee to that cruel mistress.

Unlike insurgents, Fentanyl didn't sneak up on soldiers. No, she walked right into camp. She was handed out to soldiers to manage their pain. Little did they know they were welcoming friendly fire.

Opioid addiction wasn't a new thing in the armed forces. As far back as the Civil War, soldiers had self-medicated. The advent of morphine had brought relief from more than just physical injuries. With the pain and stress a soldier took on, that mental escape offered by morphine and later synthetic opioids was welcome. Jackson was far more fearful of succumbing to that trap than he was of losing his knee.

He capped the meds and shoved them out of sight. The relief to his joints was near-instant, but it wasn't absolute. The pain cleared enough for him to get on with his day and think clearly.

Most soldiers stayed away from hard drugs. They'd lose their livelihood in the Armed Forces if it was found out they were using. But worse, using could also get them killed when all their faculties weren't online in the theater of battle.

Jackson was no longer in the fog of war. He was on another battlefield. He was trying to pave a path for the rest of his life. One that he could walk without tripping himself up. He was pretty sure that he was headed in the right direction now that he'd arrived at the Silver Star Ranch. Though walking out of the bedroom of the cabin he was staying in and into the living room, Jackson had a moment of doubt.

Posters lined the walls. They proclaimed everything from Save the Whales to Meat is Murder and Don't Support Circus Cruelty. It was as though the animal rights organization PETA had been the interior decorator for the place. Or this had to at least have been a haven for their organizational meetings, complete with yoga mats, meditation rugs, and bean bags.

This hadn't been Jackson's first choice in cabins. When he and Truman had opened the door a few weeks ago, the former sniper had backed up and run to the last cabin on the row. That left Jackson stuck here in Gunnery Silver's cabin.

He was set to marry Gunny next month. He'd already set up house in the cabin she'd built with her father and sisters. But he'd never had a conversation with the woman.

Jackson introduced himself to Gunny over email a couple of

weeks ago when the Silver sisters and the President's Men had hatched this arranged marriage plan so that they could keep the ranch. If all six sisters weren't hitched by the General's deadline, then the ranch would pass to his ex-wife, an unpleasant woman who couldn't wait to turn them out and turn the ranch into something like a parking lot. Gunny's response to Jackson's thoughtfully worded email, "Fine. I'll be there in a few weeks. But after the vows, I'm out."

Well, that did wonders for his ego. But what did he expect? To find true love like Linc and Scout? Or Jeff and Saylor? Or Wilson and Mareen?

He knew love wasn't in the cards for him. Not when he couldn't sweep a woman off her feet if he wanted to. He could barely maintain his own weight.

This was the best he was going to get. He'd give his vow to Gunny. Keep his pledge. And soldier on along this new path.

Decision reaffirmed, he paced the length of the cabin a few times. At first, his right knee wouldn't stand any weight he put on it. His knee always took a few minutes to warm up in the morning. Like a car in winter needing to idle before raring to go.

He felt no pain thanks to the medication. Just because he couldn't feel the pain didn't mean his body worked perfectly. With each determined step, Jackson's knee relaxed a bit more. His movements became smoother and less stiff. Once he stepped outside, he was walking normally.

"It looks like he has arthritis in the knee."

Jackson paused, nearly stumbling as he came to a halt. Brig leaned against a railing. Her gaze was on him, as it often was when they were near each other. She looked lovely in a sundress and flats. He rarely saw her out of jeans and boots. The outfit made her look professional, older, like a woman he might consider bringing closer to him.

"He's not showing any of the signs, Brig," said Scout.

Scout's attention wasn't on Jackson. She and Saylor were eying one of the horses. Colonel Brandon was the horse's name. Jackson knew that because the horse was a trained dancer. He hadn't known that such a thing was possible until he saw Mareen leading the horse in high stepping, choreographed movements.

"I don't see any swelling in the carpus or the tarsus," said Saylor, her gaze traveling from the horse's front and then back legs. "I don't hear any popping or grinding as he walks."

Jackson's heart slowed. They weren't talking about him. They were talking about the horse. Still, Brig's gaze remained on him.

"He's too young for arthritis," said Scout, waving a dismissive hand at Brig's diagnosis.

Jackson wanted to tell them that age had nothing to do with joint pain. If an animal was overworked or had direct impact with a joint, pain could exist. And worse, if he was a stubborn male who relied on his strength and prowess, he wouldn't want his weaknesses on display.

His gaze caught Brig's again. It was as though she was reading his mind. But then her blue gaze clouded over, and the mischief was back.

"Pain isn't always obvious," she said. "Sometimes it's in the mind."

Jackson frowned. "You think people fake their pain?"

"Not fake," she said. "Ignore."

It felt like they were having a conversation that wasn't about the horse. But she couldn't know about his knee. The other men didn't know the extent of his injury. If he was lucky, they never would, and he would be past it soon.

Jackson had hit a brick wall with the VA hospital. They gave him only two options; more pain meds or surgery. Neither was his preference. Which was why he'd made an appointment with the university medical center this Monday morning. Hopefully, this Occupational Therapy doctor at the university would have some new treatments for him that would make him as good as new without doping him up or coming at him with a knife.

"I think people often deny what they know to be true because of social acceptance," Brig was saying. "The horse knows he's supposed to work, so he does."

Brig leaned back against the railing. She and Jackson were feet away, but he swore he could feel everywhere her gaze landed on him. It felt like a burst of sunshine. Every word she said was a cool breeze as it reached his ears. Jackson shifted his weight. Unfortunately, he shifted it to his right knee instead of his left. Those penetrating blue eyes caught his wince.

"You know, Scout," said Saylor, "Colonel Brandon is favoring his right leg."

Scout rounded the horse to peer down at his long legs. Sure enough, every few seconds, he shifted his weight.

"Now that I'm thinking about it, he was stiff when I took him out," said Scout.

"Maybe it is arthritis?" said Saylor.

Saylor said it to Scout as though it was the first time either of them had considered it. Jackson looked to Brig. She shrugged as if the credit passing by her was no big deal.

"I didn't know horses could get arthritis," said Jackson.

"Just because they're big and strong doesn't mean they don't have weaknesses," Brig said as she took one and then another step toward him.

Jackson held still, certain any sudden moves would irritate his knee and give him away. "How do you treat it?"

Brig opened her mouth. But Scout cut her off. Jackson wanted to tell the other woman to keep quiet so he could listen to Brig. But he said nothing.

"Simplest way is to treat it with drugs," said Scout as she scratched behind Colonel Brandon's ear. The horse whinnied and moved away from her touch as though he didn't like the suggestion.

Jackson could relate. Drugs would likely make the horse slower and foggy. He was sure all the animal wanted was to run wild and free like when he was a calf.

"There are other ways to treat stiff joints," said Brig. "If you want to take a walk, I could tell you about some."

Jackson gave himself a shake. He wasn't sure if he'd heard her correctly. Those suggestive words should not come out of a mouth so young and innocent. Though standing before him with long legs like a colt and a lush mane of hair, Brigadear Silver looked anything but young and innocent.

"Actually, I did want to talk with you," he said. "I wanted to talk to you all about Gunny."

CHAPTER FOUR

$\mathcal{A}$ cold, steel ball clocked Brig in the face. Metaphorically speaking. Miley Cyrus's song *Wrecking Ball* blared in her mind when Jackson mentioned her sister.

She and Jackson had just shared a moment. She knew she wasn't making it up in her mind. His nostrils had flared when she'd talked about his joints. His gaze had widened when she'd suggested they go off alone together. He felt something between the two of them. He was just too fool-headed to admit it.

She'd found that most men were. Her soccer coach had been. Coach Olly had assured Brig that her feelings for him were nothing more than a teenage infatuation. He'd insisted it was pretty common. Although all the other girls on the team had been into the Portuguese phenom Cristiano Ronaldo and seethed at Coach Olly's daily two-hour drills.

Her psychology professor had said the same words in her freshmen year at the university. Though Professor Whitman had named it. Gerontophilia was a condition where someone was attracted to the elderly.

Brig knew that wasn't her jam. She simply preferred her men

tall, dark, capable, and with a touch of gray at the temples. Okay, so she might have a thing for older guys. But it wasn't like she trolled old folks' homes.

The boys her age could never hold her attention for long. All they cared about was video games, sports games, and seeing who could get the most phone numbers from girls. Not that they'd even use the numbers to have an actual conversation with the opposite sex. It was all about grammatically incorrect text messages, DMs, and PMs.

Brig had a mind that needed stimulation. Jackson got her synapses firing.

She liked how he looked out for his teammates. She and her sisters were the same way. Though her sisters rarely let her look out for them. So Brig had to do it sneakily. They never thought she had the answers, which was why she didn't take offense when they so quickly discarded her diagnosis of Colonel Brandon.

She had been right about the horse. Brig was often right. It wasn't hard when she lived with opinionated women who often shouted the answers out of turn. Brig always had time to sit back, evaluate all sides, and come to the best conclusion. By that time, her sisters were usually too riled up to listen to reason. So she whispered in their ears, playing mischief and cracking jokes until they thought the idea she insinuated was their own.

It was textbook reverse psychology take that Professor Whitman. See, she had been paying attention. Only the reverse psychology wasn't working on Jackson. And by not working, she meant she was having trouble showing the opposite of her feelings for him.

It always happened this way with a guy she liked. She'd try to play it cool and inevitably wound up throwing herself at him. Well, not this time.

"What do you want to know about Gunny?" she asked Jackson.

Jackson's gaze roved back to hers. He tugged at his lower lip as he looked down at her. That lip made her think of the berries that would soon be in bloom in the north pasture. Brig was suddenly very, very thirsty for some fruit juice.

"What's Gunny like?" he asked.

It was such a simple question. Brig could talk about her sisters for hours. And not just the surface-level stuff. Brig had liked psychology so much that she'd minored in the field. With a family as dysfunctional as hers, it was inevitable that she'd take an interest. Her parents and her sisters were a fascinating lot that could fill volumes of academic texts.

Scout with her control issues. Saylor with her care-taker needs. Aside from being guilt-ridden over the divorce, Mareen's mother had truly screwed up her self-worth. The twins, Tilly and Gunny, had lost their mother shortly after childbirth and had a whole host of abandonment issues. And don't get her started on the daddy issues all of them exhibited. Brig said none of that to Jackson.

"Gunny snores."

Jackson quirked a brow at that. Just another feat most frat boys couldn't manage. On them, the raised brow would look sleazy. On Jackson, it looked devilish.

"She's a cover hog, and she kicks," Brig continued. "I know from experience."

"So, do you," said Scout as she came up to the fence.

"I do not," Brig huffed. Then she moved in front of Scout, hoping that her body blocked out her older sister from Jackson's view.

It might have blocked Scout's face. Unfortunately, it did not block her mouth. "You wet the bed until you were six."

Brig turned and lunged for her sister. The wooden fence that stood in between them was the only thing that saved Scout. That and her cat-like reflexes that had her jumping just beyond Brig's reach.

Brig's cheeks were hotter than red clay in the summer heat. She hesitated to glance up at Jackson. But she couldn't help herself. She was drawn to him. When she looked over, she saw that he was grinning as he looked between the sisters.

Brig was not amused. The man she wanted to marry was looking at her like she was a pampers-soaking, bed-wetting, cover hog who kicked.

"You hear from Gunny?" asked Scout, her attention turning to Jackson. "How's it going with you two?"

"Nothing other than the first email that she'd be here in a few weeks."

A few weeks. That was all the time Brig had to convince Jackson that he was the one for her and not Gunny. Definitely not Gunny, who would prefer to trot the globe saving every endangered animal known to mankind. Jackson needed a woman to look after him, to stand by him, especially with whatever was going on with his knee.

He didn't speak of it, but Brig knew the signs. Horses and men weren't so different.

Unlike the man standing stoically next to Brig, Colonel Brandon took that moment to rear. He wasn't the only one. A few of the other horses who had been sedately eating their morning hay moved around in agitation.

"What's gotten into them?" asked Scout.

"Probably a storm coming," said Brig. Animals could sense changes in weather more accurately than meteorologists.

"Didn't you say you had to go into town?" Scout asked, coming closer to Brig now that the subject of embarrassing childhood stories had passed. Too bad her sister was still smart enough to stay just beyond her reach.

"Yeah, I won't be long," said Brig.

"Your tires were looking a little bald last time I checked."

"I'll get them changed, mom," Brig mocked.

"That would mean you'd have to stay twice as long," said Scout.

"I'm headed into town," said Jackson.

He looked torn as he said it. It was as though the chivalrous knight wanted to care for the damsel. But on the other side, the hardened warrior sensed danger.

See, intelligence. It was so sexy on a man. And it mostly only showed up in the grown variety. Who could truly blame Brig for being attracted to him?

It likely only took a second. To Brig, it looked like the internal battle had waged for years. Finally, the dust settled, and the outcome was announced.

"I can give her a lift."

Perfect. Things were going exactly as she'd planned.

CHAPTER FIVE

*J*ackson winced as he folded himself into the car. As his right knee bent so that his foot could move to its place near the gas pedal, the synovial fluids in the joint released. The resulting sound was similar to a Fourth of July fireworks display.

"I can drive if you'd like," said Brig.

She sat perched at the edge of the passenger seat. The hem of her dress rested just above her knees, which were pressed together primly. A flush of pink colored her perfectly rounded knee caps. She had a dimple in her left knee that mirrored the one that often made an appearance on her left cheek when that mischievous grin slid across her face. Her cheeks blushed that same rosy shade when she was up to something.

Jackson realized he was staring at her knees. He slammed the driver's side door, jammed the key in the ignition, and started the engine. The radio came to life. Miley Cyrus's voice filled the interior like a wrecking ball.

"I love this song," said Brig.

She reached over the armrest that separated them. Jackson tensed, readying to hop out the window. In hindsight, he doubted he would've laughed at his reaction. Having this slip of a girl who all of a sudden looked like a grown woman encroach on his territory would start a war. Scout Silver was not an adversary Jackson wanted or needed. Looking like he was putting the moves on her baby sister when he was all but engaged to a different sister would easily bring on her battle cry.

Brig didn't cross the invisible line between them. She reached instead for the knobs on the radio. With a flick of her wrist, she turned the volume up.

"I was a huge Hannah Montana fan as a kid."

Jackson wanted to tell her that she was still a kid. Those long legs tapping to the beat begged to differ. Why hadn't he told her to put some clothes on before allowing her to hop in the car with him?

Instead of admonishing her state of undress, he said, "I thought this was Miley Cyrus? Who's Hannah Montana?"

"Hannah Montana is Miley Cyrus," she grinned as her head bopped side to side in time to the beat. Then she shimmied her shoulders, which would draw any red-blooded man's attention to her chest.

Jackson thought of ice. He thought of polar bears in the Arctic. His mind went to the poster in Gunny's cabin where a mama polar bear and a baby polar bear walked on thin ice.

That did the trick.

With his libido under control, Jackson pulled out of the long, gravel drive and headed toward the road that would take them to the city. Miley-Hannah crooned on in a country drawl on the two-lane main road that would take them into the highway.

"It was a Disney show that Miley starred in."

Jackson's attention snapped back to the woman beside him. He hadn't noticed the song had finished. Brig was turning down the volume as she spoke. Jackson had no idea what she was talking about.

"The show was called *Hannah Montana*. Miley played the famous singer Hannah Montana, but she wore a wig so she could disguise herself so she could have a normal life as Miley at home."

"Like Jerrica Benton in *Jem and the Holograms?*"

"Who?"

Jackson clamped his mouth shut instead of describing the eighties cartoon his older sister had loved. Though on second thought, maybe he should speak up. He needed to remind them both of their age gap.

"Anyway, I liked the show because I can understand the need to pretend to be something you're not," Brig went on. "Especially when you're trying to protect others."

Jackson glanced at her. Once again, the childish mischief was replaced with clear, blue wisdom. There was more to Brigadear Silver than met the eye. It was something Jackson was not going to uncover.

"How's it going with Carter?" he said, cutting off the radio.

Brig snorted. "Ask Tilly."

Carter and Tilly were spending a lot of time together. More time than the engaged man was spending with the woman he'd agreed to fake marry. Jackson knew nothing inappropriate was going on between Carter and Tilly. In fact, if they all didn't need Carter to marry Brig, then Jackson would've encouraged the bond with Tilly to grow. Carter's attention to the blonde Silver sister was keeping his mind off his other vices.

Where Jackson refused to allow the medication that dulled his pain to become his master, Carter had long ago bent the knee. Metaphorically, speaking. Jackson couldn't blame the man. Combat was ugly and left deep wounds that didn't always heal, especially the internal ones.

"Carter's a good guy," said Jackson.

"He'd better be if he's going to marry my sister," said Brig.

"He's going to marry you."

"Wanna make a bet?" Brig cocked a brow, part question mark, part challenge.

Also, the mischief was back in that clear blue gaze. That was good. Jackson was better with the mischief than with the clarity and wisdom.

"I knew Scout and Linc would tie the knot that first day. They're both used to being in charge, so it made sense that they would join forces. Like Saylor, Jeff is a peacemaker—so that was inevitable. Mareen and Wilson both feel like outsiders, even though they are loved by the people who care about them."

Jackson snuck another glance at Brig in his peripheral vision. Once again, the mischief was gone from her gaze. It was replaced by a light of wisdom that was far beyond her two decades of living. She looked older than her twenty years.

"It took a little while to realize that Tilly and Carter were going to be a thing since they keep talking about the other guys she's dating," Brig continued to muse. "But they're both codependent. As a twin, Tilly's not used to being on her own. She'll never admit it, but when Gunny left to travel, it hit her hard."

Brig turned that blue gaze on him. Jackson felt she saw right through him. Her perceptions thus far were dead on. He didn't need her looking more deeply into him.

"You think Carter's codependent?" he said.

"I do," she said. "But I don't think it's another person he needs. I can't put my finger on it yet. But it's clear to me he and Tilly need each other more than he needs me. I'm not going to hold still and talk about eighties fashion wrecks."

"Hey, don't knock the eighties."

"Why not? You weren't born yet."

"I was born before this century began."

"So was I," said Brig. "I was born in 1999. You were born, what? 1990?"

That was the year of his birth. That gave them a nine-year age gap, not the ten he'd assumed. Still, it was an age gap. Jackson merged onto the highway, but he stayed in the slow lane.

"Truman is like a wounded animal," Brig went on. "Gunny is great with wounded animals."

"I'm marrying Gunny."

Brig turned to him with a wicked smile, but those blue eyes were clear. Clear and serious. "No. You're not."

It sounded worse than a threat. It sounded like a promise.

A horn blared, yanking Jackson's attention back to the road. He straightened the wheel just in time. He'd swerved over into a faster lane. But he hadn't picked up the pace.

"You sure you don't want me to take the wheel?" said Brig. "You drive like an old fuddy-duddy."

"I'm fine." His voice came out more harshly than he'd meant it to.

"Okay, Boomer."

"Boomer? How old do you think I am?"

"Not as old as *you* think you are."

Brig turned the radio back on. It was a Cyrus kind of afternoon. Miley's dad was crooning *Achy Breaky Heart*.

They drove the rest of the way without conversation. But Jackson's mind stayed on Brig. She relaxed next to him in the passenger seat, even closing her eyes as she hummed along to the music. She was completely trusting of him. Little did she know that he wanted to pull over and...

And what? Finally, learn what that mischievous grin tasted like? He couldn't do that. She was a child. He had to keep reminding himself of that. Except that in the conversation he'd had with her, Brig proved she might be the baby of the family in age, but not in intellect.

So why did she act so immature when there were flashes of what could only be called brilliance and insight in those blue eyes? She might think Gunny wasn't the one for him, but Jackson knew Brig could never be that woman.

CHAPTER SIX

"I'll drop you where you need to go," said Jackson.

Brig opened her eyes as the car came down to a slower speed. She was a sucker for falling asleep on long car rides. She hadn't fallen asleep just now. She'd just felt so relaxed, so right being near Jackson Bennett that she'd let her eyes close and her guard down.

"Here's good," she said, yawning. She stretched her arms over her head and arched her back to work out the stiff spot there. When she turned, she found Jackson's gaze latched on her form.

Not exactly on her face. His eyes roved from her arms over her head, down to the curve of her elbow, and finally at her raised chest.

He didn't avert his gaze as she unfurled her body and pressed her back against the cushion of the passenger seat. He had yet to blink when her arms slowly came down from over her head to rest in her lap.

Jackson was attracted to her. Even more, he wanted her. Which was just fine with Brig because she wanted him right back.

Call it gerontophilia. She didn't care. That touch of gray at his temples did something to her belly, and she wasn't ashamed. Jackson's cheekbones were starker than Cristiano Ronaldo's could've ever hoped to be. If Jackson stepped out on a soccer field, he'd win World Cups just with a grin.

He wasn't grinning at her. His eyes widened with guilt when he saw he'd been caught.

He sure was caught. Soon he'd be tied up in a nice little bow if she had her way, and Brig usually did. She'd laid hint after hint that she was a full-grown woman. Finally, the idea was taking root in that thick skull of his.

Surprisingly, manipulating a grown man was harder than it was with her sisters.

Jackson put the car in park. As soon as he cut the engine, he hopped out of the vehicle as though it were on fire.

Brig waited patiently in her seat like her father had taught her. More times than not, when she'd gone out on dates with boys her age, she found herself waiting long after they'd walked away from the car.

Not Jackson. After a slow exhale and a shake of his head, he rounded the car and opened the passenger door for her. Brig held out her hand. Jackson didn't hesitate to offer his own in assistance.

The moment their fingers touched, that guilty expression clouded his vision again. He dropped her hand like it was on fire. But he kept it hovering at her low back until they were both out of the street and on the sidewalk. Then he turned to face her.

"I'm not sure how long my appointment will be," he said. "I'll text you when I'm done."

"You can't. You don't have my number."

Jackson handed her his phone. Brig tapped into his contacts, adding her own. When she handed the phone back to Jackson, he smirked at what she'd written there.

"Brigalicious?"

She gave him a wink.

He tried and failed to wipe the grin off his face. "I'll see you in a bit."

It was a warm day with the sun shading itself behind a few clouds. Coeds were out on blankets with books and tablets. A few guys played ultimate frisbee on the lawn. Midterms had passed a couple of weeks ago, and the workload wasn't yet heavy with finals a couple of months away.

Brig didn't have many academic classes left. She'd finished all the classroom requirements of her degree over a year ago. All of her remaining coursework was practical and hands-on.

Jackson turned to walk into the university clinic. Brig trailed behind him. He looked over his shoulder, giving her a quizzical expression. "Don't you have to get to class?"

"This is my classroom," she said, pointing to the clinic.

Jackson's expression morphed from questioning to wary. Brig stepped up to the closed glass doors. She lifted her gaze to Jackson expectantly. The gentleman in him took over and opened the door.

"Hey, sweetie," said the receptionist, with a deep Southern twang.

Brig hated to be called by sugary endearments. Today's college women had a habit of calling each other *babe* and *sweets*. It turned her stomach as though she'd eaten a bunch of Valentine Sweet Tarts. But when Ronnie Mae Barton, with her cloud of gray curls and her kind pale eyes, called her sweetie, Brig couldn't muster the ire to mind. So maybe she did have a touch of gerontophilia.

"Hi, Mrs. Barton. How are you today?"

"My old bones are aching," she said. "Must mean a storm is coming."

Brig smiled at the old superstition. The weatherman had called for sunny skies all week. Outside, there wasn't a cloud in the sky.

"Good morning, sir," Ronnie Mae said, turning her attention to Jackson. "Can you sign in here please?"

Jackson picked up the pen and began the paperwork.

"Brig, sweetie, before you go Dr. Vargas wanted to know if you'd consult with her on a new patient," said the receptionist.

Brig nodded with as much nonchalance as she could muster. That consult, which she'd seen on the books when she was here last week, was her only pretense for being in the clinic today. All of her files were up to date. All of her paperwork in order.

"There's been a lot of job offers for you," Ronnie continued. "Have you made your decision on where you'll go after graduation?"

Brig still had a year left in her program. She'd been interning and volunteering in clinics all over the state for the last three years, aiming to learn all the best techniques. Now that she had them, there was only one place she'd ever take them.

"You know I'm gonna work on my family ranch," said Brig. "But I'll always be happy to consult at the clinic after graduation."

Brig caught Jackson glancing at her from his paperwork. He hadn't gotten past the first question, which was Patient's Last Name.

"Dr. Vargas, your next appointment is here," Ronnie Mae said to the petite brunette coming into the waiting area.

"Mr. Bennett?"

Jackson dropped the pen to shake Dr. Vargas's hand.

"And Brig, you're here too. I was hoping you'd consult on this case."

Jackson's gaze went wide. Wider than when he'd been caught gazing at her arched back. He opened his mouth as though ready to form a protest.

"Ms. Silver is my best student in Occupational Therapy," Dr. Vargas was saying. "Not just in this year's class, but ever. I put a lot of weight on her expertise."

"I'll be happy to sit in," said Brig. "If Mr. Bennett is open to hearing my advice."

Jackson looked at Brig as though she was a stranger. Brig was uncertain if her little game had been the best move. But what other move did she have? Before this, he hadn't seen her as the grown, capable woman she was. In this capacity, he'd have to.

CHAPTER SEVEN

*J*ackson sat on a hospital gurney. He had his shirt on, a pair of boxer briefs, and a paper-thin hospital gown. A slight chill ran through the room, but that's not what made him into a ball of tension.

"This all began with a torn meniscus?" asked Dr. Vargas.

The woman was pretty, average height, and curvy in all the right places. In her mid-thirties if Jackson ventured a guess. Not that he'd ever say so out loud. His mama didn't raise a fool who'd ask women about their age or their weight.

Still, a fool he was as he looked past Dr. Vargas and to the woman standing behind her. Brig now donned a white doctor's coat. Thankfully, that addition to her wardrobe enhanced the straight lines of her body, making her look like a young girl playing doctor. Somehow Jackson still found that adorable.

So not only did he have a thing for young girls, now he was hot for doctors? No, not doctors in the plural. Just this one doctor.

Wait? Was Brig an actual doctor? She couldn't be? She was too young.

"I tore my meniscus last year," said Jackson. "It was after an impact blast."

Brig looked out the window. She closed her eyes and exhaled. When she turned back, she caught Jackson's gaze. She knew what that impact blast had been. It had been the blast that had killed her father. Jackson had walked away with a limp. General Silver hadn't walked away at all.

Jackson held the gaze of the General's youngest daughter. Her eyes were the exact same shade as his. Her chin tilted high, just as proudly as her father's. Jackson worried that his mention of the incident had upset her. He should've known better. Brig was every bit her father's daughter. She nodded as if giving him permission to go on.

"A year before that," Jackson continued once he knew Brig was going to be all right, "I had a ligament tear. And five years ago, I fractured it."

"All on the same knee?" asked Dr. Vargas.

Jackson nodded.

Dr. Vargas pursed her lips. She flipped through a few pages on the chart. Then she tapped her pen at her lips.

Jackson should have noticed how lush her lips were. He should've thought about kissing those lips. Instead, he fought to stare at Dr. Vargas instead of doing what he really wanted to do, which was to lift his gaze and check on Brig.

"What's your diagnosis, Ms. Silver?"

Brig inhaled slowly, her gaze never wavering from Jackson's. There again, he spied the light of wisdom in those clear blue eyes. "Osteoarthritis."

"What?" The single word was harsh when it came out of Jackson's mouth. "Isn't that what old people get?"

"You'll be what? Thirty this year. That's getting up there, buddy."

Brig's tone was mocking. Jackson knew that even though she said *buddy,* what she was thinking was *boomer.* The jab should've stung. Because it was their private joke, it spread warmth through him.

"I take it you two know each other?" said Dr. Vargas peering between both of them.

"Mr. Bennett is staying on my family's ranch. Watching him these past few weeks, I noticed that the pain is usually in the mornings. He appears to go on a brisk walk at dawn to warm the joint up. I've noticed his walks going slightly longer recently, which indicates that the pain is progressing."

Jackson stared, dumbfounded. He hadn't even known that anyone was watching him on his morning walks. To hear how detailed Brig described his daily habits made him feel as though he'd been under surveillance. The woman would've been perfect for the intel division of the military.

"The joint is swelling now," Brig said as she bent down to peer at his bare leg. "There have been times when I've heard the popping of joint noise, all which tell me it's progressing."

Dr. Vargas nodded. Jackson felt like a lab rat as he sat between the two women who spoke about him as though he wasn't cognizant.

"What would your treatment plan be?" asked Dr. Vargas.

Brig turned from the doctor and looked directly at Jackson. "I know he did equine therapy at a rehabilitation ranch for veterans. It's clear that has been beneficial. I think he needs to stay that course at Silver Star. He could stay on the Fentanyl that the military prescribed, but I don't think it necessary. I think with the physical activity of riding, with added physical therapy, Mr. Bennett could be put on an aspirin regimen."

Jackson's lips parted as he looked at this woman. There wasn't a hint of mischief in Brig's gaze. He sat there under the full brunt of those intelligent blue eyes. He felt seen in the darkness that had surrounded him this past year. He felt heard, even though he hadn't spoken of his pain. His hands itched to pull her close. And then she came closer.

When her fingertips touched his knee, Jackson kicked out in reflex. Luckily, Brig moved to the side. Jackson's toes caught Dr. Vargas's charts, and the clipboard went flying.

"Sorry," said Jackson.

"No worries," said Dr. Vargas. "It's just papers."

"It's my fault," said Brig. "I should've warned you I was going to touch you. Jackson?"

"Yes, Brig."

"I'm going to touch you."

The thoughts that went through Jackson's mind at that phrase were not Disney friendly. He sat still as Brig's hand landed on his knee. Her gaze was all cool assessment as she poked and prodded his knee as countless medical professionals had done over the years.

Brig was different. Her hands on him felt right. Her proximity to him felt inevitable. He hadn't known he was in a battle until he realized he'd lost.

Brig wanted him. Of that, he was sure. Now he was also sure that she was going to have him. She was going to win this entire war if he didn't do something soon.

"Dr. Vargas." The gray-haired receptionist poked her head in the door. "I'm sorry to interrupt, but you have an urgent call."

"Excellent work, Brig. I agree with all of your recommendations. Will you finish up this chart and answer any of Mr. Bennett's questions? I'll be back to finish up once I'm done with my call."

"Sure thing," said Brig.

She took the chart and pen. The doctor and receptionist went out the door. The door closed with a quiet snick. Then it was just the two of them.

All Jackson could hear in the room was the *scratch scratch* of Brig's pen as she made notes on the documents. She didn't look up at him when she spoke.

"Do you have any questions for me, Mr. Bennett?"

"How long have you been watching me?"

She still didn't look up. But the corner of her lip quirked into that mischievous grin. "Since the day you stepped out of that truck and winced when your right foot hit the ground."

Jackson blew the breath he was holding out his nose. He emptied out his lungs and chest. Then he took a new breath and made one last attempt to win this battle between them.

"You can't treat me," he said.

"You don't think I know what I'm doing?"

Her face fell. No mischief. No intelligence. There was only hurt.

"It's clear you know exactly what you're doing, Brigadear. In more ways than one."

Brig sat the paperwork on the counter and took a step toward him. Jackson had the inclination to back down, but he knew better than to show his enemy his neck.

That thought brought his gaze to Brig's neck. It was long and slender. He wondered if she'd taste salty or sweet? She'd probably be all spice and fireworks.

"Jackson..." Brig reached for him.

Jackson held still, waiting for those fingers to impact him. He was uncertain what he'd do when they did. He was uncertain what his response would be to her words.

He needn't have worried. Before Brig's hands could reach his flesh or her words reach his ears, the entire room shook. He felt the earth move under his feet. He heard a large groan that sounded inhuman.

Jackson reached for Brig as the world went off-kilter. He brought her into his arms, sheltering her with his body, caring not for his injuries, only trying to protect her from harm as the world shook all around them.

CHAPTER EIGHT

"**I**'ve got you, baby."

The earth had literally moved, shifting Brig into exactly the place she wanted to be. She was cradled in Jackson's strong arms. She was tucked snuggly into his chest. One of his hands spanned her small back, clutching her to him. The other nestled her head into the crook of his neck. His palm was the softest, warmest cushion she'd ever come in contact with. She didn't know how she'd fall asleep ever again without it. She also knew she could never sleep if she found herself in this position.

Jackson's gaze wasn't on her. It was flitting about the room. The warrior part of him was clear in his hazel eyes. He assessed the threat to the both of them as he used his body as protection against hers.

As far as Brig was concerned, there was no threat, only fate. All of her scheming over the last couple of weeks had nothing on the power of Mother Nature. And because Mother Nature had intervened when Brig needed a miracle, it was more proof that she and Jackson were meant to be.

"It was an earthquake," Brig said. Her tone was calm because she'd grown up in Montana. Most people looked at California for its earth-shattering records, but Montana had its fair share of seismic activity each year.

Jackson's face came back to hers. He peered down at her as though just remembering that she was there. His gaze dipped to her lips.

Brig licked her lips and moistened her bottom lip. Jackson tracked the movement. His nostrils flared, a hunger in his eyes.

Brig didn't have a lot of experience with the opposite sex. She'd had no patience for the fumbling of the boys her age when they'd tried to grope her. The grown men she had been interested in had always kept at least six feet of distance between them at all times. This was the first time Brig had been in the embrace of a man she wanted to hold her.

She wasn't sure how to get him to come closer. So she did what any Silver daughter would do. She took command.

Brig lifted her head to meet Jackson's lips. The soldier in him was all reflex. He jerked back out of her reach without letting go of his protective hold. When he did so, he let out a sharp gasp of pain.

It must have been the pain that caused him to release her. Jackson rolled off her. He let her go and clutched at his knee.

Oh, no. His knee. Had he injured it more?

Brig scrambled to her own knees to get a better look. There was no blood. Just a dark flush on his brown skin where the wrinkle of his knee cap sat.

"Don't try to stand," Brig ordered. "Stay there. You need to rest it."

Jackson pried his eyes open. In those hazel depths, Brig heard the message loud and clear. It fairly shouted, *you think?*

Men in pain made for the worst patients. Brig went to the fridge, picking her way over debris left by the shaking earth. The door to the mini-fridge was open. She reached in and grabbed an ice pack.

Jackson hissed when she put the bag on his knee. Brig wouldn't have been surprised if he started wailing like a baby, like many of the other males that came into this clinic. She should've known better. After the initial harsh breath, Jackson pressed his lips together and focused on his breathing through his nose.

"I want to bandage it, to add compression."

The moment she touched his skin, he hissed again. Her gaze darted to his. She knew she couldn't have hurt him. She hadn't touched the knee, just the space above his thigh.

Then Brig realized that wasn't pain twisting his lips now. It hadn't been the first time either. It was a flare of desire, desire Jackson was trying to hide from her.

"Don't be a baby," she chided.

"Don't be a child," he struck back.

"I'm a grown woman. Did you know that I'll be twenty-one in a matter of months?"

Jackson's brows rose, giving her another glimpse of the interest he was trying desperately to hide. Brig didn't clarify that the matter wouldn't happen for nearly nine months.

"You're in my care," she said. "Which means you need to listen to me."

"I'm supposed to be protecting you," he said as she carefully wrapped the tan adhesive around his knee. "It's what I promised your father; that I'd look after all of you."

"My dad raised six capable women. I'm starting to believe he wanted us to look after the six of you more than he wanted you to look after us."

A small smile tugged at his lips. The mention of the general hailed a temporary truce between them. Jackson's posture relaxed as he leaned back against the wall. Brig curled her knees under her as she scooted closer to him to finish tying the bandage.

He winced again as she tied the end of the knot. "You need to work on your bedside manner."

"Happy to. Once I get you in bed."

Jackson's nostrils flared again before he tamped it down. Brig grinned triumphantly. He could deny all he wanted that she wasn't having an effect on him.

She cocked her head toward the gurney, eyes full of an innocence that neither of them bought. Jackson moved to get up, wincing as he did so. Brig put her arms around him.

"I've got this," he said.

"Now who's acting like a child?" she said. "Lean on me."

The set to his jaw was stubborn. "Don't you know soldiers have a hard time showing vulnerability?"

"I'm good at fixing broken things," she said. "There's a part of you that's broken. Let me fix it."

That changed his features. He didn't look relaxed. He didn't look tense. The only word that Brig could find to describe how Jackson looked down at her was resigned. She wasn't sure if that was a good thing?

He put an arm around her but didn't give her any of his weight. He winced again as they rose to stand. Brig had to brace herself against the wall to take on his weight. When she did, she realized it was her back against the wall as he loomed over her.

Jackson had her pinned against the wall. His arms boxed her in. His breathing became shallow. A bead of sweat formed on his brow.

Brig reached up and wiped it away. Jackson didn't track her movements. His gaze was fixed on her mouth once more. That's when she knew that resignation was a good thing.

Jackson wasn't giving up. He was giving in.

CHAPTER NINE

Jackson hadn't noticed the pain when he'd been holding Brig in his arms, protecting her on the ground after the quake. He'd forgotten the pain while he had her caged against the wall, her lips so close to his.

He might have been the injured party, but there was no way she could escape him. He had her well and trapped. Then a brief moment of clarity struck him when he looked into those clear blue.

Brigadear Silver wasn't trapped. She was exactly where she wanted to be. Jackson was the one with no escape.

He was going to kiss her. There was no other choice. Once he kissed her, his path would be set. He would have to marry her. Spend the rest of his days with her. Raise children with her, children with clear blue eyes and caramel-colored skin who would wreak havoc up and down the valley with their mother's penchant for mischief and his military prowess.

The world was doomed.

A loud boom sounded from the other side of the door. Jackson pulled Brig against his chest, tucking her forehead against his neck to ensure he would bear any of the brunt of the oncoming attack. She fit perfectly into the contours of his body like they were parts of a puzzle that had been pulled apart a long time ago. Now that they were back together, the frayed edges of his person felt whole.

"Brig? Mr. Bennett? Are you okay in there?"

The pounding sounded again. The rational part of Jackson knew the person on the other side of the door wasn't a threat. Still, he couldn't make his hands let Brig go. She was no help. She'd wrapped her arms around his waist and held fast.

"We're fine," she said into his chest.

"The door's jammed. Hold on, we're going to get you out."

Jackson wanted to roar at whoever was on the other side of that door. Didn't they hear Brig? The two of them were just fine the way they were.

There was a vibrant, beautiful woman in his arms. A woman looking up at him with the same desire he felt for her. It burned so hot between them that it dulled the ache in his knee. The only pain Jackson felt was the burning in his belly to claim Brig.

With brute force, the door opened. The doctor, the receptionist, and a burly security guard looked at the two of them. Their surprised looks were what finally snapped Jackson out of the dream world and back to reality.

Jackson had Brig pinned against the wall. He stood there in a shirt and his boxers and nothing else. The hospital gown had ripped off him at some point during the earthquake.

This was entirely improper.

But why?

Because he was a patient, and Brig was his doctor? No, that wasn't it.

"You okay, sweetie?" asked the receptionist.

Sweetie? The endearment that came from the gray-haired woman seemed meant for a child. Then Jackson remembered; Brig was a child. Though his brain rejected that notion as he looked down at her.

"We're fine," Brig answered.

She took a step past him. Jackson hesitated to let her go. The moment she left his hold, the pain in his knee slammed back into him. He knew she hadn't used an ounce of her strength to hold him up. He'd been the one holding her. Still, the moment she left his side, he couldn't hold on any longer, and he slumped against the wall.

Brig turned back to him. Concern etched in her pretty features. Jackson didn't like the look in her eyes. It was neither mischievous nor knowing. She looked scared.

He reached out for her, but he missed. He had a couple of inches on Brig in height, but she seemed to be growing taller with each passing second. All the while, the look in her blue eyes grew darker as her gaze widened. She was supposed to look at him as though he hung the moon. But she looked at him as though he was a sinking ship.

Because he was sinking. He was slowly going to the ground.

"He re-injured himself protecting me," she said as she crouched over him. "I bandaged the knee and had started applying ice."

"Good work, Brig," said Dr. Vargas. Her blunt fingers inspected the work at his knee. "Looks like you had a bit of excitement today, Mr. Bennet. Earthquakes are unpredictable. But Montana has its fair share of them. Luckily that one wasn't so bad."

Wasn't so bad? It had knocked Jackson off his feet. It had made him appear vulnerable and weak to Brig. That boom of the earth shaking had rattled his bones, making him feel like the Boomer Brig had accused him of being.

"Nothing's broken," said the doctor after an examination. "Just get him back to the ranch and start your course of therapy."

This was said to Brig. Jackson expected the mischievous grin to make an appearance. What made him quake in his bones was that Brig didn't grin at him. She looked at him with that clear blue gaze that unnerved him. That gaze unnerved him because it always made her look older than her nearly twenty-one years. It made her appear like she wasn't just on par with him age-wise; it made him feel like she was more than his equal. It made him feel like she was about to conquer him.

CHAPTER TEN

"You feeling better today, big boy?"

In response, the big boy in question dipped its head and snagged the apple out of Brig's palm. If only all men could be bought so easily.

Brig looked over her shoulder at Gunny's cabin. The front door hadn't opened yet today. It probably wouldn't since Jackson had been given orders by Dr. Vargas to rest his leg today after yesterday's natural disaster.

The worse the quake had done on the ranch was knock some of the tack off the walls in the barns and portraits in the houses. The main house and the cabins were all built to withstand a quake. Not to mention, the animals often gave a fair warning when something out of the ordinary was about to occur.

"We just weren't paying attention to you yesterday, were we, boy?"

Colonel Brandon took an unsteady step. He was much more agreeable today now that the ground beneath him was silent and still. Brig might not have paid attention to his behavior about the earthquake, but she was listening to the horse's complaint about his joints.

"Don't worry, buddy. We just need to work that leg out. You'll be dancing again with Mareen in no time."

The horse brushed his long nose against the side of Brig's face, much like an affectionate dog would do, only without the slobbering tongue lashing. At least the horse wasn't afraid to show her affection. Unlike some grown men who preferred to hide out in their cabins.

Jackson hadn't even allowed her to drive them home after the quake. He'd sent for Carter and Truman to drive into town to chauffeur them back. Then he'd stuck Brig in the car with Carter while he got into the passenger seat of Truman's truck.

Brig knew it wasn't the earthquake that had shaken Jackson up so much. It was that near kiss. She'd seen the spark in his eyes. It was easy to recognize since she'd felt it every time she'd looked at him these past couple of weeks.

For a few minutes the other day, Jackson had seen her. Really seen her. Seen her as more than the youngest Silver sister. He'd seen her as a capable, intelligent, desirable woman. And that had rattled him.

She wanted to stomp over there and bang on his door. But that wouldn't be the mature thing to do.

So what should she do? She was done playing the waiting game. They were running out of time.

Colonel Brandon stumbled, bringing them both up to a halt. Brig bent and ran her hand over the horse's front carpus. She breathed a sigh of relief when she didn't find any swelling. The horse held still, allowing her to massage the joint. Another difference between man and beast, the horse didn't kick out when she touched his leg.

Why was Jackson so afraid of what was between them? Was it really the age thing? They weren't that far apart in age. Both of them were in their twenties.

Maybe he had his sights set on Gunny? But he'd never seen Gunny. Brig was pretty sure the two of them had never had a conversation outside of a few lines of emails. Even if they had, she knew that her globe-trotting, save-the-animals sister was not the right woman for Jackson.

Jackson was a family man. He had set-me-down-with-roots written all over him. Brig wasn't ready to be a mother. Not yet. But when the time came, she wanted to be rooted right alongside him, whereas Gunny would never hold still in one place long enough to be caught.

"There you are."

Brig lifted her head at the sound of her sister's voice. Scout was a few yards away, but her voice carried as though she was standing right next to Brig. If Scout had joined the military, their father had hoped, she would've been the scariest drill sergeant that ever barked an order.

Brig never jumped when Scout spoke. Because as harsh as her sister's bite was, her hugs were the most comforting thing in the world. And besides, Brig knew Scout would never order her to do something that would put her in harm's way.

"We need to start talking details about your and Carter's wedding."

"Scouttie," Brig said patiently, "I'm not marrying Carter."

"Of course you are. It's decided."

Usually, Brig didn't mind her sisters trying to run her life. She was too good at covertly turning them around and steering their directives the way she already wanted to go. "You know Carter's into Tilly?"

"Their friends." Scout's tone was dismissive.

As if they heard their names called, Carter and Tilly came out of the barn. They were laughing and jabbing at each other. It was not inappropriate. They looked like best buddies. But Brig knew being best buddies was often a precursor to romance.

Scout looked at the two of them with a pinched expression as they rounded the barn and headed into the house. Scout opened her mouth as though to yell. Brig knew her sister's voice would easily carry across that distance. But that wasn't the direction Brig wanted to go.

"What if I'm into someone else?" Brig said before Scout could bark any order.

Again, Scout's features squinched into a pinched expression. "That might be for the best."

Scout's brows drew together as her gaze narrowed. Brig turned to peer in the direction of Scout's new focus. Truman walked up to Tilly and Carter. After a few seconds of what looked like a greeting, Carter went off with Truman, though his gaze lingered on Tilly as she walked up the porch steps and into the house.

"Truman's not into it," said Scout.

Brig breathed a sigh of relief. Once again, the right words whispered into her sister's ears were going to get her exactly what she wanted.

"I'll talk him into it," Scout continued. "I'll twist his arm if I have to."

Scout didn't wait around for Brig's next words. She marched off in the direction of the house. Brig didn't bother correcting her sister. Once Scout got on a path, even a path Brig tried to direct her bull-headed sister down, it was hard to steer her until she reached the end.

Everyone in this family thought they knew what was best for Brig. Sometimes they were even right. But not this time. It was crystal clear to Brig that she was going to marry Jackson, whether everyone liked it or not. And that included Jackson.

CHAPTER ELEVEN

Jackson could see Brig in the distance, but for once, her gaze was not on him. Her attention was on Colonel Brandon. She patiently walked the arthritic horse around in a slow circle. Even from this distance, Jackson could see the horse's uneven gait as his front right leg gingerly contacted the ground.

This morning, Jackson had had the same reaction when he'd put weight on his right leg. The joints there protested more than normal. Likely because of the impact of his world shifting the day before.

He'd nearly kissed Brig. He'd wanted to with every fiber of his being. Right now, every fiber, even the disjointed ones in his legs, urged him to make his way to her and complete that mission.

Laying in the bed for an entire day, Jackson had felt like he was lying in darkness. Even though the light of the sun had shone through the curtains. The moment he was breathing the same air as Brig, he felt like a switch had been turned on inside him, and he could finally see the dawn.

"You look like hell," said Truman. He leaned against the frame of the cabin next door.

"Survived an earthquake," Jackson shot back.

"You survived bomb blasts and looked better," said Carter.

"Aren't you supposed to be resting those old bones?" said Truman.

Jackson shook his head. "Doc said I needed to walk it a bit the next day."

"Which doctor?" asked Truman, his gaze turning to where Brig walked the horse.

Carter turned too. His eyes lighting up once they landed on the woman in question.

Jackson felt the urge to wring his brother's neck. He couldn't stand to have any man look at Brig as though she was the dessert he was about to dig into. The truth was that Carter had claimed that right. Carter had agreed to marry Brig. Carter would get to indulge in the sweetness of that clever mouth.

The grin on Carter's face fairly shouted that he couldn't wait. But then the clouds in the sky shifted, and Jackson saw that Tilly had joined Brig in the round pen.

An enormous weight lifted off Jackson's shoulders. The sigh of relief that left Jackson's chest was audible. He would've hated to kill one of his best friends. Especially if it had to be Carter. If he'd have had to wring the man's neck, Jackson would've been left with oily gel all over his hands.

"I take it back," said Truman. "You're looking combat-ready all of a sudden."

There was a knowing light in Truman's gaze. The sniper's vision was sharp. Not that it needed to be when Jackson was standing at close range.

Jackson looked away, but not before sneaking another glance at the pen. "I'm gonna work the knee."

"We'll come with you," said Truman.

"I don't need a babysitter."

"Really?" said Truman. "Cause it sounds like you're pitching a fit."

Jackson huffed. Once upon a time, he could outrun both of them. However, with his injury, he knew they could outpace him with nothing more than a fast walk. So, he resigned himself to being followed.

At least they didn't demand he banter with them. Carter could talk to a wall and hold an engaging conversation. Instead of walls, Carter's voice bounced off trees. Leaves rustled in the breezeless afternoon. Branches crunched underfoot.

Truman offered infrequent grunts of his inattentiveness. Jackson remained entirely mute. He was far too lost in his own thoughts to even follow Carter's monologue.

Jackson needed to figure out what he needed to do about Brig. More to the point, his inappropriate desire to kiss the young woman. She might be turning twenty-one in a matter of months, as she'd said. But she was still far too green behind the ears to get mixed up with a man like him.

But if not him, then who? Definitely not Carter. Jackson would never consign Brig to a loveless marriage, even if temporary. It was clear to anyone paying attention that Carter had it bad for Tilly.

Not Truman, either. That soldier had it bad for his old job. Truman was working hard to rehabilitate his shoulder injury. Before shrapnel had lodged in his shooting arm, Truman had been one of the best snipers in the Armed Forces. He had a single-minded determination to get that title back. Meaning there was no woman in his plan. Unless she was standing within the crosshairs of a target.

That left only Jackson.

A hand shot out in front of him. Jackson looked beside him to see Truman with his hand outstretched. His friend's gaze was on the ground. A root rose out of the earth. One more step, and Jackson would've easily caught the tree's overgrown vine. One more fall could easily take his knee out.

"Thanks, man."

Truman nodded wordlessly.

Carter kept babbling on in front of them as though nothing had happened.

Age aside, this was the other reason Jackson could never be the man for Brig. She was young and vibrant. Where his body was already giving up on him before he'd even hit thirty. He could never keep up with her.

The sound of horse hooves came near. Jackson tensed, wondering if it was Brig. Was he hoping it was her? If he was honest, he would admit that he was.

Knowing he wasn't right for her was one thing. But thinking about how right she felt in his arms was an entirely different matter.

While he lay in bed all day yesterday, all he thought about was her. The feel of her against his chest. The taste of her breath so close to his lips. He'd nearly kissed her, and man, had he wanted to. Still wanted to. Which was why he was putting distance between them.

But if she came to him?

Jackson looked up to see the rider. It wasn't a brown-haired girl. It was a brown-skinned man. Jackson and the two other soldiers immediately stood at attention as Father Matthews rode toward them.

"Afternoon, gentlemen."

"Colonel," they all intoned.

Haran Matthews shook his head at the three stiff soldiers standing in formation. The old man was a decorated war hero with more medals and stars that the three of them had combined. Father Matthews came from a line of decorated war heroes from the Buffalo Soldiers to the Tuskegee Airman. He had been a pilot himself in his youth. Now he contented himself with the care of horses while also keeping a watchful eye on his best friend's six daughters.

"I hear I'll be officiating another wedding soon," said Father Matthews, who was also an ordained minister. In fact, he preferred to be called Father Matthews.

Father Matthews' eyes landed on Carter. For once in his life, Carter was momentarily tongue-tied.

"Right," said Carter, finding his voice. "That would be me. I'll be marrying..."

"Brig." Truman supplied for him.

Carter blinked as though he didn't recognize the name.

"That's surprising," said Father Matthews. "With as much as I've seen you and Artillery about town together."

"Oh, no." Carter waved the notion away as though it were a trifling matter. "Tilly and I are just friends."

"And you and Brig?" prompted the pastor.

"Me and Brig?" Carter looked confused. "Oh, yeah, Brig's a great kid."

"She's not a kid."

All eyes swung to Jackson. He stood chewing on his lip as though chastising it for speaking. But the words were the truth.

"Brigadear is a very accomplished young woman," Jackson managed to say. "And she'll be twenty-one in a matter of months."

"I remember when her father fell for her mother," said Father Matthews. "Did you know he was ten years older than Sarah? Sarah's parents wouldn't hear of the marriage. But Sarah was determined. She threatened to elope if her parents didn't agree."

Jackson was still thinking about Father Matthews's first words before the rest of the pastor's words caught up with him. The general had married a much younger woman? And that woman had been defiant. Seemed Brig and her mother had a lot in common.

"My wife was fifteen years older than me." Father Matthews went on. "I think you boys would call her a cougar? We didn't have any children of our own. We adopted our boys. Love doesn't see age or blood. It just sees a heart like its own."

Father Matthews's gaze landed on Jackson. Those dark eyes seemed to see directly into Jackson's heart. Whatever the general's best friend saw there, it made him smile.

"Let me know about those wedding dates, boys," said the pastor as he directed his horse to walk on. "None of us are getting any younger."

CHAPTER TWELVE

"Come on, twinkle toes. You owe me a dance."

Colonel Brandon got off to a slow start as Brig walked him out of the barn the next morning. She didn't mount him yet, knowing he needed a good warm-up. His movements were sluggish as she led him around the pen. Too bad horses couldn't have canes.

"How's he doing this morning?" asked Mareen.

She and Tilly came inside the pen. Colonel Brandon immediately pulled to go to Mareen. Brig let him go. The colonel's slow start quickly picked up as he made his way to his owner and former dance partner.

As a teenager, Colonel Brandon and Mareen had taken the dressage stage by storm. The horse was already in his prime when they'd partnered up. All these years later, and the colonel's heart was still aching to move, but his body just wasn't willing. Though the body-mind connection seemed to snap back into place as he high stepped it to Mareen.

Mareen smiled at the horse, giving him a nuzzle and a scratch behind his ears. The simple wedding band on her hand left hand caught in the morning sunlight. The former society miss wore worn jeans and boots instead of her normal tailored dresses and heels. Mareen Silver Michaels looked as young, fresh, happy as the days when she'd dance with Colonel Brandon. That's what love could do for a person; change them inside and out.

"He's doing good this morning," Brig said in answer to her sister's earlier question. "He just needs some exercising."

Already, the horse's gait was easier as he walked alongside Mareen around the pen.

"Do you think it'll come to injections?" Mareen asked.

Brig said nothing. It took the silence stretching on for longer than a few seconds for Brig to realize that the question was aimed at her. She was so used to one of her other sisters shouting out the answer that it took her an additional moment to respond to Mareen's question.

"No, I don't think you need to go the pharmaceutical route if you don't want to. We can do supplements to start. Right now, I think he needs routine, exercise, and a modified diet. If we can get some of this weight off, he'll feel an immediate difference."

"Thank you, Brig," said Mareen. "For taking care of him all these years."

Brig shrugged. "You would've done the same for me."

Mareen looked pensive. For so many years, Mareen had tried to hide her true feelings. Over the past week that she'd been with her family on the ranch, that skill was getting harder and harder to maintain.

Mareen wasn't used to others having her back. Even her own mother had used her as a pawn in the divorce. That divide had left Mareen feeling alone, even though she had a big family who had always wanted to love her. Now, Mareen just needed to learn to let them.

Brig insinuated herself between Mareen and the horse. It was easy for Mareen to show her love for the horse. It wasn't so easy to show it to her sisters. At least not yet.

"Resistance is futile," said Brig as she leaned into her older sister. "I don't doubt it for a second you would do whatever it takes to keep us all safe. You nearly married a man you didn't love to keep a roof over our head."

Mareen relaxed into Brig's embrace. She was doing that faster and faster these days, after always holding herself off from her sisters. Brig had always ignored that barrier Mareen had tried to erect. She didn't believe in the term half-sisters. All five of her siblings were all hers regardless of the imaginary lines their parents and others may have drawn in the dirt.

"I didn't do the best job of saving you," said Mareen. "You still have to marry a stranger."

"Carter isn't a stranger," piped in Tilly. Her face hunkered down in her phone as usual. "Did you know he worked for Dad since he joined the military? It means he's practically our brother."

Mareen and Brig shared a glance. Tilly didn't catch it. She was often oblivious until the thing was staring her right in the face.

"I didn't know that about him," Brig said, deciding to skirt the brother comment.

"Yeah, didn't he tell you?" said Tilly, her thumbs tapping away on her phone's face.

"Carter and I have never had an actual conversation."

"Sure you have," said Tilly. "We were all talking last night."

"The two of you were talking. I was simply in your presence."

Tilly's thumbs paused, hovering over her phone. Finally, she glanced up. "What do you mean by that?"

"Do you realize Carter is the longest relationship you've ever had?" said Brig.

"Relationship?" Tilly frowned, her thumbs caressing the side of her phone case. "Carter and I are just friends."

Brig turned back to Mareen. She felt gratified when Mareen lifted an eyebrow, indicating that she was seeing exactly what Brig was seeing. Tilly was entirely clueless.

"Carter's for you," Tilly said.

"Thanks, sis," Brig scoffed. "Are you giving him to me with a big red bow?"

Tilly frowned, completely missing the jab. "You're being a child."

It was the insult often hurled at Brig when her older sisters didn't have an adequate comeback. Only this time, it wasn't going to work. Brig was tired of pretending, tired of playing this childish game of peekaboo where she was the wizard behind the curtain.

"Why does everyone accuse me of that when I tell a truth they don't like?" she said.

Tilly looked to Mareen for support. Mareen wisely kept to the other side of the pen, making sure to avoid any new lines drawn in this family.

"I'm going on a date with Sergei this weekend." Tilly held up her phone. "Which proves I'm not into Carter. And he's not into me. He's helping me plan my outfit."

Mareen crossed the imaginary line. She and Colonel Brandon stood firmly on Brig's side. It was a moot point as Tilly was back looking down at her phone.

Brig's attention wasn't on her sister any longer. Jackson was walking toward them. For the first time since he'd arrived on the ranch, his gaze wasn't on anyone and anything besides her. Jackson was looking at and walking toward Brig with even, purposeful strides.

CHAPTER THIRTEEN

Jackson's gaze slid over Brig as he walked toward her and her sisters. For the past few weeks, he'd been sure to look past her. Not today. Today, something had changed.

She wore a pair of jeans he'd seen on her many times before. The fabric molded to curves he'd never admit to noticing. The dull colors of her flannel shirt only served to brighten the mischievous glint in her blue eyes. Her toned arms moved as she expertly and confidently handled the horse in her care.

Even on the days when he'd tried not to look, Jackson had always noticed that Brig knew exactly what she was doing when it came to the horses under her care. The horses knew too, and they followed her commands without dallying. With a wave of her hand, one of the horses came to her.

Jackson felt his feet pick up their pace as he rushed to fulfill the order. The walk down the path did him good in more ways than one. His knee was feeling nearly brand new. And so was his mind, thanks to the talk with Father Matthews.

It was as though shells had fallen from his eyes. Brig stood backlit by the sun. In the glare of the afternoon light, Jackson saw the young woman in an entirely new way.

As though she felt his gaze, Brig looked up from the horse, and her eyes found Jackson's. Jackson nearly stumbled when they did.

Gone from her eyes was playfulness. Instead, her gaze was cool, medical assessment as it zeroed in on his right. Her head cocked to one side and then the other as though she was measuring each of his strides.

Jackson's back went erect. He felt every muscle in his legs working to win her approval. He almost wished for the days when she'd grin at him like a lovesick schoolgirl. When her gaze lifted to his face and met his, there was no hint of that girl. In fact, Jackson couldn't remember how he'd ever seen Brigadear Silver as a kid with all the weight of intelligence in those blue eyes.

"You're being a child."

Jackson frowned at Tilly's accusation. It didn't fit the woman standing before him. Brig stood with a strong posture. Her head high. Her brow quirked.

"Why does everyone accuse me of that when I tell a truth they don't like?"

That stopped Jackson in his tracks. He'd done the same to her the other day. He'd heard her sisters do it more than once since he'd been on the ranch.

Each time the childish accusation was hurled at her, Brig would shrug it off. She didn't now. Jackson wasn't sure what the sisters were arguing about. He could see that it was Tilly who looked like a petulant adolescent. It was Brig who looked on with the wary patience of an overworked mother.

That cracked a smile on his lips. His smile quickly fell when he saw that Brig wasn't smiling. She looked defeated.

"Fine," Brig said when they were upon them. "Have it your way."

Brig came toward them. But her gaze wasn't on Jackson. Her attention focused in on Carter. "How are you this morning, Carter?"

Carter startled. His body had been angled to keep walking past

Brig. He was likely headed for the object of his unspoken desire; Tilly. But he stopped and gave Brig a bright smile.

"I'm doing good." He paused a beat. And then, "And you?"

"I'm doing great," said Brig.

A silence descended between the two. Had it been a couple of days ago, Jackson would've nudged Carter to ask after Brig's health or to give her a compliment. Today Jackson was annoyed that Brig's attention was on his friend and not him.

"I think it's time we got to know each other," said Brig. "Since we're going to be married soon."

In that moment, Jackson knew bliss. He stood in a state of perfect happiness and joy. He was oblivious to everything around him. All he could see was his future with Brig.

Caramel-skinned cherubs with light blue eyes and wild curly hair running around his legs. His hands clasped with Brig's as he looked down into her beautiful face. Her lips pressed against his in one of a million kisses he'd steal because it was his right as her-

The record scratch of his dream made Jackson wince. Brig's words hadn't been aimed at him. They'd been for Carter.

Beside Jackson, Carter blinked. "Right. Sure. Of course."

Wrong. Doubtful. Never going to happen. That's what Jackson wanted to shout.

"Why don't we go for a walk," Carter said as he took a step toward Brig.

At least Carter had tried to take a step toward Brig. But something held him back. Jackson looked over to see that it was his arm against his friend's chest.

"No," Jackson barked. The bass in his voice was so deep that the horse took a step back. "I need to talk to Brig first. About my knee. She's my doctor."

"She's not a doctor," Tilly muttered.

"Brig?" Jackson held his hand out to her.

Brig stared at his open palm as though he was presenting her with a sparkly diamond. He didn't miss the grin as she slid her hand into his. Jackson fought to keep his hold on her light.

He failed. His fingers clasped firmly around hers, not letting in a whisper of air between them. Silence reigned behind them as they walked off toward the barn.

Great. Now that Jackson had her, he wasn't sure what to do with her. He just knew that her hand in his felt right, and he didn't want to let her go. The real question was, was he going to keep her?

The second the thought crossed his mind, Jackson realized his miscalculation. He was alone. In a barn. With Brig. A position he'd promised himself he'd never get in.

Yet here he was. A man unarmed against his most worthy adversary. The war was already decided, had been when the general had ordered them all to come here. But Jackson wasn't going down the aisle without a fight. If he didn't at least show some gumption, he wouldn't be the man deserving of the general's daughter.

CHAPTER FOURTEEN

ingles shot up and zinged down Brig's entire arm at just the touch of Jackson's warm hand on hers. When the door to the barn closed behind him, she heard his sharp intake of breath.

At first, she was concerned that it was pain. But he was moving with sure strides beside her. That wasn't physical pain he was feeling. It was something deeper. It was the sound he'd made a week ago when they'd all been playing Monopoly, and she'd bankrupted him even though he owned all the expensive, blue properties.

Jackson hadn't realized he'd been had. Right up until she had him. Once again, Brig had snuck up on him and was ready to take him for everything he had. Only this time, in return, she'd offer him her heart.

She stopped and turned to face him. Jackson was looking at her, but she wasn't sure what he was seeing. His features were a mask. She knew he had to be feeling this too. How much longer would he deny what was happening between them?

"So," Brig began once they were standing in the barn. "You got me alone. Now, what are you going to do with me?"

Jackson said nothing as his gaze appraised her. Brig noted he still held her hand in his. She'd always hated when her sisters held her hand. She knew they liked babying her, but by the time she was a teenager it had gotten old.

Of course, it felt different when a man held her hand; when this man held her hand. So, Brig didn't pull away from Jackson's hold. She wanted to be held by him.

He'd called her baby when they'd been trapped in the exam room back in the clinic. Brig had always cringed when guys tried that endearment on her. When Jackson had said it in that deep voice of his, it sounded as though she was something precious, someone he wanted to care for. Maybe even cradle in his arms.

Jackson dropped her hand. He re-schooled his features. Now he looked at her with clinical assessment.

"I want to talk with you about my care plan," he said.

"Your… care plan?"

He nodded. "I think you were right about my treatment."

"You… do?"

"I'd like to get started on your suggestions."

"Oh. Okay."

"I was thinking we could take a walk. Maybe a long one. Down by the pond between the Flying Cross and Silver Star property line. Since that's a long walk, maybe we should take a picnic lunch."

"Hang on." Brig held up her hands, needing a minute to follow Jackson's new plan. She opened her mouth to take a deep breath. The air she had been holding inside gushed out first. She had to take another moment for her lungs to refill before she could speak. "You want to take a long walk with me and have a picnic?"

Jackson nodded patiently. His features still set in that unreadable expression. "Yes, if that sounds like a good care plan to you."

"It sounds like a date to me."

His features barely shifted. Brig caught the slight wince of his right eye. Or was that a wink? She'd become very familiar with Jackson's looks of pain. There was none in the crinkle of his eye. So she decided to label that a wink.

The next thing she noted was a slight tug of his bottom lip. He wasn't frowning. Frowns were signs of distaste. People didn't lick their lip when something was distasteful. They licked their lip when they wanted to taste something.

Meaning Jackson wanted to taste her. Brig wanted to jump up and down and pump her fists for joy. But she couldn't. The game wasn't won. Yet. She was going to make this grown man cry uncle.

"I'll have to ask Carter since, you know, I'm engaged to him."

Jackson lips pressed into a flat line as though he'd tasted a rotten egg. "You are not marrying Carter."

"I'm afraid I'll have to." Brig raised her open palms in a helpless gesture. "Unless there's an alternative."

Jackson's body was so tense, so rigid, that Brig worried he might hurt himself. She would be the one to cry uncle if she sensed that he was in pain. She reached out her hand and laid it on his chest. His heart was racing.

"Are you okay?" she asked.

Jackson let out a long, weary sigh as though the weight of the world had just left his strong shoulders. "When you touch me, all the pain goes away. You make me feel like I can do anything."

His hand covered hers. It pressed her palm flat against his chest, where his heart lay. Brig wanted to curl her fingers into him. She wanted to possess this man completely, as he had possessed her the first time she'd laid eyes on him.

"You can do anything," she said. "And if you let me, I'll stand beside you as your helpmate, as your cheerleader, as your partner while you do. Every day, for the rest of my life."

Jackson's hazel gaze roamed every inch of her face. As he did so, he came closer, closer. Then his free hand shot out.

He wasn't cradling her. He was holding her so tight she couldn't tell where she ended, and he began. She didn't feel like a baby in his arms. She felt perfect. Right.

And then his lips met hers.

She'd expected Jackson to crash into her with how tightly he was holding her. Instead, his lips were the gentlest of caresses. A helpless moan escaped her lips. She'd spent all these weeks trying to bend Jackson to her will that she was surprised at her cry of surrender.

Brig had fought for his attention. She had fought for him to see her as a woman. Now the battle was won, and she was lost.

Jackson's hold on her tightened even more as he deepened the kiss. In this realm, she was out of her depths. She'd received a few light pecks, but she'd never opened to someone as she was doing now. Jackson invaded, and Brig let down all of her defenses. She laid her every weapon at his feet.

Until he was wrenched from her.

Brig opened her eyes to see a haze of brown hair and a fist flying. She tensed for impact. But the punch landed on Jackson's nose. He went down like a stone.

"Scout!" Brig shouted, grabbing at her sister's hooked right arm, which was preparing to unload again. "Stop it!"

CHAPTER FIFTEEN

One moment, Jackson was tasting heaven. Brig was sweeter than he'd imagined. With the first brush of her upper lip, the sugar rush had weakened his knees. His second nip of her lower lip sent energy beaming out from his chest and down into his legs.

He felt like he could run a marathon. He felt like he could climb a mountain. He felt invincible with this bountiful, beautiful, blooming slice of pure bliss.

Jackson pulled her closer to deepen the kiss. But instead of more bliss, he tasted blood.

"Get your hands off my sister."

The sharp pain in his face was intense after the tender feel of Brig's lips. He'd already lost his breath while kissing her. Now he needed air. His throbbing nose wouldn't let any in. Likely due to the blood filling his nostrils. The pendulum of sensations was so violent that Jackson could no longer hold himself up.

He went down. Luckily, it was his left knee that crashed into the dirt floor of the barn and not his right. It still hurt, adding to the agony of his busted nose.

"I don't know what game you're playing, but I'm ending it now."

Even with his eyes closed and his nose aching, Jackson knew that voice. It had lost its femininity and sounded much more like the general who had given him orders for years. When he opened his eyes, Scout Silver Rawlings loomed over him like an avenging angel of death.

It should've smarted that a woman had gotten the drop on him. But Brig had already brought Jackson to his knees the moment he set foot on this ranch. It had been inevitable that he would fall for the girl. So, taking a blow from her older, over-protective sister - who by the way had a mean right hook- was his due.

"She's just a kid," Scout snarled.

"She's not a kid," Jackson said at the same time that Brig said, "I'm not a kid."

Brig's arms were around him. He'd like to say that the moment she touched him, all the pain went away. If only that were true. It wasn't.

The pain did dull as Brig cradled his head in her hands. She tilted his head from side to side and then back. Jackson clamped his mouth shut from the vertigo. Then he howled in pain when she touched his injured nose.

"Ouch, Brig!"

"It's not broken."

Maybe not, but her fingers pressing into either side of his nostrils wasn't helping any. If they survived this, they needed to have a serious talk about her bedside manner when it came to treating human patients.

"You're supposed to be marrying Gunny," said Scout.

"I'm not marrying Gunny," Jackson said at the same time that Brig said, "He's not marrying Gunny."

"He's marrying me," Brig said at the same time that Jackson said, "I'm marrying Brig."

In the barn door, a crowd gathered. Linc stood just inside the barn, his arms crossed over his shoulder as he grinned at his wife's back while simultaneously wincing down at Jackson.

Tilly and Carter stood off to the side of the entrance. For once, they weren't looking down at a cell phone and cracking jokes. But like always, their heads were together as they watched the spectacle with voyeuristic delight.

In front of Jackson, Scout's right fist was still cocked. Jackson had been trying to get his feet under him. One glance at the weapon of Scout's hand, and he sat his bum down on the ground in surrender. Linc gave him a nod as though he'd made the right decision.

General Silver had taught them many lessons in combat over the years. They knew the signals of when to advance on a fledgling enemy. They knew when to press the bad guys into making a mistake that would give them a tactical advantage. They'd also learned when the odds were against them and to throw up the white flag.

Jackson's white shirt was now dripping with red. His fledgling defenses which Brig had masterfully broken down, lay in shambles. As one sister stood over him with fists at the ready, and the other continued to poke at his nose in a sign of care, he decided to let the two superior forces duke it out amongst themselves.

"You broke his nose, Scouttie."

"I'm about to do more than that," Scout huffed. "He seduced you."

Brig snorted as she glared up at her sister. "I seduced him."

Jackson winced. Not at the pain, but because Brig was right. She had put him completely under his spell, and he was quite content to stay there for the rest of his days.

"He's too old for you," Scout insisted.

"He's eight years older than me," said Brig.

"I'm actually nine years older," Jackson said. "Closer to ten. I'll be thirty this year."

"You're not helping," Brig hissed.

"It's the same age difference as your parents," Jackson said to Scout, who had taken a step closer to them.

"Again," said Brig, "you're not helping."

"I don't believe in divorce." Jackson turned his gaze from Scout and focused all of his attention on Brig. "So, if you say yes, it's for better or—"

"Yes." Brig grinned, tears lighting her eyes.

Despite the pain still lingering in his body, Jackson reached up to cup Brig's chin. It trembled at his touch. "I haven't asked the question yet."

"When you do, the answer will be yes."

Brig moved closer, tilting her head first one way then the other. Her nose still bumped his before he could taste her lips. Jackson pulled back with a pained groan. Less from the pain and more from being denied the sweet taste of the woman who would soon be his wife.

"I haven't said yes," said Scout.

"It's not your decision, Scouttie," said Brig.

"What about Carter?" said Scout.

"She'd run over Carter," said Jackson.

"Hey!" Carter said from the door of the barn.

"They're right," Tilly said to him.

That appeared to soothe Carter. He shrugged and offered Jackson a grin that said congratulations, and I pity you at the same time.

"You think she won't run over you?" said Scout to Jackson.

Jackson looked back at Brig. She was beaming at him. Her cheeks glowed in the low light of the barn. The happiness in her smile soothed every ache in his knee, every pain in his nose.

"I'm sure she will. But I can handle her."

That glow of happiness morphed into the mischievous grin that Jackson had once feared. Only now, he realized it hadn't been fear of danger or a threat. Jackson was a warrior, and the fight-or-flight part of him had known that that grin would be his downfall.

Not a fall to defeat.

The type of fall that involved his heart.

Jackson was going to fall in love with Brigadear Silver. He might already be there. He was down on the ground after all. And that grin on her face seemed to say this was exactly how she'd planned all of this to go down.

He was so screwed. And he didn't mind one bit. He pulled her to him and pressed a light kiss to her lips. Their noses tweaked, and he winced in pain, but it was a good hurt.

CHAPTER SIXTEEN

"Aren't we walking?"

In answer to Jackson's question, Brig led him inside the barn where two horses were saddled. She would never tire of the deep rumble of Jackson's voice. Nor how it rolled through her body when he spoke. She wouldn't have to worry about never getting enough of him because she finally had him. Which meant that she wouldn't have to hide her feelings for him any longer.

Jackson was hers. He'd made a promise, which for a man of his honor made it a done deal. But soon, she'd have it made official in a legally binding contract, which she'd never let him get out of.

Luckily, it looked like he was pretty happy with his acquisition. His fingers twined with hers. Just at the knuckles, not down to the webbing between each digit. It was more than enough for her.

Brig reveled in the feel of his callused hands against hers. She shivered every time his bare forearm brushed against hers. If just the touch of his elbow made her warm, imagine what another kiss would do.

Then she realized she could have his lips pressed against hers anytime she wanted. Because Jackson was hers. He was going to marry her. They would spend the rest of their days with him whispering in her ear, brushing light kisses on her mouth, and doing all the things married couples did to cause shivers.

"Brig?"

"No, we're not walking." Brig reluctantly pulled off her fiancée hat and pulled on her clinical one. "You've had enough weight on your knee for now."

"I'm not sure if you're calling me fat? Or if you're judging my stamina."

Brig giggled. Then she rested her hand on Jackson's chest. Just because she now had that right as his fiancée. Jackson didn't shy away from her touch.

"No one could get away with calling you out of shape," she said.

Jackson huffed, a dark shadow crossing his features. Part of Brig wanted to poke at that, to unfurl his brow and ask more about the shadow. She decided to focus on the second part of his statement.

"As for your stamina…"

Jackson quirked a brow at her.

"We'll have to see about that."

Brig tilted her head up, angling for a kiss.

Jackson's lips parted. Then he gulped audibly. As though he was swallowing down his desire.

Brig didn't move an inch. She didn't bat an eyelash. She held her position and waited. Her fiancé needed to figure out that the only thing standing between them was him.

"We're waiting until we're married," Jackson said, his lips hovering just above hers. Because his mouth was so close to hers, she felt his lips quiver as he said the words, as though the thoughts that made them up stood on shaky ground.

"Get your mind out of the gutter, soldier," Brig said against his lips. Then she leaned her head back so that he could see the seriousness in her gaze. "We're going horseback riding. A little equine therapy will be good for that injury."

Jackson let out the breath he'd been holding. That gush of air didn't sound relieved. It was sweet with his desire for her.

"I'm going to be a good wife to you; hopefully, a great wife. But

I'm outstanding at what I do in rehabilitative care. I'll get your knee where you want it to be."

Jackson brushed a finger across her temple. His knee brushed against hers as they stood toe to toe. "My knee is exactly where I want it to be."

His lips brushed hers in a slow caress. By the time he'd brushed from one side of her mouth to the other, Brig had forgotten where they were, why they were there, and what her name was. Before she could press him to deepen the kiss, Jackson hoisted her up and onto one of the horses.

"Hey," she protested. "No more heavy lifting, mister."

"You're light as a feather," Jackson said as he mounted his horse.

He gave her a wink before urging his horse on. Brig let him take the lead. He was a man, and they needed to feel in control from time to time.

"Sit up taller," Brig said once they were on the trails.

Jackson glanced over at her. The man swaggered in the saddle as though he were walking across the runway. It took Brig a moment before she could remember what she'd said and why.

"I'm the expert, remember."

Jackson gave her a sultry smile and did as she bade. With his shoulders back, he looked even more devastating in the saddle.

"Riding is a three-dimensional movement," Brig went on, trying to focus on his health and not how beautifully masculine he was. "Your body is moving back and forward, up and down, and side to side all at once when you're riding a horse. It's the same as when you're walking. You're using all the same neuromuscular pathways as when your arms swing back and forward, your hips move side to side, and your legs go up and down. Except now, you're not using your body weight."

Jackson adjusted his body in the saddle as he listened. Then he grinned as he looked at her. "You're good."

"No," she corrected. "I'm exceptional."

"Lean to the side," he said.

Brig grinned as she did so. The horses came to walk side by side.

Jackson leaned toward her from his mount. He brushed a gentle kiss against her lips. Brig wanted more but now was not the time.

Still, when they pulled apart, a mischievous grin lit her face. "Ready to kick it up a notch?"

"Bring it on."

Brig urged her horse up from a walk and into a slightly faster trot. Jackson did the same, still keeping his same posture. Brig watched for a moment, checking his body's alignment. When she was satisfied, she went faster. Jackson matched her pace for pace, his posture never wavering.

By the time they came to a stop, all four of them—man, woman, and horses—were out of breath. Jackson and Brig tied the horses up in a patch of grass with flowers they liked. With their rides settled, they made their picnic.

Jackson spread the blanket while Brig unpacked the food. Once the feast was spread, Jackson picked up a piece of fruit and brought it to Brig's mouth.

"Are you going to feed me like a child?" she asked. "Because if we're still on this age thing, I think I'll be the one cutting up your food in fifty years, Boomer."

"No, baby," he grinned.

The way Jackson said baby made Brig feel nothing like a young girl. That word rumbled in his mouth, making her feel like a desirable woman.

"I stopped seeing a child back at the clinic. Probably sooner than that, which is why I've been trying to avoid you the past couple of weeks. Right now, I'm feeding you this food because I want any excuse to touch your lips."

"You don't need any excuse. I'm yours."

Jackson ran the chunk of fruit over Brig's bottom lip. She opened and took a bite. The fruit's juices ran down her chin. Jackson caught the droplets with his thumb. Then he put his thumb in his mouth.

"Not as sweet as you," he said.

Brig expected that to be followed up by more kisses where they completely ignored all the food and feasted on each other. Instead, Jackson's gaze clouded over and threatened to rain on their picnic.

"You have your whole life ahead of you," he said. "Am I being selfish taking it away?"

"I want to experience my life with you at my side. I want to be by your side. You're going to need a nursemaid in your old age, boomer."

Jackson chuckled. "Hopefully, by then, you'll have learned better bedside manners, baby."

"I love you, Jackson."

She couldn't help the words. They tumbled out with a will of their own because they were the truth. Thankfully, Jackson didn't flinch at the declaration.

"Don't tell me it's too soon. Or that I don't know you well enough. I know my own mind, and I know what's in my heart."

Her sisters tried to tell her what was best for her all her life. But she knew no one would be better for her than this man. Jackson had seen right through to the heart of her since that first day. No one had bothered to look that deeply. Finally, he wasn't running from what he saw. He reached for her.

"I'm going to spend my life being worthy of your love, Brigadear. Even with these rickety, old man bones."

"Okay, boomer," she grinned.

"Come here, baby." Jackson captured her lips in that grin.

Their picnic lunch did sit forgotten on the blanket. By the time the sun began to set, both Jackson and Brig were full from feasting on each other's lips.

CHAPTER SEVENTEEN

She loved him.

The thought should send Jackson running for the hills. It should have him turning her around and pushing her back to her sisters. Instead, Jackson held Brig's hand as though it were his lifeline.

Because that's what she was. Just the touch of her hand was more potent than the pills he'd taken every morning since the blast. This morning he hadn't reached for the cursed bottle. He hadn't felt the need. After the workout from yesterday, coupled with the warmth that had suffused his limbs from holding her close and kissing her soundly, the constant aches and pains of his body had retreated.

Brig's fingers twined with his over the middle console of the truck. She hummed along to the radio in the passenger seat of the car. Her gaze was out the window. Her features were relaxed, as though she didn't have a care in the world.

Why would she have a care? She had gotten everything she wanted. One of those things was him. Because make no mistake, Jackson Bennett was wrapped around Brigadear Silver's little finger, and he wasn't making a move to unravel himself from his position.

Had he have known that being with her would put such a kick in his step and lift his spirits, he would've let her trap him the first day he'd set foot on the ranch. Right now, he brought her fingers to his lips and brushed kisses from her knuckles to her nails. Brig turned from her sightseeing out the window. When those blue eyes landed on him, Jackson knew peace for the first time in his life.

He'd thought her mischievous grin would be the death of him. He'd come to see her in a new light when wisdom brightened her gaze. Now, only love and devotion shined through.

He pulled the truck into the first parking spot he found. Then he divulged them both of their seatbelts and pulled her to him. Brig wrapped her arms around his neck with a delighted giggle.

Jackson kissed her like it was their first time. Like it was their last time. Like they had all the time in the world.

But they didn't. Brig nudged at his shoulder as she tried to pull away from him. Jackson growled and held her tighter.

"Jackson, I have to get to class."

"Of course, I'd wind up with the nerdy teacher's pet," Jackson sighed but loosened his grip.

She gave him a wink as she slung her backpack over her shoulder. "You don't have to wait. This will take a few hours."

"I'm not leaving you here stranded."

"I don't want to ruin your day. I can get a friend to drive me back or call an Uber."

Jackson cupped her chin in his hand, tilting her head back so that she would see the dead seriousness in his gaze. "First, you could never ruin my day. Second, I'm going to be your husband. That means it will be your job to inconvenience me."

Desire and delight churned in Brig's blue gaze. Jackson couldn't help himself. He leaned over the middle console to taste the emotions on her face, starting with her eyelids, then her cheekbones, and finally her lips. She was even sweeter than the last time he'd kissed her. Now that he was allowed, he couldn't seem to stop kissing Brig.

"I'll wait for you," he said when he pulled away.

"Okay," she agreed.

Jackson blinked once, twice, and then held his gaze wide. "So that's how it's done? That's how I get you to do what you're told?"

Brig leaned in, just a few millimeters from his lips. "Kiss me like that, and I'll obey your every command."

"Dutifully noted."

Jackson snuck a quick kiss, savoring the taste of her grin. Then he slipped out of his seatbelt and opened the driver's side door to round to her side. When he stepped down, he misjudged the distance to the paved street.

Pain shot up his knee. So swift, so absolute, that he felt nauseous. He made a sound at the back of his throat like a pained animal. A few people stopped walking to glance over.

"You okay?" Brig had hopped out and was beside him.

"I'm good." Jackson didn't look at her as he straightened. His gaze was on the eyes staring at him. Young eyes taking him in. Pity on their faces.

"We may have overworked it on the ride yesterday," Brig said. "Will you promise to take it easy while I'm inside?"

Jackson wasn't listening. He was glaring at the young men eyeing Brig's backside. She was still bent down, running her hands over his knee. Jackson pulled her up and into his arms in a possessive grip.

That gesture broke the young men's lurid stares. They looked from him to Brig and back again at him. Then they sniggered as they walked on.

Jackson wanted to storm over to them and teach them the real lesson they should be learning on this campus. But his knee ached. He'd probably wobble as he marched over.

"Why don't you catch a movie at the town cinema," said Brig, completely oblivious to the battle lines drawn behind her. "They have a matinee."

"Senior citizens go to the matinees."

"Then you'll be right at home, boomer."

Part of his brain knew that the nickname was a joke, a private joke shared between the two of them. But Jackson was still raw from the pain in his knee and the adrenaline pumping through his veins at the threats now jogging away from them to join a game of Ultimate Frisbee.

"I think I'll hit the gym," Jackson said.

"No, you won't." Brig's voice was loud enough to carry.

Jackson drew up to his full height, towering over her. Of course, that wouldn't deter Brig. She threw her head back and glared right back at him.

"I'm the boss of your body," she said, placing her hand on his heart. "You're the boss of my heart. If you break your body, it will break my heart."

This little slip of a woman. How did she unman him and at the same time make him feel invincible? Jackson knew there was no choice but to do as she told him.

She leaned in for a kiss. Once again, Jackson obeyed. Just because he could, he deepened the kiss, pressing her to him and giving anyone who walked by a show. Those frat boys were off catching a frisbee, but they wouldn't get their hands on this ultimate prize.

After a few catcalls, Jackson was satisfied that he had made his point. When he let her go, it was Brig who stumbled a few steps as she made her way to her classroom.

CHAPTER EIGHTEEN

"To the happy couple," said Carter, raising his glass.

Everyone around the table did the same. The entire Silver clan took up a long table in the back of the bar. Even though they were in the private area, there still weren't enough seats for all eleven of them. The three married couples didn't mind. As always, Scout and Linc, Saylor and Jeff, and Mareen and Wilson used one seat per couple.

Brig sat beside Jackson, but their chairs were so close together that she was nearly on his lap.

"And here's to you, Jackson," Carter turned to face his friend. "Only man I don't mind losing my fiancée to."

Jackson tipped back his beer as he drank to his friend's toast. His arm rested lightly around Brig's shoulders, but his fingers gripped her shoulder cap in what felt like mindless possession. Brig didn't mind at all.

"Thank you for being so good about it," said Brig, raising her Shirley Temple to Carter. The fizzy drink tickled her nose when she brought the glass to her mouth. The sugar rush made her blink a couple of times.

"You chose the better man, Brig." Carter bent down and bussed her on the cheek.

Jackson growled, giving his friend a look of warning. That low hum only served to increase the bubble of sweet happiness that Brig found herself in. Carter held up his hands in protest and backed away.

"So…" said Tilly. "What are we going to tell Gunny?"

All around the table, drinks paused on their way to mouths. Those who had taken a drink gulped down the contents. No one spoke.

"We'll tell her that she got an upgrade," Carter said, brushing imaginary dust off his shoulders.

"You'll marry her instead?" asked Tilly. She placed the phone she always held face down on the table.

"Of course," Carter said, turning to her. "It's what I agreed to."

Tilly nodded. She didn't pick her phone back up. She tapped her nails on the back of the case.

"Now you just have to land Sergei," said Carter.

"Sergei's out," said Tilly, picking her phone back up. "Can you believe he DM'd me at one in the morning with a *U up?*"

"Rookie move," said Carter.

"Right?" agreed Tilly.

"But you were up," said Mareen. "You and Carter were watching *Say Anything*. Again."

"We could hear Peter Gabriel singing *In Your Eyes* blaring like he was holding a stereo right into our window."

Mareen shuddered. Wilson pulled her into his chest, pressing his lips against her temple. The newlyweds had the unfortunate luck to be in the cabin nearest Carter's, which Tilly had built. Tilly stayed in a bedroom in the main house most nights, but she could often be found hanging out in her old cabin with Carter.

"I thought you two hated the eighties," Wilson said.

"We do," said Tilly.

"Then why are you always watching John Hughes films?" asked Mareen.

"Making fun," said Carter.

"It's called hate-watching," said Tilly.

Brig lost interest in the nonsensical conversation. Tilly had a habit of only watching movies and television shows she swore she detested. She'd talk all through them, commenting on how stupid a character was or how tragic their outfit was. No surprise that none of her sisters enjoyed going out to the movies with her. But Carter seemed to enjoy her every quip.

Brig turned from her family's back and forth to the dance floor. Her toes tapped in time to the beat. She'd been sitting at a desk all day filling out charts and reports as part of her classwork at the clinic. Now she wanted to move her body. But she didn't get out of her seat because she also was happy right where she was.

Jackson had an arm around her shoulder. She was pressed flush against his side. Every now and again, he'd lean over and brush his lips against her cheekbone in a thoughtless kiss, as though he'd been doing it all her life. Why would she pass up this spot? It was the best seat in the bar.

Party in the USA came on the speakers. Brig couldn't resist. When Miley sang about putting her hands up, Brig threw up her hands and shimmied her shoulders.

"Go dance, Hannah," said Tilly.

"Hannah?" asked Jackson.

"Hannah Montana. It was her favorite show as a kid."

"Oh, right. You told me." Jackson grinned at her. "You wanna dance, baby?"

"Do you wanna dance with me, boomer?"

"Ha ha," snorted Carter. "Baby boomer. Get it."

"Yeah, I get it," said Tilly.

Jackson ignored them both. His lips twisted as though he wasn't happy with the words he was about to say. "I don't dance."

"Oh." Brig felt her shoulders hunch. "Okay."

"The knee," Jackson clarified. "Doctor's orders."

"Well, your doctor thinks you can sway from side to side while you have her in your arms."

Slowly, Jackson's lips untwisted from their grimace and turned into a grin. "That sounds like the best medication ever."

He got up, holding out his hand to her. Brig slipped her hand in his, feeling a jolt of excitement go through her. It wasn't their first dance as a married couple. That was coming soon. It was their first dance as a couple which was more important. Not everyone would be invited to her wedding. But when the bar-goers saw them in a tight clench, everyone would know that Jackson was her man and she was his woman.

Jackson led her to the dance floor. Once in the center of the gyrating bodies, he gave her a slow twirl. Once she came back around to face him, Brig rested her hands on his shoulders. She moved her hips, but not in time to the beat. She moved in time to the beating of Jackson's heart. Jackson kept a light hand on her as she moved around.

"Your beautiful," he said in her ear when he pulled her close. "I'm the luckiest man in the world."

Brig wrapped her arms around his neck, swaying slowly to the fast-paced beat. Even though her feet were steady and Jackson's hold was firm, Brig felt like she was falling.

"When I hold you close, I feel invincible. Like I can run a marathon. Or even bust a dance move."

And then he did. He pulled away from her, crossed one foot over the other, and did a spin that would've put James Brown to shame.

"Where'd you get those moves?" called a guy. "Send them back to the seventies."

The carefree joy on Jackson's face melted away. His head snapped to the side to find the taunting voice. Brig looked over and recognized a couple of guys from campus. She'd never had any classes with them. They seemed to spend their days on the lawn playing Ultimate Frisbee and catcalling at the girls walking by. A few of the young women on campus had filed a complaint, but not much had been done.

Jackson tensed as though he was ready to do something. Brig

wrapped her arm around his bicep. She didn't want her night ruined.

She should've known Jackson wouldn't fall for such childish behavior. He gave the boys a warning glare. Then he swayed with Brig until they were away from the menace.

Brig grinned up at him. Some of the tension left his face as he gazed down at her. A second later, his back was ramrod straight, as though he was tensed to fight.

"Come on, sweet thing," said the same nasally voice. "You know you wanna hang with us instead of the old geezer here."

Though the kid might be on the college campus, he couldn't have been enrolled there. No one was that dumb. He'd riled up a trained soldier. Even worse, he was on the bad side of a Silver sister's temper.

As though they sensed danger, her sisters were already rising from their seats at the back of the bar. But by the time Brig turned back around, Jackson already had the guy in hand.

Literally. With one hand, he had the boy's shirt collar gathered in his fist. The boy struggled to breathe as Jackson lifted him an inch off the ground.

The kid was helpless. Or so she thought. Mr. Mouthy's hands slapped ineffectually at Jackson's iron grip. But when his sneakered shoe kicked out, that was all it took.

The toe of Mouthy's shoe struck Jackson right in the wrong knee cap. Jackson's grip opened, and both men went down.

CHAPTER NINETEEN

"*S*urgery."

There were words before that pronouncement. There were words after it. But all Jackson heard was that single word.

Surgery.

Nearly two hours ago, his friends had hefted him off the dance floor. They'd laid him out in the backseat of one of the cars and took off to the Emergency Room. Brig had climbed into the backseat with him. Jackson's head had rested in her lap. He'd tried to concentrate on the feel of her fingers in his hair, on his cheek, on his chest. Instead, he felt every rock and pebble the wheels bumped over on the way to the hospital. Luckily, with it being a small town, they didn't have to go far.

Jackson had refused any pain meds when they'd wheeled him in. He'd been off Fentanyl for a few days now with no adverse reactions. He didn't want to backstep. Though he knew that the time of grinning and bearing it would be cut short all too soon. All he felt were the sharp pains going up and down his leg, radiating outward from the throb in his kneecap.

There was one bright spot of relief in all of the pain. Brig. She stood at the bed beside him. Her gaze fixed on the doctor as the young man spoke.

The youthful doctor looked like he was just out of high school with his pimpled face and slim build. Was that a lisp Jackson detected as the boy said words like arthroplasty and synovial membrane? Was Jackson really going to listen to his prognosis?

No, he wasn't. He was getting up and walking out of here before this boy picked a knife and started playing with it near Jackson's knee. But even shifting on the bed caused shooting pains to run up and down his leg.

Jackson slumped back on the hospital bed. Brig leaned over him, peering into his gaze and running her hand over his leg at the same time. Her fingers were careful not to touch his knee.

A part of Jackson knew that her touch would be just the thing to heal him. Instead, the young doctor touched him. Jackson let out a howl of pain that nearly knocked him out.

Brig's blue gaze widened. There wasn't mischief in her eyes. Nor was their wisdom. Her bright blue depths dimmed to showcase dismay and dread.

"I'm not having surgery," Jackson managed to bite out. "The swelling will go down, like before. I'll just stay off it for a few days."

Brig held her tongue. And that's when the first tendrils of fear crept up Jackson's spine. Brig was never quiet. She always spoke her mind.

Unless she didn't want him to know what was on her mind. Unless she was having second thoughts about their marriage. She was finally seeing him as he truly was, a washed-up soldier whose parts were no longer in working order.

"I'm afraid you're not going to be able to walk out of here," the doctor was saying. "You'll be in a wheelchair for weeks, maybe months. After the surgery, you'll be lucky to get around with a cane."

Jackson balled his hands into a fist. He was surprised to find pain coming from his knuckles. But then he looked down at the torn skin where he'd decked the guy who'd come onto Brig. Was this going to be his life? Having to take shots at all the young bucks who sniffed around his young wife? And now he'd have to do that from a wheelchair. Or, if he was lucky, with the assistance of a cane.

"Mr. Bennett? Mr. Bennett, did you hear me?"

Jackson did not hear the doctor. The man's opinion didn't matter. The only person whose opinion mattered was being uncharacteristically silent.

And then, finally, she spoke. "Thank you, Dr. Pierce. We'll take your prognosis under advisement."

The man gave them both a wane smile before turning and leaving the room. The door to the hospital room shut. Jackson and Brig were alone.

Brig took a deep, audible breath. She let it out slow through her parted lips. Jackson tried to hold his breath so that he wouldn't sample any of the sweet air, but his body ignored him. He breathed her in, the scent of cherries, and sugar, and Brig.

"The first thing we're going to do is get a second opinion," she said.

Jackson stared at her lovely face. His immediate thought wasn't how young she looked. It was how vibrant and full of life she appeared. Brigadear Silver oozed vitality and health. She had it in spades.

"We'll start with Dr. Vargas at the university. She's not a surgeon, but I'd trust her prognosis before his. That kid looked barely out of freshman year of college."

Part of Jackson wanted to laugh. Brig thought that kid was young. He was definitely older than her.

"I do think you should spend the night here. I don't want to move you again and make it worse."

"I'll stay," said Jackson. "But you should go."

"I'm not leaving you alone here."

"Visiting hours will be over soon."

"They have to let me stay." Brig shrugged, pulling up a chair to the bed. "I'm going to be your wife."

She took his hand. Her fingers brushed over the torn skin of his knuckles. The skin torn when he'd roughed up the guy who had hit on her earlier tonight.

Jackson shouldn't have let that young buck get under his skin. But he had because the jerk had voiced Jackson's fear. And now that fear had a hold on his knee. It was that fear that had taken Jackson down. And now, he might not be able to stand back up.

"No," Jackson said, his voice strained. "No, you're not."

"I'm not what?" Brig lifted her hand from his knuckles to run them down the side of his face.

It took everything in Jackson to pull away from her touch. "You're not going to be my wife."

Brig jerked back as though he'd slapped her. He felt the sting all over his body. On the positive side, it momentarily muted the pain in his leg.

"You're going to marry Carter as planned. Unless he finally realizes he's in love with Tilly. Then I'll force Truman to do it."

"You'll force someone to marry me?"

"Yes. It's the only way I have left to protect you."

Brig stood. The chair toppled back with the force of the action. "I don't need protection. I need the man I love to come to his senses."

Jackson shut his eyes. It was the second time she'd said she loved him. He hadn't even said it once yet. But it was there in his heart.

Jackson loved Brig. He loved her so much that he knew he couldn't consign her to a life with him if he couldn't be the man she needed.

"You're being serious?" Her voice was quiet. Pain laced every word she said.

The throbbing in his knee was nothing compared to having to cause pain to the woman he would lay down his life for. But he couldn't even get up to do that act for her.

He knew better than to argue with her. Brig was the most intelligent person he knew. She would talk him blue in the face, trying to convince him to her way of thinking. Or worse, she might pull out the heavy artillery and lean down and kiss him. If she did that, all would be lost, and she would be stuck with a man who would never be her match.

"Nurse," Jackson called out to the woman in scrubs passing by the door.

The nurse ducked her head into the room, a pleasant smile on her face. "Do you need something?"

"She needs to go." Jackson chucked a thumb at Brig.

"Isn't this your wife?" asked the nurse.

"No, she's not. She's just a kid."

This time Brig looked like he'd punched her in the gut. Tears stung her eyes. Jackson had hit her where he knew it would hurt the most. But he'd had to do it. She would realize it in time. He was broken, and his path to healing was rocky at best.

Brig would heal. She was young and resilient. She gazed down at him, blue eyes wide and perceptive as always.

Did she know what he was doing? Did she understand why? Would she ever forgive him?

Jackson wouldn't find out. Brig shuttered her gaze. Then she turned her back on him and marched out the door.

CHAPTER TWENTY

*B*rig knew what Jackson was doing. She'd had enough psychology classes to understand the male mind. Especially when said mind was vulnerable and backed against a wall.

Jackson was protecting himself. Even worse, he thought he was protecting her. In a sense, it was logical. But Jackson's words to her still hurt the next morning.

She lay wrapped up in his sheets in Gunny's cabin. Even though his scent brought her comfort, she couldn't stop hearing the sound of his agony when he'd gone down on the dance floor of the bar.

Brig curled into a fetal position. She brought her legs up to her chest and hugged herself tight.

It brought no comfort. The only thing that would bring her relief was Jackson's arms wrapped around her. But he was too wrapped up in his own pain to do that.

Well, he'd have to get over that, and quick. In fact, he'd have to do it today. This minute. Because last night and the distance between the ranch and the hospital was all the space she was going to give him.

The only reason she'd left him last night was because she wanted him to feel the pain of pushing her away. Of course, then they'd both been left in agony. Him in a hospital bed with his knee in turmoil. Her in his bed, tossing and turning all night.

It was childish. If they were going to act like children, then they should at least suffer their punishment together.

Brig heard the sound of the door opening. She sat up in the bed, heart pounding that Jackson had come after her. This was the precedent she wanted to set in their relationship, that she was always right.

She breathed a sigh of relief as she sat up. All would be well. They would get married and laugh this off as their first fight.

Then reality dawned. Jackson's knee was too banged up. He couldn't walk out of the hospital, much less into the cabin.

"She's in here," called Scout.

Brig flopped back down on the bed. Then she pulled the pillow over her head. When she did, she got another strong whiff of Jackson. She felt the urge to punch the pillow. If only that would knock some sense into the man.

"Everything's going to be okay, sweetie," cooed Saylor. The bed dipped as her sister's weight landed on the mattress, and warm hands came to Brig's back.

Brig wanted to tell her sister she didn't need coddling. But the moment Saylor sat down on the bed, Brig found her head migrate to her sister's lap. Her arms went around Saylor's waist, and tears welled up again.

"He sent me away," Brig sniffed. "He said he won't marry me now. He said he's not man enough for me."

"That's the stupidest thing I ever heard," said Scout, fists on her hips as though she were preparing for battle.

"It's kinda romantic," said Mareen.

Scout shot her sister daggers with her eyes. Mareen held up her hands in placation. Though when Mareen turned from Scout, her eyes rolled.

There was a part of Brig that wanted to laugh at the two. Scout's way of fighting was to shout and bully her opponent into submission. Mareen used the silent treatment and cold shoulder. Neither of their methods ever worked. Scout would eventually tire herself out while Mareen would inevitably get lonely. In the end, they would always wind up talking things out to solve the problem—even if that chat was years in the making.

"I think what Mareen said makes sense," said Tilly.

Now Scout turned her loud glare on Tilly. Mareen turned back around with a warm smile on her face that said *I told you so*. Tilly, used to both their antics, ignored them and focused on Brig.

"Jackson wants what's best for you," Tilly continued. "Now that he's injured, he doesn't believe he's it anymore."

"If he truly believes that," said Scout, "then he's not the man for my baby sister."

"I'm not a kid anymore," said Brig. The pounding of her fist against the mattress didn't help her argument.

"We know that," said Scout. "You haven't been a kid since you said your first word."

"It was cornucopia," grinned Saylor.

It was. Toddler Brig had been fascinated by the horn that overflowed with colorful fruits and corn. She'd grown up in a family full of people, and she was used to being surrounded and wanting for nothing.

"I didn't know that," said Mareen, her voice barely audible.

Mareen had missed a lot. But she was here now. Right in the middle of this overflowing room of sisters. Sisters who would always have her back, even if she tried to turn away. Sisters who would never let her fall anytime she stumbled. Sisters who would stand by as she touched the fire they told her was hot because they'd let her learn her lesson, but they'd never let her get truly hurt.

That's what family did. Whether by blood, or by vow, or by enlistment.

Jackson had enlisted to join this family. He didn't get to suffer on his own. He didn't get to soldier a burden by himself. He was a Silver now, and he'd have to get with the program. Because he needed her. He needed all of them.

Jackson didn't know it, but very soon, his hospital room would be overflowing with his new family.

"We need to get back to the hospital," said Brig as she threw off the covers.

"I'm driving," said Scout.

"What if he won't see her?" asked Mareen.

"We're not giving him a choice," said Scout. "He wanted in this family, he's in. You don't get out that easily."

"Breaking knees is usually how the mafia let's someone go," said Tilly.

"No, it's putting them in a trunk and parking it in Long Term Parking at the airport," said Scout.

"You've watched way too much *Sopranos*," said Tilly.

"Jackson's in pain right now, Brig," said Saylor. "He's not thinking clearly. Maybe we should give him some time."

"We don't have a lot of time," said Brig. "The will—"

"Don't worry about the will," said Scout. "No matter what, we will always be a family. No matter where we are or who we marry."

"Is everybody decent?" asked a male voice.

When no response came, Carter poked his curly head in the bedroom door. Instead of his gaze going to Tilly, it searched out and found Brig. When his gaze latched onto hers, Brig took a step back.

Jackson said he wanted Brig to marry Carter. Was Carter here to finally make good on that promise? No. Carter's gaze looked worried, not resigned to marrying a woman he didn't love.

"What's wrong?" said Brig. "Is he okay?"

"They're moving him," said Carter.

Relief warmed Brig through, and she took a step forward. "He's coming home?"

"He's not coming back to the ranch," said Carter. "He's checking in at the VA clinic in the city."

CHAPTER TWENTY-ONE

*J*ackson winced as the transport set him down on pavement. His leg was extended and immobilized while in the wheelchair, but he could still feel every bit of loose gravel on the pavement as he was rolled into the VA clinic.

He'd called in the last few favors he had left in the military and had gotten the transfer rushed through. He knew he wouldn't have much reprieve before Brig came back. Jackson knew she would come back, and the next time would be with reinforcements.

Not the President's Men. They knew better than to try to change his mind. Jackson knew Brig would return with a far more formidable weapon; her sisters.

If his brothers wouldn't be enough to change his mind, he knew that the Silver sisters would twist his arm right along with his leg until he cried uncle. He'd expect nothing less of the general's daughters, which was why he'd moved fast. Or as fast as the red-taped, backed up, weighed down healthcare system would allow him to.

Then there was the tangled web of Brigadear Silver. Just another flash of her smile would cut through all the bureaucratic defenses Jackson had armed himself with. Seeing her lip tremble had hurt him, likely more than it had hurt her. But Jackson knew the woman he loved; he knew that pushing her aside might bring her down, but it wouldn't knock her out.

Brig was too strong, too smart to fall for the act for long. She'd be back. Without a vow between them, she wouldn't be able to get in to see him.

The valves of his heart twisted inside his cold chest. The pain was worse than what was going on in his knee. The damage to his knee could be fixed. The pain in his heart would be permanent.

Jackson pounded at his chest to hush the protests within. He knew that wheeling around and racing back to the ranch wasn't best for Brig. She needed a man who could protect her, who could keep pace with her. He could do none of those things.

He also knew that Brig would roll right over Carter if he took her hand. She would race mental circles around Truman if he stepped in. Still, both those men were better options than him.

Inside the waiting area, Jackson saw the fruits of war. Men and women with hands to heads and pain in their features likely suffering from undiagnosed TBIs. Others sat with missing limbs. Many stood alone in corners, no family or friends by their sides. One man caught Jackson's gaze.

He was in a wheelchair. Both his legs were missing and replaced with prosthetics. He held a wiggling child in his muscled arms. Behind him, a vibrant red-haired woman pushed the back of his chair to set the family in motion.

The wounded soldier looked up at her, love in his gaze. The woman, his wife, if the dazzling ring on her finger had anything to say about it, looked down at him the same way. The child gurgled between them, making happy sounds as he looked up at his parents.

A toy tank wheeled into their paths. The man's free hand went to the handbrake on the wheel. The toy tank passed by with another toddler chasing after it. The child's parent gave an apologetic wince as she scooped up both her child and the toy.

The red-haired wife gave the woman a grin and then leaned down and kissed her husband. The child rested a tired head against his father's chest and began to doze. The family continued on out the door as though nothing had happened.

Jackson stared after them.

He'd seen similar scenes at his time on The Purple Heart Ranch. Dylan, who had one leg amputated, and his wife Maggie chasing after dogs and children. Reed, who had had a prosthetic arm, holding his infant in one hand while tapping away at a computer code with the other. Nothing physical stood in the way of those relationships. The men and women who made their lives on the Purple Heart Ranch were some of the strongest Jackson had ever encountered.

Jackson looked down at his knee as he sat in the waiting room. The joint throbbed, though no weight or pressure was on it. He might be in this chair for a long time. He might have to depend on a cane for the rest of his life.

If he remained in the chair, Brig would likely insist on riding on his lap as he wheeled them along. If he had to rely on the cane, she'd probably decorate the device, and they'd ride horseback most places.

But Brig wasn't here. He'd told her to go. And she had.

He'd put another obstacle in their path. First, with the years between them. And now with his knee.

Jackson came to a horrified realization; he'd blown it. He was the toy tank whizzing between them. An obstruction that might cause him a moment's discomfort, but it would not have taken him down permanently. No, he'd done that all by himself.

"Sir, are you checking in?" A tired-looking man behind the reception counter called to him. He had a clipboard in one hand and a pen in the other.

Jackson wasn't interested in taking either. He wheeled his chair around and headed for the exit. His knee throbbed from the quick action, but he ignored it. He would spend the rest of his life in pain if he didn't correct his mistake.

When he got outside, he realized the mistakes were coming at him from more directions. He didn't have a car. Even if he did, he couldn't drive himself anywhere with the state he was in.

Add to that that he didn't have a cellphone. He hadn't seen it, much less thought about it, since he'd collapsed onto the dance floor last night. He'd have to go back inside and ask the receptionist to use the phone to call the ranch.

As his hands moved down to the wheels of the chair to turn himself around, Jackson saw two familiar trucks pull up to the front of the clinic. The trucks swerved to a stop, lining up side by side as only stunt car drivers, or a trained unit, could pull off. It was his unit and the Silver sisters.

Brig stumbled as she got out of the truck before the engine was shut off. Jackson wanted to shout at her to be careful, to look both ways before crossing the street, to hurry on over into his arms because he couldn't get to her fast enough.

But Carter caught her. His hand wrapped around her upper arm, and he pulled her back to him. Jackson saw red.

His body demanded he stand. To take his friend down and claim what was his. A second later, Jackson's view of both Brig and Carter was blocked off when an ambulance wailed by them.

Once the danger passed, Brig and Jackson's eyes locked. Jackson held out his arms—but not before looking both ways down the street. Brig's head didn't swivel in either direction. Her gaze was only for him. She ran into his arms, climbing onto his lap just as he had dreamed she would.

"I'm sorry," he said, breathing in her scent of sweetness and sunshine.

"Good," she huffed into his chest. "Because you were an idiot."

Jackson didn't disagree with her. Because, as per usual, Brig was right. Jackson chuckled, and then he groaned in pain.

Brig hopped up off his lap. She looked down at his legs, blue eyes narrowed in that clinical assessment that Jackson found hot. His pain forgotten, he reached for her again. The tears in her eyes cooled his ardor.

"I am an idiot," he said.

Brig's head cocked to the side in the universal language of *duh.*

"But I was also right last night," Jackson continued. "I'm not the man you need."

Brig's eyes closed, pain raining down her features like clouds moving in to storm all over a parade. Jackson reached for her hands. He gave a tug, but she didn't come to him easily. For the first time since he'd known her, Brig resisted his pull.

"I'm not the man you need," he repeated. "But I want to be. I will be. If you'll be patient with me while I grow up."

Brig still hadn't opened her eyes, but she let out a low sigh. It sounded like relief. It had to be since the pain that had crisscrossed her features a moment ago was quickly evaporating.

And then she was gone.

The wheels of Jackson's chair were set in motion. Brig had disappeared behind him and was now propelling him into the clinic.

What did this mean? Was she trying to get rid of him? Was she finally giving up on him?

"Let's get your knee fixed," Brig said. "I don't want there to be any excuses when I knock you down the next time you try to run from me."

"Won't ever happen again. A man can't run without his beating heart."

The chair jerked as though the person pushing it had stumbled. Brig quickly recovered and pushed harder. The hard push resulted in a jolt of pain in Jackson's knee.

"Ouch," he groaned.

"Serves you right," Brig muttered. "You have to work on your maturity. I have to work on my bedside manner."

"We'll figure it out, baby."

"Okay, boomer."

Brig leaned down and brushed a kiss over Jackson's lips. The pain in his knee didn't magically disappear. It throbbed away, demanding all of his attention. But Jackson was too happy to pay it any mind.

He finally had something to fight for, something that made him feel like a man again. He pulled Brig closer and deepened the kiss. Soon they would cut open and replace parts of his knee. That was fine with him because now he knew the reason he would one day stand tall again was because of the woman who had brought him to his knees in the first place.

EPILOGUE

"*J*just find most women can't live up to my high expectations."

"Maybe because they're too busy looking down at you?"

Carter snorted into his glass as he eavesdropped on the couple at the table next to him. It was a hilarious thing for the guy to say to the woman who easily had a foot on him. The blonde across from the short stack was a knockout, a woman who was beyond any man's expectations.

As though she'd heard his thoughts, Tilly glanced up at Carter. She narrowed her gaze at him, giving him a sharp glare. In response, Carter grinned back at her.

"I think you're different, Artie," her date was saying.

Tilly's attention snapped back to... whatever his name was. The man had deigned to ignore her nickname and give her one of his liking. That was one of his many mistakes tonight. This date was going to crash in burn in a matter of minutes. Like he had been doing for the past two months, Carter would be there to pick up the pieces.

"You're pretty enough. You were early for our date, which shows eagerness. You ordered a steak, which shows me you're healthy. But you'll need to cut back on the calories before things get out of hand and you balloon up. I won't be one of those husbands who'll stand to let his wife go after I put a ring on it."

Carter snorted again. He grabbed his dinner napkin and dabbed at his face. But a few other diners looked over at him. One woman half rose from her seat as though she were eager to give him mouth to mouth CPR. Carter sat his dinner napkin down and smiled politely at the eager woman.

The woman took a step towards him. But a white flag went flying through the air. The dinner napkin landed on the floor.

Carter stared at it for a moment. It was Tilly's signal. She'd had enough of her date and it was time for him to step in and save her. Or save her date from being strangled. Whichever.

Giving the woman who wanted to resuscitate him an apologetic grimace, Carter bent his form to pick up Tilly's napkin. "Excuse me, ma'am, I think you dropped… Artillery? Artillery Silver, is that you?"

"I'm sorry," Tilly pressed her hand to her chest. "Do we know each other?"

"Do we know each other?" Carter turned and gave her date a chuckle. "How could you forget me? We met at fat camp when we were teens. Don't you remember?"

There was a sputtering cough. It didn't come from Tilly or Carter. Tilly's date was choking on his drink after Carter's pronouncement of Tilly as a formerly overweight person. Carter didn't hear the flimsy excuse the man gave to get out of there.

Carter used the discarded white dinner napkin to dust off the vacated chair. He was mildly surprised that he didn't see a puddle in the seat after the occupant's hasty retreat.

"Can you believe the nerve of that guy? Not one thing from his profile was true." Tilly poured herself another glass of wine from the opened bottle on the table. She tilted the bottle to Carter, but he put his hand over the top of the glass nearest him. "Right, I keep forgetting your one glass rule."

Carter hadn't finished the glass that was still sitting on the other table. He'd never been much of a drinker. In any of its forms, alcohol tasted the same to him; like a bitter astringent that was best used to strip a car's engine. As he watched Tilly's throat work to take the liquid down, he began to feel a thirst that he knew the red liquid would never quench.

When Tilly dabbed at her lip to catch a wayward droplet of the red ambrosia, Carter looked away. It wasn't the alcohol he wanted. No, he wanted something he had never tasted, could never taste.

A tremor ran down the length of his right arm, causing his index finger to tremble. He clenched his fingers around the fork to hide it from her. Tilly was usually a very observant woman, but he'd managed to keep the occasional shakes and twitches from her over the past two months.

"You're being too hard on..." Carter paused. "What was his name again?"

Tilly opened her mouth to respond. Then she frowned. "I gave up trying to remember after he told me my figure reminded him of his mother."

Carter's gaze went from the red stains on her bottom lip, to the crinkle between her brow. The little lines that drew in there formed the center point of a heart where the two halves met in the middle. Her blue eyes rounded at the top part of the heart. Her bottom lip completed the shape.

Oh no. He was back looking at her mouth again. He had to stop doing that; looking at Artillery Silver's perfectly kissable lips was mission impossible. Because he was never going to kiss those lips. He'd never know how soft they were, or if they were sweeter than the wine she sipped.

"That's sad," he said. "You don't know the name of your future husband."

Tilly scowled at and snatched the fork away from him.

That single touch sent a jolt of awareness through him. Carter's pinky finger joined the fluttering dance of his index finger. To hide the involuntary movement, he returned to his table to grab his own cutlery. By the time he took his seat across from Tilly again, his fingers were behaving.

When he looked up, he found Tilly's gaze on him. She wasn't looking at his hands. She was looking at his face.

That furrowed frown turned into a pointed glare. What Tilly didn't know was that Carter found that her glare made her even more beautiful. Her blue eyes blazed like the hottest part of the fire, making Carter want to forget any caution and get burned.

"He probably lied about his name, too," Tilly huffed. "How can you trust someone who misleads you or keeps secrets?"

A spasm rocketed through Carter's palm. He dropped the fork, letting it clatter to the plate. Then he shoved his trembling hand under the table like the dirty little secret it was.

Tilly had been carving a piece of meat. Her gaze tracked to the edge of the table where his hand had disappeared. She pursed her lips as though she were about to ask him what the matter was?

"Was it the height or the bald head that did it?" Carter needled, trying to get her attention back on her awful date.

"I have nothing against a bald head. Look at Vin Diesel, or the Rock. And what modern woman hasn't had a fantasy or two about Peter Dinklage in his role as Tyrion Lannister?"

"Peter Dinklage? I thought you would've been a Warwick Davis kinda girl."

"Why would you think that?"

"You made me watch Willow last weekend."

"Made you?" she scoffed. "You're the one that swore that Val Kilmer hit his peak as Doc Holliday in Tombstone. I had to counter that with the brilliance of his acting in the role of Madmartigan."

"Proving once again that you like the villain to turn into a hero."

The frown was back. It always came back when he'd bested Tilly in the language she knew best; filmology.

"Let's face it, you're the only woman I know whose favorite John Cusack film isn't Say Anything."

"Because it's a sappy 80s film."

"You and your dark heart love Grosse Pointe Blank."

She grinned at the mention of her favorite film. "Who in their right mind doesn't love that film? Rebel son returns to his hometown for his high school reunion where everyone else has a family, a house, and a dog. But Martin Blank has become a professional hitman with a score to settle because he was an overachiever."

Carter chuckled. Trust Tilly to find the good in a trained assassin. She would've been perfect for his best friend Truman, who was an actual trained sniper. But the thought of Truman holding Tilly set his entire arm to shaking.

"I'm surprised you didn't go that route," Tilly said.

"What? An assassin? Unlike our hero in your favorite film, when I took the Army's psych exam, it showed that my moral compass was pointed due North."

"How lucky for Gunny."

The mention of Tilly's twin was like a bomb between them. A tremor went through Carter's entire body and a piercing pain in his head made him wince.

"You're still on board to marry her, right?" asked Tilly. "I mean, now that Brig and Jackson are together, she's the only one of us left."

"And you." Carter pressed his lips together. He hadn't meant to say that out loud. But the two words hung between them.

"I'll be fine." Tilly waved away the inconvenience of her single state in the face of only three weeks before the deadline to keep their family ranch. "I've got a few more dates lined up. I'm sure one of them has to be my Mr. Right."

"Yeah, sure." Carter's tone lacked any kind of certainty. "Or you could run after your date. I'm sure he hasn't gotten that far."

Tilly tossed her dinner napkin at him. Carter caught the white flag. He wished it meant her surrender.

But it didn't. Tilly saw him as a friend. In truth, that's all he could ever be to her. She was already close enough to him that she might see the secrets he was hiding from her, from everyone. At least when he married Gunny, that particular Silver sister would only stick around long enough for the ink of the wedding license to dry.

Then she'd be off, returning to her quest to save the world, and all its endangered species.

The upside to the deal was that Carter would have a place to stay, a place to work, and he'd still get to hang out with Tilly and watch movies, or talk about nonsense. He couldn't ask for much more than that in this life. It was likely more than he deserved.

~

This date is going to end with a kiss;
a kiss between Carter and Tilly!
But you won't believe what happens after these two share their first kiss.
It's the stuff of movie magic complete with a music montage from a boom box blaring a Peter Gabriel ballad!
You don't want to miss "His Pledge to Have,"
Book Five from the Silver Star Ranch romances.

SHANAE JOHNSON

HIS Pledge TO Have

A SILVER STAR RANCH ROMANCE

CHAPTER ONE

"Can you believe I've never been in a long-term relationship?"

Artillery Silver could believe that about the guy who was sitting across from her. His name was Chet. Or -wait? Was it Chaz?

Whatever it was, it certainly wasn't the name he'd given on the dating app they'd initially connected on. On the popular app, Meet-Cute, individuals could use nicknames. Tilly had used her actual nickname of Tilly. Charles—or was it Chester?—had called himself MomApproved. Tilly was starting to wonder if the moniker boasted that the mothers of the women he dated approved of him? Or if it was only his mother who approved of him?

"Most women aren't honest about who they are on these dating apps, you know. When you meet them in person, you often get a big shock."

Christian -or maybe it was Chase?- only barely resembled his profile picture. In his current state, he sported a comb-over that barely had enough wisps to complete the trek to the other side of his forehead. He was five inches shorter than his dating profile claimed and forty pounds heavier. That picture on his profile had to be at least ten years older than the man who sat across from her at the dinner table.

All that evidence led Tilly to think it must have been his college picture... or maybe his high school yearbook photo. Whenever the picture had been snapped left Tilly in no doubt that Clarence—or maybe it was Clinton?—had been telling the truth about one thing; it was easy to believe he'd never been in a long-term relationship.

"I find most women can't live up to my high expectations."

"Maybe because they're too busy looking down at you?"

Tilly hadn't muttered the words under her breath. She'd said them loud enough for the guy at the next table to hear her. Like her, her next-table-neighbor didn't bother to mute his reaction. The dark-haired man laughed out loud. His sensual lips parted, allowing a few red droplets to fall back into the wineglass he held partway to his mouth. Most of the droplets seemed to cling to the flesh of his quirked lower lip as if the liquid was unwilling to part from him.

Light green eyes met hers. They twinkled with mirthful delight. A second laugh escaped him, sending more droplets. A few of those droplets landed on Tilly's arm.

Tilly glared at the man. He grinned back at her. She had to turn away quickly before he made her laugh too. The way he lifted his right brow in a perfectly arched upside-down V of mocking never failed to elicit a giggle out of her.

"I think you're different, Artie," her date was saying.

Tilly's attention snapped back to... whatever his name was. The man deigned to ignore her nickname and gave her one of his liking. She saw no reason to exert herself any further over trying to remember his.

"You're pretty enough." MomApproved leaned to the side and gave her seated frame a once over as though to confirm his words. "You were early for our date, which shows eagerness. You ordered a steak, which shows me you're healthy. But..." He held up a finger and wagged it at her as though she'd been a naughty child. "... you'll need to cut back on the calories before things get out of hand and you balloon up. I won't be one of those husbands who'll stand to let his wife let herself go after I put a ring on it."

Tilly's fingers pinched at her wineglass stem. Her eyes narrowed on the bright, bald spot on her date's forehead. It made an excellent bull's eye. She bet she could hit that marker with her eyes shut.

The man sitting at the table next to them cleared his throat. The sound was loud enough to bring a few of the other dining guests' attention to him. Not Tilly's date, though. He went on and on about what he expected of his wife-to-be as their next-table-neighbor began to cough.

The coughing man wasn't in any distress. His gaze was locked on Tilly's hand. Belatedly, she realized she'd raised her wineglass an inch off the tablecloth. The contents of the glass were nearly empty. But really, who could blame her with the tediousness of this date. Still, what was left in the glass would make a splash if the contents met with MomApproved's bloated face.

The guy next to them coughed a little louder. Tilly distinctly made out the words *Don't, Cause*, and *Scene* in the midst of his theatrical hacking. To punctuate his whooping Morse Code, he narrowed those light green eyes at her.

Tilly huffed as she set the glass back down. The man was right. She wasn't on this date to cause a scene. Her date was doing exactly what she had planned for him to do; he was proposing marriage.

Tilly needed to get married, and soon. She'd been going through dating apps like a horse quidding hay. She chomped at each straw of a man she came in contact with and spit out the wet bundles of rejects. But just like with a horse that wasn't properly swallowing his food, Tilly had to put a stop to the practice because she wasn't getting what she needed to keep her livelihood going.

Her father's will stipulated that she and her five sisters had to get married within three months of the reading of his will if they were going to keep the ranch they'd grown up on. It was the only home they'd known. And in two weeks, their time would be up. So, Tilly couldn't afford to be picky about who she would wind up rolling around in the hay with.

"I would suggest we go Dutch on dinner," her date was saying. "But, since you ordered the more expensive item on the menu, I think we should each pay our own way tonight. Like it says in my profile, I'm a feminist. I believe in equality of the sexes, and that includes financially."

Tilly lifted her wineglass again. Her hand didn't jerk to empty the contents in his face. She pressed the rim of the glass to her mouth and took a healthy gulp of what remained of her drink and her pride.

She had to do this. Her sisters were counting on her. Already four of the six Silver sisters had married. Only Tilly and her twin Gunny were left. And Gunny had a fiancé.

"Why don't we take this back to my place," said MomApproved. "My parents will be out until midnight playing bridge, and we'll have the whole basement to ourselves."

Annnnnd cut scene. That was a wrap on this date. Because, nope, she couldn't do it. She could not spend five more minutes with this joker, much less the rest of her life. She had only one choice left. She threw up the white flag.

Not just metaphorically. She tossed her white dinner linen to the floor.

Her neighbor at the next table lowered his left eyebrow as he looked down at the crumpled signal at his feet. Where lifting the right brow was always done in amusement, lowering the left brow was a sign of exasperation. His expression read, *Are you really giving up?*

Tilly wanted to glower at him that, *Yes, she was giving up, and he'd better do something about it.*

With the same pouting sigh he'd affected when she'd asked him to watch *Grosse Pointe Blank* for the tenth time—even though she knew he loved it, Carter Shane lifted his long form from the chair. Tilly took a moment to admire the play of muscles under his fitted black shirt as his lean fingers smoothed out the fabric.

Tilly knew firsthand what those muscles felt like under her cheek. She'd fallen asleep more than once while leaning against him on the sofa as they watched old movies. She'd even woken up a couple of times, laying fully against his chest with his arms wrapped snug around her, the television blaring static at them.

Now Tilly watched as Carter bent his form to pick up her napkin. "Excuse me, ma'am, I think you dropped... Artillery? Artillery Silver, is that you?"

"I'm sorry," Tilly pressed her hand to her chest. "Do we know each other?"

"Do we know each other?" Carter turned and gave her date a chuckle. "How could you forget me? We met at fat camp when we were teens. Don't you remember?"

There was a sputtering cough. It didn't come from Tilly or Carter. The man that only his mother would approve of was choking on his drink after Carter's pronouncement of Tilly as a formerly overweight person.

She would've killed her friend for this if she managed to keep herself from laughing. Gotta hand it to Carter. Her sister's fiancé knew how to clear Tilly's unwanted dates quickly and efficiently. After all, he'd been doing it for weeks now.

CHAPTER TWO

Carter Shane used the discarded white dinner napkin to dust off the vacated chair. He was mildly surprised that he didn't see a puddle in the seat after the occupant's hasty retreat. He was also surprised that Tilly's date moved so fast to the exit with the extra weight the man carried.

"He may not have been lying about his level of physical fitness," Carter mused as he folded himself down in the chair across from Tilly.

"You're one to talk about fitness having been a fat camp dropout." Tilly lifted her wineglass as though to down the remaining contents, only to find that the glass was empty.

"Oy, the politically correct term is Health Resort." Carter snagged Tilly's fork and speared a chunk of meat. It was in his mouth before she could swat his hand away from her plate. "You didn't think my hail Mary save was free, did you?"

"Can you believe the nerve of that guy? Not one thing from his profile was true." Tilly poured herself another glass of wine from the opened bottle on the table. She tilted the bottle to Carter, but he put his hand over the top of the glass nearest him. "Right, I keep forgetting your one glass rule."

Carter hadn't finished the glass that was still sitting on the other table. He'd never been much of a drinker. In any of its forms, alcohol tasted the same to him, like a bitter astringent that was best used to strip a car's engine. As he watched Tilly's throat work to take the liquid down, he began to feel a thirst that he knew the red liquid would never quench.

When Tilly dabbed at her lip to catch a wayward droplet of the red ambrosia, Carter looked away. It wasn't the alcohol he wanted. No, he wanted something he had never tasted, could never taste.

A tremor ran down the length of his right arm, causing his index finger to tremble. He clenched his fingers around the fork to hide it from her. Tilly was usually a very observant woman, but he'd managed to keep the occasional shakes and twitches from her over the past two months.

"You're being too hard on…" Carter paused. "What was his name again?"

Tilly opened her mouth to respond. Then she frowned. "I gave up trying to remember after he told me my figure reminded him of his mother."

Carter's gaze went from the red stains on her bottom lip to the crinkle between her brow. The little lines that drew in there formed the center point of a heart where the two halves met in the middle. Her blue eyes rounded at the top part of the heart. Her bottom lip completed the shape.

Oh no. He was back looking at her mouth again. He had to stop doing that; looking at Artillery Silver's perfectly kissable lips was mission impossible. Because he was never going to kiss those lips. He'd never know how soft they were or if they were sweeter than the wine she sipped.

"That's sad," he said. "You don't know the name of your future husband."

Tilly scowled at him, then snatched the fork away from him.

That single touch sent a jolt of awareness through him. Carter's pinky finger joined the fluttering dance of his index finger. To hide the involuntary movement, he returned to his table to grab his own cutlery. By the time he took his seat across from Tilly again, his fingers were behaving.

When he looked up, he found Tilly's gaze on him. She wasn't looking at his hands. She was looking at his face.

That furrowed frown turned into a pointed glare. What Tilly didn't know was that Carter found that her glare made her even more beautiful. Her blue eyes blazed like the hottest part of a fire, making Carter want to forget any caution and get burned.

"He probably lied about his name, too," Tilly huffed. "How can you trust someone who misleads you or keeps secrets?"

A spasm rocketed through Carter's palm. He dropped the fork, letting it clatter to the plate. Then he shoved his trembling hand under the table like the dirty little secret it was.

Tilly had been carving a piece of meat. Her gaze tracked to the edge of the table where his hand had disappeared. She pursed her lips as though she were about to ask him what the matter was?

"Was it the height or the bald head that did it?" Carter needled, trying to get her attention back on her awful date.

"I have nothing against a bald head. Look at Vin Diesel or the Rock. And what modern woman hasn't had a fantasy or two about Peter Dinklage in his role as Tyrion Lannister?"

"Peter Dinklage? I thought you would've been a Warwick Davis kinda girl."

"Why would you think that?"

"You made me watch *Willow* last weekend."

"Made you?" she scoffed. "You're the one that swore that Val Kilmer hit his peak as Doc Holliday in *Tombstone*. I had to counter that with the brilliance of his acting in the role of Madmartigan."

"Proving once again that you like the villain to turn into a hero."

The frown was back. It always came back when he'd bested Tilly in the language she knew best; filmology.

"Let's face it, you're the only woman I know whose favorite John Cusack film isn't *Say Anything*."

"Because it's a sappy 80s film."

"You and your dark heart love *Grosse Pointe Blank*."

She grinned at the mention of her favorite film. "Who in their right mind doesn't love that film? Rebel son returns to his hometown for his high school reunion, where everyone else has a family, a house, and a dog. But Martin Blank has become a professional hitman with a score to settle because he was an overachiever."

Carter chuckled. Trust Tilly to find the good in a trained assassin. She would've been perfect for his best friend Truman, who was an actual trained sniper. But the thought of Truman holding Tilly set his entire arm to shaking.

"I'm surprised you didn't go that route," Tilly said.

"What? An assassin? Unlike our hero in your favorite film, when I took the Army's psych exam, it showed that my moral compass was pointed due North."

"How lucky for Gunny."

The mention of Tilly's twin was like a bomb between them. A tremor went through Carter's entire body, and a piercing pain in his head made him wince.

"You're still on board to marry her, right?" asked Tilly. "I mean, now that Brig and Jackson are together, she's the only one of us left."

"And you." Carter pressed his lips together. He hadn't meant to say that out loud. But the two words hung between them.

"I'll be fine." Tilly waved away the inconvenience of her single state in the face of only two weeks before the deadline to keep their family ranch. "I've got a few more dates lined up. I'm sure one of them has to be my Mr. Right."

"Yeah, sure." Carter's tone lacked any kind of certainty. "Or you could run after your date. I'm sure he hasn't gotten that far."

Tilly tossed her dinner napkin at him. Carter caught the white flag. He wished it meant her surrender.

But it didn't. Tilly saw him as a friend. In truth, that's all he could ever be to her. She was already close enough to him that she might see the secrets he was hiding from her, from everyone. At least when he married Gunny, that particular Silver sister would only stick around long enough for the ink of the wedding license to dry.

Then she'd be off, returning to her quest to save the world and all its endangered species.

The upside to the deal was that Carter would have a place to stay, a place to work, and he'd still get to hang out with Tilly and watch movies or talk about nonsense. He couldn't ask for much more than that in this life. It was likely more than he deserved.

CHAPTER THREE

"What do you think you're doing?" Tilly demanded.

"Hailing a cab?" said Carter. "What does it look like?"

Tilly's indignation turned into a scowl as Carter brought his wallet from his pocket and onto the dinner table. The waiter sat the check down on the table, placing it in front of Carter, which Tilly took offense to as well.

Sure, she had just dumped a guy because he'd suggested they go Dutch. But at least... Seriously, what had his name been? At least MomApproved had brought up who would pay. Carter just took charge of the situation, swiping the check away from Tilly before she could get her fingers around it.

Carter thumbed through his wallet. Tilly couldn't help but notice that his bills were organized by denomination. A few one-dollar bills, followed by a number of fives and a few twenties. Carter pulled all of the twenties from his wallet and slipped them into the billfold.

"Keep the change," he said, handing the billfold back to the waiter

"No," said Tilly. "I can't let you pay for my date."

"Date? That was my night's entertainment, a live-action romcom. You played your part brilliantly. But I think casting got the leading man wrong."

Once again, the man disarmed her with his jokes. Carter was right, though. The wrong man had been cast in tonight's episode of her disastrous dating life. In fact, this whole past season of Tilly's Dating Adventures would've likely been canceled after the pilot episode. The only thing saving the show was the introduction of her sidekick, Carter Shane.

Carter stood and brushed imaginary crumbs off his shirt and pants. Tilly's gaze tracked the movement. Unlike the men she dated, Carter fit the profile of a man any woman would want to go on a blind date with. In fact, a few of the women looked away from their dates to appreciate the man's form.

"You're showing off," Tilly said to Carter.

"What do you mean?" The look of innocence was fake as he slid his jacket over his form.

One thing Tilly knew about Carter Shane was that the man knew how handsome he was. Moreover, he was not above using his looks and charm to get what he wanted. Case in point, the table next to where they sat had been reserved. But a few words to the hostess and Carter had been seated there just a few moments after Tilly and her date.

"You're the only man I know who women might pay to watch put clothes on," she said as he buttoned his jacket.

Carter grinned at her. It wasn't the same grin that he'd given the hostess. Carter never flirted with Tilly. Likely because soon after they met, he'd been assigned to marry her baby sister Brig. When Brig fell for and pursued another member of their unit, Carter had been reassigned to marry Tilly's twin sister Gunny. And so, because nothing could ever happen between them, Tilly and Carter became something else. They became friends.

It was their friendship that made Tilly feel the urge to hiss at each of the women looking at him. Not a verbal hiss like a cat. More of a visual hiss where she cut her eyes at them—like a cat.

Carter was taken. Not by her. By her sister. Gunny would be thanking her lucky stars when she arrived home in a couple of days to exchange vows with the man.

When their father's will had been read a little over two months ago, and the Silver sisters had learned what they'd have to do to keep their home, each and every one of them had balked at the idea that they'd each need to hitch their wagons to a man to keep their childhood home. It had gone against everything their father had taught his six daughters. Lessons like you can do anything a man can do, and that includes building your own home.

To prove that lesson, the general had made each girl build a cabin on the ranch. The Silver sisters were no strangers to hammers, nails, and power drills. Now, all of a sudden, they each would need a man to keep what they'd built with their own hands?

It had made no sense. Until the six men of their father's unit had strode onto the ranch. As each Silver girl and President's Man teamed up, it appeared their strengths and weaknesses meshed into something that made the pair even stronger.

Except Tilly. She'd already been casually dating a couple of guys at the time. She was sure she could get one of them to marry her. Especially since Truman, the sixth man of the unit, had no interest in holy matrimony.

Tilly hoped that Carter might be the glue to finally make her twin sister come home and stay for good. After all, Tilly looked forward to hanging with Carter each day, watching old movies and television shows, looking through magazines at fashion do's and don'ts, and people watching when they went into town.

"Hey, what do you think about them?" Carter nodded his head toward a couple in the corner of the restaurant. "First date? Or an old married couple?"

Tilly looked over at the two people Carter indicated. It was a silly game they played, one she loved. "Newlywed couple."

Carter looked at the couple anew. The pair leaned toward each other, not quite touching but near enough that they could. The man looked down at his dinner companion with total admiration. She looked up at him with patient amusement.

"Yeah," said Carter. "I think you're right."

Tilly was a good read of people. She could size up a person within the first five minutes of meeting them face to face, hence why she went on a lot of dates. Tilly had never wanted for male attention. She went out with a new guy each week. Sometimes two. Getting the first date was no problem. It was the second date she had trouble with.

People could easily hide behind their online profiles. But when they stood before her in real life, everything became crystal clear. Crystal clear that, most of the time, they'd been lying on their profiles. Tilly, and her razor-sharp internal lie detector, couldn't abide lying.

"You ready?" Carter held out his hand to Tilly. His fingers were immaculately groomed, clean, and cut in even half-moons.

His fingertips were also soft to the touch. Tilly knew that because he always offered her his hand when she was getting into or out of a car. She also knew his large hands spanned her waist because he'd helped her down from a horse a few times. She even knew the exact temperature of his palm because he'd rest it there whenever they crossed a street, and he switched sides with her, always making sure his body was between her and the street traffic.

It was old-world gentlemanly behavior, the kind her father told her a man should exhibit if they wanted to date her. Not one of her dates over the past couple of years had offered his hands in any of these manners. They mainly wanted to grope.

When Tilly took Carter's hand now, a tingle went to the center of her palm. It stayed there, sizzling and radiating warmth. The heat made her shiver.

"Cold?" Carter asked.

They had stepped out of the restaurant into the warm evening air. There were still rays of the sun in the sky. Her date with what's-his-face had been early in the evening. Tilly supposed she knew it would be a bust. Now her whole night wasn't spoilt.

She didn't answer Carter's question. She didn't want to lie and say that she wasn't cold. Not when she had already anticipated what his action would be. Not when she craved what he was about to do to her.

Sure enough, Carter tugged off his jacket. Tilly's gaze was riveted to the rippling of his muscles under that dark, fitted shirt. Then she was engulfed in his scent and body heat as Carter draped his jacket over her shoulders.

Vanilla mixed with citrus hit her nose like she'd walked in a garden of exotic plants. She felt drugged by Carter's scent. Her mind went to the scene in *The Wizard of Oz* when Dorothy and her crew walked through the poppy fields. That's what she felt like as Carter's heady scent filled her.

Tilly closed her eyes and breathed him in. She knew she had to be quick about it. She couldn't let Carter see the effect he had on her. They were friends. They were soon to be in-laws. Friends and siblings smelled each other. Right?

"Hey, look out," Carter shouted.

Tilly's eyes slammed open, guilt rising hot to her cheeks. She expected to see Carter glaring at her for what she'd been doing. But she was slammed into his chest.

All she saw was the dark color of Carter's shirt. Her gaze landed on a sliver of his exposed skin. She saw the beat of his pulse in his collarbone. She smelled that super sweet scent of him mixed with a musky note of aftershave. Men shouldn't smell like flowers. Tilly's belly grumbled even though it was full of steak and wine. She wanted to taste the salty-sweetness of him for dessert.

"Are you okay?" Carter wasn't looking down at her. His eyes were blazing as they looked after a group of kids on skateboards zooming down the sidewalk.

"Those idiots are going to hurt somebody," Carter growled

He still wasn't looking at Tilly. So she had a few more seconds to savor the feel of being in his arms. Of imagining that this was how her date would end, with a kiss from this man.

And then his gaze turned down to her. The anger was snuffed out like a match being blown out. But the flame was too strong, and it struck back to life. And this time, it burned brighter.

CHAPTER FOUR

Carter knew how to disassemble an M4 carbine rifle. He could do it in the dark with just the feel of his hands. In this moment, his hands couldn't figure out how to unlock their hold on Tilly's frame.

Instead of straightening and lifting off the woman, Carter's fingers clenched her to him. Instead of unlocking his arms and pulling away from her, Carter's muscles tensed, readying to tighten their hold.

Just like guns, Silver women were not toys. They were not meant to be played with. If one of them went off, people would get hurt.

Carter needed to disengage. He needed to step back. The responsible thing to do would be to point Artillery Silver in a safe direction.

The problem was that her lips were within striking distance. For weeks he'd sat, stood, or walked close to her. The temptation had always been there. But he wasn't fool enough to act on it.

He was supposed to be marrying Brig, or Gunny, or one of the other sisters. But not her. It had never been Tilly. Even though the moment Carter had lain eyes on her, his heart had said *This One*.

Tilly had barely glanced at him on that day. Now he had her full attention. He knew that if he acted on what was in his heart, she would never speak to him again. That—her silence—he couldn't abide.

Still, his entire body ached to do it. To bend down and kiss her. But Carter stepped back.

He unlocked his hands. Then his arms. Finally, he managed to put space between himself and Tilly.

Instantly, he felt like he was crashing down into withdrawal. They had to get home soon, or his symptoms would become noticeable. Not that Tilly ever looked that closely at him. If she had, then she would not only see how he ached for her, she would also see the general ache in his bones when he was off his meds.

His hands were shaking with want of her, but mainly they shook as his body demanded another hit of his pain meds. He needed to get back to the ranch to get a dose in his system. He sometimes didn't think clearly between long stretches between pills.

"Sorry," Carter said. "I didn't mean to—"

"I wasn't paying attention—" Tilly said at the same time.

"You're alright?" Carter reached a hand out to her cheek. His fingers trembled in the space between them. He brought his hand back to his side.

"I'm good. You?"

Carter nodded. "We should probably head back and—"

"You want dessert?"

Carter couldn't finish his sentence. He choked on his words. Had she heard his thoughts? Did she know that the only thing he wanted to curl up with and sample were her lush lips?

"I have a craving for something sweet and salty," Tilly continued. "I want to satisfy that craving before heading back."

He could only stare. His green gaze latched onto her blue, and he swore he smelled scorched earth from the heat coming between them. But no, someone had just tossed a cigarette butt into the street.

"So, how about it?" Tilly asked.

Carter opened his mouth to shout yes. Yes, he wanted to satisfy his sweet and salty craving for her.

"How about some ice cream?"

Carter gulped down his desire. It stuck in his throat. "Sure."

That was the only word he could manage. He had to put all his energy into concentrating on walking. His whole body was on fire, the fire of an unfulfilled desire along with the fire of the need for his meds.

Carter pushed the fire of the withdrawal down. The longer he stayed in town, the longer he could be with Tilly. They wouldn't get this much time alone in a few days. Her sister would be coming, and then Carter would be beholden to the vows he promised to make to Tilly's twin.

They walked to the end of the block where an ice cream shop was. It was a quaint one-story shop, like most of the establishments in the small town square. Everything in the town was within reach. The grocer in the center of the square. The police station at the edge of the block. The courthouse right next to it.

It was the kind of place Carter had grown up in where everybody knew everybody. It's also why he was in no hurry to go back to the home of his birth. He didn't want anyone in his current business.

His parents would inevitably find his medications and question his use. It had been nearly a year since the incident. But pain would forever be his constant companion. Not the physical pain, something deeper. An ache in his very bones that never quite went away and pestered him in his sleeping and waking hours.

The men in his unit understood. That's why they asked no questions. His civilian parents wouldn't understand that. So it was better for him to stay on the ranch with a wife who would leave soon after their vows were stated.

It would be the perfect relationship. Not only because Gunny wouldn't hassle him over the pills. Because Carter would have an excuse to see Tilly every day.

Carter kept his hands to himself as he crossed the street with

Tilly. He made sure to keep her on the inside of the sidewalk. Though he worried about the pedestrians on the walk as well, now that they'd almost been run over by a reckless kid on a skateboard.

His reactions had been slow after the blast that had taken his team down and killed the general. Carter had walked away with no limbs lost. But everything in him constantly ached. The doctors had prescribed a low-dose pain killer. Unfortunately, the pain kept creeping back. So Carter had doubled and now tripled the dosage. Looked like soon he'd have to make his daily pill regiment into quadruplets.

"I'm buying the ice cream," Tilly said as they came inside the establishment.

"Seeing as I'm a feminist," Carter pressed his hand to his heart, "I'll let you pay my way."

Tilly snorted. "I can't believe I lasted as long as I did on that date with a straight face. Do men really think like that?"

"I'll have you know that men are a very diverse breed of humans."

Again, Tilly snorted.

"Some of us even do our own laundry," Carter went on.

Tilly threw back her head and laughed. Carter didn't tell her that he still messed up his white and color loads sometimes. He'd let her believe some men were more evolved than they actually were.

"He was all wrong for you," Carter said. He didn't mention that most of the men Tilly chose from the dating app were wrong for her. It was as if she was purposefully not trying to get married. "He said his favorite movie was *Psycho.*"

Tilly winced. "Yeah, it explained a lot. Son who killed his mother and then talks to her corpse." She tilted her head and looked off in the distance. "You know his shirt did look a bit feminine."

"You think it was hers?"

"She would probably approve."

The two of them bent over with laughter. A few of the customers in the ice cream shop turned to stare. Both Tilly and Carter shrugged at the outsiders who didn't get their inside jokes.

"Not everyone is a Cusack fan," Tilly said once she sobered. "Too bad you don't have a brother."

"I do," said Carter. "But he's into WrestleMania as a grown man."

Tilly looked horrified. She rested a hand on his shoulder. "I'm so sorry for your family."

Another laugh bubbled up through her elegant throat. This was Carter's favorite part of every day since he'd come to the ranch. Making Tilly laugh. Seeing her smile. Having her ruin a movie for him as she talked over the dialogue. It was the highlight of his every day.

"Gunny isn't into movies," said Tilly. "Unless it's a wildlife documentary."

It took Carter a moment to comprehend what, and then, who a Gunny was. Right. His fiancée.

"She's more of a *National Geographic Special* kind of girl."

"Well, Morgan Freeman narrated *March of the Penguins*."

Tilly smiled, and Carter was dazzled. It wouldn't be so bad marrying Gunny. Not if she had Tilly's face.

The shopkeeper handed over two cones to them. Tilly took a bite of her ice cream. The dollop brushed against her skin, leaving her a creamy beard. She giggled and began dabbing at her chin.

"You missed a spot," Carter said. "Here, let me…"

His hand was already moving before he could think better of the motion. His thumb reached her cheek. He didn't feel the cold of the ice cream. All he felt was the silky warmth of Tilly.

At the same time as he touched her, Tilly canted her head. Her tongue snaked out of her mouth and caught the same dollop of cream as his thumb. When her tongue made contact with his thumb, shots were fired, and Carter's brain short-circuited.

Gone was the data on the woman he was supposed to marry. All he saw in front of him was the woman he was going to claim as his own. No matter what the fallout.

CHAPTER FIVE

Tilly had been coming to Castro's Creamery since she was a kid. Old Mr. Castro had fled communist Cuba before she'd been born. The dapper gentleman made his way to the Midwest, married a cowgirl, and opened this beloved shop where people came from miles to try his flavors.

Tilly made it a point to try each flavor at least once. And because Old Man Castro kept inventing new and inventive flavors, there was always something new to try. Today's special was Cereal Milk. As the creamy concoction touched her tongue, Tilly was transported to Saturday morning in front of the television with a bowl of Fruit Loops in her lap.

She'd been reveling in the fruity sweetness of the ice cream when a few drops dribbled down her chin and met with Carter's thumb. It was a complete and total accident that her tongue brushed his thumb in its effort to lap up the cream that had dribbled from her lips. And like a cat who'd had one taste of sweet, frothy ambrosia, Tilly wanted to go back for more.

The first time had been a mistake... Hadn't it?

If she did it a second time, it would be on purpose... Which would be a bad thing, right?

But why would it be so bad? Tilly couldn't remember? However, she knew the reason that it was bad was important.

It couldn't be that to lick another person's thumb was bad manners. Carter's hand was still on her face. He hadn't pulled away. Which had to mean he didn't mind it the first time.

If he'd have minded, he would've told her so. He told her everything. Because they were friends.

But friends didn't use each other's flesh as a topping on a sundae. Right? She was only mildly sure that was a rule.

Maybe if she asked him really nicely, he'd agree to give her another taste.

They'd shared popcorn on their movie nights. Their fingers had touched in the bowels of the buttery goodness. Had that spice been there those times she'd popped kernels in her mouth?

When they'd been out at a bar the other night, and Carter had saved her from another disastrous date, she'd had a sip of his cocktail. Belatedly, she remembered that the drink had made her eyebrows raise to her hairline. It had to have been the same spicy kick.

So it had happened more than once already. What would one more time be? It was just a small thing between friends. Because that's what they were. Since he was going to marry…

Tilly let out a low sigh. Her shoulders slumped as she set the ice cream cone in a dish on their tabletop. The realization of why she couldn't have another taste of Carter punched her in the gut where there had been nothing but sweetness and spice before.

Carter was going to marry her sister. He was going to be her brother. She couldn't want to eat ice cream out of her new brother-in-law's hand. That was highly inappropriate.

She needed to back off. She needed to put distance between them. She needed to remove her face from his hand so that the temptation was no longer there.

Wait?

Carter still hadn't removed his hand from her face. In fact, his thumb swiped at her chin, where the ice cream had dripped. The cream was gone, but Carter's thumb was still there.

His thumb wiped higher and higher. It brushed the flesh just under her bottom lip. It skated along the spot at the corner of her mouth where her bottom lip met her top lip.

Tilly held herself entirely still. She couldn't have another mishap with her tongue. The problem was Carter's thumb was coaxing her tongue out of her mouth, like a snake charmer playing a flute.

Did Carter know that that's what he was doing to her? He had to? He often anticipated her needs, like having a selection of DVDs of her favorite movies after a long day of chores. He sometimes completed her sentences. True, most of the time, she was quoting a movie. But he was always there with the punch line. Always there to say the thing she was thinking. Or sometimes not saying it but clearly thinking it and nudging her with his elbow until she giggled first.

Though Tilly had been born a twin, she had never had this kind of connection with her sister. Gunny was far too serious. She was always concerned about saving an endangered animal or plant. Gunny never sat back and watched life for its entertainment value.

Gunny often didn't get Tilly. Which meant Gunny would never get Carter. Because Carter was so very much like Tilly.

If Carter and Gunny got together, it would be a bad date that would never end because they'd be married. There would be no white dinner napkin thrown on the floor to save either of them. It would be a catastrophe.

Tilly knew what she had to do.

"You can't marry Gunny," she said at the same time as Carter said, "I can't marry Gunny."

Tilly glanced up into his eyes. What she saw there took her breath away. Carter's gaze was latched onto her face, roaming over her features with a familiarity that she had never felt with another person.

Carter's gaze was both soft and fierce at the same time. Wanting something but afraid to reach out and touch it. Tilly read his emotions easily because it was exactly how she felt.

She felt his pulse quicken because he still held her chin in his hand. She felt the slight tremor in his thumb as the tension increased between them. She felt a spark, a tingling as electricity zapped between them.

"Why?" Tilly asked him. "Why can't you marry my sister?"

Carter gulped. It wasn't a gulp of uncertainty or guilt. It looked as though he swallowed down a huge helping of desire. Tilly read the action easily because it was exactly what she was experiencing.

"Because you told me not to," he said.

"You do everything I tell you?" she asked, wanting him to say the real answer that she knew to be true because she heard it in her own heart. "Because I distinctly told you not to watch *The Matrix* sequels, and you did."

Carter chuckled, his caress on her face heating. Then his other hand joined until he was holding her steady in his grip. "I would do anything you tell me." He paused and then added, "From this moment on."

The admission sounded like a national security secret he was letting her in on. He was whispering to her, even though there were hardly any people in the ice cream shop. Old Man Castro had gone to the back after he'd handed over their scoops.

"If you tell me to marry your sister because you believe it's the right thing for her and for me, then I'll do it."

Now Tilly gulped. It wasn't a gulp of uncertainty or guilt. She was swallowing down a huge helping of desire, only to have more of the sensation fill her throat, her mouth. "I think it would be the right thing…"

Carter's head dipped low. Tilly couldn't help but grin. Even in this serious moment, she couldn't help riling him up.

"It would be the right thing for the ranch," she continued in a somber voice. "But it wouldn't be right for you. And it wouldn't be right for me."

Carter's head lifted, eyes shining bright with hope.

"I think I might be in love with you, Carter."

Tilly caught a flash of his grin before she was tasting it. Sweet, salt, spicy, and heat met her lips. Tilly gulped it down and took another taste. She was greedy for more.

She wrapped her arms around his neck and pulled him closer. He was sweeter than the ice cream. Sweeter than a bowl of the most sugary cereal. And it wasn't enough. She needed more of him.

A throat cleared. It had probably cleared more than once before Carter let Tilly go. It had to clear one more time before Tilly let Carter go.

Old Man Castro stood behind the counter. He raised a bushy brow at them. "This is a family-friendly place. You two take that outside."

There was no bite to his heavily accented words. Tilly had no problem following his instructions. She wanted to be alone with Carter so that she could indulge uninterrupted in her dessert dish.

CHAPTER SIX

As soon as they were out of the shop, Carter pulled Tilly to him again. He wrapped one arm around her waist and the other he used to capture her chin. He brought her to him and did what he'd wanted to do since laying eyes on her nearly three months ago.

He kissed her.

He kissed her like it was the first time.

He kissed her like it was the last time.

He kissed her like he had all the time in the world. Because now he did. He didn't have to deny or hide his feelings any longer. The freedom of being able to touch her without pretense made him dizzy. Or maybe that was the heady, rich taste of her.

Sugary breakfast pastry to zap him with energy in the morning and the last rays of sunshine before curling up for the night. That was what Tilly Silver tasted like to Carter.

When he broke away, she grinned at him. He grinned at her. They had spent weeks together with a never-ending commentary running between them. But for the first time in their acquaintance, they both were at a loss for words.

Carter tugged Tilly into an alleyway between the ice cream shop and the tailor shop. The work day was coming to a close. It wasn't quite five o'clock, but a few workers were sneaking out early. Not that the town had much of a rush hour. People probably were simply eager to get home to be with their families.

Looking down at Tilly, there was no place else that Carter wanted to be. He kept his hand cradled at the back of her head as he pressed her into the brick wall. He didn't press his suit or try for another kiss. He simply looked down at her. His expression was unguarded as he allowed her to see everything he'd been feeling for the past two-and-a-half months.

Had she said she loved him? Or had he imagined that? He never would've dreamed that she would, that she could. But maybe his luck was finally changing.

"I don't have much, Tilly. Just a bunch of DVDs and a few VHS tapes. But everything that I have is yours."

"Hmmm," she hummed, toying with the top button of his shirt. "Would any of those DVDs feature one John Cusack?"

"I have *High Fidelity, Con Air, Serendipity*. The theatrical releases and the director's cut."

"So you plan to keep me up all night," she grinned, "watching all versions?"

The grin Tilly gave Carter nearly unmanned him. He felt his knees buckle under the weight of his desire for this woman. He wanted to cuddle under the sheets with her, allowing her total control over the television remote, and never leave.

"Marry me," was all he could say.

Tilly's grin softened. Tears pricked her eyes. Her lips moved, but no sound escaped.

"I'd say we should probably go on a date first, but I think that's what we've been doing these past two months."

She closed her mouth. She closed her eyes, but it was too late. A sigh escaped her lips. A single tear fell from the corner of her eye.

"There's no one else for me but you. I know that for certain." Carter caught the tear, brushing it away. "I would've married your sister to save you and your family, but my heart would've always been yours."

Slowly, Tilly lifted her head. Gradually, her lashes lifted to reveal that startling blue. Haltingly, her lips parted, and she spoke. "Carter?"

"Yes, Tilly?"

"Would you have let me marry one of these jokers I've been dating?"

His grin was one part mischief, two parts caveman. He realized then that the only reason he had let—yes, *let*—her go on these dates was because he knew not one of those jokers had been in contention for her hand.

"I think either you or I would've kept sabotaging those dates," he said.

Tilly's lips quirked upward as though she finally realized the zero-sum game they'd been playing these last two months. Then she winced.

"What is it?" Carter looked around. "Is Clifton back?" Maybe her date had come back for his doggy bag?

Tilly's wince cleared in an instance. "Clifton? Right! That was his name."

The man that only his mother could approve of was not on the prowl. Then what was Tilly wincing about?

"No, it's not about him. It's Scout."

That was worse. Scout Silver was a force that Carter didn't want to reckon with. Tentatively, he peered out of the alley and looked in both directions. He didn't see the general's oldest daughter marching on the street.

"This will ruin her plan," said Tilly. "She's going to kill us."

Oh, that was her worry. If Carter was no longer on board to marry Gunny, that left them a man down. Right now, Carter didn't have the brain space to worry about that. He pulled Tilly to him. Now that he had the right to do this, he wasn't giving it up. Ever.

"The plan is still the same," he said. "The players have changed. We get married, and we'll find a guy for Gunny on the dating apps."

"Gunny will probably do it if she gets back in time. And if the man is not cruel to animals, environmentally conscious, and drives a hybrid." Tilly rested her head on his chest. "In the meantime, Scout will argue us down."

Scout could argue all she wanted. It wouldn't change a thing. Carter would not budge from his hard-fought position. Still, weariness hovered just over his skin like a cloak blowing in the wind.

It was late in the day. Carter should be feeling the full effects of being late for his medication dose. But all he felt was the warmth of Tilly. The rightness of her. This woman was the most powerful medication. She took away all of his aches and pains and worries. She was the only thing keeping both his symptoms and the side effects at bay.

A bell tolled, announcing the half-hour. Carter's attention went to the bell tower. It sat above the courthouse. When the bell came to settle, an idea had sprouted in Carter's mind.

"She can get mad," he said. "But if we're already married, there's nothing she can do about it."

Tilly lifted her head to meet his gaze. Carter tilted his head to the courthouse. Tilly followed the direction he indicated. Her brows lifted as understanding dawned.

She turned him, a grin on her face. He didn't need to ask if she was in. He saw it there in her eyes.

Carter held out his hand. Tilly took it. It was as if she was already shouting *I do*. They stepped out of the alley and rushed across the street. The building would be closing in less than thirty minutes. They had to make it in time. Carter couldn't spend another moment without having Tilly as his wife.

CHAPTER SEVEN

illy looked up as she climbed the stairs to the courthouse. The classical style of the building screamed for the people by the people. The tall marble pillars that extended from ground to ceiling were imposing as they stood solitary and independent. Above the four pillars was an ornate roof of sharp angles that boasted of stability and longevity. The two pieces would fall without the other's support.

Tilly's steps faltered as she ascended the last step. Carter caught her elbow and brought her to him. She could've managed to right herself. She'd been standing on her own two feet all her life. But having the support and shelter of him beside her, surrounding her, Tilly knew she now wanted to be permanently attached to this man.

"Second thoughts?" Carter asked, brushing a strand of her hair out of her face.

One look in his eyes and she forgot her train of thought. All she saw was him. How had she ever seen any man but him?

"No," she said. "I'm not having second thoughts. I'm eager to make this official."

A grin split his handsome face. The divot at the top of his upper lip and the twin dimples on his cheeks fairly twinkled at her, beckoning her closer. Tilly couldn't help herself. She kissed him.

The sweetness from the ice cream was still on his bottom lip. It mixed with that heated spice she had accidentally tasted earlier, that taste that had finally brought her to her senses and lead them both to this inevitable conclusion.

"We have to hurry," Carter said, breaking the kiss far sooner than Tilly would've liked. "They're closing soon."

It was almost a quarter to the hour. It would be a miracle if they made it to the judge in time. Neither of them wanted to go back to the ranch without that marriage certificate as their armor.

It looked like they were in luck. Inside there were hardly any people in the lobby. Most of the men and women ambling about were clearly workers headed home for the day. They had coats and purses slung over their shoulders and forearms and were headed for the exits.

Carter tugged Tilly to a desk occupied by a young man who was still busily typing. The title placard over his head read Clerk. The clerk's coat was slung over the back of the chair. An open briefcase sat at his feet. He tapped a key with his index finger definitively and reached up to the monitor of the computer as though he were about to turn it off.

"We're here to get married," said Carter.

"We're shutting down," said the clerk without looking up. He pressed the button, and the screen went black. "Best to come back tomorrow."

"We still have fourteen minutes," said Carter. He held up his cellphone and waved it under the clerk's nose. "It says on the city website that it can take as little as ten minutes to get married."

"It's quarter 'til," said the clerk, finally giving Carter his attention.

"Which means we have plenty of time," Carter grinned.

The clerk huffed, setting his mouth in a grimace that screamed denial. But then his mouth went slack. "Tilly? Artillery Silver? Is that you?"

It took her a minute which was time they didn't have, but slowly

Tilly recognized Ryan Burns. They'd dated in high school. Well, dated was a strong word. She'd gone out with Ryan a few Friday nights. But she'd also went out with his good friend Dave Graham a few Saturday nights. When they found out, they demanded she choose. She'd stopped dating them both and insisted they could all stay friends. Although this was the first time she'd seen him in years.

"Hi," Tilly said, waggling her fingers.

"He knock you up or something?" Ryan chucked his thumb at Carter.

Tilly set her mouth to say no, but then thought better of it. This was a shotgun wedding, but only because they were trying to avoid Scout aiming at the both of them. So she decided to stick as close to the truth as possible.

"If Scout finds out we're doing this now, she'll kill us. I'd like to die a married woman if it's all the same to you."

That piqued his interest. So much for staying friends after the breakup. He looked between the two. Whatever he decided, Tilly knew that the whole town would know about this before she and Carter made it back to the ranch tonight.

"All right," Ryan finally said. "Hand over your driver's licenses. I can get the paperwork, but I can't guarantee the judge will make time for it."

Ryan bent over, rifling through a drawer under his desk. Out of his view, Carter gave Tilly a fist bump. After her knuckles touched his they each opened their fingers wide and wriggled them like an explosion.

It was happening. She was just a few minutes away from being Mrs. Carter Shane. Tilly Shane. Artillery Shane. She liked the sound of it.

Two precious moments later, they'd finished filling out the paperwork and, with a loud thud of his official stamp, Ryan handed the document over. Tilly's fingers shook as she took the marriage license. The lightweight of the sheet felt heavy in her hands.

Carter took the other end as though to balance his share of the weight. The paper stopped shaking. Everything felt steady.

Once again, the feeling that this was the right thing swept over Tilly. It was rash, and it was sudden, but it was exactly the direction she wanted her life to go in.

"You'll need two witnesses for the ceremony," said Ryan.

Carter winced. Tilly knew what he was thinking. Even if they called their friends and family on the ranch -which they didn't want to do- none of them could get here in time.

Tilly glanced up at Ryan. "Would you mind?"

The guy she'd went out with a handful of Friday nights all the way back in high school smiled warily, but he nodded. Then his wary smiled turned downright mischievous as he looked over Tilly's shoulder and raised his hand as though to get someone's attention.

"Mel, wait. Don't leave yet. You'll want to see this. Tilly Silver is getting hitched."

"Tilly Silver?" came a high-pitched voice filled with disbelief and a hint of disdain. But at least it was female and not male.

It wasn't another guy she'd dated. It was worse. It was the wife of another guy she'd dated. They hadn't been married at the time, thank all that was good and holy. Though Melanie might have been dating Al Hopper at the time. Tilly had never been sure. He certainly hadn't said so.

Melanie Hopper scratched at her jaw, using her left hand. The diamond on her finger sparkled. She looked at Tilly's bare left hand and smirked.

"This I gotta see," Melanie said, her tone laced with superior scorn.

Tilly's lips hurt as she held onto her polite grin. She needed this woman's presence for the next five minutes. Her dislike was preferable to her sister's temper.

The unlikely bunch walked down the hall and knocked on the judge's door. Tilly wanted to urge them all into a fast trot. They had just under ten minutes left.

CHAPTER EIGHT

arter held firm to Tilly's hand as they came up to the door of the judge's chambers. He gave her hand a tender squeeze. She turned and rested her chin on his shoulder. He wanted the world to stop while he gazed into those blue eyes.

"What is it, Burns?" A tall man with snowy white hair stood in the doorway to the chamber. "I was just headed out for a dinner date."

"Sorry, Judge Blair," said the clerk. "We have a last-minute request for a marriage ceremony."

"At this hour?" The judge looked past the clerk, and his snowy white brows rose to his hairline. "Tilly? Is that you?"

"Hello, Judge Blair. It's been a long time."

"I haven't seen you since your father's..." The judge allowed that sentence to dangle as pain crept over both his and Tilly's features. "Well, I'm delighted to see you, dear girl. Are you dining with us tonight?"

"No." Tilly shook her head, tightening her grip on Carter's arm. "I'm here to get married."

Now those bushy brows over the judge's eyes drew together. His head canted as he took in Carter. Carter remembered the first time the general had looked at him. General Silver had an uncanny way of looking right into the heart of the men who served him. As though he could see past their qualities and any sins they might possess. The judge's assessment made Carter feel as though he were back on base, squirming in his combat boots.

"I thought Haran was performing ceremonies for you and your sisters," said Judge Blair.

"Not this time," said Tilly.

"What's the rush?"

"We're in love," Tilly said at the same time as the clerk stage whispered, "She's in the family way."

Tilly's cheeks heated, her lips pursing together. She didn't correct the guy who clearly still carried a torch for her. Carter had ignored the dig earlier when he'd thought it would hurry the process along. Now, he worried the incorrect assumption might bite them both in the shins.

"You took advantage of this little girl, son?"

The judge's eyes were laser-focused on Carter. Even though he was being accused of something he hadn't done, Carter felt as though he was standing directly in the fire. Sweat broke out at his temple and under his armpits.

"No, Judge Blair," said Tilly. "I took advantage of him."

There was a slight cooling sensation as all gazes went to her.

"Not in the way you think," she said. "He was going to marry my sister."

The brief cooling period was followed by another flash of heat. More heads came out of office doors. People stopped in their strides toward the exit and lingered to listen.

"But then we realized we're perfect for each other," Tilly continued.

"Which sister was he going to marry?" asked the judge.

"Brig," said Carter, at the same time as Tilly said, "Gunny."

Carter wondered if there was any central heating and cooling in this building. His fingers were chilled to the bone while his chest was dripping with sweat. He wanted to get out of his clothes. He wanted to get out from under the judge's glare.

"None of that matters," said Carter. "What matters is I love her, and she loves me. And we want to get married, sir."

The judge stared between the two. The courthouse workers looked between the judge and the couple with bated breath. The clock on the wall ticked toward the new hour.

"If this is really that important to you and you're truly in love," said the judge, "then there's no harm in waiting."

Carter felt Tilly's shoulders deflate. They'd have to go home and face her sister. It would be tough, but they'd get through it.

"It's all right," Carter said to her. "We'll come back tomorrow morning."

"No," said the judge. "You can come back in two months."

"Two months?" both Carter and Tilly said at the same time

"That's my decision," said Judge Blair.

"There's no rule that says we have to wait that long," said Tilly.

"To the contrary, I'm making sure that no rules are being broken," said the judge. "I heard a disturbing report that you Silver girls were abusing the institution of marriage to cheat an inheritance."

Both Tilly and Carter opened their mouths to deny it. Though they were in love, and each and every one of the general's daughters had eventually fallen in love with one of his President's Men, that was technically true.

But how could the judge know such a thing?

As if in answer to Carter's silent question, the clack of heels coming toward them sent a shiver down his spine. He turned and saw a familiar face.

Carter didn't know much about General Silver's ex-wife. The man had rarely spoken of her. But Carter had heard the general speaking to her over the phone on more than one occasion.

Speaking was putting it lightly. When the general spoke to his former wife, Catherine, he was often yelling. His normally calm features reddening, and the hairs of his buzz cut on end from scrubbing his fingers through his hair.

When Carter had come to the ranch months ago, he hadn't heard Catherine's name mentioned by the Silver girls.

Or so he thought.

Cruella was the name the Silver sisters gave to their step mom.

When Carter had met Mareen a couple of weeks ago, he'd seen a shade of her mother in Mareen's cold attitude. Though he could barely reconcile the ice princess Mareen had been a few weeks ago with the rosy-cheeked, smiling woman she was now.

Carter felt Tilly's hands go cold the moment she saw her stepmother. Even before he'd agreed to make her his wife, he'd put himself before anything that threatened her happiness. Which was why he'd insisted on tagging along on her dates. But now, just the act of wanting to marry him could be used against her. He had to do something to protect the woman he loved.

So, like any fool who thought he was Prince Charming, he threw himself into the wicked witch's path.

"Mrs. Silver."

The older woman's back stiffened. "It's Ms. Chesterfield."

She didn't turn to face him. All Carter got was her profile. Just that partial look was enough to freeze a glacier and, at the same time, melt an iceberg.

"My apologies, ma'am."

Another blast of chilly air went through the room at the use of the word ma'am. Carter wondered if he could put a right foot forward with the woman.

"I worked with your husband—"

"Ex. Husband." Her voice was clipped enough to separate the hyphenated word into two.

"His dying wish was to do what was best for his daughters."

Now Catherine turned to face him. Carter flinched under the weight of her glare. He felt Tilly standing beside him, offering her strength and support. He'd faced down men with automatic rifles, but he hadn't felt truly afraid for his life until this singular foe.

"You should know that Wilson loves your daughter," Carter said. "Mareen is very happy."

"My daughter's future has been ruined because a down on his luck, washed up soldier, with no name and no money has her living in a dirt cabin all so he and the rest of you can pick over my ex-husband's remains."

"That's not what happened, and you know it," said Tilly.

"No?" Catherine turned her attention to Tilly.

Instinctively, Carter shifted to block the icy chill from reaching the woman he loved. But he couldn't help the shiver in his bones reminding him that he was past due for his medication.

"So I'm mistaken in believing the only way the ranch will pass to you girls is if you get married?" Catherine asked with a false note of innocence.

Tilly opened her mouth and shut it. That was the truth of the matter. But it wasn't the dirty plot that Catherine was making it out to be.

"Exactly," Catherine said, taking the judge's arm. "You're all marrying under false pretenses to steal my dearly departed husband's property from me."

"Dearly departed?" Tilly sputtered. "You hated my father."

Something crossed over Catherine's features. It was there and gone in an instant before Carter could make out the emotion. If it had been an emotion.

"What I hate are lies and deception," Catherine said. "And that's what you girls are engaging in. I won't allow what you're doing to put a stain on Abe's name. Despite our differences, he was a good man. He would turn over in his grave if he knew what his men were doing to his daughters."

Now it was Tilly holding Carter back. Those men Catherine was disparaging were all good and brave soldiers who had risked their lives to save the general. Not only that, they'd each kept their promise of checking in on the general's daughters after his death. By all looks of it, Catherine hadn't done that once in her ex-husband's absence.

Judge Blair glanced between the three of them. The onlookers moved their mouths wordlessly as though they were eating popcorn at the movie theaters.

"These are serious allegations," said the judge. "Out of respect for your father, I won't bring this into chambers immediately. But I'll be by to talk with you and your sisters soon."

With that stay of judgment, Judge Blair led Catherine down the hall. Catherine shot them a cruel smirk of certain victory as she and the judge walked out the exit.

The license in Carter's hand wouldn't be put to use today. The judge might call all of their marriages into question depending on how Catherine whispered lies into his ear. They thought they'd get an earful with their marriage from Scout. Now everything might be in jeopardy.

CHAPTER NINE

he truck came to a slow stop in the driveway of the ranch. Tucked safely in the passenger seat, Tilly could see the lights on in the dining room. She could hear the laughs of the couples inside. Once she and Carter stepped out of the truck and inside the house, all joy would cease.

Carter put the car in park and cut the engine. Neither of them made a move to unstrap their safety belts. It was as though they both knew the real ride was still in motion, and things were about to get bumpy.

When Carter's hand found hers, Tilly should've felt like she could take on the world. Instead, she only wanted to stay inside the vehicle where they were together. Where a woman who was meant to love her and her sisters like daughters would be giving her advice for her wedding night, not trying to prevent it from ever happening.

Tilly didn't have a lot of memories of her stepmother, Catherine. What memories she did have were of a woman too beautiful to be real glaring down at her. Catherine rarely smiled. The few times Tilly had seen the expression, it had brought her nightmares.

Catherine would've melted the Wicked Witch with one of her grins. Her smile would've poisoned the Wicked Queen without the apple. Instead, her Wicked Stepmother was intent on locking all of the Silver girls, her own daughter included, away from their princes.

"Everything will be alright," said Carter.

Tilly heard his words. She felt the warmth of his fingers as they squeezed hers. She also felt a tremor in his hand.

Carter's words sounded a little slurred. He often sounded that way when it was late at night. He shivered a lot, too, during the cooler nights. She supposed his body temperature always ran colder, but he was always warm whenever she'd managed to rest her head against his shoulder and cuddle up next to him.

Tilly realized she wouldn't need any more pretext to cuddle up next to him. He was going to marry her. He loved her. Pretty soon, they might be cuddling up in this car because they'd be homeless. But it would be worth it.

"You know what you need?" said Carter.

"What?" Tilly asked.

Carter brought her hand to his lips and brushed a kiss across her knuckles. "Shakabuku."

Tilly snorted a laugh at the silly, made-up word that she knew so well.

"You know what that is, don't you," Carter grinned. "A swift, spiritual kick to the head that alters your reality forever."

"Did you just quote Martin Blank from *Grosse Pointe Blank* to me?"

"It seemed fitting," he kissed each of her fingertips.

"Wow. I am so in love with you."

Carter grinned. "That's good because we might be headed head over heels in the bad way when your sister gets her hands on us."

"It's not our fault," said Tilly. "Though we probably made it worse."

"Yeah."

Carter brushed his thumb over her lower lip. Tilly would much rather stay in the truck and let him kiss her silly. They both looked at the lights in the house. Still, neither moved to unbuckle their seatbelt.

"You know, technically, this is Mareen's fault," said Tilly.

"You have a point there," Carter agreed. "It's her mother that's causing trouble."

"If Mareen had just married Steven—"

"I think his name was Stephán."

"—then her mother would have no reason to come to the ranch. In fact, Catherine would be none the wiser."

"You make a very valid point."

"I know, right?"

"Beauty and brains."

"You're a lucky guy."

"That, I am."

Tilly leaned over the console. Carter met her halfway. With her lips pressed to his, she felt like she could conquer the world.

Yes, kissing was far better than facing her sister. What was that saying? Making love, not war. Such good advice.

"What the heck is going on here?"

Tilly and Carter broke apart at the sound of Scout's voice. Tilly felt like she was back in high school and had been caught necking with a boy. In fact, hadn't she gone parking with Ryan Shane? And Al Hopper?

Man, karma was not her friend today.

"I can explain," said Carter, unbuckling his belt and getting out of the car.

Tilly knew she should follow him. She reached for the button of her safety belt. With a press of her thumb, she was free of the belt. However, with one look at Scout's face Tilly held the freed strap in place, so it looked like she was still strapped in. This ride was about to surpass bumpy and get downright treacherous.

"You bet you will explain," Scout was saying. "Explain why you're kissing one sister when you're supposed to marry another."

"Didn't this whole scenario just play out last week?" said Truman from the porch.

He stood next to Jackson, who leaned heavily on his walking cane with one hand while the other was wrapped around Brig. Brig and Jackson grinned at each other. Then they turned their attention back to the show in the parking area.

"I'm in love with Tilly," Carter said.

"Told ya," said Brig. She reached out her hand to Truman, making a come hither motion. Truman reluctantly handed over a bill. Then he gave Carter a scathing look.

"My bride is the smartest of the bunch," said Jackson, looking adoringly at Brig. "Never bet against her."

"Now that Tilly and Carter are settled, that just leaves Gunny and Truman," said Brig.

"Nope," was the only sound Truman made before he leaped off the porch and blended into the night.

"Artillery?"

Tilly turned her attention from the spot where Truman had disappeared to the place Carter was standing. It was dangerous territory as he was faced off with her sister. Scout did not look in the slightest amused.

"A little help here?" said Carter.

Right. Tilly was still in the truck while he was facing off against her sister. Honestly, Tilly liked her spot. It was warm in the cab of the truck. Nicely upholstered seating. That safety belt that only needed to be refastened to hold her steady. And there was also that lovely key in the ignition that would help her make a fast getaway.

Unfortunately, she couldn't do that. She couldn't leave Carter behind to face her family. They were in this together. And so, Tilly took a deep breath and climbed out of the truck.

"You love him?" said Scout.

Tilly nodded, not sure of her voice.

Scout raised her head skyward and shook her head. She took in a deep breath, filling her lungs as though preparing for a long, loud lecture. But when she lowered her head, she let out a sigh and opened her arms.

Tilly didn't hesitate. She went into her big sister's arms. She took all the comfort Scout was willing to give at this moment. Because, even though Tilly had braced for a hurricane of emotions, she knew this was still the calm before the storm.

"We have bigger problems," said Carter.

Tilly wanted to glare at the man she loved. She wasn't ready to have her peace doused. But they'd stalled long enough.

"When we went to the courthouse to get married..." Carter began but broke off abruptly. His body shivered as though the memory was physically painful to him.

"You what?" Scout's embraced turned painful as she pulled away enough to glare down at Tilly.

"Our stepmother was there," Tilly picked up where Carter had left off. "Catherine's trying to convince the judge that all of our marriages are fake. That we're trying to pull a scam. If Judge Blair believes her, we might lose the ranch, anyway."

The rest of her sisters and their husbands had all gathered on the porch. Everyone looked around at each other with worry and fury on their faces. Tilly turned to Carter, but he was doubled over as though in pain.

"Carter? Are you okay?"

CHAPTER TEN

arter felt like he was underwater. He felt like he was in a tub of boiling water. But he was still freezing cold.

He tried to move his feet to propel him out of the depths. He tried to reach his arms over his head to break the surface. But his entire body felt weak, weary, and worthless.

He was tired. So tired. He knew that if he just rested for a moment, he'd be able to gather his strength and try again.

He had to try again. He had to break free. There was a very important reason for him to be free.

"Carter? Are you okay?"

Tilly. That was his reason. His reason for waking up. His reason for dreaming. His reason for breathing.

He had to break free of what was holding him so that he could hold her. She needed him to hold her, to be there for her. None of the men she met on those apps were even half as qualified as him for the job.

Except, Carter couldn't even lift a finger, he couldn't even move a toe to get to her.

Because he was drowning.

Not in water.

Not in cold.

He was trapped inside of himself. The only thing that would set him free was another dose of his pain meds. The same meds that were holding him hostage now.

"What's wrong with him?" came Tilly's urgent voice.

Were her words accompanied by sobs? He'd never heard her sob before. The sound broke the hold the withdrawal had on him. He tried to reach for her. But just like her voice sounded far away, her entire body was far away.

He was being lifted. Carried away. Away from her.

No. He couldn't let that happen. He tried to fight, but he was being held down.

Strong arms caught his feeble attempts to get free. They weren't Tilly's arms. He knew that for certain. They were bigger, rougher, and a bit hairy.

"I've got him," came Wilson's grizzly bear of a deep voice.

"Let's move him to the cabin," came Linc's directive.

"I'm coming too," Carter heard Tilly say.

He couldn't make out who told her to stay back or the argument that ensued. The only thing Carter heard clearly as he was being carried away was Tilly sob again as she said, "I'm going to be his wife."

"Just give us a second," said Jeff. "It's an old injury. He won't want you to see him like this."

Carter heard the door shut. And then silence. Linc and Wilson were speaking to him. He didn't hear Tilly's voice. Without the sound of her voice, nothing else mattered.

Well, nothing but the pounding in his head. The shivers that made him feel both hot and cold at the same time. His labored breathing where he felt like he couldn't gulp down enough air to fill his lungs. He had never let it get this bad.

"Where are they?" Wilson demanded.

Carter didn't pretend to misunderstand. "Under the mattress."

He heard Wilson's heavy boots on the floor. Then the creak of the mattress. Finally, the twisting pop of the cap coming off the medicine bottle.

A glass of water was pressed in one hand. A pill in the other. Carter wanted to tell his friends that he needed more than a single pill, but one would suffice for now.

The relief was near instant as the synthetic opioid dissolved onto his tongue, into his bloodstream, down to his very soul. His breathing returned to normal. The pounding in his head ceased. The fog retreated from his brain.

When his vision cleared, Carter saw his friends staring at him. There wasn't judgment on their faces. They each knew what he had gone through in combat to bring him here. Each of them had taken this pain reliever at some point in their military career.

Linc should still be on the medication for his TBI, but he'd declined any more refills before he was discharged. Wilson had only taken it during surgery. Jackson had come off it not too long ago. As far as he knew, Carter was the only one still reliant on the meds.

"Did you tell her?" asked Wilson.

"No, I didn't," said Carter. "There's no need because I'm going to quit."

He'd determined that the moment he'd tasted the sweetness of Tilly's lips. He'd suffer through any pain if that was his reward. He'd just needed to get through that last bout of withdrawal. This would be his last dose.

When he looked up, he was met with silence from his friends. They didn't even bother to glance at each other. They only stared at him. Still no judgment.

In the military, doing hard drugs was a no-no. Soldiers couldn't get away with it with the frequent drug tests they had to undergo. Besides, it would be disastrous to be under the influence when your life, the lives of your buddies, and innocents were on the line.

Pain medication was a different story.

"I'm going to quit," Carter said again. "For her."

"Fine," said Linc. "Then you won't mind if I take these." He held up the bottle of his meds.

Carter wanted to tell his friend that that wasn't his only bottle. He didn't need to. He was quitting. So he nodded.

"Search the cabin for another bottle," Linc said to Wilson.

Wilson was already moving before the full sentence was out of Linc's mouth. Wilson was a bloodhound. Carter knew the man would find his stash. And so Carter said nothing. Because he was serious about quitting.

"Withdrawal is going to suck," said Linc. "But it won't kill you. You've got a good twenty-four to thirty-six hours before the withdrawal symptoms kick in. You need to tell her by then."

Linc was wrong. If Carter had been taking the recommended dose, he would've had that much time. These days, if he didn't have his tripled dose, he would be feeling the withdrawal again in hours.

Already, he'd been without his normal dose all day, and it had hit him this hard. How was he going to make it through the night without another hit? But worse, how was he going to face Tilly and tell her this secret he'd been keeping from her?

CHAPTER ELEVEN

"What are we going to do about Cruella?" said Scout.

Tilly nearly voiced aloud that she could not care less about their wicked stepmother. Catherine could swoop down on her broomstick right now with a legion of flying monkeys, and Tilly wouldn't care. All she wanted to do was to get back to Carter.

In all her weeks of knowing the man, she'd seen him sluggish in the morning, irritated under the afternoon Montana sun, and drained as the moon rose high in the late night. But Tilly had never once seen Carter unresponsive.

It had been as though he couldn't speak. As though he couldn't coordinate his movements. As though he wasn't himself.

She'd reached for him, tried to hold on to him. But the weight of him had been too much for her. She'd had to relinquish her hold to his friends. And then they'd shut her out. Physically shutting the cabin door in her face.

Tilly had grown up with a house full of sisters who had each other's back without questions. A neighboring ranch filled with strong men who would back them up if they sent up their secret call. But for the first time in her life, Tilly felt utterly alone.

She wanted to march back over to the cabin, but she felt drained.

Inside her chest, her heartbeat had slowed. Her throat ached. But from somewhere, she felt a soothing balm making its way through her.

Looking up, Tilly saw Mareen. Her sister's hand was stroking her back and offering comfort. Tilly had expected that comfort to be coming from Saylor, the peacemaker of the family. Mareen, who had been an outsider of the Silver clan nearly all her life, was still finding her footing now that she was inside the household.

"I'm surprised that Wicked Witch didn't swoop in on her broomstick already," Scout was saying.

"Scout, be nice," said Saylor.

"What?" asked Scout, her blue gaze blazing with indignation before they landed on Mareen. "Oh, no offense, Mo."

"None taken," said Mareen, her attention still on Tilly. "Not if my mother is planning to do what I think she's planning to do."

"What do you think she's up to?" asked Saylor.

"She's going to try and convince the authorities that we're all pulling a scam. If she can get the judge to believe it, then he'll call for an investigation."

"But we have nothing to hide," said Brig. "All of our marriages were for love."

"True," said Mareen. "But they didn't start that way. I'm not sure what Stephán told her, but she could probably use that against us too."

Mareen and her former fiancé had appeared to part on good terms. But Stephán had taken the long drive with Catherine back into the city. Tilly was sure that ordeal was enough to turn the man's goodwill to bad.

Tilly couldn't focus on Mareen's old fiancé. She was too busy worrying over her own. She couldn't see any movement in the cabin. She turned to Jackson, who sat in his wheelchair, his walking cane balanced on his knees.

"What injury does Carter have?"

Jackson pursed his lips. He rolled his cane over his knee as though pushing out the pain of his injury. "He should tell you that himself."

"He tells me everything," said Tilly. "But he never told me about this. Is he dying? Is it cancer?"

"It's not cancer." Jackson rolled the cane back up his thigh.

"Then what?"

Jackson wouldn't meet her gaze. "He should tell you himself."

Tilly didn't need her degree in animal nutrition to know that she was being fed a load of crap. Jackson knew something. They all did. And the fact they wouldn't tell her, let her know that it was bad.

Before Tilly could interrogate the only soldier in the house, his backup arrived. Linc and Wilson came in through the back door. Their faces were stoic, revealing nothing.

"What's wrong?" said Tilly. "Is he okay?"

"He's fine," said Linc. "He's resting now."

"Tilly, where are you going?" said Scout.

"To check on my fiancé."

Tilly was already at the backdoor. Scout slipped her body between Tilly's hand and the knob before Tilly could reach it.

"What?" Tilly didn't bother trying to hide the annoyance in her voice.

Scout had an inch over Tilly. That used to matter to Tilly, adding to Scout's arsenal as an authority figure. Now Tilly was ready to shove her sister aside, extra inch and all.

And just to imagine, she'd been fearful of her sister finding out that she was getting married only an hour ago. Now Tilly didn't care what anyone thought. She should be with Carter. What injury could he possibly have that would make him nearly pass out? She'd known him for two months and never seen any symptoms. Had she?

"If you go, I want you back here by ten," said Scout.

"What?" Tilly repeated. Her annoyance was gone this time. It was replaced with confusion.

"You're not spending the night with that man."

"That man is going to be my husband."

"He's not yet. I won't have any shenanigans going on under this roof. Especially not now with our stepmother breathing down our necks."

"Shenanigans? Who are you? Donna Reed all of a sudden? It's not the first time Carter and I have spent the night together."

"Yeah, but you were watching movies." Scout's gaze narrowed. "You were just watching movies?"

"Saylor and Jeff spent the night together before they got married," said Tilly.

"Yes," agreed Saylor. "But all we did was sleep."

"Look, Carter isn't feeling well. I'm going to go and look after him, which will be a part of our marriage vows."

"Are you really going to marry him?" asked Scout.

That drew Tilly up short. "What are you implying?"

"Just that you have a bad track record with commitment."

The room of opinionated sisters fell silent. The tension grew thick.

"Two months ago, you were going to marry Sergei from the dating app," said Scout, holding up her hand and raising her thumb.

Tilly got a bad feeling in her stomach that it was her thumb that her sister raised. Normally if someone were making a point, they raised their index finger. Because Scout had started with her thumb, it indicated that she had more than one point to make.

"Last week, you swore some guy named David would make the perfect temporary husband. A couple of weeks ago, it was a Sean. Before that—"

"Enough." Tilly drew herself up to her full height to face her sister. Somehow, with the moral high ground, it seemed Scout had a good two inches on her now. "Do you know the only constant with all of those guys? Carter. Every time I went on a date, I always came back and told Carter about it. Or discussed the guy with him before. I realize now that it was his attention that I wanted. Now I have it, and I want to keep it. I've never felt like this before, Scout, and I don't want to lose it."

Scout took a slow inhale as she regarded her. Tilly tilted her chin. She wasn't above bodily removing her sister if it came to that.

"Scout," said Linc, "let your sister go and speak with her fiancé alone."

Linc wasn't a man of many words. He also didn't bother to try and boss Scout around. He seemed more interested in simply watching her go about the day as she took charge of anything and anyone around her. This was the first time Tilly could remember him making a demand of his wife.

"The two of them need to talk," Linc continued, coming closer to his wife. He leaned down and whispered in her ear. "I need you to come remind me of something."

Linc pressed a kiss to her earlobe. Scout's eyelashes fluttered. With a second kiss, she sighed and melted into her husband's arms.

"Thank you," Tilly mouthed to Linc.

Scout reached out her hand before Tilly could grab the doorknob. "Tilly, just know if you change your mind, it's going to hurt us all."

"Gee sis, thanks for your vote of confidence."

"We're your family. We'll always be here for you. Marriage, despite how our parents did it, should mean forever."

That was just it. Tilly didn't like the idea of a forever without Carter. Scout moved her hand from the door. Tilly turned the knob and dashed out.

"Congratulations, Tilly," Saylor called behind her. The belated sentiment was echoed by her other sisters. Tilly barely paid them any mind. She was more focused on getting to Carter.

CHAPTER TWELVE

Carter heaved a heavy sigh, letting his forehead fall into his hands. The medication was in his system. Like a car that had been running low on gas, now that his tank was refilled, the engine of his heart revved in his ears. His blood rushed through his head, lubricating his thoughts and giving him back his sense of clarity. The heat from all his sensors now firing cooled his skin and calmed his nerves.

All should be right with the world. Except it wasn't. Carter knew the high he felt wasn't about the turn his life had taken with regards to his personal life. His racing heart had nothing to do with the woman who owned it. It was all due to the medication.

Before tonight, he wouldn't have cared where the relief came from, only that it came. He spent so many of his waking hours in pain that any relief was welcome. His movie nights with Tilly had been a source of relief. His helping her with her daily chores around the ranch had offered relief as well. But to do those tasks, to be witty when they watched a film, to remember the details of what they spoke of, Carter needed his daily dose.

Wilson had found Carter's secret stash. But he hadn't found all of it. Carter held a handful of pills in his palm.

He stared down at the pills. He knew he couldn't hold on to the pills if he wanted to hold on to Tilly. It was an easy decision.

Or at least it should have been.

What if Carter couldn't be the man Tilly loved without the pills? She had only ever known him when he was on the medication. Maybe to have her, he needed to have the pills as well?

"Carter?"

Carter shoved his hand behind his back at the sound of Tilly's voice. She stood framed in the doorway, her beautiful face highlighted by the moon. Her blonde strands looked like moonlight. Her bright blue gaze in contrast to the dark sky.

Carter ached to touch her. But he couldn't. His hands were full of pills.

"Are you okay?" Tilly's steps to him were tentative. They had never been before. She'd never hesitated to come up to him, to sit down next to him.

"I'm fine." Carter clenched his fists. The pills in his palms ground against each other. The sound was like fireworks in his head. Could she hear them too?

"Then tell me what's going on?" Tilly closed the distance between them.

Carter reached for her. Then he drew his hands back to his side, his right hand still clenched in a fist with a handful of dirty little secrets inside.

"What injury?" Tilly looked his body up and down, searching for signs of a wound she would never see.

Carter shoved his hands in his pocket, depositing the pills there. When he pulled his hands from his pocket, he could feel a bit of the chalky stains on his palm. He rubbed his hand against his pants leg. Some of the residue stained the fabric. But Tilly wasn't looking down. She was looking him straight in the eye.

"Where are you hurt?" she asked, taking another of those tentative steps toward him. "And why didn't you tell me?"

Carter had never had to explain this to anyone. The guys all got it, and none of them questioned his need for the pain meds.

Though he had increasingly felt their concern as the months had gone by.

How to explain this to someone who never had to keep going through the pain and residual effects of combat because their life depended on it?

"I was injured," he began. "Then they put me on medication to help me heal."

There was just an inch between them, but it felt like a gulf. Tilly waited, blue eyes trusting as she looked at him. Carter didn't want the next words out of his mouth to be *I'm a drug addict.*

Because he wasn't a drug addict. This medication was prescribed by the military. It was helping him.

Though he didn't need it anymore. Not now that he had her. He would flush those pills down the toilet and go through withdrawals and what may come.

"I had a bad reaction to the medication," Carter continued. That wasn't a lie. But it did keep the uglier part from her. "There may be a few more bad reactions until it's out of my system."

"Do you need to see a doctor?" She reached out to him, but her fingers only managed to traverse half of the inch between them.

"No." Carter caught her fingers in his hand, bringing them to his heart. The organ leaped at her touch, proving it was Tilly that it beat for and not the meds. "It's just flu-like symptoms. Nothing to worry about, I promise."

"What can I do?" She brought her other palm to his face, cupping his chin. Everything in his mind cleared out, leaving behind only thoughts of her, proving that it wasn't the meds that brought him clarity. It was her.

"Watch *Say Anything* with me."

The concern that had been written all over her features leeched from her face. Carter couldn't bite back his mischievous grin.

"Really? Really, Carter?" Tilly snatched her hands from his chin and chest. She put them both on her hips in the cutest sign of indignation he'd ever seen.

"It would make me feel better," he said.

Carter wrapped his arms around her waist and tugged her to him. She didn't resist. She did pout.

Tilly blew out a sharp breath. "Okay, fine. But the first time I have the flu, we are watching *The Grifters*."

Carter should want to groan at the thought of watching the John Cusack film about con artists. There was hardly a love story in it. It didn't matter. He had his own real-life love story playing out before him.

"Hey?" he said, resting his forehead against hers.

"Yeah?" she said, wrapping her arms around his neck.

"I'm going to marry you," he whispered.

"I know," she said with a grin.

"You still okay with that?"

"Depends. Can we watch *Con Air* instead of *Say Anything*?"

"Not on your life."

Tilly giggled, and it was the sweetest sound Carter had ever heard. He led her to the couch and then pulled her down with him, tucking her into his chest. Then he grabbed the remote and thumbed through the streaming app until he found *Grosse Point Blank*.

Her sigh of happiness let him know he made the right decision. Besides, he was in the mood to watch a hitman return to his hometown to fight for his true love while leaving a body count along the way.

"What happened to your pants?" Tilly asked, brushing at the white stain on his thigh. "Did you spill something on them?"

"It's fine." Carter grabbed a blanket and tossed it over both their legs, hiding any trace of the medication. "Hush now, the movie's starting."

CHAPTER THIRTEEN

There was a throbbing in Tilly's skull. The kind where she'd slept wrong all night and would need to down a couple of aspirin alongside a jug of coffee to feel halfway right for the day. The crick in her neck begged her to roll her head and pop some of the tendons.

She didn't. She couldn't. Tilly had no desire to move from the warm, soft spot she was in. In fact, she shifted her body until she was even more dug into the uncomfortable, spine crunching, neck bending position. She inhaled deeply and smelled the sweet citrusy scent of Carter.

Not for the first time, she wondered how such a manly man could smell so delicate and pull it off? Because Carter did. There were vanilla notes to his scent. A touch of cocoa and a hint of mint. It reminded her of poppy flowers.

There was a patch of them in the northern pasture that grew like weeds. They made sure and kept the horses away from that bit of land as the flowers were dangerous to the animals if consumed in large quantities. But they were still pretty to look at and lovely to smell.

Whenever Tilly went out there, she imagined herself as Dorothy from *The Wizard of Oz* falling to sleep in the poppy field. Instead of a lion, tinman, or scarecrow, she had her very own Prince Charming in her arms. Not even the Wicked Witch could tear her from this dream.

The problem was that her stepmother was trying to rain down on her happily ever after. So Tilly peeled open one eye. When she did, she had not a single regret because the waking world was better than the dream one.

She was lying in Carter's arms. Her head rested against his chest. When she tilted her head to look up at him, her nose brushed the warm flesh of his neck. Even from this angle, Carter Shane was a beautiful man.

His hair was mussed from a night cuddling on the couch. His lips were parted, a slight snore rattling from his nose. It wasn't irritating. It was entirely darling. Just like the man.

Unfortunately, the throbbing in her head was still there. It was actually getting louder and three-dimensional. When Tilly lifted her head from Carter's chest, she realized it wasn't her head that was pounding. It was the door.

"You two had better be decent," called Scout's voice from the other side of the front door.

Both Carter and Tilly groaned, pulling the covers over their head. The sound of the door creaking open was muffled from under the threadbare sheet. The light of the new day shone through. A dark shadow cast over them in the form of Scout, who promptly yanked the sheet from them.

"Good," said Scout. "Still fully dressed."

Tilly and Carter had fallen asleep sometime after the end of *Say Anything* and near the beginning of *Con Air*. Tilly had woken in the middle of the night and retrieved the blanket. She hadn't wanted to wake Carter to move to the bedroom. Besides, they'd fallen asleep many times on this couch. Though last night had felt different.

Last night there had been many stolen kisses between the movie scenes. Last night, they had laced their fingers together with a tightness that had no space for friendship. Last night they had held onto each other with the knowledge that this was how they would spend the rest of their lives together. Today was the first day of the rest of her life with this man. Tilly wanted to get started on forever.

"Scout, go away," Tilly said, curling her fingers into Carter's shirt.

"It's past sun up, and there are still chores to do," said Scout as though she hadn't heard Tilly. "And then we need to figure out how to handle Cruella."

Right. Reality. Tilly wished the credits could roll, and she and Carter could skip to the happily ever after instead of going head to head with the villain of their story. But this was the real world.

"Mareen needs some help with Mr. Tilney. She said he's been acting strange lately."

Tilly loosened her hold on Carter with a sigh. A sick horse was the only thing that would part her from Carter right now. And Mr. Tilney was one of her favorites.

"The guys are replacing the fences in the northern pasture," Scout continued.

"I'll be there in a second," said Carter. He rocked to lift his body, but he slumped back. When he readied himself to try again, Tilly pressed him down.

"You're not going anywhere today," she said. "I don't want another relapse."

She expected a chiding smile. Instead, something dark and defiant crossed his features. In an instant, it was gone.

"I'm fine," he said with a grin that didn't light his eyes like normal.

"Yes, you are," Tilly said, letting her appreciative gaze skate over his disheveled form.

Carter's brittle grin widened into a solid smirk. The light in his eyes became a spotlight that nearly blinded her with his feelings for her. He reached for her, cupping her face in his warm palm.

Except his palm wasn't warm. It was cold and clammy. Tilly pressed the back of her hand to his forehead. He wasn't hot, but he was a few degrees above cool.

"I'm fine," he repeated.

"And you're going to stay that way," she said. "At least wash-up and have some breakfast first, okay."

"Is this how our marriage is going to go? You bossing me around?"

"Did you really imagine there was any other way?"

Carter chuckled as he pulled her to him. He brushed a kiss over her mouth. His lips were the perfect temperature. Aside from that, they tasted sweet. Vanilla, mint, and a hint of chocolate. She felt like she was being pulled back under, like when she lay in the poppy fields and she was all too happy to-

"Okay, okay," Scout barked. "Enough of that. We have to keep this ranch going, and then we still have to save it. Work to do, people. Work to do."

Her older sister marched out of the cabin, leaving the two of them there. At least there was blessed silence again.

Tilly stood, brushing the wrinkles out of her clothing. It was a losing battle. Carter had seen her rumpled before. The way he was looking at her now made her certain he wanted to rumple her a bit more.

He made to stand. But once again, he wobbled. He reached for the side of the couch for support and closed his eyes as though the world were spinning.

"What is it?" asked Tilly.

He tried to smile in the way he did when he wanted to brush something off. But the smile turned to a wince. "Dizziness. It's one of the symptoms."

Tilly ran a hand across his brow. Carter turned his face into her palm and let out a long sigh.

"That is the best medicine," he whispered against her fingers. He turned his head until he met her eyes. "Are you freaked out? Changing your mind?"

"I promised in sickness and health." Tilly wrapped her arms around his neck.

"We haven't actually said our vows yet." Carter stood. His legs were sturdy now, and he didn't wobble as he held onto her.

"I vow it now."

A beep sounded from the table. They both looked over to see Tilly's phone on the surface. It lit up with a text message from the MeetCute dating app. It was the guy she'd been planning to see tonight.

Tilly grabbed the phone. With a few taps of the keys, she deleted the app. When she was done, she held the face of the phone up to Carter.

"Now, you're stuck with me," she said.

"That makes me the luckiest man in the world."

Carter set the phone aside and held her tighter. Without any warning, his lips crashed down on hers. It was now Tilly who felt dizzy and unsteady. She leaned into him for support, and he gave it.

That's how she knew that the two of them would get through any of it, through all of it. She trusted Carter with her heart, her body, and her soul. He'd never pretended to be something that he wasn't. Which was perfect, because she loved the man that he was.

CHAPTER FOURTEEN

*C*arter made his way to the northern pasture. He was feeling on top of the world since leaving Tilly. The nagging withdrawal symptoms would be nothing so long as he had her kisses, her touches, her voice whispering in his ear that she would be with him for the rest of his days.

He felt like Lloyd Dobler sitting next to Diane Court on the plane at the end of *Say Anything*. Any minute now, he would hear the ding announcing he could take his safety belt off and move around the plane. Because everything in his life was turning out fine. The turbulence of the past was behind him. There would be smooth sailing from here on out.

The northern pasture was large, but the guys weren't hard to find. Their voices boomed in the morning air like a bugle announcing the command to charge.

Carter pressed his fingertips against his temples before joining the fray. With a few circular rubs, he managed to wrangle the burgeoning headache into submission. The turmoil that the pills had caused was a distant, weak memory. One he was able to smooth away with just a few rubs of his fingers.

"What are you doing up?"

Carter opened his eyes. It took a couple of seconds for his vision to come into focus, and Wilson's large frame came into view. "Scout said you were out here. I'm here to help."

"I think you should take it easy today, buddy."

"I said I'm fine," Carter snapped.

All chatter stopped. All eyes were on him. His friends' faces were carefully blank. That's what bothered Carter the most.

He couldn't hide from his brothers. Each and every one of them knew what he was going through. It might have been easier if he'd seen judgment in their gazes. But not a single one of them judged. Their blank faces waited for his cues, letting him know that they would follow his lead on this road to recovery.

Fentanyl addiction wasn't deadly. It was just going to be a miserable few days. But Carter wasn't miserable. He was happy. Why couldn't they see that?

His head began to pound. When he lifted his hand to rub out the pressure, the world tilted off its axis. He was toppling over. Somehow he didn't hit the ground.

"Easy there. We got you."

Carter wasn't sure which of his friends said those words. He wasn't sure whose hands were around him. What he did know was that though he loved each and every one of these men as his brothers, he didn't like them seeing him in this vulnerable state.

They were soldiers. They were strong men. Showcasing any of their pain could be deadly. It could get them all killed on the battlefield.

But they weren't on the battlefield anymore. They were on a ranch. Making a border of wooded fencing. Not to keep enemies out, but to keep the gentle horses who roamed this lands inside.

Suddenly Carter felt nauseous. His body itched everywhere like a thousand ants were crawling on him. He just needed a moment of relief. One pill would do it.

His heels itched to about-face and go back to the cabin, back to where he'd hid those last few pills. He'd intended to throw them in the trash after Tilly left this morning. But then he reasoned that keeping the pills and not using them would prove him stronger.

And now he was in a moment of weakness.

"I'm sorry," Carter whispered.

"You're good," said Jeff, in his calm voice. "You're standing on your own two feet."

And he was. Carter stood center in the circle of his brothers. They were all at a distance where they could reach out to him if he faltered.

The throb in his head had silenced. The blur was gone from his vision. The fog cleared from his mind. All was right with the world.

"It passed," said Linc.

"So, get your lazy butt to work," said Wilson, in his deep, gruff voice.

Carter huffed a short laugh through his gritted teeth. And just like that, they were all fine. He knew his buddies wouldn't let him fail. He also knew they wouldn't let him slip backward.

He was fine.

He had this.

Carter moved slowly and carefully. The dizziness kept creeping back, but not so much that he could hold it at bay with a shake of his head. He noted that the guys gave him the light end of the work. He decided not to complain. He was taking the first steps toward getting clean. He couldn't be expected to run headlong into the action. This was a process, and he'd work the steps.

The sound of a branch breaking behind him made his heart skip a beat. All of the men in his unit were in front of him. That meant an enemy was approaching from behind.

Carter reached for his gun. It wasn't at his side where he normally kept it. He was unarmed, and the enemy was at his back.

Down on the ground was a hammer. He scooped it up and spun to face his attacker.

A dark-skinned man came into the clearing on a horse. There was no fear in the old man's eyes. The horse was another matter.

The beast reared. The old man held fast, leaning into the horse's neck. Once all four of the horse's feet were back on the ground, the man expertly soothed the horse.

Truman came up around Carter. He moved slowly, holding his hands in full view. Carter heaved a breath and lowered his hands. Truman grabbed his arm and took the hammer from him. Then he laid a hand on Carter's shoulder and forced Carter to look in his eyes.

Carter took a few deep breaths, letting reality wash over him in slow waves. He'd been pulled back into battle. It had been a long time since he'd had a PTSD episode. The fentanyl had kept most of those emotions at bay. Without the drug in his system, his entire being was vulnerable to attacks from all fronts.

"Sorry, sir," Carter said to Father Matthews who had gotten his horse under control and was now towering over him.

Father Matthews' gaze raked over Carter. It felt like the old soldier was seeing into Carter's bruised and battered soul. That penetrating gaze was also seeing inside Carter's veins where the last vestiges of the opioid were slowly making their retreat and realizing there would be no reinforcements.

Father Matthews dismounted. He handed the reins of his horse to Truman, then turned to Carter. "Walk with me."

Carter followed the man's orders. He followed behind the old man whose strides were long and measured, like the commanding officer that he was. Once they were at a distance from the others, Father Matthews turned to face him.

"It's a cool day," said Father Matthews. "But you're sweating like it's a hundred degrees."

Carter didn't need to look down to see the pit stains on his shirt. He felt like his entire body had been submerged under water and he'd come out dripping.

"Your pupils are small," Father Matthews continued. "And you slurred your words back there."

He had? Carter hadn't noticed anything amiss with his speech.

"I know opioid withdrawal when I see it," said the old soldier. "You tell Tilly?"

The shame was bitter on Carter's tongue. He wanted to stand at attention with a straight back, but he felt so weary. "No sir, not in so many words."

Father Matthews's gaze was hard. Carter felt his resolve weakening. His entire body was threatening to shake like a petulant child until he got his fix. The tantrum would just have to come. He wasn't going back.

"I quit. I'm going clean. The guys have my back. She has other things to worry about. I don't want to worry her with this."

"You're going to marry this woman? And you're already keeping secrets from her?"

Carter pursed his lips. It wasn't a secret if it was no longer a factor. Carter was going to stay clean, he was going to marry Tilly, and they would keep the ranch from Catherine.

"Judge Blair gave me a call," said Father Matthews. "He wants me to come in and talk about the marriages and the will."

As if this day couldn't get any worse.

CHAPTER FIFTEEN

"Thanks, Mr. Pete," Tilly called as the trailer pulled off. "Say hi to your wife for me!"

Mr. Pete honked in acknowledgment as he ambled down the road. Tilly turned her attention to the hay he had delivered. Normally, she'd take the tractor out and make the hay for the ranch. But there had been an accident a couple of weeks ago, and the vehicle had been put to rest for nearly decapitating Mareen.

So delivery it was. But she still needed to mix some of her special blends into the bales. She had a legume blend of alfalfa which was higher in proteins and calcium for the older horses. There was a Kentucky bluegrass blend for one of the horses who was still suffering from colic.

Off in the distance, Saylor and Brig worked with a new horse that had been dropped off a couple days ago. Like most of the horses here at Silver Star, the newly named Elton was a former racehorse who had outlived his usefulness to his owners. Those losers looked at Elton as though he was washed up. Little did they know that here on this ranch, the horse was about to begin living his best life.

Scout sat on the porch with binders and a calculator spread out around her. Unlike all of her younger sisters, Scout hadn't gone to college. There had never been time. Instead, she'd gotten on-the-job training and did a couple of courses online. Scout always had a singular mind about what she was meant to do, and that was to run this ranch.

Scout picked up a post-it note. The singular concentration leached from her face, and she smiled. No doubt the note was from Linc, who had a habit of leaving the sticky scraps around for her to find. Tilly had blushed at a couple of notes she accidentally found. Now everyone averted their gazes when they came across any of the adhesive, square reminders.

In the distance, Tilly saw Mareen. She was dressed in a pair of jeans and flannel. It was so unlike the high society miss that always came to the ranch in delicate fabrics and heels. Now Mareen was happy to get out in the dirt and make a mess of her clothing.

There was a smile on Mareen's face as she tilted her head to the sunlight. In her hands was a lead as she walked with a horse. From its coat, it looked like Mr. Tilney. Tilney was a docile and gentle creature. So when he reared on Mareen, Tilly rushed to her sister.

Tilly knew that Mareen could handle a horse. The woman had won medals in dressage for years. It was Mr. Tilney that had Tilly's attention. Mareen had the horse under control before Tilly reached them.

"I might be a little out of practice." Mareen looked off toward the house. But Scout had left the porch, likely following the directive on the Post-It and searching for her husband. Mareen sighed with what sounded like relief.

Tilly knew that Scout and Mareen were still getting their footing in their relationship. For so long, there had been a wedge between the two sisters. That wedge had been Mareen's mother, who was now inserting herself into all of their relationships.

"You're doing great," said Tilly. She gave Mareen's arm a quick rub before her attention turned to the horse.

"I'm pretty useless here," said Mareen. "All I know how to do is teach a horse to dance, and I'm pretty rusty at that."

Mr. Tilney pawed at the ground. He yanked at the lead as though agitated. His breaths came out in fast spurts as though he'd just been galloping.

"Did you ride him?" Tilly asked.

"No, we were just walking back from the north pasture."

"You're always such a gentleman, Mr. Tilney. What's got into you?" Tilly ran her hand over his side. She could feel the horse's heartbeat racing.

Mr. Tilney backed away from her, flattening his ears. In any horse, it was a sure sign of aggression. In this horse, it was entirely out of character.

"You said you took him to the north pasture?"

Mareen nodded. "I noticed Wickham and Heathcliff constantly running him off his food. I figured he could have a few mornings of eating in peace."

The horse let out another huff of air. On his breath, Tilly smelled the sweet scent of flowers. Not just the airy perfume of any flower. She smelled hints of vanilla, citrus, and cocoa.

"Oh," Tilly sighed. "That's why you're behaving this way."

"Why?" asked Mareen. "What did I do wrong now?"

"He's been eating poppy flowers."

The plant contained opiates and could act on horses the same way that it acted on humans, making them feel sedate, lethargic, and dazed. Or conversely giving them a sense of euphoria that made their hearts race. The animals normally stayed away from the bitter-tasting plant, but if that was all they had available, they'd eat it.

Mareen's shoulders deflated. She looked crestfallen as Tilly explained the situation.

"So," Mareen sighed, "in short, I screwed up."

"You didn't screw up. You were trying to help."

"You mean like when I asked my fiancé to buy this place, and he brought my mother who figured out what was going on with the will and is now actively trying to prove all of our marriages are a fraud?"

"That's not your fault," Tilly insisted. "None of this is your fault.

None of this is any of our faults. We are not our parents. We're certainly not going to make any of their mistakes by hiding emotions, not being honest, and hurting the people we claim to love."

As if she'd called out to him, Carter came out of the woods toward them. He was flanked on either side by the rest of the guys. But all Tilly could see was her guy.

"We're going to fight for this place," said Tilly. "No matter what your mother does, I think both of our futures look bright."

Wilson jogged up to them. He came to stand before his wife and swept her off her feet. Only to put her down a second later and tilt her chin. "Why are there smudges of dirt all over you? Did you fall?"

Mareen pinched her lips together, but she couldn't hide the smile there. Wilson was overprotective. And who could blame him when Mareen had almost died three different ways on the day he'd met her.

Wilson took Mr. Tilney's lead with one hand while he held onto his wife with the other. He led them both toward the stables and disappeared inside. When Tilly looked up, she and Carter were alone.

"We need to talk," said Carter.

Tilly waited for her heart to drop. Those were not the best words to hear in a new relationship. She'd said them herself with the intent of cutting all ties to guys she'd been dating. But everything in her heart told her that Carter wasn't dumping her.

He reached out a hand to her, and she felt his fingers tremble. He blew out a huff of breath. She noted the normal vanilla and citrus scent of him was fading. Probably due to the excessive amount of sweat collecting on his shirt.

Tilly wanted to rail at him. Hadn't she told him to take it easy today? He was still getting over his injury. Though he looked perfectly fine, better than fine. Aside from the sweat. And the trembling of his hands. And his pupils looked very dilated. He reminded Tilly of Mr. Tilney's behavior. Perhaps Carter needed a change in his diet, too.

"What do you want to talk about?" she asked Carter.

"It'll keep," he said. His gaze was not on her. It was over her shoulder. "We have another problem."

Tilly turned to see a sleek car pull up to the ranch house. When the car came to a stop, she saw Judge Blair step out of the driver's side. He rounded the car and handed out Catherine, who wore a grin that would've scared Maleficent.

CHAPTER SIXTEEN

Carter wrapped his hand around Tilly's and squeezed. To those assembled, they presented a united front. He needed to feel her solidarity, but he also needed to disguise the trembling of his body.

Sweat beaded on his forehead. It pooled under his armpits. That he could excuse from working out of doors all morning. The blurry vision and headache he couldn't explain. Luckily, no one could see those symptoms. Still, he felt that all eyes were on him.

The living room of the main house was packed with bodies. On a normal day with the six soldiers and five Silver girls, it was a tight fit. This afternoon they had three other guests added to the fray.

Catherine sneered at the glass of lemonade her daughter set in front of her. The older woman wrinkled her nose as though the glass were dirty or the contents were poisonous. Likely, she thought both instances were the case.

The two men who were guests happily gulped down the offered drinks. Father Matthews, who was a regular guest, emptied his glass and unabashedly held it out for more. Mareen filled it, offering the man a wane smile. The old man ran a gnarled hand over hers, causing Mareen's smile to increase.

Judge Blair took a polite sip. His lips turned up in appreciation, and he took a few more sips before setting the glass down.

"I believe you all know why we're here," said the judge. "Serious accusations have been leveled against you young ladies."

All eyes went to the cause of those accusations. Catherine sat stiffly in her chair. Perched as though she believed the fabric would stain her expensive dress.

"I've determined to speak with you in your home instead of in my courtroom out of respect for your father."

"What exactly are the allegations?" asked Linc. He stood behind Scout, a hand around her waist. Everyone present knew that her husband's hand was the only thing restraining Scout at the moment.

"Marriage fraud," said the judge.

"Isn't that often to do with immigration?" asked Tilly. "One party marrying to get a green card."

Her sisters' gazes all settled on her. As did the soldiers'. The judge's and Father Matthews's too. But not Catherine's. She brushed an imaginary piece of lint from her immaculate skirt.

"What?" Tilly said to everyone gaping at her. "We watched the movie *Green Card* a couple weeks ago."

Carter remembered that night. Tilly had fallen asleep against his shoulder. He'd sat and gazed down at her slumbering form for the second half of the movie before carrying her in his arms, tucking her into bed, and leaving. But some of the movie penetrated through his brain.

"We're all American citizens," he said. "Half of us have served this country with honor. The Silvers are a military family who has paid the ultimate sacrifice."

The judge shifted uncomfortably in his seat at the mention of the general's passing. It was easy to believe the two men had been friends. They were of the same generation and appeared to have the same family values. And each man had had his ear tugged by a woman who didn't think twice about twisting the world to suit her needs.

"All of these marriages are a sham," said Catherine. "Each and every one of you married under false pretenses with the intent to keep me out of my dear late husband's home."

It would've been impossible to hear a pen drop in the room. The intake of sharp breaths would've deafened the impact of the metal clattering to the floor. Not even a hammer falling could be heard during the indignant gasps of the Silver girls.

"Your *dear* husband?" said Mareen. She'd taken a step in front of Scout. But Wilson tugged her back into his arms.

"Abe's will states that the property will come to me unless all of his daughters marry before his deadline," Catherine went on. "That's clearly a ridiculous notion; the girls all getting married. So it stands to reason he wanted the property to come to me."

Carter looked up at the sound of a scuffle. Linc now had both arms around Scout. He turned her body so that her face was buried against his chest.

"I'm fine," Scout hissed. But when she turned her head, she shot Catherine a murderous gaze. Luckily, her husband didn't loosen his hold on her.

"Haran," said Judge Blair, turning to Father Matthews. "You're the most familiar with this matter since I believe you were in possession of Abe's will."

Father Matthews looked around the room. His gentle gaze taking in each man and woman in turn. When his gaze came to Tilly and Carter, there was a slight crinkle in his eyes as they narrowed on Carter.

"Yes." Father Matthews nodded. "Abe said the girls would inherit the ranch equally after they all married."

"Then soon after, these soldiers showed up," said Catherine. "They'd been in service to Abe all these years, but this was the first time they deigned to visit."

"We were a little busy protecting this country," said Wilson, his arm around Mareen.

"And now you're aiming to steal from the great man who gave your life purpose," said Catherine. "My daughter had been engaged for a year when you turned her head with your lies."

"What lies?" said Wilson. "That I love her and will give my life to protect hers." Wilson gazed down at Mareen with a love so bright that it hurt to look at.

Catherine was undeterred. She turned her venom on Scout and Linc. "Scout married this man within a week of meeting him."

"Because she's stubborn," said Linc. "It took that long to convince her she was in love with me. I knew on the first day."

The animosity that had been aimed at Catherine leached out of Scout's blue eyes when she turned to look up at her husband.

"Saylor left a relationship of five years to marry an invalid," said Catherine.

"I left an abusive relationship to go into the arms of a man who lifted me up," said Saylor. Her normally pleasant features were screwed into distaste as she shook her head at her stepmother.

"And they gave the child to an old man," said Catherine, turning her ire to Jackson and Brig.

Jackson lifted a brow. He was seated in a chair on the opposite side of the room. His walking cane was leaned against his injured knee. He didn't bother to speak. Instead, he tilted his head to look up at Brig.

Brig shook her head sadly as she regarded her stepmother. "Despite what you think, our father did care about you."

Now the pen could've fallen with a resounding crack of a hammer in the quiet of the room. Mouths hung open with no sound coming out. A few hands flew to chests as though to hush racing heartbeats.

"We care about you," Brig continued. "We could probably even love you. If you let us."

There was a bit of rustling. As though no one was certain of those statements. But neither were they ready to deny them outright.

Catherine's face turned so still her features looked like glass. She reminded Carter of a mannequin in a department store window. An expressionless lump of plastic with a beautiful garment. That was until her gaze turned from Brig and landed on him and Tilly.

"You're running out of time," said Catherine, her voice as cold as her gaze. "I'm assuming that's why you went to the courthouse."

"Going to the courthouse was impulsive," said Carter. "I've been prone to do things without thinking them through in the past. But not anymore."

His voice was steady even as he felt tremors running through his arms and hot and cold across his shoulders. His head pounded in his skull, but he held onto the one thing that mattered to him; Tilly. Her hand was still in his, lending him all the strength he would need to get through this.

Carter's gaze found Father Matthews. Carter felt the man saw straight into his soul. That was good. Because Carter needed the man to know that he was worthy of Tilly.

As though his prayers had been both heard and answered, Father Matthews gave a slight nod. It was all the approval Carter needed.

"We were being selfish the other day," Carter said, turning to Tilly and taking both of her hands in his. "Family is the most important thing in this world. When I promise to honor and protect, to obey and cherish, to have and to hold this woman for every day of my life, I'll do it with our entire family as witnesses."

"With all your family here, why not do it now?"

That hadn't been Scout's commanding voice. It hadn't been a directive from Linc. It came from Judge Blair.

"I don't know exactly what's in that will," said the judge. "What I can see is that there's clearly no fraud going on here. Just young love. Impetuous, a bit impatient. But love, nonetheless."

"You're making a mistake," said Catherine. Finally, her ice features cracked to reveal anger and indignation. "They'll all divorce after they get the deed."

"There will be no divorces here," said Linc. "We're building something. Why not be a part of it? You'll be a grandma someday soon."

Apparently, Linc didn't notice the murmur of *retreat* that came from the girls. Or the hand waving to get down that came from his own wife. The Silver girls all moved a step closer to him as though to block the incoming missile.

Catherine looked murderous. She stood, giving everyone, including her daughter, a once-over that left them all feeling dirty. "Cameron," she hissed at the judge, "take me home."

"It looks like I have a ceremony to perform, Catherine," said the judge. Like Linc, he didn't realize the minefield he was treading on.

The look Catherine gave Judge Blair would melt a glacier. The judge actually cringed. To prove he had a good sense of judgment, the man rose from his chair and offered Catherine his arm.

"It's fine," said Father Matthews. "I'll take it from here."

The judge looked saddened. Sad because he would miss the vows? Or sad because he'd have to be confined with Catherine in that car on the drive out? Whichever it was, Carter didn't care.

His heart was pounding with happiness. His head was throbbing with joy. His hands were trembling with the knowledge that he would be able to hold Tilly Silver to him for the rest of his days.

He knew these symptoms of the withdrawal wouldn't last long. He knew he wouldn't need any more pills to get through the day. Nothing was worth losing this woman. And he'd tell her what he'd been through, what he was going through.

Now clearly wasn't the time. He made a vow that he would. She'd already promised him in sickness and health. So, he'd tell her right after their vows.

CHAPTER SEVENTEEN

Tilly held Carter's hand in hers. He'd been shaking since they'd come into the house. She grinned to know that he was more overcome with emotions than her.

"Dearly beloved," intoned Father Matthews's deep voice. "We are gathered here today to witness the joining of this man and this woman."

Now it was Tilly's hands that were shaking. She bounced on her toes, shifting her weight from one foot to the other. Carter pulled her closer until her hands rested on his heart. Through his shirt, she felt the organ beating wildly. It matched the rhythm of her own racing heart.

Neither of them ran for the door, intent on escaping their future. Instead, they held onto one another until the trembling ceased and their hearts slowed down and came into synch. This was where they belonged, together.

Looking down at her, Carter blinked a couple of times as though she wasn't in focus. Tilly could understand. There were tears in her own eyes. She kept waiting for the feeling that this wasn't right, that there was something more, somewhere something greener. Looking into his green gaze, she didn't want to be anywhere else.

"In this union, the two of you will have to push forward through the times that make you want to withdraw and turn back."

Carter lifted his gaze from Tilly and focused on Father Matthew. Tilly watched as his green eyes adjusted and became clear. With a slight gulp, Carter nodded once at Father Matthews, who then turned to Tilly.

"Trust that your love is stronger, despite the odds you will face. Love each other through the dark moments, which will threaten your wellbeing. Have faith that you can recover through any fall."

It felt like Father Matthews was giving a sermon. Which Tilly would've appreciated at another time and place. But this was her wedding day. She wanted to skip to the good parts.

"You will be inextricably intertwined. You will be family."

She and Carter already were both those things. Even now, his fingers were laced with hers. Though his were trembling again, and sweat covered his brow.

Tilly squeezed his hands tightly, trying to let him know that she was here for him. That she was his. And he was hers. That this was right. That this was forever.

"I Artillery Silver, take thee, Carter Shane to be my wedded husband, to have and to hold from this day forward, for better, for worse, for richer, for poorer, in sickness and in health, to love and to cherish, till death do us part."

Carter closed his eyes and let out a sigh. A tear formed at the corner of his right eye. Tilly unlaced her fingers from his just in time to catch it. When he opened his eyes, they shone with a love so bright her knees felt weak.

"I Carter Shane, take thee, Artillery Silver to be my wedded wife, to have and to hold from this day forward, for better, for worse, for richer, for poorer, in..."

He coughed at this next part. Tilly's hand was still on his face. She cupped his cheek, letting him know with her touch that she was here for him, would always be.

"In sickness and in health," he continued, with a renewed strength in his voice. "To love and to cherish, till death do us part."

Tilly tilted her head to seal that deal with a kiss. Before her lips touched his, a throat cleared.

"We haven't gotten to that part yet," said Father Matthews.

"I'm pretty sure it's the next part," said Tilly.

The old man smiled at her. Tilly tried to hold on to her patience, but it was a losing battle.

"You let me know when you get there," she said. "I'm way ahead of you."

And with that, she claimed her prize. Carter chuckled against her lips, but he accepted her kiss. They might not have gotten here the conventional way, but they were here. They were together. And that's the way it would be for the rest of their lives.

"I now pronounce you man and wife. You may now kiss the bride."

Carter swayed a little as he ended the kiss. Instead of letting her go, he pulled her to him as though she was his anchor. When he opened his eyes, his green gaze was steady, as was his large body. His trembling had stopped. His skin was no longer clammy with sweat.

"I love you," he whispered before he captured her lips again.

Tilly wasn't able to respond with words. She was able to respond with her mouth. She used her lips to tell him that her whole heart, her entire body, all of her soul was his.

Carter's breath was shuddery as he broke the kiss. Tilly opened her eyes slowly. Her gaze was hazy. Looking across the room, she thought she was seeing double. Though she'd never be caught dead in khakis and hiking boots.

"Gunny?"

Tilly broke from her husband and peered around his shoulder. Sure enough, her twin stood in the entryway to the parlor. Gunnery Silver had a duffle bag slung over her shoulder as she regarded the scene with quizzical interest.

Tilly went to her twin and wrapped her up in her arms. Gunny smelled like she hadn't showered in a week, along with a hint of dark roast coffee. Tilly inhaled deeply. She might have just given herself to a man, but she had missed this part of herself. With her twin in her arms, Tilly felt whole.

"You're married," said Gunny.

Tilly followed her sister's gaze to Carter, her husband. "I am."

"That's Carter?" asked Gunny.

"Hi," said Carter with a wave.

Gunny waved back before turning her attention to her twin. "Wasn't I supposed to marry him?"

Oh. Right. That had been the plan.

"Well…" Tilly began and stopped. "Technically, you were supposed to marry Jackson."

"And which one is Jackson?" asked Gunny.

"He's mine," said Brig, taking a seat on Jackson's lap.

Gunny looked around the room at her sisters. "I've been on a plane for the better part of two days to get here because you all said I had to come home and get married. And now that I get here, there's no one for me to marry?"

With that, Tilly saw Truman slip out the back door. Father Matthews chuckled. All the sisters launched themselves at Gunny in a hearty Silver family welcome.

They were all here. They were all together. Now they just had to figure out how to keep it that way.

CHAPTER EIGHTEEN

"What are we going to do about Gunny?" Carter asked as he and Tilly made their way to the cottage.

He held her hand in his. As he rubbed his thumb back and forth over her knuckles, he noted the absence of a ring there. He'd have to remedy that oversight soon. He wanted everyone in the whole world to know that this woman was his.

"We'll figure something out," Tilly said. "Who knows? Maybe she'll be interested in MomApproved?"

Carter chuckled. Had that disastrous date only been yesterday? Yes, just twenty-four hours ago, and he'd been sitting by watching as the woman he loved sat across from a man who would never deserve her. And now, here he was, standing beside her as her husband.

The world was a strange place. It didn't matter how crazy things got. He could weather anything with Tilly beside him. The shakes had calmed the moment she'd made her vows. Alongside the sweating and his racing heart. The only thing he couldn't control was her Wicked Stepmother's aim to take the ranch from them.

"We don't have much time left," Carter said.

"You don't think Truman will come around to the idea of marrying Gunny?"

"Your twin is an animal rights activist and anti-gun protestor."

"She's not anti-gun. She knows how to use one. She just doesn't believe in the Second Amendment."

"You do know that Truman is a trained sniper who wants back in the military?"

"Well, yeah. But opposites have been known to attract."

"Not if one is in the North Pole and the other is on Mars."

They came to the door of Tilly's cottage. Carter supposed it was both of theirs now. This is the place where their friendship had blossomed. This is the place where their married life would begin. He was ready to take this first step toward the rest of their lives. But when he opened the door. Tilly waited outside.

"What?" he asked. Was she already having cold feet about their marriage?

"I'm your new bride," she said. "You need to carry me over the threshold."

"Right," he said but hesitated.

"Unless…" Tilly reached a tentative hand out to him. "Are you still feeling ill?"

The withdrawal symptoms had loosened their grip on him. Carter knew that wouldn't last. It was still going to be a rough couple of days before he got all of the poison out of his body. Another side effect of the opioids was that it was a high chance he wouldn't be able to perform as a husband should on this important night. Might as well set that expectation now and then come clean with the rest.

"Yes, I am still feeling ill." Carter took her hands in his. "That's something I want to talk to you about. Come on inside."

He gave her a tug. They walked across the threshold of the cottage, hand in hand.

"There's something I didn't tell you," he said.

Tilly tensed. Carter could feel protective walls erecting around her. They were the barriers she put up between herself and the other men she'd gone out with on first dates. The boundaries she would erect to ensure that no foundation could be set between them.

"No," Carter said the word forcefully. "Don't do that."

He didn't have to clarify what he meant. They knew each other too well. There had never been walls between them. There never had been any reason for them. Tilly took a deep breath, and Carter felt the boundaries crumbling around them.

"Tilly, I've never lied to you. But there is something that I neglected to tell you about myself."

He saw the struggle on her face. She wanted to put something between them. Instead of a mental brick barrier, she grabbed for a pillow from the couch where they sat most nights watching old movies.

Carter placed a hand on the pillow she held against her chest. "It's something personal. We weren't together, so I didn't think you needed to know it and—"

"Stop stalling, please." The quiver of her lip nearly did him in. "The more you do, the worse I imagine it is."

"It was bad. But it's not a factor any longer."

"Carter!" She tossed the pillow at him.

Carter caught the fluffy missive and set it back on the couch. "I had a fentanyl addiction."

The only hint that she'd heard him was a minute twitch of her brows.

"Have," he corrected himself. "I have a fentanyl addiction."

"Fentanyl? That's an opioid?"

Carter nodded.

"Like heroin?"

"No. Not heroine. I didn't get drugs off the street. They were prescribed to me by the military for pain management."

"Because you were injured."

Carter inhaled. "I was. It healed. But the pills... I developed an addiction. I began to need them to function."

Tilly looked at him as though seeing him anew. "The smell."

"What smell?"

"You. Your smell. Vanilla and citrus with a hint of cocoa. You smell like poppies, which is where opium comes from in nature."

Carter didn't answer. Trust the nutritionist would figure it out with the help of a plant.

"The twitching and trembling," she continued. "The sweating and headaches. Those are all symptoms of withdrawal. How did I not see that?"

"I'm sorry," he said. "For all of it. Especially for not telling you."

"I wish you had," she snapped.

Carter snatched the pillow away before she could use it as a weapon again.

"I would've supported you." She jabbed a finger at his chest. "I was your friend before I was anything else."

"I didn't think I had a problem." Carter took that finger and wrapped it in his hand. "I thought I had it all under control."

"What changed?"

"You. I wanted you more than I wanted the pills. So I gave them up."

"For me?" Tilly sighed and pressed her palm against his chest.

"I'd do anything for you. I want to be the man you need, the man you deserve. That man is not a drug addict. So no more pills, I swear."

"You're going through withdrawals now? Is it dangerous?"

"It's going to be uncomfortable. But it's not dangerous, not life-threatening."

"Okay," she said after a long pause.

"Okay?" Carter asked. "I was expecting a big blowup. More than a pillow grenade and a finger poke. You hate lies. Including ones of omission."

"That was your one pass." She poked him in the chest with her finger. "It'll have to last a lifetime."

"I'll never keep anything from you again."

"You better not, or—"

She picked up a pillow and aimed it for his chest. Carter pulled her to him and kissed her soundly. The pillow fell to the floor with an inaudible thud.

"So, I know we can't sleep together because of your condition," she said. "But we can still *sleep* together, right?"

"Yes."

As though he was letting her be anywhere without him again. Carter guided Tilly to the bedroom. The bed with her comforter was made up with military precision. His things were tucked neatly in corners. They'd have to expand if they were going to live here together. But all that would wait. All he needed was a good night's sleep with the woman he loved tucked securely in his arms. Then he'd wake up and conquer the world for her.

That thought dulled any effects of the withdrawal. In fact, he couldn't feel a single symptom. His head was clear. His heart beat slow and steady. He was no longer sweating, though he could use a shower to wipe away the residual effects.

When Tilly came out of the bathroom, he was surprised to find her in the same messy state as when she'd went in. He wondered if she needed a night shirt. The thought of her in one of his t-shirts made all the symptoms come back, but not as a result of the withdrawals. These were all due to desire. Maybe he could perform his husbandly duties after all?

When Tilly opened her hand, palm up, all his desires turned cold. In her hand, Carter saw three white pills. The reserves he'd sworn he wouldn't use.

"You said you got rid of these," Tilly said.

"I did… Those were just… I wasn't going to take them."

Carter heard the flimsiness of his argument. In real-time, he saw the protective walls erecting around his wife, the ones she used when she saw that her dates were liars who had misrepresented themselves.

"Tilly…" He reached out to her, but even though she was so close, she was beyond his touch.

She set the pills on the counter. The small white shapes merged in his eyes to resemble a white flag being thrown down. If only he were here to save himself. But she'd turned her back on him, was headed for the door.

CHAPTER NINETEEN

e'd lied to her. And not a bald-faced lie. It was worse because he'd hidden the truth until the last possible second, revealing it only when he was caught in the web he'd spun.

Tilly couldn't stand looking at Carter's profile any longer. She could barely recognize the man that had been her friend for the last couple of months. She definitely couldn't see the man who had become her husband.

She turned on her heel and ran. She'd expected Carter to reach out and grab her, to haul her back to him, to wrap her up in his arms and tell her it had all been a mistake.

He did none of those things. He let her go.

So that he could stay with his drugs. Clearly, they were more important than she was. So important that he'd lied to her about them.

The cool evening air whipped strands of hair about her face. Tilly brushed her locks aside, but they refused to be captive. Her hands fell to her sides, and she looked about the ranch, unsure where to go.

She didn't want to go into the house. Everyone was still up celebrating her union with Carter and likely visiting with Gunny. If she walked through the door, even with a fake smile plastered on her face, her twin would know something was wrong.

Tilly couldn't talk about it. Not with her sister. The only person she did want to confide in about her heartbreak was the one who'd broken the organ.

Her feet took her to the stables. Inside, the horses were settling down for the night. Mr. Tilney put his head over his stall.

There was a bit of slobber at the horse's mouth. His breaths came out raspy. His large eyes drooped with lethargy. The poor animal was still suffering the effects of his accidental poppy consumption.

"You'll be fine once it's out of your system," Tilly said, giving the horse a soothing pat. "We'll take care of you."

She could take care of Mr. Tilney because the horse wanted to be taken care of. If he'd had another choice, Mr. Tilney would not have eaten that bitter-tasting plant. Unlike Carter, who had other choices and nearly a dozen hands that would offer help. But instead, he'd chosen to lie.

Mr. Tilney whined. He gave a shake of his head and backed away from Tilly. Belatedly, she realized her comforting pats had turned to a rougher grip.

"Sorry, buddy. I'm not fit for company right now."

Tilly didn't want to wreck another horse's slumber. She didn't want to talk to her family. She definitely didn't want to see her husband right now. What she needed was anonymity and a drink. There was only one place to get that.

She headed to the driveway, found her car, and climbed in. Pulling out onto the road, she headed into town. As she drove down the long and winding road, Tilly pressed her temple with one hand. She felt something grainy against her forehead. When she looked at her palm, she saw that there was still residue from Carter's pills there.

How had she not seen this? How had she not known that the man she was falling in love with had an addiction?

She knew how. It was because Carter had been hiding it from

her. Just like the men who put up misleading details on their dating profile.

Her stomach twisted in knots at the realization. She'd trusted Carter. She'd trusted him completely, blindly.

The fluorescent lights of the bar didn't help to clear her vision. It just made things a bit bleary. The bar was at the edge of the town square. Down the street, Tilly could see the bell tower over the courthouse.

Had it just been one day ago that she and Carter had left the restaurant, grabbed an ice cream, and then headed up the steps to the courthouse to be married. All the while, he'd been lying to her.

Tilly climbed out of the car and headed into the bar. She wasn't much of a drinker, but she needed something in her system. If not to help her think clearly, then to help her stop thinking entirely.

"What's a newlywed doing at a bar on her wedding night?"

Tilly had only just taken a seat at the bar. She hadn't even placed her order yet. So she knew she wasn't drunk. Still, she didn't trust what her eyes told her she was seeing.

Catherine stood next to her. She looked down at the empty barstool beside Tilly. With a look of utter distaste on her lovely face, she pinched the edges of a napkin and wiped the seat of the barstool off. Frowning at the smudges that stubbornly remained, she sat perched at the edge of the seat.

It took Tilly a few more seconds to find her voice. "What are you doing in here?"

"I asked first." When Tilly didn't answer, Catherine went on. "I was leaving the courthouse after Judge Blair dropped me at my car when I saw you come in here. Without your husband."

Tilly looked down into the drink the bartender sat in front of her. She didn't want to talk to her wicked stepmother. This would just be more fodder for her to try and use against them. But Tilly's marriage was already over before it began, so Catherine had won.

CHAPTER TWENTY

arter didn't chase after Tilly. Not because he didn't want to. He physically couldn't. His body was not cooperating with him.

He felt hot and cold. Dizzy and nauseous. All at the same time.

He barely made it to the bathroom before giving up his lunch. His head swam as he praised the porcelain gods. The bile didn't leave his throat, not even after he managed to wash his mouth out. The bitter taste of his lies of omission clung to his tongue.

If only Carter told Tilly what he was going through early on in their friendship. But he hadn't even had the courage to tell the men in his unit. The only reason they knew was because they had seen it or experienced it themselves.

Carter was the weak one. He was the one who had grown dependent on the medication. He'd used it as a crutch long after he was healed. And look at what those pills had done; they had broken him.

The woman of his dreams had slipped through his fingers because he hadn't been able to let go of the pain meds. No, scratch that -the drugs.

The fentanyl had stopped being medicinal a long time ago. They were drugs, and he was an addict. He'd been more devoted to the drugs than he was to himself, to his friends, and to the woman he loved.

Carter would need to seek forgiveness from all wronged parties. Starting with himself. He had lost control of himself. He recognized that now. He also recognized that it would be a fight to regain mastery over himself.

Despite the fact that he knew he didn't want the pills any longer, he had to finally admit the power they'd had over him. His friends had seen that when he couldn't. He owed them an apology at the least, a debt of gratitude at the most.

Carter knew he could get to work on making amends with himself and his friends immediately. It was his wife's forgiveness that would be the hardest. He'd broken Tilly's cardinal rule; no lying or omissions. He knew that about her, and he'd done it, anyway.

Carter felt wretched. He felt untethered to the world. His body started to shake and tremble. He felt hot and cold at the same time. And tired. Oh, so tired. He knew only one thing would take this pain away.

The pills sat where Tilly had left them. They were like white pearls that would ease his suffering, help him think clearly, make everything feel better.

Carter picked one up. He studied the white tablet. He expected the pill to burn his fingers. But it was cool to the touch, almost an inviting feeling. So familiar.

There was no judgment from the pill. All it wanted to offer him was relief. It was a door, an escape. He just needed to walk through. And by walking through, he'd simply need to put it in his mouth and swallow.

Carter had lost Tilly. She wasn't here now. She likely wouldn't be back until tomorrow if she came back to him at all.

She wouldn't know if he took it. It would be his only comfort. His consolation prize for trying to do the right thing and failing.

Only he didn't want a consolation prize. Carter wanted Tilly. He wanted his wife. These pills were standing in the way of him getting her back.

They were standing in the way of him getting himself back. Carter wanted both of those things equally. But he couldn't have one without the other.

He was not this man. He was not beholden to this drug. But the truth was, the drugs still had a hold on him.

He was strong. But this tiny tablet had an edge on him, an edge that could bring him to his knees. He finally had to admit it. He couldn't do this alone. He needed help.

There was a knock at the door. When Carter called out, the door to the cabin opened. On the threshold stood Tilly. She was bathed in moonlight. She looked tired and haggard. There wasn't love in her gaze. There was suspicion.

With an ache that tore through his heart, Carter realized the worst possible outcome. He'd already lost her. She'd closed herself off to him, just like she'd done with the guys from the dating apps when she was done with them. After she realized that they'd lied or misrepresented themselves.

There had to be someway back into her heart. Carter had never felt this way about anyone. He wasn't about to let her go. He looked at her again, ready to beg and plead. Until he realized…

"You're not Tilly."

"I saw her leave," said Gunny. "It felt like something was wrong. It's the whole twin connection thing. What happened?"

CHAPTER TWENTY-ONE

"He lied to me," said Tilly.

"So soon?" Catherine turned her nose up at the glass of wine that was sat before her on the bar. "And I thought Abe had the world record on that."

Tilly held her own shot glass in her hand. The tumbler was full. Though inside, her gut twisted with acid and fire. She ached with need, but she knew the alcohol wouldn't quench her thirst. So she turned her attention to her stepmother.

"Why do you think my father lied to you?"

"He said he loved me."

Tilly waited. But it appeared that was the beginning and the end of Catherine's accusation. "My father did love you."

Catherine shoved the wine glass away with a scoff. A few droplets spilled over the top of the glass. The white wine splattered onto the wood surface of the bar. But the instant they hit, they dried without leaving a trace.

"My father didn't always keep his word," said Tilly. "Not because he didn't want to. Because he had a habit of over-committing himself."

"He shouldn't have married me if he was still in love with that woman." Catherine grabbed the wineglass and took a gulp.

"He told us that he loved you."

"If he loved me, then he wouldn't have divorced me," Catherine took another gulp. Her eyes were vacant as she gazed out the window.

"*You* divorced *him*."

"Because he loved that woman." Catherine slammed her empty wineglass down on the bar top.

"Yes, he did. He loved Sarah. And he loved my birth mother. And he loved you. A man can love more than one woman in his lifetime. The man had six daughters."

A myriad of emotions skittered over Catherine's features. Confusion, anger, doubt, hope. Not one emotion stayed longer than a full second. It was as though she didn't believe that all those statements could be true at the same time.

Abe had loved each of his wives. Of that Tilly was sure. Her father had failed a lot in his personal endeavors with the women in his life. He'd made promises that he wasn't able to keep. He'd broken his word countless times. But he'd never once done it maliciously. He'd tried his best. But his best wasn't always good enough.

"So, your man is in love with another woman?"

It took Tilly a few seconds to break out of her silent reverie over her father's failings. She blinked at Catherine, repeating her question over again in her head. Was Carter in love with another woman? Tilly knew that answer without a doubt.

"No," Tilly said. She knew she was the only one in Carter's heart.

"Is it a financial thing that broke you up?"

"No."

And they weren't exactly broken up. Were they? This was a fight. A big one because he'd lied to her. He'd said he'd quit, and she found evidence to the contrary.

"A communication thing?" asked Catherine. "He doesn't talk to you and tell you his feelings?"

"We talk about everything." Everything except his addiction.

I didn't think I had a problem. I thought I had it all under control.

Carter should've told her what he was going through. She would've helped him. She didn't have any experience with drug addiction. She knew it had to be hard. Something someone shouldn't do alone.

But she'd left Carter alone when he was clearly struggling.

"Those are the top three reasons for marital trouble," Catherine was saying. "What else could it be."

"He has a... a problem."

Catherine cocked her head one way and then the other. Then she grimaced. "Oh. I see."

She did?

"That's why you're at a bar on your wedding night. Bad luck on you."

"No, not that."

Well, yes, *that*. But *that* wasn't the point.

Tilly had fallen in love with Carter before she'd ever kissed him. She loved him for his wit and his attentiveness. She loved that he could finish her sentences and even begin her thoughts. She loved the way his body curled around hers when they sat next to each other. She loved the sound of his voice, the whisper of his breath, the way he looked at her like she was the only person in the world who understood him. She loved that no one else in the world understood her the way he did.

"Well, whatever it is, best you learn now there's no such thing as true love or happily ever afters," said Catherine. "I tried to teach my daughter that. That soldier will break her heart one day, and she'll come crying back to me."

The warm and fuzzy feelings in Tilly's heart had migrated down into her gut and soothed it. She felt herself heal from the inside out with just the thought of Carter. But her ears stung at Catherine's words.

Tilly looked at her stepmother. Catherine had tried to get Mareen to believe something that simply wasn't true. And while Mareen had believed it, it had hurt her.

I didn't think I had a problem. I thought I had it all under control.

Carter's words rang in Tilly's mind. She could tell that he believed what he'd said. But he'd been wrong. He'd been hurting for months, and she hadn't known it, hadn't seen it. He was hurting even worse now. And she'd abandoned him.

"It would seem I'm the only mother you have left," Catherine was saying. "So let me give you some advice."

Tilly was sure that she didn't want to hear Catherine's advice. Advice that there was no such thing as true love. Tilly knew that was false because she'd felt a connection to Carter the first time she'd met him. It hadn't presented itself as love, but now she recognized it clearly. She loved him, and he loved her right back. And that was never going away.

"Divorce is an ugly affair," said Catherine. "So, stay with him."

Tilly was surprised at her stepmother's words. She'd expected Catherine to tell her to annul the marriage and take him for everything he had—which Tilly knew wasn't much—except those few VHS tapes, which she kinda wanted. Maybe Catherine had grown? Maybe she could step in and finally be the mother they all needed?

"Stay with him and make him suffer for every ounce of pain he brought on you."

Tilly reared back at Catherine's words. She waited for the wicked grin on her stepmother's face to turn her heart cold. She waited for the cruel glint in Catherine's eyes to make her gut twist again. But Tilly's lie radar was back in working order, and she smelled a rat.

"I don't believe you," Tilly said.

Catherine shrugged with a nonchalance that also tickled Tilly's radar. The older woman's shoulders were too rigid. Her half-smile too bland.

"No, I mean, I don't believe you are this person. You work too hard to be cold and unfeeling. I see the strain on you."

"Not possible," Catherine sniffed. "I have an excellent plastic surgeon."

"Mareen loves you. We could all love you if you let us. We could be your family if you just come home with us."

Catherine might want to get a new surgeon because there was a crease that formed at the corner of each of her eyes. But it was straightened in a blink. "Go back and live in your fairytale, little girl. There may be five of you married, but your twin sister isn't even back in the country. And unless she brings someone with her and gets married by next weekend, you won't make that deadline, and the ranch will be mine."

With that, Catherine got up with all the grace of a queen. Heels clacking against the sticky linoleum, she stormed out of the bar.

Tilly couldn't spare her much more emotion. Catherine had made her choice. But Tilly had also made her choice, and she needed to get back to him.

CHAPTER TWENTY-TWO

*C*arter stood in the crowded parlor of the main house for the second time tonight. He was sweating even more than when he said his vows to Tilly. His fingers trembled without his wife by his side. But if he had any hope of saving his marriage, if he had any hope of saving himself, he had to go through with this.

"I've been keeping a secret," he began. "I had... *have* an addiction."

The Silver women gasped softly at the news. There was a collective sigh of relief from the President's Men. They weren't surprised at this admission. They all knew. The relief was likely that Carter was finally owning up to it.

"I was prescribed a pain killer after my injuries in the blast," Carter continued. They all knew what blast he meant. He didn't have to elaborate.

"Is it fentanyl?" asked Brig. "I've been reading about that particular medication. The military prescribes it to many soldiers for pain management."

"Fentanyl?" said Scout. "Isn't that an opioid?"

"Yes, it is," said Carter. "In small doses, if you follow the directions, it's helpful to ease the pain of injuries. But if you abuse it, it can become an addiction."

"You abused it?" asked Saylor, her voice full of concern and empathy.

"I did," Carter admitted. "For months now. But recently, I've been trying to get clean."

"He gave us his last prescription," said Linc.

"I did," Carter admitted. "But…"

"Let me guess," said Wilson. "You had a few pills left."

Carter nodded.

"Tilly found them?" said Gunny.

It was hard for Carter to look at his wife's twin. He would never confuse the two women. Tilly's blue eyes were soft and full of humor. Gunny's were filled with hard judgment. Instead of looking into those judgmental blues, he focused on Gunny's shoulder as he nodded.

"That's why she left." It wasn't a question. Gunny stated the words as the facts they were. "You never told her before tonight?"

Carter shook his head.

"She's going to have a hard time forgiving you," said Scout. "Tilly hates liars."

"I'll face those consequences and spend the rest of my life earning back her trust. But first, I have to get well."

Carter opened his hands and showed the pills in his palm. They were in a plastic baggie so that the white powder couldn't rub off and onto his sweaty palms. The contact would've been the same as a hit, and he was done pulling his punches.

"I'm struggling," he continued. "I'm sure if I keep trying to do it on my own, I'll keep struggling, and then I'll fail."

"You're not on your own," said Saylor, getting up and taking the pills from him. "We're all here for you."

"We're your family," said Scout. "We're not going to let you fail."

Four Silver sisters surrounded Carter. Gunny remained on the outskirts, as though she was still unsure of him. That was fine. He had time to win her over. First, he had to win his wife back.

In the meantime, he leaned on the rest of the Silver sisters' strength. It was almost comical. He was a big, tough soldier. Relying on these women's courage, stability, and unconditional love made Carter feel like he could move a mountain with them behind him.

"And don't worry," said Brig. "Tilly will forgive you in time."

"She already has forgiven him."

They all turned to the front door to see Tilly. Her blue eyes looked heavy, as though she'd been crying. There was no humor there because Carter had turned their happy little romcom into a near tragedy.

Carter wanted to run to her. To scoop her in his arms. To set her in front of a television and play a stream of John Cusack comedies. But he wasn't sure he had the right any longer.

The door shut with a snick behind Tilly. And then she was running to him. She wrapped her arms tightly around him. The impact of having her back in his arms nearly knocked Carter over. He used the remainder of his strength to hold them both steady.

"I'm sorry," he said.

"I'm sorry," she said at the same time.

"I should've told you."

"I should've known."

Carter pulled away to peer down into her eyes. "How could you have known? I hid it from you. I hid it from all of you. I didn't want you to see it. I didn't want you to see me as weak. I wanted to be strong for you."

Tilly pressed kisses to his forehead, each of his eyelids, and finally his mouth. Carter felt soothed by her touch. He felt strengthened by the love she was showing him. But he needed to get it all out so that there were no more gaps between them.

"I don't have any more secrets," said Carter. "I will never leave anything out or hide anything from you ever again."

"I believe you."

Something in Carter's chest caused him to choke. He hadn't realized until now that that was his greatest fear. But he hadn't lost Tilly's trust. Those three little words let him know that they would weather this storm.

"I realize that you meant well, Carter," she said. "You over-committed, and you couldn't deliver on your promise to yourself, to your friends, and to me. But I know you always had the best of intentions."

"I do."

"I believe you," she said again.

Those three little words hit him harder than her saying, *I love you.*

"Tell me what I need to do to help you beat this?" she said.

"Hold my hand," he said. "Stand by me and never leave."

"Done."

"And, I hear romcoms are great therapy for recovering addicts."

Tilly pulled away from him, rolling her eyes. "Don't even—"

"I'm sure a *Say Anything* marathon will be just the thing I need."

"This marriage is doomed," Tilly groaned, but she didn't let go of his hand.

Carter laughed as he pulled his wife to him and kissed her. His world might still be off balance. His body might still be in withdrawal. He might still be craving the unnatural comfort the pills could bring to him. But nothing would ever have a stronger hold on him than the love of this woman.

EPILOGUE

ruman Bates sunk into the quiet of his surroundings. Even the insects seemed to hush as he laid his form against the cool earth. The four legged mammals made no sound either. The metal resting against his shoulder proved that he was the biggest, baddest predator out in these woods today.

There were no claws at the ends of his sure hands. No deadly antlers protruded from the cap covering his dark hair. He was even clean-shaven, not possessing the funk that would ward off any oncoming foe. It was the metal behemoth that kept all others at bay.

However, Truman's finger was not on the trigger of his rifle. It was on the microscopic lens that doubled as his eyes. He rotated the scope using the grooves on the wheel. All of his focus was on his target. The exercise right now was training his eyes to find the details in plain sight of the scope.

With his vision magnified, Truman could see the details that even an owl couldn't pick out. The turn of the blade of grass in the light breeze. The fall of a leaf as its weight got too heavy for the tree limb. The movement of a pebble as an insect carved a path in new growth.

Nature continued its business in quiet activity. This was how

Truman had learned most of his training as a sniper for the US Military. Snipers were masters of hiding in plain sight. They excelled at watching over, or even under, both a target they aimed to take out as well as the person whose back they were tasked with protecting. A sniper's ability to become one with their environment trained them to spot enemies and to take out threats without being detected by man, beast, or even owl.

There were no owls high up in trees today. No snakes slithering through the grasses. Only a bull's eye placed a thousand meters away. It was a little over half a mile. On his best day, he had managed twelve hundred meters. He was hoping his better days were ahead of him. For now, he needed to manage this distance.

With his eye in the scope, Truman fingered the trigger. When he was ready, he pulled his index finger back. The zip of the bullet whizzing through the air hit his ears as the kickback of gun hit his shoulder.

Truman grunted, tamping down as much of the pain as he could. It still hurt. The injury may have shouted, but so did the target. Truman had managed to hit the bull's eye.

He couldn't hear the thud of the impact. But he could see it. A perfect black hole in the center of the yellow paper.

Silence was all that cheered on his victory. Until Truman let out a low sigh, that turned to a groan. The groan became a grunt as he rolled onto his back.

Now that the tension was released, all he felt was the recoil that had hit his injured shoulder. Truman's calculations had been perfect. He'd accounted for everything thing but that.

There was nothing wrong with his aim. The only problem rested tireless in his shoulder where he could no longer lift his rifle without pain. Right now the ground was taking on the weight of his weapon.

Unfortunately, the job of a sniper didn't always call for him to lay in wait with a surface under him to take the weight of his weapon. If he couldn't lift the rifle in protection of anyone in his unit, then he was as good as dead. Which was how he felt at this moment while his shoulder throbbed at the blow the rifle had dealt it.

Instead of letting the rifle go, Truman clung to it. For so many years it had been his constant companion. Never letting him down, until that fateful day when he could no longer carry it.

The sound of gunfire. Of his brothers' shouts. Of women screaming. Of the blast that stole the general's last commands. Those sounds played in repeat inside Truman's once quiet head. So, when the sounds of twigs breaking and footsteps approaching reached him in the present moment, it was too late for him to react.

Someone was coming. It was clear to him that that someone wasn't a soldier. Each of the President's Men knew he was shooting out here. They knew he was trying to recapture his precision, his strength. They knew he didn't want company as he tried to dig himself out of this particular hole.

Because they all knew that, they would announce their presence by calling out to him. Which meant that whoever was coming wasn't one of his fellow soldiers. Whoever was coming was coming in hot.

Truman reached for his weapon. He rolled to his side, wrapping his arms around it. Then she rolled onto his back with the rifle in toe.

Too bad his grunt of pain was just as loud as the encroaching enemy. Truman grimaced as his shoulder protested the weight of the gun. It mutinied when he ordered the muscles to arrange themselves in the position he needed to hold the weapon in order to defend himself. He managed to rest the stock of the rifle against the ground, giving him leverage to get in position when a form came out of the bushes.

Wild blonde hair flew into view. Followed by blue eyes blazing so bright, they were all that would be seen before the storm swept in.

It was Tilly. What was she doing out here? Shouldn't she be holed up with Carter, her knew hubby?

But no, this wasn't Tilly. Tilly wore pretty sundresses and make up. Which was why she was perfect for Truman's best friend who was fastidious when it came to his dress and appearance.

This Tilly imposter wore ill-fitting cargo pants, combat boots, and a rainbow t-shirt with animals frolicking underneath the rays. There wasn't an ounce of makeup to mask her irate features.

"Gunnery?" Truman asked, naming Tilly's twin sister.

In answer Gunnery kicked the rifle out his hand. Had his shoulder been what it was, the move would've never worked. But as it was, the gun clattered out of his hands and onto the ground as he muttered a curse of discomfort and incredulity.

Truman had just been ungunned by a slip of a girl. Well, she was a Silver. The daughter of a General who took no prisoners. So he could always claim that as his excuse if the rest of the guys, or even her older sister Scout, ever found out.

"What do you think you're doing," Gunny hissed.

~

Gunny and Truman are the last two holdouts to meet the General's deadline.
They're gonna get together.
But not without an epic war of wills!
And the real question is, will they get down the aisle in time?
You don't want to miss the epic conclusion of The Silver Star Ranch Romances
with "His Pledge to Hold."

SHANAE JOHNSON
HIS
Pledge
TO
Hold
A SILVER STAR RANCH ROMANCE

CHAPTER ONE

ruman Bates sunk into the quiet of his surroundings. Even the insects seemed to hush as he lay his form against the cool earth. The four-legged mammals made no sound either. The metal resting against his shoulder proved that he was the biggest, baddest predator out in these woods today.

There were no claws at the ends of his sure hands. No deadly antlers protruded from the cap covering his dark hair. He was even clean-shaven, not possessing the funk that would ward off any oncoming foe. It was the metal behemoth that kept all others at bay.

However, Truman's finger was not on the trigger of his rifle. It was on the microscopic lens that doubled as his eyes. He rotated the scope using the grooves on the wheel. All of his focus was on his target. The exercise right now was training his eyes to find the details in plain sight of the scope.

With his vision magnified, Truman could see the details that even an owl couldn't pick up. The turn of the blade of grass in the light breeze. The fall of a leaf as its weight got too heavy for the tree limb. The movement of a pebble as an insect carved a path in new growth.

Nature continued its business in quiet activity. This was how

Truman had learned most of his training as a sniper for the US Military. Snipers were masters of hiding in plain sight. They excelled at watching over, or even under, both a target they aimed to take out as well as the person whose back they were tasked with protecting. A sniper's ability to become one with their environment trained them to spot enemies and to take out threats without being detected by man, beast, or even owl.

There were no owls high up in trees today. No snakes slithering through the grasses. Only a bull's eye placed a thousand meters away. It was a little over half a mile. On his best day, he had managed twelve hundred meters. He was hoping his better days were ahead of him. For now, he needed to remaster this distance.

With his eye in the scope, Truman fingered the trigger. When he was ready, he pulled his index finger back. The zip of the bullet whizzing through the air hit his ears as the kickback of the gun hit his shoulder.

Truman grunted, tamping down as much of the pain as he could. It still hurt. The injury may have shouted, but so did the target. Truman had managed to hit the bull's eye.

He couldn't hear the thud of the impact. But he could see it. A perfect black hole in the center of the yellow paper.

Silence was all that cheered on his victory. Until Truman let out a low sigh that turned to a groan. The groan became a grunt as he rolled onto his back.

Now that the tension was released, all he could feel was the recoil that had hit his injured shoulder. Truman's calculations had been perfect. He'd accounted for everything but that.

There was nothing wrong with his aim. The only problem rested tirelessly in his shoulder, where he could no longer lift his rifle without pain. Right now, the ground was taking on the weight of his weapon. Unfortunately, the job of a sniper didn't always call for him to lie in wait with a surface under him to take the weight of his weapon. If he couldn't lift the rifle in protection of anyone in his unit, then he was as good as dead. Which was how he felt at the moment while his shoulder throbbed from the blow the rifle had dealt it.

Instead of letting the rifle go, Truman clung to it. For so many years, it had been his constant companion. Never letting him down until that fateful day when he could no longer carry it.

The sound of gunfire. Of his brothers' shouts. Of women screaming. Of the blast that stole the general's last command. Those sounds played in repeat inside Truman's once-quiet head. So, when the sounds of twigs breaking and footsteps approaching reached him in the present moment, it was too late for him to react.

Someone was coming. It was clear to hear that that someone wasn't a soldier. Each of the President's Men knew he was shooting out here. They knew he was trying to recapture his precision, his strength. They knew he didn't want company as he tried to dig himself out of this particular hole.

Because they all knew that, they would announce their presence by calling out to him. Which meant that whoever was coming wasn't one of his fellow soldiers. Whoever was coming was coming in hot.

Truman reached for his weapon. He rolled to his side, wrapping his arms around it. Then he rolled onto his back with the rifle in tow.

Too bad his grunt of pain was just as loud as the encroaching enemy. Truman grimaced as his shoulder protested the weight of the gun. It mutinied when he ordered the muscles to arrange themselves in the position he needed to hold the weapon in order to defend himself. He managed to rest the stock of the rifle against the ground, giving him leverage to get in position when a form came out of the bushes.

Wild blonde hair flew into view. Followed by blue eyes blazing so bright, they were all that would be seen before the storm swept in.

It was Tilly. What was she doing out here? Shouldn't she be holed up with Carter, her new hubby?

But no, this wasn't Tilly. Tilly wore pretty sundresses and

makeup. Which was why she was perfect for Truman's best friend, who was fastidious when it came to his dress and appearance.

This Tilly imposter wore ill-fitting cargo pants, combat boots, and a rainbow t-shirt with animals frolicking underneath the rays. There wasn't an ounce of makeup to mask her irate features.

"Gunnery?" Truman asked, naming Tilly's twin sister.

In answer, Gunnery kicked the rifle out of his hand. Had his shoulder been what it was, the move would've never worked. But as it was, the gun clattered out of his hands and onto the ground as he muttered a curse of discomfort and incredulity.

Truman had just been ungunned by a slip of a girl. Well, she was a Silver. The daughter of a general who took no prisoners. So he could always claim that as his excuse if the rest of the guys, or even her older sister Scout, ever found out.

"What do you think you're doing?" Gunny hissed.

CHAPTER TWO

S o, she was back home. Second time in less than a year. It was a record.

Gunnery Silver tilted her head back and looked out at the splendor of the Silver Star Ranch. All she could see was green. A green so lush it looked like it could be a mirage. Just a few days ago, she would've sworn it was.

Just last week, she'd been in the Namib Desert. Tracking and studying the Namib Desert Horse. The creature was native to the African continent, but only by way of transplant. Likely thanks to German cavalry horses.

Not only were the horses a magnificent athletic specimen, they had evolved to withstand the harsh desert climate. Most of the time, they thrived in the harsh, barren conditions. Unless there was famine. Or drought. Or worse, human interference.

It never ceased to amaze Gunny how much damage humankind did to this planet. Mankind roamed around bulldozing, flattening the lands as if they truly owned the entire Earth. But no one could ever own land, not truly. Not even when they produced a scrap of paper with some ink on it. Because they had to wait for that same scrap of parchment to sprout from the earth just to claim the land.

It was idiotic.

Still, no matter how much she shouted, most people didn't care to listen to her. But Gunny still railed at the top of her lungs. She had to. The animals, the environment, neither had a voice of their own. If she didn't fight with all her might, more lands would turn to waste, more animals would become endangered.

Some fights she won. Some fights… well, she wouldn't say she'd lost. She just moved on to another battle and would come back another day. A fight was never over until she had won it.

The Silver Star ranch was the only place she didn't have to fight. There was no danger of her home turning into a human wasteland where trees withered and animals disappeared. The place was as vibrant as the day Gunny had learned to walk on the land. From every corner, the ranch teemed with life. The funny thing was, she was the endangered species on the property.

Gunny was the last single Silver daughter. All five of her sisters were married. Except her. And if she didn't get married soon, they would lose this haven for flora and fauna.

It was almost contradictory. Because as she'd said, Gunny didn't believe that land was owned, not truly. But she did know that if her wicked stepmother got her hands on this land, then Catherine would definitely raze it to the ground. Not a green shrub would remain after Cruella flew by on her broom. Not a horse would have a place to eat its hay. Not a bunny would have a hole to hide in.

Her beliefs aside, Gunny couldn't let that happen. So, she'd get married. And then she'd be out of here.

She just had to wait for her sisters to figure out which soldier she was supposed to marry. Already the two men that had been earmarked for her had been swiped up by her sisters. So much for their lessons in sibling sharing.

But one look at her baby sister Brig with her hubby Jackson, and Gunny knew the two were meant to spend the rest of their days together. Only a slightly older man could handle the maturity that Brig and her intelligence brought to the table.

Gunny had had her doubts about her twin's beau, Carter. But

when she'd witnessed the devastation in the man's eyes that he'd potentially lost Tilly, Gunny knew the man was hopelessly in love and would move heaven and earth to get Tilly back and keep her. Plus, he was far too groomed for Gunny's tastes.

She needed a man who liked the outdoors. A man who didn't mind a little dirt under his fingernails. A man who loved animals and wanted to preserve the Earth as much as she did.

There was one soldier left. She had yet to meet Truman Bates. She doubted the man would live up to her list. But he didn't need to. She just needed to marry him to get the deed, and then she was out of here. It didn't matter if he had a preservation consciousness or not.

A crack split the air. Followed by a whizzing hiss. Then the sound of a thud as the impact was made.

Gunny froze. She knew that sound. It was unmistakable. But what was it doing here in her backyard?

Using the senses and skills she'd learned from her general of a father, Gunny zeroed in on the location. She could see a bull's eye in the distance, but not the shooter. Someone was shooting on her land.

It had to be one of the soldiers. How dare he? She would give her new brother-in-law an earful about hunting on this land that was purposed solely for horse rehab and not for killing any living soul.

But that would only be if she could find the man. She saw the bull's eye, but she didn't see any human tracks. He couldn't be far. No one could shoot more than a thousand meters and hit a bull's eye.

Gunny was starting to wonder if she had been hearing things when she nearly stumbled over the body. When she looked down, she saw the face of a stranger. He wasn't one of the five new brothers-in-law that she had met. He didn't seem brotherly at all, not with the rifle trained on her.

Indignation got the better of her. Gunny kicked the gun out of his hands with her boot. Surprisingly, it fell out of his hold. Then, even more surprisingly than the gunman letting loose his weapon, he hissed in pain.

She had no idea why? Her boot hadn't made contact with his skin—yet. She'd only kicked the weapon.

Slowly, the gunman's gaze narrowed on her in recognition. "Gunnery?" he asked.

"What do you think you're doing?" she hissed. "There's no shooting on this land. You might've hurt something."

"Something?" he said, rolling to his haunches. "There are no people or animals out here. And if there were, I wouldn't shoot them."

"You can't control a bullet."

"I can if it's coming from my weapon." The man stood up. And up. And then he straightened to stand a bit more up.

He was tall. Tall enough to rival the trees surrounding them. Tall enough to block out the sun.

Gunny gave herself a shake to focus on the matter at hand. The man had been shooting on her family ranch. No one from town would have the audacity.

"Let me guess," she said. "You're the sixth soldier from my father's unit?"

"Truman Bates, sniper of the President's Men, at your service."

He didn't hold out a hand for her to shake. It was still gripping his shoulder. Gunny wouldn't have taken his hand if he had offered it to her. Not in greeting. Not in matrimony.

"No," she said.

"No, what?"

"No, this is not going to happen." She waved her hand, motioning between them. But he wasn't looking at her. He was reaching for his weapon. Not with his right hand, which had been the shoulder he'd been holding. He reached with his left hand. The move was awkward, as though he were right-handed by nature and was picking up a pencil with his left.

"Look," he said, once the weapon was clutched in his left hand.

"Scout said it was fine if I shoot as long as I come all the way out here."

Did Scout really think Gunny would marry a sniper? "Well, Scout was wrong."

"Are you calling me a liar?"

"I'm not calling you anything. Especially not husband."

Truman blanched as he looked at her. And suddenly, Gunny wondered if she had it all wrong. Her sisters would've known she would never marry a gunman. Not to save her family, not to save all the animals and land in the world. There simply was no way.

And then Truman the Sniper opened his mouth and confirmed the facts as they stood. "I have no plans to marry you."

CHAPTER THREE

Truman looked between his gun and Gunnery. In another life, he may have gotten a kick out of that. A woman named after his favorite pastime in the world. The term gunnery meant the use of guns. But as Gunnery Silver sneered down at Truman's most prized possession, his gun, he got the distinct impression that she wasn't a fan of either of them.

Her round pink lips were curled down at one end, flashing a hint of sharp incisors. Her heart-shaped nose was wrinkled, as though she smelled something foul. That slender swan's neck of hers undulated as though she were finding it hard to swallow something. That was not the look of a woman who enjoyed shooting.

"I have no plan to marry you," he said.

And he didn't. True, he had no plan to marry anyone. Definitely not a woman who was clearly his exact opposite.

Gunny Silver looked like a tiny warrior standing over him. But the worst kind of warrior. She believed that peace came at no cost. She was wrong. Truman knew the price of peace firsthand as someone with personal knowledge of the balance sheet of the ledger.

"At least that we can agree on," she said.

She crossed her arms over her chest. Truman's eyes were drawn there, and he immediately looked away. Not because he didn't want to be caught staring at her chest. More because the sight hurt his eyes.

For such a tiny woman, Gunny was loud. Not just in her voice but in her clothing as well. She wore green camouflaged pants that only came to her mid-calf. There was a patch of toned leg exposed before the eye reached her hiking boots.

The camo pants were all well and good out in nature. What Truman couldn't understand was why she would couple them with a bright pink shirt that read *Be Kind to Every Kind*. Green was every-where and could hide her. But there was no shade of pink like that in nature, not unless nature was a drugstore full of Pepto Bismol.

"I could never bring myself to let a man with gunpowder on his hands touch me," she said.

"Now, now," Truman tsked. "That doesn't sound very kind to one of my kind."

He pointed at her shirt. When she looked down to follow the trajectory of his index finger, it looked as though he was pointing at her breast. Truman retracted his finger.

"I don't think killing is very kind," she said, those blue eyes shooting fire at him.

Little did Gunny know that blue was the hottest part of the flame. Or maybe she did know that, and that's why she was shooting those sparks at him with her eyes. What she didn't realize was that it was making Truman warm all up and down his limbs.

He needed to shake this insane feeling. The woman had just called him a killer. And she wasn't wrong.

The military had trained him to take out bad guys swiftly, effi-ciently, and quietly. Those were his best and brightest skills. His only skills. If he didn't regain his proficiency—and soon—he had no idea what he'd do with the rest of his life.

He knew for certain that he wasn't going to marry this Silver woman. He had no intention of following the path of the other President's Men. He was still a fighter.

So why did his heart kick against his chest at the thought of not marrying Gunny Silver? Why did his blood elevate at the thought of another man taking on that job?

She was not his type.

Not in any way.

First off, she was a civilian. Truman had only ever dated women in the service. They knew the score. They didn't question his job. Or his absences. Or the bloodstains that wouldn't come out of his shirts.

Secondly, Gunny stood against everything that he crept through hostile environments to defend. Truman had no qualms with the rights of animals. So long as they were served on his plate or kept in the backyard. Environmental protection was a concern of his, but only when it came to guarding the borders of his country and the boundaries of his homestead. And peace? Well, peace was the ultimate goal.

Third—and by far the most important reason that Gunny Silver was not for him—was that she required a ring. Truman was a young, virile man, even with his injury. He had dated much and looked forward to getting back on that saddle. But he planned never to be saddled with a wife, not with his line of work.

And so, with that, he took a deep breath into his chest. With an exhale, his blood settled back to its normal temperature. He pulled his weapon to his chest, preparing to get away from this vociferously dressed and roaringly opinionated woman. But as the full weight of the gun came up against his shoulder, he winced and stumbled backward.

"Are you hurt?" Gunny asked. The pinch in her brow gone. What was left was a smooth line of concern as she reached out to him.

The sweet scent of cloves filled his nose. The strong earthy scent reminded him of his mother rubbing Tiger Balm on his chest when he had a cold. Truman had continued the use of the topical cream whenever he had any aches and pains. It was also an insect repellant for when he was in the field.

For a moment, all of the pain in his shoulder went away. Along with his cares about getting cleared. All that mattered was the scent and sensation of the woman at his side.

With his mind so preoccupied with the peace she brought, Truman failed to react when Gunny took his gun from his hand. Never before had anyone, friend or foe, managed to disarm him. But this protesting, prismatic, pint-sized woman managed to with little resistance.

"I'm fine," Truman said, reaching for his weapon. Only, his hand didn't make it very far. Because his eyes liked what he was seeing.

Gunny was looking his rifle up and down. Truman felt as though she was examining him as a man, measuring his worth and value in the weapon he used to defend himself and make his livelihood. She'd been holding the rifle sideways in her inspection. Now, she turned it upright, tucking it against her side.

She didn't aim it at him. She aimed it at the ground. And then, with practiced fingers that moved as though the digits had done this a thousand times, she flicked her thumb over the selector switch, ensuring the weapon wouldn't discharge automatically or accidentally.

Truman watched her. He should've been livid that she held his gun. Or at least ill at ease. But once again, his heart was kicking inside his chest. Harder this time, as though it wanted out of its cage. His blood was scalding hot in his veins, as though it knew the blue of her eyes was the only thing that would cool the heat.

Truman stood staring at Gunnery Silver with her bright camouflage that would never hide her. And he liked the look of her with his weapon in her hands.

CHAPTER FOUR

The feel of the cool steel in her hand made Gunny's chest feel hollow. Her palms dampened, and she worried the weapon might fall from her hands. The next thing she knew, the rifle was removed from her hold.

Gunny looked up into eyes, the same cool steel color of the death machine. She saw loss in those gray eyes. She saw pain and torment.

Instead of feeling that this soldier had got his due, Gunny felt the sudden urge to wrap her arms around Truman and rub up and down his back. Just like her second mom Sarah had done for her anytime Gunny had awakened in the night with phantom memories of the birth mother Gunny hadn't gotten the chance to know.

Roxanne Silver's eyes had been gray. Gunny knew because she'd seen pictures. Her birth mother had been beautiful, though frail. She'd never understood why her father, a strong and commanding general, had picked Roxanne. But Gunny was grateful because her father's choice had brought her Sarah and all of her sisters.

Now her sisters would lose everything if Gunny didn't follow her father's outrageous demands and find a husband before the end of the week. Looking at this man with gun metal eyes, Gunny could see the appeal another woman would find in him.

Along with those arresting eyes, Truman Bates had a strong square jaw. There was even a dimple right, smack dab at the center of his chin that Kurt Russell would've envied. A five o'clock shadow darkened his cheeks. A few tendrils of dark hair escaped his camouflage-colored cap.

Truman was a handsome man. By the looks of him, he was a capable man. If only he didn't cradle that rifle like it was his long-lost lover. That was so not cute.

He'd said he was fine when clearly his shoulder was sore. Gunny had caught the grimace when she'd kicked the gun. She caught it again when he retrieved his weapon from her with his right hand. He was injured, but just like a man, he wasn't owning up to it.

"Of course you'd say you're fine," she said. "Pain is fear leaving the body, right? My dad used to say that all the time."

"My mother said it, too."

A grin lit up his features. That steel gray felt like a ray of sunshine at the mention of his mother. His smile looked soft and welcoming, like a pillow Gunny wanted to rest against her forehead, against her nose, against her mouth.

"She was in the Army," he continued. "One of the first female snipers."

Gunny was hard-wired to form a bad opinion of anyone with a gun. She preferred to use her words to solve the world's problems, not weapons. She'd start with trying to have a civil conversation. When that didn't work, she began to shout. When that didn't work, she picked up a pen. Instead of pouring ink down her adversaries' throats, which she often daydreamed of doing, she penned letters instead. Letters of protests. Letters to legislators. Letters to conservation and humanitarian organizations.

"I'm not sure how to feel about that," Gunny said. "One part of me wants to cheer for her addition to the cause of women's advancement in the workplace."

Truman's bright grin turned to a smirk. The way he parted his lips made Gunny's brain stutter for a second. She gave herself a shake and found more words to hurl at him.

"But those same cheers she deserves for breaking down one barrier are clashing with my activism side for gun control."

"She was killed in the line of duty by a thirteen-year-old child soldier. The gun he carried was bigger than he was."

"I... I'm sorry."

He blinked, as though coming back to the present. That steely gray gaze focused on her. His eyes roamed her face, searching for... she didn't know what he was hoping to find. But she held still for him.

"She took him out before she succumbed to her injuries." His voice sounded hollow as he spoke. "The kid and I were the same age, and she had to shoot him so he couldn't hurt anybody else."

Gunny did reach for him then. Her hand landed on his shoulder cap. His right shoulder cap where she knew he was hiding even more pain.

Truman pulled away from her touch. He sat down, pulling the rifle onto his lap, and began disassembling the weapon. His fingers were fast and sure, as though he'd done this a thousand times. Because he likely had.

"This is why I'm for gun control," she said. "A bullet doesn't just hurt the one it's aimed at, it hurts entire families and societies for generations."

It was the wrong thing to say after he bared his pain. She knew that. She knew it as she was saying it. But it was a truth she believed so wholeheartedly that she didn't think twice.

"Ever notice how bad guys don't follow the laws," he said. "It's kind of their thing."

"If world governments made it harder for the bad guys to get their hands on weapons, then it wouldn't be their thing."

Truman stood up. And up. And up.

He'd only been sitting for a few moments, but in that time Gunny had forgotten how tall he was. Now that she was so close to him, she saw how broad he was as well. He blocked out the sun. The only source of illumination were those silver-gray eyes. And they were cloudy as they narrowed on her.

Gunny braced herself for battle. Though something in her quaked and shook loose. She had a feeling that Truman Bates would be a worthy opponent. She'd have to bring her A-game. Likely her B and C game as well.

Except then he pulled a move she didn't see coming from miles away. He pulled her to him, wrapping his arms around her body and tucking her head into his chest.

The quaking and shaking made its way up from the heel of her boots. It grew until her knees knocked together. Her heart rate didn't increase, but she felt the thumps like fists against her rib cage.

What was happening to her?

"Don't worry. I've got you."

It was the sound of Truman's deep voice that brought her back to her senses. It was the ground that was shaking, not her. That kind of rumbling could only come from one place. Gunny lifted her head and saw confirmation.

Off in the distance, she saw a herd of wild mustangs running across the land. Black-coated stallions. Majestic brown steeds. White-haired beauties. They ran as a group, kicking up dust in their wake.

All Gunny could do was stand there and watch as they raced by, free as the day they were born. She could hear the rhythm of life beating strong as she lay her ear against a strong chest.

Wait! What? Her ear was against Truman's chest. She was still wrapped up in Truman's embrace as they both watched the scene play out before them.

He must have thought they were in danger from the horses. Though it was never wise to approach a wild horse, they preferred to avoid humans. And besides, it was Gunny who had fought for their freedom years ago.

Since she was in no danger from the animals, there was no reason for her to be in this soldier's embrace. She lifted her head and immediately missed the musicality of his heartbeat. She took a step back and instantly missed the heat from his body.

When gray eyes met blue, she felt lost in a land she knew like the back of her hand. She cleared her throat once, twice. Finally, she was able to get out the only words that mattered.

"I'm not going to marry you," she said.

Truman swallowed a few times. His Adam's apple bobbing as though it was having trouble getting words past his throat. "I'm not going to marry you, either."

"Glad that's settled."

"Me, too."

They stood staring at each other. The horses were long gone, but their dust was still floating in the air. It felt like tumbleweeds had rolled through in a western stand-off.

The gun was a dividing line between them on the ground. Her sisters thought she would marry this man? Not if he was the last man on earth. Luckily, he wasn't.

"Well," she said, "have a nice life, Truman Bates."

"Same to you, Gunnery Silver."

Gunny turned her back on him. She'd come out here for a reason. In the distance, she could see the Flying Cross Ranch. There were six perfectly good specimens of men who'd grown up next door. Surely one of them would help an old friend out to save Silver Star.

CHAPTER FIVE

Truman turned the knob to head inside his cabin. Technically, it was Scout's cabin. Before moving in here a few weeks ago, he'd been staying in Brig's cabin. But once she and Jackson tied the knot, he gave them that space.

Scout's cabin was spartan and utilitarian. Much like the woman who had built it. It suited Truman's needs just fine, as he didn't have many belongings and didn't require that much space. The life of a sniper demanded few attachments.

Truman clenched his fist and then shook out his fingers. Unfortunately, the move didn't mute the feel of having a woman in his arms for the first time in… he couldn't even remember how long it had been since he'd last held a woman. He knew not one single time could compare to pressing Gunny Silver's curves against his form.

He'd been surprised to find supple arcs and contours inside those two contradicting fabrics she wore. Gunny was built nothing like her namesake. Truman's trigger finger itched to bend her form to him once more.

But they'd already agreed. Neither wanted to marry the other. Though Truman was seriously shaky on his pronouncement.

He knew it wasn't meant to be. He was headed back to the military. She was headed to the Flying Cross Ranch to make a deal with one of Father Matthews' sons.

Truman wasn't even aware that any of the old man's boys were at home. He'd never met a single one of them in the months he'd been living at Silver Star Ranch. So why did he have the urge to punch out any one of them who might take Gunny up on her offer of a convenient marriage?

Truman didn't like the woman. He couldn't even stand being in her cabin. He'd taken one look in Gunny's cabin two and a half months ago and backpedaled it out of there like a cartoon character. PETA posters had been plastered over the walls. Along with *Save the Whales* and *Let Wild Horses Roam Free*.

It wasn't that Truman disagreed with any of those sentiments. He preferred to do his hunting in grocery stores like a normal twenty-first-century man. Guns were for protection, not sport. What his country needed to be protected from most were terrorists and extremists. Which meant his attentions, and the barrel of his gun, were aimed at bad humans and not animals.

He was certain he could never explain his views to Gunny Silver. She probably thought the United States Military should work out their problems with Jihadists while holding hands and singing *Kumbaya*.

So, nope, the two of them would never suit. Not even if the feel of her breath against his neck had sparked a fire in him that was still messing with his head. He went to the small fridge and pulled out a cold beer. Instead of drinking it, he pressed it to his forehead.

It wasn't that Truman had never thought of marriage and a family. He had. For his friends. Not for him. He would be happy being Uncle Truman, teaching the little girls to shoot and the young boys how to hide in plain sight.

But a wife of his own? That was impractical since he planned to spend all of his days fighting alongside his brothers and sisters in the military. His family would never see him. That method worked great for his role as a sniper, but not for a wife and kids.

Truman heard voices outside. He sat his unopened beer down

and went to the window. Linc and Jefferson rode horses side by side. They brought the horses to a stop and chatted to each other.

As always, neither man could see him. Truman had always been in the shadows as he had their backs. But he'd failed them on that last mission.

It didn't seem like any of them cared. They weren't concerned about their backs any longer. Not when they each looked forward to a future with their wives.

The war was over for them. This, this ranch, these Silver girls, this was their reward.

A knock came at his door. Before Truman made his way over to open it, Linc strode in.

"This came for you," Linc said.

The envelope in his hands was from the latest recruiter Truman had been working with. Though all of his unit had been medically discharged due to their injuries, Truman wanted back in active duty. He craved the action, needed the responsibility. But he needed a waiver to do so.

For the past year, Truman had been told that the type of waiver he'd need would require a shipload of paperwork. The person who'd told him that hadn't exaggerated enough. The paperwork had been mountainous. The work wasn't for the faint of heart. Truman had gone through two other recruiters who'd given up on the insurmountable task in a matter of weeks. Until he'd found one who'd stuck it out with him.

This latest recruiter had streamlined the paperwork and gave Truman hope. Truman was told he simply needed to find a surgeon who would clear him for duty. A feat which was easier said than done.

Truman had been to surgeon after surgeon in the last four months. Each one had expressed doubt over his ability to perform his duties. Until Dr. Hunter.

True, the man had been practicing in Cancun. And the degree on the wall looked as though there was a smudge of white-out on the document. But Dr. Hunter had told Truman what he'd wanted to hear. Beyond that, the good doctor had written a report to the recruiter.

In that envelope was the military's final decision. Truman reached for it. He winced at the dull pain in his shoulder as he did so. That didn't deter him from tearing the thin document out.

And then the small pain in his arm was forgotten. His heart dropped to the floor after the first line.

Denied.

Limitation in motion.

No appeals.

It was over. Truman wasn't sure what crumpled to the ground first? Him or the letter.

"There's always contract work," said Linc, who had sat down beside him.

Truman wasn't sure how long they had sat there? Maybe a few minutes? Maybe an hour?

Truman looked up at his friend. Linc was always ready with a plan. The problem was contract work wasn't in Truman's plan. Those men were often more loyal to a paycheck than their country.

"Or, there's the original backup plan," said Linc. "You marry into this family."

Truman opened his mouth to speak, to tell Linc that it would never work between him and Gunny. Truman wasn't sure if his mouth shut before it could lie or if Linc cut him off.

"It would be the only marriage of convenience, which there's no law against. You two wouldn't have to see each other after the ceremony. She'll be going back overseas. You'll be looking into contract work. But it'll keep us all intact. It'll give you both a home you can always come back to."

That's what did it. Truman couldn't break his team up. At least this way, he would have their backs one last time.

CHAPTER SIX

Gunny took the long way round to the Flying Cross Ranch. She needed the walk in nature to cool her temper. Her boots left the wildflowers her stepmother Sarah had sprinkled in every corner of the ranch, only to crunch over dry, caked earth that had been left unattended for years as she drew nearer to the edge of the property line.

The nerve of that man. Had Truman really questioned her intelligence? Of course, she knew that bad guys didn't follow laws. But sometimes, it was the bad guys that made the laws.

Gunny snapped her fingers. That's what she should have said to him as a comeback. She had half a mind to turn around, march back up to him, and deliver the line.

Only she knew he was long gone. Packed up his killing machine and gone back to his cabin. Belatedly, she wondered whose cabin he was sleeping in?

The thought of Truman Bates curled up in her eco-friendly, zero waste, organic eucalyptus sheets made her blood heat. Not in an angry way. In the way where she had to lift both her hands and fan her face.

What was wrong with her? She couldn't be attracted to him. His coworker was a rifle. The man had a body count for crying out loud.

He was a gun-toting, war-loving fascist. Or worst, capitalist. She had no problem with communism and socialism. The roots of the words implied family. Though her sisters had miscalculated if they thought she would've ever considered Truman the Sniper for a real marriage or even a sham one.

Which was why Gunny would have to take matters into her own hands.

At the edge of the Flying Cross Ranch property line, Gunny saw movement. It was a movement of the four-legged kind. But these two animals weren't large enough for her to mount. Two deer roamed just beyond the fenced boundary; a mom and her fawn.

Gunny stood and watched the pair. Even though the film *Bambi* had traumatized her at a young age. Scout should've never shown that film to a child who had lost her mother shortly after she'd been born. Gunny was certain that movie had imprinted on her and pointed her on her life's mission to save all the world's animals from hunters' guns.

All over the world, mankind was ravaging forests, jungles, and valleys that were once sacred to all kinds of flora and fauna. Hunters killed for sport, not for sustenance. The never-thinning human herd was laying waste to much of the world's natural resources and life forms. Gunny was resolved to put a stop to it.

She had lost two mothers, but she would not lose her home. Which was why Gunny needed to protect this land. She might not want to stand still on the Silver Star Ranch, but this was where her roots were planted. She wasn't going to let anyone take this away from her family.

Marrying that gun-happy soldier was a bridge too far. Truman could've shot and killed Bambi himself. He'd been close to taking out one of the wild horses that ran freely through all these lands.

He had been a good shot. Seeing as the only thing he aimed at was the target, and he'd hit it. Still, he was far from her type.

Gunny wasn't exactly sure she had a type. The few men who

joined her in her crusades were either old hippies with gray hair and poor hygiene. Or they were young hipsters with top knots and floral-scented soaps. She couldn't take a man with a ponytail seriously.

No, Gunny had a better idea. Which was why she marched onto the land of the Flying Cross Ranch. She still couldn't fathom why her sisters had married those strangers when there had been six Matthews boys next door. The Silver sisters had always been able to get the Matthews boys to do what they wanted. Now, in their time of absolute need, should be no different.

As Gunny made her way up the drive, she saw a familiar vehicle in the driveway next to Father Matthews's beat-up, old truck. The other vehicle was a minivan that had seen better days. But those days had to have happened long before Gunny had been born because the vehicle was at least twice her age. Bright Horizons Foster Care was painted on the side. The yellow paint of the sun's rays was chipped. And it looked as though someone had spray-painted a gray swirl of smoke from the smiling sun's lips to make it look as though the star was having a cigarette. Or at least Gunny hoped that was meant to be a cigarette.

Climbing the stairs, she heard a familiar voice coming from within the house. The voice was deep and raspy, making the owner sound like she was a longtime smoker. Gunny had heard that voice sing the most soulful tunes before.

"The city is saying the federal government is taking the land. Which means they're going to demolish the foster home, and we'll all be kicked out."

Savy James stood with her hands on generous hips. Even in a pair of worn jeans and a tank top, Savy looked like she'd just walked out onto a stage to give a concert to a packed house.

"Can they even do this?" Savy handed a stapled packet of paper to Father Matthews.

Father Matthews's gnarled fingers trembled as he took the documents. Gunny noticed there was some strain at the corners of his eyes. He looked tired like he hadn't been sleeping well.

She wanted to go to him, to fuss over the man that had always been as much a father to her as her own had. In some cases, more of a father than the General. Because Father Matthews was always just on the other side of the fence.

"They can't kick us out?" asked Savy. "Can they?"

Father Matthews drew in a deep breath as his dark gaze scanned the documents. He had a big heart where Bright Horizons was concerned. That's where all six of his sons had come to him from.

"No, they can't kick you out," said Gunny. "Not if we put up a fight."

They both turned to the door. Gunny came into the screen door without knocking. She'd fairly lived here when she was younger. She couldn't remember a time when she had knocked, less even when the door was locked.

"Gunny? Is that you?" Savy opened her arms, and Gunny embraced her old friend. "What are they feeding you out in the desert? You need to come by for a good meal."

Even though Savy was just a few years older than Gunny, the woman had always had a maternal instinct. Which was likely why, after her career as a singer, she'd returned to the foster home that had taken her and her sisters in when their mother had died.

"Let's worry less about my eating habits and more about how to stop these land-grabbing officials from stealing the foster home. First thing we'll do is start a petition."

Savy threw back her head and laughed. Her dark curls bounced as she did. "If you're on it, then I'm not going to worry about it any longer. I still remember when you chained yourself to the science lab cabinet to protest dissecting frogs."

"It was inhumane."

"It saved my GPA because I knew I'd pass out if I held a scalpel. You home for good?"

"Nope." Gunny shook her head. "I'm here to get married real quick, then I've gotta hop on a plane to Australia. The human population is encroaching on the Brumby population there."

"Right." Savy nodded, but there was clear confusion in her hazel eyes. "Did you say married? Who's the lucky guy?"

"Well…" Gunny turned her attention to Father Matthews, who sat with the documents in his lap. "I was hoping I could convince one of the Matthews boys to be my sacrificial lamb."

Both Savy and Father Matthews blinked.

"Not Charlie, of course," said Gunny.

Savy took a step toward the front door, crossing her arms over her chest. "Oh, that's over. So over."

She cleared her throat once, twice. She opened her mouth, then closed it. Finally, she affixed a bright smile. But there was a wobble at one side that made the smile look lopsided. Savy James and Charlie Matthews might not be together, but those two were so not over.

"I'll just let the two of you look over that paperwork," Savy said, backpedaling out the door. "I've gotta get back. Who knows what the kids have been up to while I've been gone. Let me know what you find. And good luck with your marriage, Gunny. Thanks, Father Matthews."

She was already in her van before she'd finished speaking. Gunny grinned after the woman as she pulled off. It must've taken Savy a lot of courage to drive out to Flying Cross after her and Charlie's last break-up. But Gunny supposed the woman must've known that the eldest of the Matthews boys wasn't at home.

Gunny turned to Father Matthews. "So, you got any sons hanging around that I can borrow for a few months?"

Father Matthews chuckled, which turned into a cough. Then turned into hacking. Gunny grabbed a tissue box from the fireplace and handed it to him.

"It's nothing, just a little cold." Father Matthews waved the box away and cleared his throat. "None of my boys are here right now. Otherwise, I'd offer one of them up along with some lemonade."

"Well, which one is the closest by? I just need a day, a couple of hours at most."

Father Matthews smiled, but he didn't attempt to laugh. "I'm afraid none of my boys will be back until Thanksgiving at the earliest, which is after your father's deadline."

Gunny cursed—in her head, not under her breath. Father Matthews was not only a father figure to her, he had a direct line to the man upstairs—her father. The last thing Gunny needed was the General haunting her over foul language.

"What's wrong with Truman?" asked Father Matthews. "He's a good man. Certainly good enough to pass your father's muster."

Again, Gunny decided the best tactic was to hold her tongue. The General looked down on lying as much as he looked down on cursing.

"I'm starting to think Abe had a plan all along with those men and his girls. You might grow to love Truman as each of your sisters has grown to love her own young man."

"Love him? I don't even like him. I could very possibly hate him."

"Love and hate are two strong emotions. There's a very thin line separating the two, which makes it easy to fall from one side to the other."

"Isn't hate the opposite of love?"

"No. That's apathy; which means not caring at all. Besides, you're both leaving soon, heading back to your careers."

Was that why Truman was out shooting this morning? Trying to get back in shipshape so he could take down live targets? Gunny's lip curled at the thought. She could not marry that man. But she just might have to. He was the only man around that could meet her goals and her time frame.

She could marry him and then never see him again. It wouldn't be the worst thing in the world.

CHAPTER SEVEN

*I*t was the worst thing in the world.

Truman never thought he'd see this day. He was getting married. He had to. He had no options left. Not if he wanted to still be of use.

The military wouldn't have him, no matter how many tests the doctors ran. The tear in his shoulder would always show up on x-rays and shout in black and white pixels that he was no longer good enough. There was nowhere to hide from the x-ray. No cover he could take.

So, this was his only option. He'd stay where he was needed. Where he could at least be of use. Here on this ranch.

Maybe it wasn't the worst thing in the world?

Working the ranch was good, honest work. Even though he was about to come by it on a dishonest route.

Marriage.

To a woman he didn't love.

To a woman he didn't even like. But that was part of combat. Soldiers signed up to do the things that others found distasteful or were too scared to do themselves. All in protection of the many.

At least he would be the only sacrifice for his friends. He owed them that much after failing to spot the bomb that had ruined all their lives and took the general from them. This would be his payment.

He'd lay down his gun and put a ring on Gunnery Silver's finger. Then she'd leave, and the two would likely rarely see each other. She'd head back overseas on whatever animal rights or environmental crusade she was on. He'd stay on the ranch and keep this home front safe. One day they might reunite to sign divorce papers.

That thought left a burn in his chest. Though he wasn't in love with Gunny, he didn't like the idea of divorce. It felt too much like giving up.

"You sure about this?" Linc said as Truman stepped out of the cabin.

The men lined up outside, all dressed in military finery. It was the last wedding ceremony. There wouldn't be a need to get this gussied up again.

"Yeah," he said. "I'm sure."

Truman had loved serving with these men. It had been the privilege of his life to have their backs in combat. It would be worth it to stand by them now.

"He meant about Gunny," said Jeff. "The two of you don't seem to get along."

Truman shrugged. "We don't have to. We won't be in the same place after this week."

"She's leaving that quick?" asked Jeff.

Her flight was booked. As soon as the ink was dry on the deed to the ranch, she was out. To some place in the Australian Outback. Truman scratched at his chest.

"It's not right. We all fell in love. But you…?"

Truman knew he wasn't meant to fall in love. It wasn't in his character. Not for a man that was so good at hiding and taking out the target. Love's arrow could never find him, and he was fine with that.

Because he was so good at lying in wait, he was also good at sensing danger. He saw Catherine walk up to them, a sly smile on her beautiful face.

"Looks like you're going to make my late husband's requirements in time," she said. "Just by the skin of your teeth. How convenient."

Her smile was false. It was brittle, like the porcelain of her face. She eyed each of the men in turn, but her gaze latched onto Truman.

There was nowhere for him to hide the sweat on his brow. There was no cover he could take. He was out in the open.

"The other five of you might claim a love match," Catherine continued. "But the PETA princess and a decorated sniper? You can't expect me to believe you two fell in love?"

Truman felt Linc and Jefferson at his back. He could tell when Linc opened his mouth and prepared to stand up for their entire family unit. But this wasn't Linc's place. It was Truman's.

"It's true," he said. "The first time I saw Gunny, I wanted to run in the other direction."

In fact, he had gone in the other direction when she'd walked into the house. It was just as her twin Tilly and Carter were saying their vows. When Truman saw Tilly's twin standing in the doorway, he got the sense that his time as a single man was almost up.

"But over this past week, we spent some time together." True, that time had been short-lived. But the most impactful of that time they'd spent together had been when Truman had been out shooting. When he'd seen Gunny with his rifle, when he'd held Gunny in his arms, and she'd clicked into place against him. "I knew she was the one for me the moment I touched her. I think that the general knew exactly what he was doing when he paired the six of us with his six daughters."

"My husband was not a romantic," said Catherine. "The man was married five times."

Truman looked at the woman. He really looked at her, which was difficult. There was so much makeup on her face. He wondered if Catherine had ever shown the general the real woman beneath that facade.

Catherine's gaze narrowed as though she knew what was going through Truman's mind. Her frosty glare didn't shake him. He knew when someone was hiding.

"There was something about you that drew him to you," Truman said. "But maybe you hid it away? Maybe he went searching for it? Maybe you never showed him again?"

Catherine jerked back as though Truman had struck her. He supposed his words had struck a chord. But just as quickly as she jerked back did her features settle.

"You and Gunnery are exact opposites," Catherine said. "A sniper and an animal rights activist? The others might have feelings for each other, but the two of you? This is a lie and fake, and it will be found out. If not today, then soon after, and this ranch will be mine."

She turned on her heel and walked away. Not to the field where the cars were parked. She walked toward the backyard, where the ceremony would be held.

There were only a few guests seated. Mostly neighbors from nearby ranches and a few townsfolk to make it look official. Now, Truman and Gunny would have to look at each other like they were officially in love. Or like they at least liked the other's company.

For the past couple of days after agreeing to go through with the fake marriage, he had barely seen his betrothed. Truman spent his days working on Linc's improvement projects in the north pasture. While Gunny had spent her days working with the horses in the eastern pasture. They'd barely seen each other except at dinner time, where they studiously ignored one another.

"You make an excellent point," said Linc. "You and Gunny are hiding from each other. Have either of you shown the other the real you?"

Before Truman could answer, he looked up, and there she was. Gunny stood on the porch in a white sundress and sandals. Her blonde hair was pulled up in a swirly bun with tendrils escaping to frame her face. But the best accessory she wore was a smile.

It was so bright that Truman felt blinded. When she threw her head back and laughed, he forgot how to breathe.

"Never mind." Linc clapped him. "I think you just got your first glimpse."

CHAPTER EIGHT

Gunny never thought this day would come. Not that it couldn't come. She had just never spent any length of time thinking about her wedding day. Yet here she was, standing in a white dress with a bunch of wildflowers in her hands.

She was getting married. It had to be done. But did she really have to wear the dress and heels? Gunny reached down to unstrap one shoe, only to have her twin slap her hand away.

"The shoes stay on," said Tilly.

"You were in cowboy boots for your wedding," Gunny said. "Can't I at least wear boots for mine?"

"Boots won't go with that dress," said Mareen, as she stuck another pin in Gunny's hair.

"Great," said Gunny. "Then let's lose the dress, too."

"You look perfect," said Saylor, slapping Gunny's hand away from the zipper on the side of the dress.

Gunny was surrounded by enemy combatants. She was too far from the exit, and she was out of options.

Despite tracking down and calling each one of the Matthews boys, each had politely turned her down. Well, Joe had laughed until he dropped the phone. Topher had hung up on her, stopped answering when she tried to call back.

So much for all the childhood pacts where they'd sliced open their palms with a pocket knife and spit-shaked on promises. Seemed their oaths to have each other's backs only went so far. And that was not down the aisle.

Gunny would be walking down the aisle toward a stranger. Because even after being home for nearly a week, she and Truman Bates were still nothing more than strangers. And she had no problem keeping it that way.

She would marry him. Her sisters would get the deed to the ranch. Then she would be on the next flight out. And that would be that. She'd likely only see her husband on holidays when she came home. If he was even still around.

"Truman's a good guy," Tilly said to her.

"He's a sniper," said Gunny.

"He was a sniper. He's not anymore. They won't have him back because of his shoulder."

Truman hadn't said as much when they'd agreed to this, but Gunny had suspected. She still remembered him wincing in pain when she'd come upon him at their first meeting. That had been five days ago. Their father's three-month deadline expired at the end of the day today.

They were now pushing it close. But in under an hour, the last Silver daughter would be married. The deed would pass into their hands. And all would be right with this part of the world. That would mean Gunny could leave for another part of the world that needed her.

"All being a sniper proves is that he will always have your back," said Scout, "even when you can't see him."

Gunny didn't need Truman to have her back. Because by next week, all he would be seeing would be the back of her.

"You should be in love," said Tilly with a wistful sigh of a woman who saw cartoon hearts anytime she looked into the blue sky.

All of her sisters were starry-eyed with bubbling, floaty hearts.

But all of her sisters wanted to be tied down to one place and push out babies. That had never been Gunny's dream. Gunny's roots were planted deep on this ranch, but she had always wanted to fly free and far.

The truth was, Gunny didn't want love. Love was a powerful feeling. She'd felt it with her birth mother, even though she couldn't remember her. Then she'd passed.

She'd felt it with her second mother, Sarah, as if the woman were her own flesh and blood. And then she'd passed. Each time Gunny's heart had broken. With her father's death, she was certain another crack would leave the organ irreparable.

What man would look twice at a woman with a broken heart? Or even once at a woman who vowed never to have children of her own? Or even blink at a woman who could never love him?

Gunny only had space in her heart for her sisters, her work, and this ranch. She was full up. Luckily, she was gussied up enough to be a presentable bride.

"Can we get this show on the road?" she said.

Gunny stood, and her sisters backed off. Behind her, she heard much sighing and oohing and ahhing. Gunny ignored her sentimental sisters and stomped toward the back door. Only to remember that she was wearing heels and, when she stomped her heels the shoes pinched her toes.

The backyard was filled with a few people from town. She recognized a few faces from this distance, but most were a blur. Before she could get any closer, a tall, dark figure slipped in front of her.

She looked up to see Truman. He was smiling down at her. Those gray eyes bright. Those full lips curved up as though they held a secret, a secret she wanted to know. The flash of teeth he showed her was so dazzling that it momentarily stunned her. That had to be why she didn't protest when he scooped her into his arms and twirled her.

He twirled her. Like, around in a circle. With her feet off the ground and her full weight in his arms. She had never been twirled. She wasn't that kind of girl.

She heard a grunt of pain from him. It must be from the shoulder injury he still hadn't told her about. She weighed more than his rifle. So what was he thinking?

Truman set her feet on the ground. But she was wearing heels, and the weight distribution was all wrong.

Thankfully, he didn't let her go. He pulled her to him and whispered something in her ear. Before her brain could make out his words, his mouth moved from the cone of her ear, brushed the contours of her cheek, and then his lips were covering hers.

Truman was kissing her. It started as just a light peck on the lips. On another day, that wouldn't have been a big deal. Gunny had been kissed before. She'd never enjoyed the encounters and put a stop to them years ago. She hadn't seen the point of dating when she found most men useless.

But Truman's lips? They were plush, like a down pillow. It was nice to rest against them. She felt as though she could lay right where they stood and take a nap against his mouth.

Except there was also the heat. There was a warmth to Truman's mouth. As though he'd just had a warm cup of morning coffee and was now spreading that curling steam that came with a good cuppa through her.

Man, that was pleasant. The curling hot tendrils of coffee layered over the plush of a pillow. Did other guys know that kissing could be like this? Truman must have kept the secret of kissing all to himself. Otherwise, women would be throwing their faces at him as he walked down the street.

Then he was pulling away. Taking that delicious heat and snuggable pillow with him.

Gunny wrapped her arms around his neck. She just needed one more touch of warmth, one more second of lush comfort.

Truman didn't resist. He leaned into her. Introducing his hands and arms to the game. The embrace took the kiss to the next level. Until the sounds of whoops and catcalls pulled them apart.

"You two can't wait a few minutes until you at least get to the altar?"

Gunny wasn't sure who said it. Her brain was still trying to rewire itself from that kiss. That kiss. What had that kiss been about?

CHAPTER NINE

He hadn't meant to do that. Well, he had. But he hadn't meant to let it get that far.

That kiss. Man, that kiss.

Was it over? Truman wasn't sure? He could still feel the impact of Gunny on his lips. Hot and spicy with an earthy kick to it that he shouldn't have liked, but he desperately wanted another taste of.

Truman, trained soldier that he was, had not been prepared for that. He'd been in areas that were bombed, and he hadn't felt as shaken as he had at the impact of her lips. Bullets had whizzed past his head, but his heart hadn't raced this much.

When he let her go, he was shell-shocked. His body felt fractured, as though he were coming apart at the seams.

He had just meant to give her a light peck for show. Now hunger claimed him.

It had to be because he hadn't been with a woman in so long. He'd been so focused on healing his injury and getting back into the game. He hadn't had time to date. But that one long moment of having Gunnery Silver in his arms had shattered him.

And so help him, he wanted more.

Gunny was looking at him with a startled expression. Under that startled expression, he saw the unmistakable spark of desire. And she was rattled by it. By the looks of her, she was far more rattled than he was.

She wanted him too. Was that even possible for two people who were so different from one another? For two people who didn't even like one another? For two people who had planned a union where they would be on opposite sides of the world from one another?

Truman took a step back. But his legs weren't working. His hands were still holding onto her. Because he was never letting her go.

Just let her try to get on that plane next week. Either he would find a way to keep her here with him. Or he would be riding shotgun beside her.

First, he had to get them both down the aisle so he would have the right to be wherever she was.

"Are we doing this?" Truman asked.

"It's the only option," Gunny said after clearing her throat.

Right. The only option. He saw Catherine seated at the back of the rows of seats. She looked smug as though the show of affection hadn't convinced her.

Well, it had convinced him. Truman was hoping maybe it had convinced Gunny. After he'd whispered in her ear that Catherine was here and watching, he had expected Gunny to play-act with just a peck. But she'd thrown herself into that kiss with everything she had. So maybe she would give a piece of herself to him?

Their steps were steady as they walked down the aisle toward Father Matthews. Truman hated being visible to so many eyes. He was used to being in the shadows or behind bushes. He wasn't used to being so visible. In the back of his mind, he kept searching out places where he could hide and blend in. But he couldn't do that. Not when he was the star of the show.

He decided to focus on his friends at the front. That's why he was doing this, why he was placing himself in such a vulnerable position. This wedding, this marriage, was to protect his friends. It was supposed to be a sham. Only, with every step he took, it felt more and more real.

Truman's grip tightened on Gunny's arm. He liked the feel of her fingers tucked inside his elbow. Her index finger pressed against his bicep like it was a trigger aiming him forward. They came to a stop when they reached Father Matthews.

The old man smiled down at them. Truman noted the dark circles under the man's eyes. There was also a fine sheen of sweat on his forehead in the overcast sky.

Father Matthews loved these girls like they were his own. The stress of these last few months must've taken its toll on him as well as the Silvers. After this, they would all be able to rest easy.

"Dearly beloved," said Father Matthews. "I was there as each of these girls came into the world. Their parents passed them onto me and asked me to look after them as I would my own as their godfather. I have done that. I've handed each off to the man who became her husband. This is my last official job as their caretaker. I will be going on a much-needed vacation after this ceremony."

A light rumble of laughter went through the crowd. Gunny smiled up at the man who was her godfather. Truman was entirely captivated by her smile. His mind reeled with tactics on how to trigger such a reaction with her that was aimed solely at him.

"The couple has provided their own vows," Father Matthews was saying.

They had? This was news to Truman, since he hadn't written anything down to provide. He slid a glance over at Gunny, who smirked as she avoided his gaze. Truman knew then and there that life with this woman was going to be interesting.

"As is the Tibetan Buddhist way—"

Wait! Buddhist? Who was Buddhist?

Gunny's grin spread in a way that didn't read peaceful to him. It was all mischief.

"—the couple will answer the first set of vows together."

Oh? That didn't sound so bad. Truman had expected chanting and candles and chakra alignments. Call and response he could deal with.

"Truman and Gunnery, do you pledge to help each other to develop your hearts and minds, cultivating generosity, ethics, patience, enthusiasm, concentration, and wisdom as you age and undergo the various ups and downs of life, and to transform them into the path of love, compassion, joy, and equanimity?"

"We do," said Gunny.

Truman was still stuck on *developing his heart and mind*. What did any of that mumbo jumbo even mean? But in the silence, which was peppered with snickers from the men in his unit and the thudding taps from their wives to be quiet, Truman realized he had to answer.

"I… I mean, we do."

Father Matthews nodded sagely. He wiped at his forehead, catching sweat there with a cloth, and then continuing on. "Recognizing that the external conditions in life will not always be smooth and that internally your own minds and emotions will sometimes get stuck in negativity, do you pledge to see all these circumstances as a challenge to help you grow, to open your hearts, to accept yourselves, and each other; and to generate compassion for others who are suffering?"

Generate compassion for others? Was he getting married or opening an animal shelter?

"We do," said Gunny. Her own lips twitching along with her brothers'-in-law.

Was she for real? Or was Truman getting punked? It didn't matter because his gaze was fixed on her mouth.

What Truman realized was there would be a part of this ceremony where he would get to kiss that mouth again. Having his lips pressed against hers was worth any vow he was making, even if it was to some elephant-headed god and many-armed goddess.

"We do," Truman agreed.

Truman had to wait a long minute for the next section as Father

Matthews took a minute to clear his throat. And then grabbed a water bottle for a lengthy sip. The man was reading a tome with words that didn't go together, so Truman didn't begrudge the man his need for a brief interlude between passages.

"Understanding that just as we are a mystery to ourselves, each other person is also a mystery to us, do you pledge to seek to understand yourselves, each other, and all living beings, to examine your own minds continually and to regard all the mysteries of life with curiosity and joy?"

Now Gunny was out and out smiling at the confused look on Truman's face. Truman let the words roll over him. He would simply have Gunny explain their meanings later. While she did, he'd have the pleasure of watching her lips press together and open. He'd lie in wait, hiding in plain sight, until he could make his attack and kiss her soundly to satisfy his curiosity and joy.

"We do," he said.

"Do you pledge to preserve and enrich your affection for each other and to share it with all beings? To take the loving feelings you have for one another and your vision of each other's potential and inner beauty as an example, rather than spiraling inwards and becoming self-absorbed, to radiate this love outwards to all beings?"

"We..." It was Gunny who hesitated now.

Truman found he actually liked that part. Something in his heart told him that loving feelings for this woman was within reach. He wanted to spiral toward her. He was already becoming self-absorbed in everything she did. He was certain his growing feelings for her were radiating outward.

"We do," both Gunny and Truman said.

They stared at each other in silence. The silence seemed to stretch. Was that it? Were they done pledging their intentions and afterlives and next lives so that they could get to the good part? Surely, there had to be a part where they were pronounced man and wife, and he could kiss the bride.

Truman looked over to Father Matthews to determine the holdup. The man seemed to be struggling for breath. One of Father

Matthews' hands was clutching his Bible, the other his heart. In slow motion, the older man's body began to crumple.

Truman let go of Gunny and reached for him before the man hit the ground. "Call an ambulance," he shouted at his friends. "He's having a heart attack."

CHAPTER TEN

he smell of antiseptic made the hairs of Gunny's nostrils burn. The yellow of the fluorescent lights hurt her eyes. The intermittent beeping and squeak of shoes on linoleum made her head throb.

She'd been in too many hospitals in her life. She began her life in a hospital as a preemie as her mother lay dying down the hall. She'd been back to the hospital when Tessa Matthews sickened with breast cancer. The last time she'd been here was with Sarah, the woman who had raised Gunny and Tilly as if they were her own flesh and blood.

Gunny had mourned Sarah's loss as though her heart had been ripped from her chest. Her father had prepared them all for the possibility of him making the ultimate sacrifice. It had never occurred to Gunny that Sarah could be taken from her. And then, in a blink, she was gone.

If memory served her correctly, Gunny had been sitting in this very hall when the doctors had come to tell the Silvers of Sarah's passing. Gunny thought she remembered staring at the same painting on the wall when she'd come to visit Tessa Matthews for the last time. And now she was waiting for word of her second father, the last parental figure she had in this world.

The ticking of the clock was in tune with the pounding of her temples. Already it was late at night. Or maybe it was the next day? She wasn't sure? The hands of the clock blurred, and Gunny didn't have the energy to make out which was the hour and minute hand. Not that it mattered.

They'd been here for hours and still no word on Father Matthews. The doctors had wheeled him into an OR upon arrival. The doors had closed, and they were all left on the other side, waiting.

A shiver skittered across Gunny's shoulders. The large waiting room was cold, with AC units blasting. Alternately a burst of hot would knock her back to the wall when the sliding glass doors that led to the outside world opened to admit new patients and visitors. The mix of cold and hot left the air tepid for a time. Until, for a long time, the doors to the outside world stayed shut, and the cold got under her skin.

Arms came around Gunny's shoulders from behind. She wasn't sure which of her sisters embraced her. She didn't care. Their body blocked the AC vents, shielding Gunny from the blast of cold air. Gunny needed the reprieve from the chill to get her bearings.

She hated this part. The part where she had to hold still and wait for the results. That's why she was always mobile. She started the fight, and then once everything was in motion, she moved on and left the battle to others.

She'd gotten Father Matthews to the hospital. She'd raised her voice until she got the attention of everyone in scrubs or a white coat to get Father Matthews the attention he needed. Now the fight was in the OR, in the hands of the very best surgeon in town.

Gunny's work here was done. It was time to move on. Time to find a new fight.

Except she couldn't move. She didn't want to move. Not yet. Her sister's arms bade every cell in her body to wait, to rest, to relax.

Those arms whispered that she wasn't alone, never had been, never would be.

It was probably Tilly holding her up. The two had come into this world together. A pang of guilt pinched Gunny in the chest that she didn't always stay in constant contact with her twin. It wasn't for lack of a satellite link -not in today's interconnected world. Often, Gunny simply found it easier to be on her own.

Looking across the waiting room, she saw Tilly wrapped in Carter's arms. In fact, all of her sisters were wrapped up in their husband's arms. So who was holding Gunny?

Truman.

She had completely forgotten about Truman. The man who had just pledged himself to examine the mysteries of life as well as both their inner beauties together. Gunny almost snorted at the memory of his face when he'd heard those vows. She'd pulled them off the internet the day before. She'd figured if they were going to pledge themselves in this ridiculous union, then their vows should be ridiculous.

Although his strong arms, the comfort of his chest, the strong beat of his heart against her spine, none of that felt ridiculous right now. It felt right. It felt necessary.

Gunny took a step away from him. She didn't get far. The effort was halfhearted to begin with, so it ended with her pivoting in his embrace to face him.

He looked tired. There were creases at the edges of his eyes. His lashes covered half of his gray eyes like a window shade had been pulled down at sunset.

Her gaze lowered to his mouth. His top lip rested on his bottom lip, like a soft pillow atop a firm mattress. Gunny knew the two textures of his mouth. She vividly remembered the softness, the insistence, the hunger.

Her face heated. She lifted her heel to step away from him. Before her toes could leave the floor, Truman tightened his embrace.

"He's strong," said Truman. "He'll come out of this."

Gunny shook her head. "My mother was strong, both of them. And they both died here."

Truman didn't argue with her. He pulled her closer. A hand lifted to her temple. He brushed a few tendrils that had come undone from her updo out of her eyes. The light brush of his fingertips stopped the pounding in her temple.

It was too familiar. It was too comfortable. Gunny didn't do attachments. It was hard to fight while being weighed down by another body. And she needed to fight. She needed a cause. Some corporate demon to shout at. A tree to chain herself to. A pen to write a strongly worded letter.

"My dad was strong too," she said. "But he was taken out by a bomb."

Truman stiffened. When he did, his hold on her loosened. Finally, she was able to pull away.

It was clear by the stony look on his face that she'd struck a nerve. Well, it was better this way. No attachments. She might be one who saved lives, but she was far from a nurturer. Best her husband learn that now.

CHAPTER ELEVEN

He was stalking her. He wasn't ashamed to admit it. She was hard not to follow. White dress and heels. There was no camouflaging someone like her.

Truman's gaze tracked Gunny as she walked down the street and away from the hospital. Her sisters had started to protest her leaving, but when they'd seen Truman on her heels, they'd all quieted.

It was good that they all trusted her safety to him. Not that there was much danger out in the small midwestern town. Even if Gunny had decided to walk through the nursery, Truman would've followed.

He wondered if those vows of hers had cast some sort of spell on him. By agreeing to understand the mystery of her, to examine her mind, had he irrevocably linked his soul to hers.

Well, they were married. So he supposed so. Despite their particular brand of vows not including the phrase, he was still honor-bound to protect her. Because more than anything, Truman wanted to have Gunny. He wanted to hold her. To comfort her, of course.

Father Matthews would recover. The man was a warrior. His heart was too big to give out. It would mend.

Then Gunny would have no reason to stay. She would leave. Which was the plan.

So why was Truman clenching his fists?

As Gunny ambled down the street, Truman saw men leering at her as she walked by. True, she was wearing a white wedding dress. Those slender shoulders were exposed for the world to see. The toned muscles of her arms made Truman's mouth water.

Yes, he wanted to hold his wife. More than that, he wanted to feel her strong arms around him. And he definitely wanted to taste that lush mouth again.

One of the leering men craned his neck all the way to get another look at her. When the leerer's shoulders followed his head, Truman picked up his step. He caught the man's bicep in a grip before the pervert could take a step toward Truman's wife. The look in Truman's gaze screamed *Mine*. The man must have heard it loud and clear because he put his hands up in surrender and backed off.

Truman picked up the pursuit of his prey. But Gunny had disappeared. There weren't many places she could've escaped to.

There was a florist shop setting out bouquets on an outdoor display. The ice cream shop wasn't yet opened. Surprisingly, the bar was.

The bell over the door still jingled, leading Truman to believe that that was Gunny's likely destination. He slipped inside the establishment but didn't spot a woman in a white wedding dress.

He'd lost her. How had she gotten past him? Truman had never missed a shot. Even now, his hand itched for a weapon that wasn't at his side. His shoulder ached, but not from any of the strain of the previous day's events. Truman ached to have Gunny back in his arms.

He caught a flash of white across the street. Looking up, he saw the town hall. It was the only other place that she could've ducked into. Truman dashed up the steps, keeping to the shadows at the side of the building out of habit.

He slipped inside behind a man in a suit with a briefcase. Not that Truman could blend in much. He was dressed in uniform. But no one gave him a second look. Truman doubted he would've noticed in any regards. He scanned the room, his gaze like a scope. When he saw her moving with purpose toward a man behind a desk, Truman stalked toward her.

He no longer bothered to stay out of sight. He wanted everyone around to know that he was on the hunt. His prey was within his crosshairs.

"Excuse me?" Gunny said.

The man with a young face but a thinning hairline turned. He wore a bright customer service smile. That smile dropped the moment his gaze locked on Gunny.

"Oh, no." His shoulders slumped. "You're back."

"What?" said Gunny.

"Tilly?"

"No. I'm Gunny."

"Gunnery? Gunny Silver? Is that you?" The smile crept back over his face, unwrinkling his features. "It's me, Ryan Burns. From high school. I dated your sister."

"Okay," Gunny said noncommittally.

"We were pretty serious for a couple weekends."

"Sure. Fine. Listen, Ron."

"Ryan," he corrected, leaning in. "So, how've you been?"

Truman didn't like the way the man's gaze roamed over his wife's form. It looked like he was about to put the moves on her. Then the man's gaze widened as he took in her state of dress.

"You're in a wedding dress?"

Gunny took a step back from the desk. She ran her hands down her dress as though just remembering that she was wearing the garment. Then she put her hands on her hips. Before she could speak, the clerk went on.

"Don't tell me you're here to get married. Your sister was in here last week."

"I'm already married." Gunny waved her hands as though it was an inconvenient truth.

"You're married? Who's the guy? Another soldier?" The clerk looked up. Likely because he felt Truman's glare. "To him?"

Gunny looked over her shoulder. The pose she struck when she looked at him reminded Truman of a blonde-haired Wonder Woman. All she needed was the lasso of truth on her hip. Not that he needed to be roped in. He was already wound tight around her finger, as evidenced by his need to be near her.

She frowned at Truman. She only spared him the one glance before turning her attention back to Ryan, the clerk.

"Ron." She snapped her fingers to get his attention. "I'm here to file a petition. The government is trying to take over the Clearwater Valley lands where the Bright Horizon's Foster Home is."

Ryan blinked and then smiled. "You know, I remember back in middle school when you protested that Harry Potter got banned from the library by the PTA."

He leaned to the side to speak directly to Truman. The clerk chucked a thumb at Gunny as he spoke, as though he and Truman were sharing an inside joke and leaving her out.

"The moms were opposed to the evils of magic in the book, but Gunny wrote up a speech about censorship that made it into the local paper. Then after reading the book, she launched another protest because the books dealt with the enslavement of elves."

Yup, that sounded like the woman Truman was coming to know. But to make sure this guy didn't think he sided with him, Truman stepped up beside Gunny. He placed a hand at her low back. In his mind, he heard a click, like the safety being set to the off position. All pistons were ready to fire. He just needed to remove the obstruction out of the way.

"Ron, will you go and get my wife the paperwork she needs?"

Ryan opened his mouth, likely to correct Truman on his name. It was likely the expression on Truman's face that let him know that neither Truman nor Gunny could care any less. The man turned on his heel and disappeared into another room.

"You following me?" Gunny asked.

"Yes," Truman admitted.

"Just because we're married doesn't give you the rights to my business."

Actually, it did. But Truman didn't want to argue that. "We've all had a shock with Father Matthews's heart attack. I didn't want you to be alone."

"I don't need you to coddle me, Truman. I can take care of myself."

She crossed her arms over her chest, but she didn't back away from his touch. Instead, she seemed to sink deeper into the palm of his hand. Before she had a chance to respond, Ryan came back out.

"You can't file a petition on the Clearwater Valley lands," said Ryan.

"Why not?" said Gunny. "It's my First Amendment right."

"Well, yeah. It is. It's just that you already filed a petition years ago. Looks like it's been approved."

"What?" Gunny snatched the documents from him.

"Yup, says there the federal government has approved the Clearwater lands as protected property since they have wild horses running on them. Congratulations."

CHAPTER TWELVE

Gunny felt the walls closing in on her. She couldn't draw in a deep breath to fill her lungs. Her legs felt like jelly as she tried to move. To get away from the walls. To find a place where she could breathe.

The dress she was wearing felt itchy on her skin. The shoes she wore pinched her toes. The pins in her hair made her temples throb.

She needed to get out. To get away. To shout. To raise her fist.

But at who? And to what end?

Finally, she found the door to the building and pushed through. The sun warmed her face, but the rays didn't penetrate through to her shivering bones. The fresh air hit her nostrils, but she couldn't gulp down enough.

If she couldn't breathe, she couldn't shout. If she couldn't shout, she couldn't launch into a formal protest. Protesting is what had gotten her here.

It was all her fault. She'd saved the wild horses, which was great. Those majestic creatures needed a hero. But so did the kids at the foster home.

Gunny turned in a circle. She was unsure which way to go. In the end, strong arms stopped any forward motion and pulled her into a cocoon of firm, cushiony muscles.

The hard and soft sensations further scrambled Gunny's brain. That had to be why she didn't fight being overtaken. She surrendered to Truman as he brought her tightly against him.

"Breathe," he crooned. "Just breathe. I've got you."

She didn't need him to have her. She was woman. Hear her roar. Instead, what came out of her was a whimper.

"This is my fault." The words were said into Truman's chest. "Those kids are going to lose the only home they know. And it's all my fault."

"You were trying to do a good thing for the horses. Sometimes there's only the choice between the best bad option or the irreconcilable good."

His words weren't making much sense. The only bad or good option she wanted right now was to not move from this space. It was bad to let him hold her like this. After all, Gunny was getting on a plane in just a few days. But right now, in this moment, it simply felt so good to let someone else have her back.

"Seems to me," Truman went on, "either the horses have to move or the people do."

Two bad decisions. The horses had roamed that land for decades. Over the years, their habitat had been threatened by the encroachment of humanity. The resources they thrived on were in stark competition with herded cattle and domesticated horses. Their long-term survival was in serious jeopardy.

The same could be said for the kids that Savy and her sisters took care of at Bright Horizons. The place was a haven for kids who were sent from the inner cities, often as a last resort. The James girls worked magic that reform schools and juvenile halls envied. It was no wonder. They'd come up out of the foster care system in that same house years ago.

"If the paperwork is already filed, there is no choice," Gunny said.

She knew what she had to do. But before she did it, she allowed herself one last second in Truman's embrace. One last deep inhale of his heady scent of outdoor and aftershave. One last circular rub by his hand at her low back.

Then she took a step back. Truman let her go, but not far. He continued to crowd her space like he belonged beside her.

"Where are you going?" he said as she turned to walk down the street.

"To talk to Savy and her sisters."

"I'll drive you."

"I can walk."

"In those shoes?"

They both looked down at her heels. The white shoes were smudged from her walk to city hall. They wouldn't survive the trek across town to the foster home.

"Fine," she said.

They walked in silence back to the hospital. At some point, his hand returned to her low back. Gunny decided she'd allow it. Only because of the high heels and cracks in the sidewalks.

She was going to have to break Truman of this habit soon. She'd be leaving him in a few days. His sure fingers would be far beyond her low back by then. And wasn't that too bad.

Gunny had never wanted a husband. Had never actually given the matter any thought until the reading of her father's will. Now that she had one, it didn't seem all that bad.

She'd especially liked that bit with the kissing. Truman had had both his hands on her body at that time. One at her upper back and one at her lower back.

She should've offered up a protest then, but she hadn't been able to find the words. No, she hadn't wanted to find the words. Because she'd liked his mouth against hers.

Maybe she could get another kiss out of him before she had to leave? It wouldn't be too much to ask for a goodbye kiss. Would it?

They arrived at the hospital parking lot. Truman opened the passenger door of his truck for her. Gunny climbed inside and slumped back into the bucket seat. It had already been an eventful morning, and the late afternoon was looking bleak.

Had she really only gotten married just earlier today? Her dress looked like she'd been out working the ranch. She'd told her sisters it was pointless to put her in white. But this day had been more about them than it was about her. She'd saved the day with her vows. She'd saved her home with one set of words, but another family would suffer because of words she'd said long ago.

The truck pulled up to the outskirts of the town. The paved street ended a mile back. The dust cloud of gravel still plumed behind the truck from the dirt road. The Bright Horizon's Foster Home was just on the edge of civilization before the land went to all things wild. The town's residents preferred it that way. The kids who wound up at the foster home were often more feral than anything. Gunny knew that firsthand. She'd grown up next to six prior residents.

Truman put the truck in park. Gunny didn't immediately leap out of her seat. She stared beyond the dilapidated ranch house to the splendor that surrounded it. Brown earth bloomed into green foliage that raced up blue mountains capped with white clouds. It looked like a dream world where peace came for a holiday. But the raised voices, racing feet, and banging could be heard from inside the house, which shook with activity.

The natives were restless. Which made this the best time to go in. Savy and her sisters would be distracted with the rambunctious kids they managed.

Gunny's foot tapped against a metal box. She looked down and noticed that her heel had become hooked on the handle. She reached down, but Truman beat her to it.

"Let me get that for you," he said, brushing her hands away.

Their hands and her foot tangled together. As fingers and heels lifted and tugged, Gunny's shoe came off, and the metal box clanged open. The contents that spilled out turned Gunny's blood cold.

"It's secure," he said.

"Not if my shoe could free it. Why do you even have a gun in the car?"

"I always have a gun."

"Were you armed at our ceremony this morning?"

"Are we going inside?"

Gunny noticed he didn't answer her question. Instead, he reached down to shove the metal box back under the passenger seat.

"You can't leave that here," she protested. "There are children inside."

Truman gave her an exasperated look. He brought the gun out of the box, pulled out the magazine. Checking the safety, he put the gun in his back waistband and the magazine in his pocket.

"Satisfied?" he asked.

Gunny wanted to tell him that she would be satisfied if there were no longer any guns on the planet. But she had a bigger battle coming. She'd need all her strength to face the James sisters and tell them it was her fault they were losing the only home they'd ever known.

CHAPTER THIRTEEN

he steel of the gun was cold against his low back. He could feel the heat of Gunny's glare on it as he climbed out of the truck. He rounded to the passenger side door to help her out. Of course, she'd already hopped down and was headed for the ranch-style house that looked like a strong wind would blow it over.

When he caught up to her, Gunny turned and looked at him quizzically. "You can go. I'll find my way back."

"I'm not leaving you out here in the middle of nowhere," he said. "Shoes, remember?"

She didn't look down. She glared at him, hands on her hips just like the first time she'd stood over him. "I've spent most of my adult life out in the middle of nowhere."

"Well, now you're my wife, and I'm rolling with you."

"Are you going to keep throwing that in my face?"

"Throwing what in your face?"

"The matrimony thing. You realize it's temporary."

All his life, Truman Bates had been known as a calm person. His mother had told him he rarely cried as a baby. His grandmother, who'd raised him after his mother's untimely death, often bragged to her Canasta friends that her grandson never once threw a tantrum. As a young man, Truman never raised his voice in the heat of an argument because he rarely found reason to debate.

Things had always been black or white for him. Never shades of gray. The haze of gray was a place where disagreements could brew. So, Truman never ventured there.

Until this past week when he agreed to this fake marriage with Gunnery Silver.

It should've been cut and dry. Instead, it was a whole, wet mess of feelings in his chest that alternately warmed and went cold. He constantly wanted to push her away and pull her close. He wanted to hear her voice, but none of the arguments. He wanted to gaze into those clear blue eyes but not deal with any of the judgment. And he couldn't for the life of him remember when he'd promised her temporary?

Gunny could call him temporary all she wanted. What she'd soon learn was that her new husband had the patience of a tiger, an animal that moved slowly and quietly, stalking their prey for extended periods of time before pouncing. Gunny was in Truman's crosshairs, and she would soon learn that he never missed a shot.

For now, he stayed quiet. He watched and waited. Meanwhile, she snuck glances at him as they climbed the porch steps.

Truman was really liking the annoyed pinch she got to her mouth. He wondered if he caught her lip, if he could straighten that pout out? He really wanted to try. But the woman wouldn't even let him open a door for her. He doubted she'd let him steal another kiss.

The house shook with a thundering boom. Truman pulled Gunny into his arms, pressing her face into his chest. A child wailed. Another screamed the word *no*. Then a calm voice of reason interjected between the two.

"Either you two work it out amongst yourselves with words, or I will bring out scissors, and we'll handle this like the good King Solomon."

"But Ms. Savy, it's *miiiiiine*," screeched the wailer.

"It's not yours," said a slightly less high-pitched voice. "You're an orphan, so you can't own anything."

"That's enough out of both of you," said the reasonable adult by the name of Savy. "Keep it up, and you'll be eating Ms. Tricksy's cooking for dinner."

The wailing and moaning stopped instantly.

"Thought so," said Ms. Savy, in a chipper, singsong tone that reminded Truman of Mary Poppins.

"If you're done feeling me up?"

That voice was not the soprano of Julie Andrews or Ms. Savy. Truman looked down at Gunny. She had a quizzical expression on her face. But he wasn't looking at her whole face. He was looking at her lips. That sassy mouth was so close to his. He could taste her breath. He remembered the sweetness he'd found there this morning, the peace that whispered on her breath. He wanted to press them both into the wall and stay hidden there while he kissed her senseless.

Gunny's breath caught, as though she knew exactly what he wanted to do. She didn't push him away.

"Ms. Savy, there are people making out in the parlor."

That childish voice made Truman let go of his hold on Gunny. But he didn't back off completely. He stayed at her flank. These kids were clearly out of control, and he wasn't sure how many of them there were. Whoever the kid was that called them out dashed around a corner before Truman could get a good look at them. The shouting was coming from the right. He heard footsteps to the left as well.

A dark head of curls came at them from the right. Ms. Savy was a tall drink of water with golden tanned skin that called to an island climate. Her hazel gaze had a tilt that matched the curve of her full lips. Her footsteps faltered and her bright smile dimmed when she saw Gunny.

"Did you come from the hospital?"

"No," said Gunny. "Oh, God no. He's fine. Well, not fine." Gunny took a breath and tried to start again, but Truman picked up the mantle instead.

"It was a heart attack," he said. "He's in stable condition, but he hasn't woken up yet."

Savy nodded at Truman before returning her gaze to Gunny. "The boys?"

"Charlie and Joe should be here by tonight."

Savy nodded again. She twisted a band on her left ring finger. It wasn't gold or silver. It looked like plastic, like it came from a Cracker Jack box or toy store.

"And who is this?" asked Savy, her gaze landing on Truman as she twisted her ring.

"This is Truman," said Gunny. "He's my… husband."

Savy raised a brow. Her lip followed the same upward curve of approval. "Good luck with that."

Truman wasn't sure who Savy directed the comment to. He decided to take it as a well-wish for a long and happy marriage. Because that's now what he intended to get out of this union.

"If you're not here about Father Matthews, then you must have found something out about the government's rights over this land."

Gunny nodded, but she didn't say anything else. Just as she opened her mouth, another crash filled the silence. Followed by a yelp and a string of curses that no child should know.

Both Gunny and Truman looked to the left. Savy ignored the crash and the language. Her attention stayed on Gunny.

"Well?" prompted Savy. "Did you find a way out of this?"

"I found the original petition. It was filed years ago."

"Okay, that's a start. No one knows their way around a petition like you."

Gunny took a deep breath, let it out, then took one more. "The original petition was filed by me."

CHAPTER FOURTEEN

Gunny closed the door behind her. The moment she did, the shouts and yelling of the kids began up again. Before that there had been fifteen minutes of silence.

Not a blessed silence. There had been nothing peaceful about the quiet conversation Gunny had had with Savy. It had been a tense one-sided conversation where Gunny had to *mea culpa* for a cause she believed in, a cause which was her very life's purpose -saving wild horses from humanity's encroaching progress.

Gunny stumbled over her words as she showed Savy the five-year-old petition that Gunny had drafted as a high school senior with dreams of changing the world. Or at least the valley beyond the borders of the Silver Star Ranch and the Flying Cross Ranch. Seventeen-year-old Gunny hadn't known that the Bright Horizons Foster Home, the place where the Matthews boys had spent the start of their lives, and the James sisters had come back to take over, sat just at the edge of Clearwater Valley where the wild horses ran free.

What was the saying? Ignorance of the law excuses no one.

"I'm so sorry, Savy."

"You didn't do this on purpose."

Savy reached out and squeezed Gunny's shoulder, but the move was halfhearted. Like a mother giving a child an absent pat on the head while they looked over the stack of unpaid bills on the table. Savy had bigger concerns to worry over than the paper Gunny had written years ago.

One by one, heads poked around corners and out of cracked doorways.

"Are we gonna be homeless again?"

"Ashton's going back to juvie."

"They'll probably split us apart."

"Noooo, I don't want you to leave, Denny."

"That's enough you all." Savy clapped her hands in quick succession. She didn't raise her voice, but her words carried. In the silence, she turned back to Gunny. "Let me deal with this. We'll catch up later."

Gunny wanted to tell the kids that the fight wasn't over. This was just the first round. Unfortunately, they didn't have years to wait and come back around for another bout. They'd have to be out in months, maybe weeks.

There was a part of Gunny that wanted to stay, to figure out a strategy and fight. But she'd already done enough. Her helpfulness was what got them here. She felt a tug toward the door, and the shame in her allowed herself to be pulled.

The moment the door closed behind her, the children's voices erupted again. It sounded like wild animals had been let out of their cages. She didn't envy Savvy her job. Animals weren't that noisy out in the wild. Their lives depended on their silence.

Truman walked beside her, quiet as a mouse tiptoeing around lions. That was one thing Gunny could say about her husband. He didn't make a lot of noise.

Her husband. This man was her husband. It appeared the bonds of matrimony were tight because she couldn't seem to shake him.

He had been a steady presence beside her all day. Truman had been the one to catch Father Matthews before he'd hit the ground. He'd done CPR to ensure there were life signs while they waited for the paramedics. Meanwhile, Gunny and her sisters had stood by in horror as the man who had been often closer than their father struggled to breathe.

Gunny stumbled now as the memories assaulted her. Coupled with the guilt over the petition and she lost her footing. Truman's arms were around her, bringing her into his hold.

She knew she should fight to get away from him. She didn't want to be this close to anyone right now. She felt so weak, so weary.

"I'm fine," she said. Although she wasn't sure she was loud enough. Even her voice was wobbly, weighed down by the stress and strain of the day.

"I think we should get you home," he said. "You've had a long day."

Truman's arms tightened around her. Instead of feeling trapped in a vise, she felt as though she were being tucked into a bed made of memory foam. Soft and firm at the same time, his chest seemed to conform to her body.

Which would be impossible since they'd never done this before. He'd never held her or wrapped her up tightly like she was precious. He'd never tucked her head against his heart and rested his cheek at her temple. So why did it all feel so familiar, like they'd been doing this for years? Why did it all feel so right?

"I don't want to go home just yet," she said after long moments in his embrace. "I need some fresh air."

It wasn't lost on Gunny that they were standing outside. The freshest air in the valley lifted the escaped tendrils of her hair. Truman loosened his hold on her. Slowly, like a tricky knot unraveling.

Once they were disentangled, he looked down at her. She couldn't meet his gaze. Instead, she turned on her heel and started off down the trail.

She would be the first to admit that traversing through the wild in heels wasn't the smartest thing in the world. But she wasn't going to admit that out loud today. She picked her way carefully on the well-tread path. Truman gave her some space but kept her within arm's reach.

"You don't have to follow me."

"It's beautiful out here," he said.

His gaze was on his surroundings, but Gunny got the sense that he kept one eye on her. In the far-off distance, a lone horse grazed on a patch of green grass at the edge of a watering hole. To the far end of the water, more of the herd rested or drank. The horses were a rainbow of stark whites, mahogany browns, and midnight blacks. The animals had no idea that a long-fought battle had been won for them. Or that their champion had caused irreparable harm in their name.

"You're not responsible for every endangered or displaced animal in the world, and that includes the human variety."

"I don't regret fighting for the horses or winning." Gunny turned her back on the horses and looked toward the path they'd come from, the path that led back to the soon-to-be-demolished foster home. "I just need to figure out how to save those kids now."

"I don't know Savy very well, but I get the sense she's going to figure out a way to protect those children. Maybe let her handle it?"

Gunny shook her head, the wheels in her brain already turning over possibilities. "I move quicker on my own."

"You sound like a sniper." Truman grinned. "Without a gun. You just have your words and your will. You could probably topple a whole government with just those two weapons."

Gunny was too busy with her own thoughts. That had to be why she missed the oncoming assault. Truman's hands cupped her cheek, one on each side. His palms were softer than she would've expected for so physical a man. Just like the memory foam soft-firmness of his chest, the flesh of his hands was a cushion that conformed to the contours of her face.

She wanted to rest in his hold. To fall asleep and leave all her cares and worries to the setting sun. No, that wasn't the sun setting. It was her eyelashes sinking downward as she allowed herself to relax in his embrace.

"Gunny?"

"Hmmm?"

"I'm going to kiss you."

Her eyes blinked open. Gun-metal gray was all she could see. Gray had always been a cold, dreary color in Gunny's mind. Until she saw the heat in Truman's gaze.

"Why?" She had to clear the huskiness from her throat and try again. "Why are you going to kiss me?"

"A man and woman—husband and wife, actually. Out alone in the woods. Seems like what should naturally happen. Don't you think?"

"I... I..." Gunny was supposed to say no. Problem was, she'd have to close her mouth to make that sound, and her lips refused to back down and make the motion.

It had to be the shame, or the guilt, or the stress of the day. Why else would she be eager to have this man's lips pressed against hers? She didn't even like him.

Except she knew she wouldn't still be on her feet without him at her side. She was only standing because he'd kept a hand on her back. He'd had an arm wrapped around her shoulders. Now his fingers were warm against her skin.

He was right. It did seem like the most natural thing to have happen right now. Truman's head came toward hers slowly, allowing her to make a run for it if she wanted.

For the first time in a long time, Gunny Silver held still. Once again, she felt certain that Truman felt familiar. His mouth against hers was more than a memory. It was a plan, an outline for a future that was hers for the taking.

Her fingers dug into his shoulders as though in protest of past separation. Her chest pressed against his, resisting any attempt of air to come between them. Her breath was the signature that sealed the deal that she was in this for the long battle.

CHAPTER FIFTEEN

Truman's senses were on high alert. That was typically the way when he was staking out a spot. The world would slow down so that he could pick out every minute detail.

He smelled the ripe berries on the breeze from the east.

He felt every fist-size rock under his shoe, which he kicked aside to have a level playing field.

He heard the melodic chirp of every bird, the busy rustling of every bug.

His gaze filled with sunlight, blonde rays of light shining brighter and brighter as each strand came to set around tan shoulders while the sun overhead began its slow descent toward the horizon.

All that was left was to taste.

Truman's trigger finger was on Gunnery Silver's chin. No, not Gunnery Silver. She was Gunnery Bates.

She was his. He'd tracked his quarry. He'd acquired his target. Now he had her surrounded. He just needed to pull the trigger.

He brushed his lower lip against hers. The shuddery breath she let out nearly made him blow his cover. That cover being that this marriage was fake. That cover being that he would let her get on a plane in a couple of days. That cover being he didn't want to possess this woman with the whole of his being.

With a groan, Truman covered her mouth with his. He couldn't be silent in his attack. He couldn't be stealth in making this advance. Truman wanted this woman too much. He wanted to come out of the shadows and proclaim that he needed her. That he never wanted to be apart from her. He felt himself attaching to Gunny like he was now her shadow.

He pulled her closer, deepening the kiss. He expected a fight from this firebrand of a woman. She put up no defense. Instead, Gunnery Silver Bates gave in.

Her hands rested against his chest. Her fingers snaked around his neck and into his hair. Then she tugged, pulling him closer as though she couldn't get enough of him.

Truman understood the sentiment. He couldn't get close enough. He couldn't get enough, period.

The rock under Truman's foot ground into pebbles as it cracked under the added weight of having Gunny in his arms. The berries smelled overripe next to the sweetness of Gunny's breath. The birdsong became noise next to the small gasps that Gunny made with each new kiss. Truman's eyes were closed tight in an effort to give him some reprieve from the onslaught of sensory overload. Even still, behind his closed eyelids, all he could see was a bright light.

His every instinct told him to go into that light. If death was on the other side, he'd die a happy man and thank his Maker for those few moments of bliss with that angel.

A new sound penetrating. This rustling was heavier than a bug. It was too loud to be an insect or a small mammal. This was something bigger.

Truman did not want to stop kissing Gunny. The soldier in him urged him to pay attention. It was more important than anything that she was safe. That thought alerted Truman to the fact that there was a threat at his back.

He pulled away from her, just enough to allow a breeze of air between them. Even that half an inch was too much. A war for his attention broke out in his head.

Truman knew he should look up and assess the danger he was sensing. But he couldn't turn his gaze away from Gunny. Her head remained tilted, waiting for the next kiss. It took everything in Truman to turn away from those lush lips and seek out the potential threat.

Please let it be a bunny hopping by, he thought to himself. *Or a curious deer that posed no threat.*

When Truman turned his head, he did see fur. Unfortunately, it was not the soft white fur of a bunny rabbit. It was not the gangly four legs of a deer. What Truman saw was a large, dark creature eying them curiously. Its paws were the size of his head. It's black fur bristled.

The bear took a step forward. Truman knew better than to make any sudden movements. He avoided eye contact, which was hard when he wanted to proclaim his dominance in this situation. There would be nothing that could stand between him and protecting Gunny.

He knew they had to walk away slowly. He knew he couldn't scream or yell. Laying down and curling his body into a ball felt like an anathema, but he would do it if it would protect his wife.

Truman reached out to Gunny to begin their descent to the ground. Only Gunny had pulled away from him. Truman turned his head slowly to let her know what they were up against. When he turned, he heard a click and was met with the barrel of his own gun.

Somehow Gunny had managed to get the gun and clip from his waistband and pocket. She held the weapon out, aimed squarely at the bear. There were tears in her eyes, but her hand was steady.

Her lips were moving. Just slightly. The whispered words were shaky as they left her mouth.

"Please, go. Please, go. Don't make me do this."

Truman had pulled the trigger of a gun many times in his life. There was a silence each time, a certainty that came after. He'd been following orders each time, orders he believed in and would die for.

This standoff was against everything his wife held dear. She held a weapon in her hand. It was trained on an animal she likely had fought to protect.

Truman could not let her take this shot.

Behind him, he heard more rustling. Curling into a ball was no longer an option. Neither was looking away. Truman dared to turn around.

The bear had turned. It was moving away from them. Its paws crunching into rocks and silencing the birds overhead and bugs below.

The gun wobbled in Gunny's hand. For the second time since he met her, Truman stripped a weapon from Gunny's hands. This time when he did, she didn't cock her hands on her hips. She shook from the impact of what she'd almost done.

Part of him wondered if he should be upset that she hadn't batted an eyelash when she'd aimed the gun at him. But Truman knew that Gunny would've never put a bullet in him. Though she had been prepared to put a bullet in that bear if it had attacked. To kill an animal would've hurt her on a soul-deep level.

Truman pulled Gunny to him. She said nothing as she came into his embrace. He kept his arms wrapped around her as they walked back down the trail. He kept a lookout for more danger. All the while, he remained her shadow. Intent he would never let this woman out of his sight.

CHAPTER SIXTEEN

unny let Truman deposit her into the truck. He might have even carried her there. She wasn't sure. Her legs were shakier than a fawn taking its first steps.

Faintly, she heard the raised voices. The running of small feet against creaky hardwoods. Savy's melodic voice pressing for calm and order within Bright Horizons.

The click of metal against metal made her jump in her seat. The thick strap of the seatbelt kept her in place. That leather strap let her know that she was inside the cab of a truck and not back out in the wilderness facing off against a bear.

She'd been prepared to pull that trigger. She'd been a second away from doing so. For all her time spent standing up against armed hunters and poachers, Gunny had never once taken a gun and aimed it at another living thing. She'd never even considered it a possibility.

Until the bear had interrupted her make-out session with this man.

Truman's hands were at her midsection. His knuckles brushed against the fabric covering her belly button as he snapped the seatbelt into place. For some unknown reason, Gunny didn't feel trapped by the strap. She felt safe, secure, tethered where she had been tossing and turning.

When she looked up, she looked directly into his gaze. There were so many questions there. Questions she wasn't ready to answer.

Questions like, was she okay?

She had no idea if she was okay or not. Her mind was so full thinking about others. There was Father Matthews, who they still had no news from. There was Savy and the foster kids. There was the bear whose life she'd nearly ended.

Questions like, would she really have pulled that trigger?

Gunny still felt the cold steel of the gun in her palm. Her index finger had been on the trigger. Her entire body had shook, but not her trigger finger. That had been steady.

Truman brushed her hair out of her face, but he didn't say anything. He let her have her silence. The passenger side door slammed, shutting out the rest of the world. For the first time in her life, Gunny felt alone.

Solitude was a strange, foreign feeling for a twin. Stranger even for the sibling of a big family. Through all her travels across the world, Gunny had never felt alone.

The driver's side door of the truck opened, letting in a breath of fresh air. On the currents of that slight wind came the scent of turned earth, gunpowder, and the spicy scent that belonged to Truman.

The door shut and out went the feeling of solitude.

Truman slanted Gunny a look. It wasn't a smile. It wasn't a frown. It was simply a brush of his gaze over her face. When he was done, he gave her a slight nod as though she'd given him the answer to a question. Then he started the engine.

Gunny sat face forward as Truman pulled out of the foster home's drive and onto the main road. They drove in silence. The radio wasn't on. The windows weren't down for the breeze to intrude. All she could hear was the even breathing coming from his mouth.

She'd kissed that mouth. It had been an amazing kiss. The best of her life. Not that she'd had much practice to begin with. Clearly, Truman had.

Any man who could kiss like that—so thoroughly that they didn't hear the danger approaching them out in the woods. So passionately that she'd been prepared to kill when they'd been interrupted. Well, that was some skill.

"I'd rather not leave you alone tonight."

Gunny turned away from the sound of his voice. She couldn't let him see how her cheeks heated at not just the sound of his voice but those words. They had every right to spend the night together. They were married, man and wife.

"I hope you're not expecting your husbandly rights," she said.

From the corner of her eye, she caught the small smile that tugged at his lips. Truman's smiles were always small, as though they were hard-fought. She felt a slight thrill race over her skin that she'd won a few.

"You've been through a lot today," he said, gaze still on the road. "Marriage to me. The ER. The foster home. And then there was the bear."

"Yeah," Gunny agreed, "that wedding was the most trying part of the day."

Again, she got another smile. This one a little bigger than the last. Truman looked over at her, and her breath caught.

She knew she looked a fright. She was still in her wedding dress, but it was no longer white. Her makeup had melted off under the day's sun. Her hair had come undone during either the march to City Hall or the trek through the woods of Clearwater Valley.

This is what life with her would be like. Gunny was always getting into a mess. It was always on purpose. Because it was often messy to save others. Gunny had no desire to live a pristine life.

"I am your husband," Truman said. "But I have no expectations of that role tonight. Other than to look after you."

"I'm not domesticated."

"I'm pretty feral myself."

"I can't stand still for long."

"There we differ," he said. "I can lay still for hours, days."

"While you wait for the perfect shot?"

"Yes." There was no apology in his voice. "I'm a very patient man. I know how to line up the perfect shot, and I never miss."

It didn't sound like he was bragging. It sounded cautionary, like he was warning her of an oncoming storm. Here she sat in the calm of the eye as they ambled down a country road.

"I don't need looking after," she said.

Truman pumped the brakes. With a flick of his wrist, he pulled the truck over to the side of the road. He placed the vehicle in park but left the engine running. Once all that was settled, he turned and faced her.

"I see you," he said.

Gunny jerked back as though he'd struck her. In a way, he had. Truman's steel gaze was like a bullet right to the chest. She felt her heart explode under the assault. The funny thing was, she didn't feel in pieces. She felt whole.

"I see you," he repeated. "And I'm pretty sure I can hold on to you."

Gunny was great at arguing. Before she'd become an activist, she'd been on the high school debate team. Other school teams would groan when she took the podium. But right now, in this moment, she couldn't craft any manner of argument. Only one word managed to escape her mouth.

"Why?"

"We're already married," he said. "So why not?"

That was not the answer. She could tell by looking at the twinkle in that gray gaze. The gaze she'd once thought was cold and unfeeling was anything but. Truman's eyes shone brightly at her, letting her see all his secrets and pressing into some of her own.

"You need someone watching your back," he said, leaning over the middle console.

He was close enough for a kiss. Gunny pressed her lips together, as though she could will them to not want what every part of her—

her heart, her mind, even her soul—wanted from this man. Her body betrayed her as she let out a gasp of air.

Truman was going to kiss her again. There was nothing she could do about it. Not if she was at war inside herself. Only it wasn't a war. There was no line in the sand inside of her. Every part in her stood to one side. It was the side of the starting line of the race. All that was left was for someone to shout, Go!

No one said go. Neither of them said anything. They simply leaned into each other, meeting halfway until their lips touched.

She could have this. She could have him. Even if only for a little time. Or maybe a little while longer if she took an extended vacation at home. Or maybe even after that if she could convince her husband to come with her to Australia.

He'd made promises in those vows. Promises to grow with her, promises to face challenges, promises to open his heart. He'd scoffed at first as the vows were read, but by the end, she'd seen the shift in him. He'd started taking them seriously.

What if he was serious about them? He sure was kissing her like he had no plans to let her go anytime soon. Gunny was giving as good as she got. What if she had no plans to let him go anytime soon?

They didn't need to let go. They were man and wife. Father Matthews had proclaimed them so.

Gunny pulled back. Her whole body, along with Truman, protested the disconnection. "Wait!"

"What?" he said as he reached for her.

"He never said it."

"Who never said what?"

"Father Matthews. He never proclaimed us man and wife. Does that mean we're not married?"

CHAPTER SEVENTEEN

*S*tars were poking out of the dark sky when Truman pulled up to the hospital for the second time today. The tiny pinpricks of light shone down and settled on Gunny's face. She looked like an angel of the night, even with the smudges of dirt on her face, her unraveled hair, and the stains on her white dress.

There was a strong possibility that she wasn't his.

Even before the entire thought formed in his mind, he rejected it. The unspoken vows meant nothing. He didn't need to have an official make the proclamation. Truman knew with every fiber of his being that this woman was meant to be in his arms, by his side, for the rest of his days.

The real question was, would she make the same vow to him?

Gunny stumbled as she walked beside him. Truman reached out to her, wrapping an arm around her waist and bringing her into the protection of his body. She came without protest, as though they'd been walking side by side for years. As though they would continue to do so for years to come.

No matter what Father Matthews had or hadn't said, they were a unit. They would remain a unit. It didn't matter if they were legally married or not.

Only it did. Because this was the last day to meet the deadline of General Silver's will. If their union wasn't legal, the family, his unit, they would all lose everything. Worst of all, Gunny would have no reason to stay.

For now, Gunny let him hold her hand as they walked through the hospital. He rubbed at her index finger. The same finger that had rested on the trigger of a gun. The same finger that had been prepared to end the life of an animal if it had charged him.

She felt something for him. The least of which was indifference. So why was she tugging her hand away from him and running to another man?

"Charlie!" Gunny called as she flung herself into a dark-haired man's hold.

"Hey, Gunny Bunny," said the man as his arms wrapped around Truman's wife.

Or possibly his not-wife. Even if Gunny wasn't his legal wife, she was still entirely his. Even if she had yet to fling herself into Truman's arms.

"What happened to you?" asked Charlie, looking her up and down. "You look like you fought a bear."

"Not too far from the truth. I was at Bright Horizon's talking with Savy and—"

Charlie straightened as though a lightning rod had zipped up his spine. "Savy? How is she? Is she okay? She didn't do this to you... did she?"

"No, we... It's a long story." Gunny sighed, placing her hands on either side of Charlie's face. "I'm so sorry about your dad."

Charlie closed his eyes and rested his forehead against Gunny's. "He's stable. The doctors say he's going to be okay. He just needs to wake up."

They were talking about Father Matthews. Truman searched the man's face for any resemblance between the two men. He couldn't find a single one in Charlie Matthews's tan skin and angular nose.

The other man must have felt Truman's stare. He looked up, his arms still wrapped around Gunny. "I'm sorry? Are we blocking your way?"

Truman grit his teeth and prayed for calm. Other than the familiarity the man had with his wife, or possibly not-wife, there was no reason to gut him. Not when his father was lying ill in a hospital bed.

But Truman couldn't stop glaring at the hand Charlie Matthews had at Gunny's hip. Until he saw the plastic ring on his hand. It looked like it came out of a Cracker Jack box. It was the second of its kind Truman had seen today.

"Charlie, this is Truman," said Gunny. "He's my…"

"I'm her husband," said Truman.

"Well, we don't know that for sure," said Gunny.

Truman knew it for sure. Gunny was his. It didn't matter if another man had declared it or not. It was simply a fact.

"They told me he was performing a wedding when this happened," said Charlie. "It was your ceremony?"

Gunny nodded. Guilt clouding her blue gaze. She crossed her arms over her chest and rubbed her forearms as though seeking comfort. She couldn't think this was her fault? Could she?

Truman took a step to bring her into the comfort of his arms. Charlie Matthews got there first.

"It's not your fault, Gunny Bunny," Charlie soothed. "If it's anybody's fault, it's his sons. We left him there to do all that work by himself."

It was a touching moment. Truly, it was. The boy next door comforting the girl next door. Except the female neighbor in question belonged in Truman's arms.

"He didn't finish the ceremony," Gunny said, stepping out of Charlie's arms. "He never pronounced us man and wife."

Behind him, Truman heard Scout curse. He turned to find Scout, Linc, and the rest of the Silver sisters and President's Men coming from what looked like the hospital cafeteria.

Charlie looked past Gunny to Truman. His gaze was one part quizzical, one part assessment. Not as though he was sizing up a rival. More of an appraisal of his worth to date this particular Silver sister. That's when Truman saw the resemblance to Father Matthews.

Charlie Matthews was just as protective of the Silvers as his father. Truman straightened his own spine to show he was strong enough for Gunny. He stepped forward, standing shoulder to shoulder with his wife to indicate that they were a unit, vows or not.

"It's okay," said Charlie. "When he wakes up, I'm sure he'll be more than happy to do it."

"We don't have that much time," said Gunny. "My father's deadline for us all to get married so that we could keep the ranch was today."

Charlie gave a shake of his head, but confusion still marred his brow when he focused on Gunny. "Exactly what did I miss while I was away?"

"You're a preacher's son," Gunny said, ignoring his question. "We had a ceremony, so that makes us married. Right?"

"It's not the ceremony that makes you legally married," said Charlie. "It's the paperwork. Once you file the marriage license, that's when you're actually married."

"Where's the license?" Gunny turned to face her family.

"Father Matthews took care of it with each of our weddings," said Scout. "It's probably with his things."

"I'll go ask about his personal effects," said Charlie as he took off down the hall.

But as Charlie disappeared around the corner, another voice spoke up. "I have them."

It was the second time today that an enemy had snuck up on Truman. Now his pulse sped up to triple time. He felt the heat of a target on his back. Instinctively, he pulled Gunny into the circle of his arms. He didn't miss that each man of his unit did the same to his own wife as Catherine walked toward them.

Her stilettos impacted the parquet floor like bullets firing from an automatic rifle. Each impact reverberated through Truman's head. He itched for a weapon to protect himself, to protect Gunny, to protect their family. All the while, he knew there was none.

Catherine held in her hands the only thing that would've protected them all from her. The single sheet of paper crinkled in her painted claws. Because she held Truman and Gunny's unfiled marriage license.

CHAPTER EIGHTEEN

G unny stared at the sheath of paper in her stepmother's hands. She'd often stared in fascination at Catherine's hands. Her nails were always impeccable. Perfectly rounded points with a pale color that always matched her outfit and makeup to perfection. Gunny's nails always matched her clothing and what was on her face as well. Because what was always on her clothes, her face, and under her nails was dirt.

Today was no different. She stood in her wedding dress that was now artfully decorated with grass stains from when she'd knelt beside Father Matthews at her ceremony. There was dust from when she'd stormed into the City Hall. There were spats of dry dirt from her trek into the woods.

"It's too late for you to file it today. The courthouse closed over an hour ago," Catherine continued. "Which means that you girls didn't meet your dear dad's requirements. So, the ranch goes to me."

The air conditioner clicked on overhead. The chilly gust blew down on them, causing the stiff sheet of paper to bend downward. It made a crinkling sound as though the fibers were about to crack under the pressure of remaining in Catherine's grasp.

"Mother, you don't want to do this." Mareen stepped to the front of the lines, Wilson close on her heels.

"I didn't do anything," said Catherine. "I've only sat by and watched this all play out just as I told you it would."

"We all did what our dad wanted," said Scout. "As twisted as it was. It worked out for all of us. We all found love."

Catherine cocked her head as she took in Scout and Linc. Linc wrapped Scout up in his arms, smiling down at her with complete adoration in his eyes. Catherine's gaze lighted on each of the couples. Jefferson had one arm wrapped around Saylor, his lips resting against her temple, which was scrunched in worry. Jackson leaned heavily on a cane with one hand, but the other was wrapped tight around Brig, who clutched at the fabric of his shirt. Tilly and Carter were wrapped around one another like they were one heart beating.

"Not all of you," said Catherine, her gaze landing on Truman and Gunny.

When Gunny looked up at Truman, her heart beat steady. Not missing a single beat. Truman didn't wrap his arms around her as though they were madly in love. Because they weren't. They weren't even married.

But he never left her side. He kept his hand at her back, a steady presence letting her know she would not face this alone.

"We did what our father wanted," said Scout. "You can't swoop in on your broomstick on a technicality."

"There are no participation trophies in life," said Catherine. "You either win, or you lose."

"You're wrong, mother," said Mareen. "You're about to lose if you do this."

"I've tried to tell you that there are no happily ever afters. That's not the way the world works."

"I'm pregnant." Mareen place her hands over her still flat belly.

Catherine's stony face went impossibly still. She didn't blink. She didn't breathe. She only stared at her daughter's midsection.

"If you take away the ranch, if you take away your grandbaby's home… I don't think I could ever forgive you. That ranch is where all my best memories are. It's the place where we will always belong. That ranch is where our family is."

With that word *family*, Catherine blinked. It was as though any emotion she'd been trying to hide was leeched from her porcelain features. "That ranch is a money suck."

"Is not," Scout said, taking a step forward. Linc held her back.

"Despite what you girls think," said Catherine, "I am doing this for your future. I'll sell the land and reinvest the money. That is true security for your futures when these fake marriages all fail."

Gunny expected each one of her sisters to shout. For at least one of them to stomp her feet. For all of them to deny Catherine's words about anything fake.

No one spoke up. They all looked at the older woman as though she were a child who could not be reasoned with.

Catherine held out the marriage license to Gunny. Her pale pink nails were a compliment to the sepia tone document. Both her and Truman's names were printed with a swirl of dark black lettering. The name of the document was embossed in gold.

It looked official, even though it meant nothing outside of the filing cabinet of the courthouse. What was karma up to with her? One document she had filed years ago, and it came back around today to wreak havoc on a family. Another document she needed filed an hour ago, and because it hadn't been, it would wreak havoc on her family.

"Do you still want it?" Catherine said, her red-coated lips curling as she spoke. "Not that it matters."

Gunny's gaze fixated on Catherine's lips. A poisoned red apple came to mind. Though Catherine looked nothing like an old crone in a black cloak, and they weren't out in the woods. Still, Gunny felt certain this had to be some kind of trick.

If she reached for the proffered prize would it turn into a snake and bite her? Sending poison through her veins that would settle her down for a long, motionless sleep that made her entirely dependent on a long-awaited prince? If she didn't reach for the fancy piece of paper, would she be the only one unscathed by the witch's spell, free to continue on her quest to save the world?

Gunny didn't have to decide. Truman took the document from Catherine's hands. There was a sharp protest at the exchange of hands. Gunny's heart stopped at the thought the paper would rip. Then there would be nothing—real or fake—holding her and Truman together.

Was that what she wanted? They had lost this battle. Her third loss of the day behind Father Matthews's heart attack, Savy losing the foster home, and now this; her marriage wisping away like a fanciful little girl's dream.

The sheet of paper straightened and went silent in Truman's hold. He didn't crumple into a heap at the touch of the document. His eyes didn't close as he fell into a deep slumber. He remained alert and vigilant as ever. He reached out his free hand and settled it again at Gunny's low back.

Gunny felt entirely awake at his warm touch. She felt like no harm could befall her. Not from a poisoned piece of fruit, a wicked witch, or even her stepmother.

However, that wasn't the case for the rest of her family. Behind her, Gunny heard the shaky sighs of defeat at Catherine's words. She saw the winces in the eyes of her sisters. She watched as each of their husbands helplessly pulled their wives to their chests, as though their bravery might still save them, might still save the ranch.

CHAPTER NINETEEN

Truman should be car sick with how many times he'd been in a vehicle today. For a man who was used to trekking through all forms of terrain and then lying low for hours, even days on end, it was more movement that he'd had to manage in over a year. His body did ache. But not because of the fourth car ride of the day.

His world was off its kilter.

He wasn't married. In his heart, yes. Legally, not at all.

That was any easy fix. They would simply file the paperwork in the morning. The real trouble was the fate of the ranch.

They pulled into the gates of the sprawling homestead well into the dead of the night. Scout and Linc had stayed behind with Charlie Matthews to be with Father Matthews in case he woke up. They wanted to be sure the old man had family around when he opened his eyes.

A few lights were on in the main house when Truman put the truck in park. He was dirty and sweaty and tired, but the day was far from over for him. He turned to look at Gunny in the passenger seat.

She looked like a fallen angel to him. Not fallen due to any deeds, just the dust that settled about her halo of blonde hair, the smudges on her white dress, and the scuffs on her shoes. In her lap sat the marriage license. She ran her thumb over the B on his last name.

"We should talk," he said.

Gunny startled. She glanced up at him as though she had forgotten he was there. There was a cloud hovering in the depths of her blue eyes. Truman smelled an oncoming storm.

"There's no need," she said, placing the license on the dashboard of the car. "I need to get packing."

She reached for the handle and hopped out of the truck. Truman was so stunned by her words that it took him a precious second to move into action. He was out of the truck and around to her before she'd taken more than two steps.

"Packing?"

Again, those blue eyes glanced up at him as though she'd already forgotten his very presence. "Yes, I need to pack. I think I can move my flight up a few days. I don't have many of my belongings here, so they won't need my help to pack up my cabin."

"You're leaving?"

"Yes," she said, stepping around him.

Truman took two more steps, which was enough to bring him back into her direct line. Gunny stopped in her tracks and looked up at him. Now that he was there, words escaped him.

He didn't need her to repeat herself. He'd heard her clearly. She was going to pack. Going to pack to leave him.

He didn't need clarification that she was going on a weekend vacation. She was leaving the country. Going somewhere in the Outback, and because she wouldn't have this place to come home to, he might never see her again.

"What?"

The word was a whisper that rattled on her tongue before it came out. That single word impacted him right in the chest. It pierced his heart, like his chest was a target, and she'd hit her mark.

"What?" she asked again, her voice growing louder, more firm.

He couldn't find any words. He was out in the open. There was no cover for him.

When she shook her head and went to step around him, Truman's arm shot out to catch her. His right arm. There was no pain when he lifted his arm.

"What do you think you're doing?" Gunny said as she looked at his fingers grasping her arm.

Those were the first words she'd ever said to him. It had been right after she'd kicked his weapon out of his hold. His shoulder had ached then. It didn't ache now.

"Truman, let me go. It's over."

"No."

"No, what?"

"No," he said, "this is not going to happen."

They were having a repeat conversation from the first time they met. Truman was determined this would not be the last time they spoke.

"We're fighters, you and I," he insisted, pulling her close. "We're not giving up."

"We've lost," she said, pulling away from him. "It's time to move on."

"Is that what you're going to tell Savy and those kids?"

Her back went ramrod straight.

"What about Father Matthews when he wakes up. Or your sisters when they have to pack up their whole lives."

"This isn't your life," she said. "This isn't even your fight. You were going to be out of here soon after me. This is just a house. My sisters will find new homes. So will Savy and those kids. But there are animals out there who are just going to die. At least I can do something about that."

"What about us?"

"There is no us. You're free to go and do whatever you were going to do."

The ache grew in his shoulder, allowing her to pull away from him easily. For the first time in his life, he'd taken a shot. And he'd missed.

"I see it now," he said. "This is what you do. This is your pattern."

"What pattern?"

"You start a fight, and then you leave."

Her shoulders jerked. He hadn't missed the shot this time. Unfortunately, Gunny stayed true to her pattern.

She took a step back, preparing to walk away from this battle. Truman mirrored her, mimicking the retreat. Gunny stepped back until she was at the door to the main house. Truman backed away from her until he blended into the shadows.

CHAPTER TWENTY

"*O*oof."

Gunny came awake from a heel to the back of her head. She and her twin had been laying head to foot in their stepmom's old bed. Though they'd never called Sarah Silver stepmom. Because she had been the only mother the twins had ever known.

All of her sisters had piled into their mom's old bed last night. They'd huddled together as they did when one of them was sick, or upset, or simply because it was a random Tuesday, and they'd stayed up all night gabbing and fussing and fighting and loving each other in that way that no one who wasn't a Silver would understand.

Gunny disentangled herself from the arm Saylor had slung over her midsection. Her older sister curled her fingers into Gunny's dress—the white sundress she'd worn at her wedding nearly twenty-four hours ago. One by one, Gunny unfurled Saylor's fingers until the slumbering woman let her go.

Next, Gunny had to climb over Scout, who was spread out like a starfish at the edge of the bed. Scout wasn't so much hogging the mattress as she had a hand or a toe reaching out to touch each of her sisters. That was Scout's way; she had to have her hand in each of her sister's lives.

Brig had opted for the old rocking chair near the window. The baby of the family had always striven to strike out on her own. But in her independence, Brig was always close by her sisters.

Mareen lay curled in a fetal position in the center of the bed, her hands protecting her belly. A new generation of Silvers would be here in less than a year. But the new kids on the block wouldn't have a field of honeysuckles to run in. They wouldn't get to see wild horses run at the edge of their property.

Of course, her sisters intended to fight their stepmother's claim to the ranch. They were Silvers, after all.

Gunny stood at the door of their mother's bedroom door. She looked out at her sisters sleeping peacefully in the knowledge that even though they'd lost the battle, they were gearing up for a war. A war they intended to win with the only weapon being their unity.

The space on the bed where Gunny had slept still held the shape of her body. She'd only fallen asleep a few hours ago, and her body was still tired from all the stress of the previous day. A part of her ached to go settle back in that spot where she knew she was safe and surrounded. But the itch that had always been inside of her agitated the bottom of her bare feet. She needed to get moving.

Moving where, she wasn't sure? Hopping on a plane and flying halfway around the world did not sound appealing. But neither did standing still. She just wasn't sure which way to turn?

"You looking for Truman?"

Gunny looked up to see Linc with a steamy mug of coffee in one hand and a pad of Post-it notes in the other. She set her lips to say the word No but choked on the response.

Truman was the last person she wanted to see. He'd accused her of being a turn tail last night. She wasn't a runner. She was a fighter.

That was her whole business model. She'd swoop in, show the locals how to fight the power, then she'd be off to the next fight. That wasn't running. It was delegating. There were so many fights, and she couldn't be everywhere at once.

"He went out to get some target practice in before we head out to look at some other properties."

"Other properties?" said Gunny.

"We're making contingencies for a Plan B," said Lincoln. "In case we can't win the deed back from your stepmother."

Can't win? Gunny knew this was going to be a battle, but she'd never considered losing it. What if Catherine actually made good on her threat of selling the ranch? What if she could never come back to this place again?

Even worse, if this place wasn't here, then she might never see Truman again. They weren't legally married. He had no reason to stay. After last night, she wouldn't be surprised if he was already planning to leave.

Gunny's mind was a whirl. She didn't want to never see Truman again. But she didn't want to stay put. She didn't want to give up this ranch. But could she stay and fight the long-drawn-out war with her sisters?

Shame rolled over her that that was even a question in her mind. Already she'd caused a mess with Bright Horizons and the wild horses of Clearwater Valley. Was she truly going to leave Savy and those kids to blow in the wind?

No. No, she was going to stay and fight this out until the end. But first, she was going to find her husband and tell him that. He needed to know that he was wrong. That would be the first fight she'd win today.

CHAPTER TWENTY-ONE

Truman couldn't sleep. The silence on the ranch had been deafening last night. Even now, in the bright light of a new day, the animals seemed to know there was something wrong.

The horses were restless in the pen. Birds were quiet up in the trees. So too were the insects. Either an earthquake or storm was coming. Or the animals knew the wicked witch would be flying in soon on her broomstick.

Truman chided himself for that uncharitable thought. The girls might call Catherine evil, but he'd seen the look in her eyes when Mareen announced she was pregnant. That was the look only a mother would give to her child when she wanted to reach out.

They might lose the ranch, but Truman knew that his brothers and their wives would never fall out of touch. The only if in that equation was his wife. Because despite the unfiled paperwork, Gunny was his.

He'd come to this ranch wanting nothing more than to fulfill the dying wish of his commander and help his daughters. All while rehabilitating his shoulder to get back into active duty. Now the only duty Truman wanted to act on was fighting to get Gunny to stay in his arms.

He was a master of disguise. He could hide in plain sight and watch over her every move. He was prepared to follow her to the ends of the earth.

Gunny might have a habit of starting a fight and leaving. But Truman had a habit of stalking his quarry and never missing a shot. He wasn't about to let his wife ruin his perfect record.

He lay on his belly out at the edge of the property. The target was within his scope, not that he needed to magnify the bull's eye. He spied the yellow center of the bull's eye. Then a flash of white came into his sight.

Truman blinked, trying to clear his vision. But even after he wiped at his eyes, the apparition didn't dissipate.

Gunny stood in front of his target. She was still dressed in the white dress she'd worn for their wedding. Though calling it white was a stretch as the garment had picked up even more dirt and dust from her trek out to this part of the property.

"Don't shoot," she said.

Truman was already laying his weapon down and clamoring to his feet. He'd been prepared to hunt her down. To stalk her. But there she stood. With her hands raised in the air in the universal sign of surrender.

He closed the distance between them and was on her in a heartbeat. Truman scooped Gunny up into his arms. His shoulder protested the move, but he ignored the ache. The one in his heart had his full attention.

"Hey," she said from inside the cradle of his arms.

"Hey," he mimicked, tightening his hold.

She wasn't squirming to get away. In fact, she was holding entirely still. Likely because of the way he was holding her, her feet dangled off the ground.

He didn't set her down. He wasn't taking any chances of her getting away now that he'd caught her.

"I'm supposed to get on a flight tomorrow," she said.

"I know." Truman was already in the process of booking his own flight to Australia. He wasn't entirely sure of Gunny's itinerary. But he had no doubts of his tracking skills. He would find her wherever she went.

Although maybe now that he held her captive, he could simply ask her where she'd be.

"I was thinking I should postpone the trip, though." She avoided his gaze. Her fingers played with the collar of his shirt. Still, she made no move to get away from him. "There are things left unfinished here that I feel I should attend to."

"Things?"

She nodded, now playing with the top button of his shirt. "The foster home, for one. I can't just leave Savy to deal with that on her own. Not when I started the fight."

"I'm sure Savy and those kids would appreciate your help and expertise in that matter. Is that all?"

"Then there's Father Matthews. He's going to need some help when he gets out of the hospital."

"Is there any other matter you want resolved before you leave, Gunnery?"

Gunny's blue gaze finally lifted and caught his. "There's the matter of us."

"Us?"

"We should probably figure out... you know, our legal standing. Since we're not technically married."

Truman spanned his hands over her back, pressing her closer to him. His shoulder had stopped protesting long ago. He wanted to carry this particular load for the rest of his life.

"We made vows to each other," he said. "We pledged to develop our hearts and minds together. I don't see what the law has to do with any of that."

"You still want to... do all of that?"

"I'm already doing it," he said. "My heart is yours. Whether you want it or not. You get on that plane, I'll be in the aisle seat beside you."

"I hate the window seat," she said.

"Fine, then you take the aisle. I'll just have to deal with being trapped on an eighteen-hour flight."

"You were going to come with me?" she asked.

"Yes. Right after I took the marriage license to the courthouse. I want the right to stand by your side, even if you wanted to get rid of me."

"I don't want to get rid of you."

"You were never in any danger of that." He pulled her to him. "I'm in love with you, Gunnery Silver Bates."

"Technically, it's still Gunnery Silver."

"Not for long."

Truman set Gunny down on the ground. He had to if he was going to keep his balance and ravage her mouth at the same time. The moment his lips touched hers, he knew he'd made the right decision because his knees wobbled with the impact.

The taste of her upper lip was like the fire from a gunshot. Her lower lip set off detonations inside his head that would rival the Fourth of July. When he deepened the kiss, his entire body jerked like the kickback of his rifle. Only there was no pain, no ache anywhere in his person. He wanted more. Now he knew he was going to have as much as he ever wanted because she was his. She had surrendered to him long after he'd surrendered to her.

"I love you too, Truman," she said. "I was going to fight for you. I just wasn't sure how to do it."

"You've already won me over," he said, brushing a kiss to her temple. "I'm pretty sure it was when you stripped my gun from me that first day."

She laughed, her lips spreading into a wide grin. Her eyes crinkling at the corners. It was the first time Truman had seen the expression. He was determined to have a repeat performance every day for the rest of their lives.

"We're going to win this fight for the ranch," she said when she sobered. Once again, a fierce warrior. "But after we do, I'm going to want to travel again and save more wild horses and endangered animals."

"I already had plans to stalk you. Now I don't have to be as stealthy. We'll face all these new battles together."

Gunny wrapped her arms around his neck. "I think I'm gonna like having you at my back."

"You'll have to fight me to keep me away from you," he said.

"This is a fight I'll be happy to let you win."

"*Let* me win?"

She grinned. Truman decided to give up this battle and claim another kiss from the woman who his heart had developed an unbreakable bond with. Later today, they'd go into town and make it legal. That would put an end to this particular fight and start them on their journey to forever.

EPILOGUE

$\mathcal{S}$cout walked the length of the solicitor's office. The office wasn't on the main street of the small Montana town she'd lived all her life in. The town was only considered small due to its population. The square footage of Honor Valley could fit the island of Manhattan inside a couple of times. But the people could all fit into the high school football stadium with enough elbow room to be comfortable. Though they'd all likely be hugging each other while mixing and mingling.

In fact, in the dining room just down the hall, there was a good portion of the town's population. From this distance, Scout heard her sisters' high-pitched gabbing and their husbands' deep grumbling assent. Mixed in with the President's Men's low tones were voices she'd known for years. A couple of the Matthews boys had come home now that their father was out of the hospital, though not entirely back on his feet.

Scout's gaze went to the photographs on the wall. There were many crackled, sepia tone images of soldiers throughout history. From the Buffalo Soldiers and Tuskegee Airman of Haran Matthews's past. There was also a large framed picture of a young Father Matthews with his wife, Tessa. The couple was surrounded by six boys of varying skin tones. Each boy smiled a big toothsome grin as they hugged one of the adults or each other. Behind the patchwork family stood the Bright Horizon's Foster Home where the boys had spent the beginning years of their lives before the Matthews had adopted each one.

Father Matthews sat behind the ancient oak desk under which Scout had never been found in games of hide and seek. The old man's eyes were closed as they both waited. The lines that had been at the corners of his eyes and the dark circles that had been below had faded now that he'd had a few weeks of rest at home.

The man was itching to get back out in the field. It took all the Silver girls, all the President's Men, and half of the Matthews boys to keep him inside and seated, if not lying down in bed. Though Scout suspected he was sneaking out at night to walk the lands.

She couldn't blame him. She hated to be away from the land for long. If things went wrong today, she would no longer have any rights to walk Silver Star Ranch at any time of the day or night.

A sleek town car pulled into the drive. A pair of six-inch heels smacked down against the dirt. Catherine climbed out of the car, dressed in a pale pink dress that wouldn't last five seconds if she didn't get inside and out of the dust storm.

The wind kicked up, swirling a small cloud of dirt at her heels. Catherine lowered her sunshades and glared at the tiny tornado. The dirt dropped where it had risen. Thus confirming what Scout believed all along; that her stepmother was the Wicked Witch incarnate. She just drove a Bentley instead of a broomstick.

"I have a bad feeling about this," Scout muttered under her breath.

"Just give her a chance," said Father Matthews, his eyes still closed as though he was talking in his sleep. "She might surprise you."

Catherine came into the office. Her gaze didn't go to Father Matthews, who now sat upright in his chair. Neither did it go to Scout, who stood at the opposite end of the room. Catherine's gaze landed on the picture on the wall. The old photograph featured a skinny Black man with his arm around a barrel-chested white man. Both men sported the modern camouflage style of military fatigues, handle-bar mustaches, and broad, toothsome grins that told the viewer that they were solemnly up to no good.

"Good afternoon, Catherine."

"Haran, how are you feeling today?" Catherine's gaze softened as she looked at Father Matthews.

"Ticker's still ticking. That's all I can ask for."

Catherine offered him a smile. Scout had to blink a couple of times at the warmth she saw there. Catherine was never warm.

As confirmed when her gaze landed on Scout. Her light gaze didn't exactly chill over, but it definitely dropped a few degrees.

"Let's get this over with, shall we," Catherine said, taking a seat.

"This won't take long at all," said Scout, taking the seat opposite her stepmother. "This is a check for the value of the ranch."

Each Silver sister and her husband had emptied out their checking and savings account. They had gotten loans, pawned valuables, begged, and borrowed until they'd scrounged up enough money to outbid the highest buyer for the ranch.

Catherine looked down at the massive check Scout held in her hand and sniffed. "I'm not interested."

The words should've left Scout cold. Instead, she felt her skin overheating. The fingers holding the check with the obscene amount of zeros trembled in her hands as she glared at Catherine.

Father Matthews wore a serene smile, as though he had not a care in the world. Scout wondered if the doctors had messed with the old man's heart. This was the worst news in the world. What if Catherine was going to sell the ranch to a dude farm? Father Matthews would never have any peace with city slickers falling off horses at every turn.

"This offer is more than fair," said Scout. "Unless you're just being spiteful."

"What I am going to be is a grandmother." Catherine shuddered at that word. "Though I think I'll prefer to be called Grammy, like the solid gold statue. Yes, I think that would suit me more."

Scout could only stare in utter disbelief. Catherine was determining what Mareen's unborn child would call her while leaving that child homeless.

"However, I don't want my grandchild to run around my house with sticky fingers in that stocky form I know they'll get from that father of theirs. I have too many precious things in there that are breakable."

With Scout so busy staring, she didn't have enough brain cells to react when Catherine snatched the check out of her hand... and then tore it in half.

Scout gasped as the zeroes were split in half and then fluttered to the floor. "What the... how could...are you...?"

"I've decided the best investment will be if he or she be raised on the ranch," Catherine continued as though Scout hadn't spoken. "I've placed the deed in a family trust that is to be shared equally by Silver females."

Catherine took a document out of her expensive purse. The title at the top of the document did, in fact, read Deed. There was a lot of legal mumbo jumbo, but Scout knew what a premise of a deed was. It was the part that laid out the parties. In that part were the words Silver female descendants.

Scout's emotions vacillated from shock to disbelief. If she was understanding Catherine right, they weren't going to lose the ranch. Everything was set to rights, and they wouldn't have to leave their home. And wonder of wonders, there didn't appear to be a catch. No strings attached, like they had to turn over their firstborn children.

"Since I was once a Silver female," Catherine continued, "that means I still retain an equal share to the land."

Ah. Here was the catch.

"Which means I can come and go as I please... to see my grandchildren, mind you. I can't have the next generation being raised entirely feral."

That was it? Catherine just wanted the right to see her grandchild? Scout could've told her that all she'd ever need to do was knock on the door. Mareen would never keep her baby from her mother.

Over the last few months, Mareen had grown increasingly nostalgic about her times with her mother. Scout did wonder if some of the stories she told were confused due to baby brain. Though the woman who sat across from Scout now faintly resembled the doting mother of Mareen's imagination.

"On behalf of your daughter and stepdaughters, we accept. But you should know there will be more than one feral grandchild running around next year."

"Mareen's having twins?" Catherine looked to the door of the office where the low murmur of voices could still be heard.

"No, she's not. I'm pregnant, as well." Scout rested her hand over the small bump at her midsection. "So is Saylor and Tilly. Looks like you're getting four Grammy's."

"Wait? No. You're not my... I'm not your..."

Catherine couldn't complete the sentences. Because even through all the ups and downs of the years, the divorces and marriages, they were hers. She was theirs. They were family. And it was high time they started acting like it.

The grin on Father Matthews's face told Scout she had finally learned the lesson of the day. It always came down to family. Love them or leave them, but you could never break those bonds.

"Too late, Catherine," said Scout. "The paperwork is signed. You're a part of this family. In perpetuity according to this deed."

Catherine took a deep breath. Then she let it out slowly. Her regal shoulders went back. The glare she gave Scout didn't have the same bite that Scout remembered from her childhood.

"Fine," Catherine said.

"Fine," Scout said.

"Fine," Father Matthews chuckled. "Now that Abe's plan is complete, and all of his girls are cared for, I know he's resting in peace."

"You really think this is what he had planned all along?" asked Scout. "To get all of us together?"

Father Matthews shrugged. "Whatever he planned, it worked out for everyone. His daughters, his men, and his remaining wife are all taken care of on the land he loved. Who knows? I might even take a cue from my old friend when it comes to my boys."

∼

The Silver sisters' stories are complete.
But the Matthews boys' stories are about to begin.
Only the Matthews boys can step in and save the foster home where they began their lives.
But they'll each need to make a big commitment to the women who run the home to do so!
Find out how in
The Flying Cross Ranch Romances!!!

ALSO BY SHANAE JOHNSON

ALSO BY SHANAE JOHNSON

Shanae Johnson was raised by Saturday Morning cartoons and After School Specials. She still doesn't understand why there isn't a life lesson that ties the issues of the day together just before bedtime. While she's still waiting for the meaning of it all, she writes stories to try and figure it all out. Her books are wholesome and sweet, but her are heroes are hot and heroines are full of sass!

And by the way, the E elongates the A. So it's pronounced Shan-aaaaaaaa. Perfect for a hero to call out across the moors, or up to a balcony, or to blare outside her window on a boombox. If you hear him calling her name, please send him her way!

You can sign up for Shanae's Reader Group and receive a FREE NOVELLA in this world at

https://shanaejohnson.com/ReaderGroup

ALSO BY SHANAE JOHNSON

The Brides of Purple Heart

On His Bended Knee

Hand Over His Heart

Offering His Arm

His Permanent Scar

Having His Back

In Over His Head

Always On His Mind

Every Step He Takes

In His Good Hands

Light Up His Life